CHARLOTTE BINGHAM

The Nightingale Sings
'A novel rich in dramatic surprises, with a large cast of vivid characters whose antics will have you frantically turning the pages'
Daily Mail

To Hear A Nightingale
'A lovely sprawling saga with a heroine you can't fail to love'
Prima

The Business
'Probably more sun-tan lotion will be spilled on the pages of Charlotte Bingham's *The Business* than any other book this summer . . . The ideal beach read'
Homes and Gardens

In Sunshine Or In Shadow
'Superbly written . . . A romantic novel that is romantic in the true sense of the word'
Daily Mail

Stardust
'Charlotte Bingham has produced a long, absorbing read, perfect for holidays, which I found hard to lay aside as the plot twisted and turned with intriguing results'
Sunday Express

Nanny
'It's deckchair season once again, and Charlotte Bingham's spellbinding saga is required reading'
Cosmopolitan

Change Of Heart
'Her imagination is thoroughly original. This book has a fairy-tale cover containing a fairy tale, which is all the more delightful as it is not something one expects from a modern novel . . . It's heady stuff'
Daily Mail

Debutantes
'A big, wallowy delicious read'
The Times

Also by Charlotte Bingham:
CORONET AMONG THE WEEDS
LUCINDA
CORONET AMONG THE GRASS
BELGRAVIA
COUNTRY LIFE
AT HOME
BY INVITATION
TO HEAR A NIGHTINGALE
THE BUSINESS
IN SUNSHINE OR IN SHADOW
STARDUST
NANNY
CHANGE OF HEART
DEBUTANTES
THE NIGHTINGALE SINGS

Novels with Terence Brady:
VICTORIA
VICTORIA AND COMPANY
ROSE'S STORY
YES HONESTLY

Television Drama Series with Terence Brady:
TAKE THREE GIRLS
UPSTAIRS DOWNSTAIRS
THOMAS AND SARAH
NANNY

Television Comedy Series with Terence Brady:
NO HONESTLY
YES HONESTLY
PIG IN THE MIDDLE
OH MADELINE! (USA)
FATHER MATTHEW'S DAUGHTER

Television Plays:
MAKING THE PLAY
SUCH A SMALL WORD
ONE OF THE FAMILY

Films:
LOVE WITH A PERFECT STRANGER
MAGIC MOMENTS

Stage Plays:
I WISH I WISH

GRAND AFFAIR

Charlotte Bingham

BANTAM BOOKS
LONDON · NEW YORK · TORONTO · SYDNEY · AUCKLAND

GRAND AFFAIR
A BANTAM BOOK : 0 553 50500 9

Simultaneously published in Great Britain by Doubleday,
a division of Transworld Publishers Ltd

PRINTING HISTORY
Doubleday edition published 1997
Bantam edition published 1997

Copyright © 1997 by Charlotte Bingham

Extracts from *The Wind in the Willows* by Kenneth Grahame
copyright © The University Chest, Oxford, reproduced by permission
of Curtis Brown, London.

The right of Charlotte Bingham to be identified as the author
of this work has been asserted in accordance with sections 77 and 78
of the Copyright Designs and Patents Act 1988.

All the characters in this book are fictitious,
and any resemblance to actual persons, living or dead,
is purely coincidental.

Condition of Sale
This book is sold subject to the condition that it shall not,
by way of trade or otherwise, be lent, re-sold, hired out or
otherwise circulated in any form of binding or cover other than that
in which it is published and without a similar condition including
this condition being imposed on the subsequent purchaser.

Set in 10pt Linotype Plantin by
County Typesetters, Margate, Kent

Bantam Books are published by Transworld Publishers Ltd,
61–63 Uxbridge Road, London W5 5SA,
in Australia by Transworld Publishers (Australia) Pty Ltd,
15–25 Helles Avenue, Moorebank, NSW 2170
and in New Zealand by Transworld Publishers (NZ) Ltd,
3 William Pickering Drive, Albany, Auckland.

Reproduced, printed and bound in Great Britain by
Cox & Wyman Ltd, Reading, Berks.

For the Junior Bears and Matt Mulligan

Prologue

It was always the same. She was standing beside him, there was a warm breeze blowing, their faces were lightly tanned, and they were both smiling and looking up the street. Stretching ahead of them lay a row of classical villas, square-fronted, porticoed, palely painted. Lying ahead of the villas on the horizon she could see a sky, distanced and pale, in parts very slightly pink, and yet the light that she could see around them was definitely that of midday on a sunny morning, and they were both in shirt-sleeves. And they were very happy. Sometimes she thought that they were expecting someone, or it might be that they were merely waiting to go towards what lay so invitingly ahead, waiting to round the corner of that street which had no cars and no people, which was empty of everyone but themselves.

Because of the light breeze she could feel on her face she sensed that they must be near the sea, that if they rounded that corner ahead they might perhaps find an endless expanse of bright water, a tantalizing mixture of turquoise and azure, of cerulean and isamine blue, and yet she could not say why, because there was no smell of salt in the air and no sound of the nagging cries of seagulls, no shells adorning the stone decorations around the porticoes of those classical square-fronted houses, no trees blown into the dwarfed and cowed shapes that seaside trees so often assume. And yet she was always so sure that the sea was very near.

Just as she was sure that when they did eventually reach

the corner of that street and turned to the left they would find a house facing the water, and palm trees and flowers and a green sward running down to a pebbled beach. And there would be the constant sound of gentle waves running up towards the garden, reaching out towards the grass, trying to touch its lush green edge before falling back once more with a sigh as if saying, 'If not this time, next time I will reach you.'

Part One

Where do you come from, baby dear?
Out of the everywhere into the here.

Victorian. Anon.

One

London, 1948

The young doctor stared across the body of the dead girl on the bed.

'She should have gone to hospital,' he told the midwife, half accusingly, and then seeing the expression in the poor woman's eyes he immediately regretted what he had said.

'Yes, she should have gone to hospital,' Mrs Proctor agreed, 'but I was called too late for that, Dr Bailey. The baby was halfway out when I arrived, see? I wouldn't be here only for one of the neighbours passing her door and thinking they heard her cry out and that, and so she sent for me. Poor child, she was five fingers already when I arrived. I don't like losing a mother, not even with a breech birth, Dr Bailey. It's years since I lost a mother, really it is. Can't think when it happened the last time.'

Mrs Proctor's voice, normally quiet, was raised in anxiety as she finished cleaning the baby and quickly wrapped it in some cheap striped towelling from her bag, for the room in which they stood was perishingly cold, so that as they were speaking they both looked as if they were smoking, so quickly did their breath turn to mist in the freezing air.

Dr Bailey sighed inwardly. Of course it was not the midwife's fault that the girl had died. Called out at the last minute, the woman had evidently done all she could. He looked down at the dead girl. She must have been a pretty young thing, long dark brown hair, slender build, too slender probably, too young certainly.

'It's this wretched darn winter, everything at sixes and

11

sevens since the snow, can't get an ambulance, can't get nothing,' Mrs Proctor went on, giving the tip of her finger to the baby to suck and at the same time rocking it gently to and fro to keep both of them warm. 'I've cleared up as best I can, Dr Bailey, but truly there was nothing more I could do for her. All I could do was try and save the baby. I'd no change even for the telephone in the hall, nothing. That's how quick it all happened. It's not easy in this neighbourhood, being a midwife, I tell you. Sometimes they call you out and there's nothing happening. Two in the morning, four in the morning, you wouldn't believe it. They don't mean to, of course, but there it is, there's nothing to be done now, the poor girl's dead as a nail and no more to be said.'

Looking round the room, which was indeed surprisingly spotless now, Dr Bailey had never been so glad that he was only the locum, that he was not going to practise in London. Tomorrow, whatever happened, he would be moving on from the dark brown neighbourhood of Notting Hill to the light and beautiful Scilly Isles, and not a day too soon.

He gazed round the chilling starkness of the room in which they stood, dreaming of the warmth he imagined lay ahead, of sunshine and spring flowers already blooming, although it was still only January. He couldn't help contrasting those imagined scenes of light and beauty with the room in which he stood, its walls decorated with cuttings from cheap magazines and old calendars which its occupier – perhaps in some desperate effort to cheer the place – had pasted onto pieces of cardboard to make believe they were paintings.

And the fact that she had cut out so many pictures of green fields, of old-fashioned cottages with roses and wistaria climbing artlessly over their exteriors, of blue and white jugs filled with pale pink roses, made them seem unbearably poignant, set about this cheerless room with its curtains of old black-out material and its poor threadbare

12

carpeting and its bare light bulb hanging from the yellowing electric wire in the bathroom.

'Poor child. She must have gone into labour very much sooner than she expected,' he murmured.

'Trouble is, a young girl like her – may she rest in peace, but they often think they can manage these things on their own.' Mrs Proctor shook her head. 'Frightened to tell anyone, too ashamed and that.'

Young Dr Bailey sighed again, this time aloud, as he looked at his watch and proceeded to write out the death certificate. Then he closed his bag and went to the window in the vain hope that somehow by now the snow would have stopped falling, which it had not. Still, at least it had covered the dreary muddle of buildings, giving it not only a new disguise but a quite alien beauty. And the street lighting too seemed softened, less stark, penetrating the cheerless room so that what with the quiet outside and the quiet inside, the sounds of the baby sucking at the midwife's finger and the sight of the dead girl on the bed – because of the snow, it all appeared less real, thank heavens, more as if they were all just figures in a painting.

Dr Bailey turned back.

'I'm afraid I really must go. I have two more calls to make before the night is out. I wonder . . .' He hesitated, not wishing to impose, yet genuinely anxious to reach his next emergency call. 'I wonder, could you possibly take the baby to the hospital for me? I have to go in quite the opposite direction.'

'Oh, that's no trouble, Dr Bailey,' Mrs Proctor agreed, only too eager to help out because she was so contused with the guilt of losing the mother. 'I can put the poor. mite in my bicycle basket, all wrapped up, and push her there. It's not that far.'

'I just hope my car will start again.'

But so sudden and thick had been the continuing snowfall that they were forced to return to the miserable

13

little room, the midwife still carrying the box in which she had placed the baby.

'It's against the rules,' Dr Bailey said suddenly, as, having lit the gas fire with the aid of a few shillings and found further towelling for the baby, they warmed their own hands and feet in front of the two bars. 'Against the rules entirely, but I really think we do need a little *eau de vie* if we are to survive this long, cold night.'

Mrs Proctor did not know what the doctor meant by *eau de vie* until he produced a half-bottle of whisky from his very new black leather bag. He found a couple of plastic mugs in a cupboard and poured them both a generous tot.

'Someone here must have a bottle of milk we could give the baby. It really should have something soon,' he said, after they had both drunk a little too readily from the toothmugs. 'I know I heard a baby crying just now. On the ground floor.'

'That'll be Mrs Mac. She's got three boys of her own, and helps people out now and then with their children. So many night workers around here, what with one thing and another,' she added discreetly.

Dr Bailey nodded. 'Yes, I should imagine there's a Mrs Mac to every tenement building in every street round here. They seem to run London, the Mrs Macs.'

'This one's called Mrs O'Flaherty, but everyone calls her Mrs Mac after MacDonagh's the shop on the corner, you know? She goes in there every day as they close, for the staling bread, and the tins that have a dent in them, anything to feed those kids. Not just her kids, everyone's kids. She's done more for the neighbourhood than the blessed government ever will through all these days of rationing, I always say. Not that she wants to stay here. No, she's an eye on moving to the country, like this girl seems to have had, wouldn't you say?' Mrs Proctor looked round the room at the magazine pictures. 'Everyone with children wants to take them to the country. I was brought up in the country myself,' she added, almost to herself,

14

because she could see the doctor's attention wandering.

'Why not leave the baby with this good lady for a few hours, then? With this Mrs Mac? It'll be much better off in the warm, rather than going through the snow in the cold.'

'Well, it would be better. 'Specially since I heard the hospital's had an outbreak, so it really wouldn't be the place for the poor little mite at the moment, I don't suppose.'

'At least it's worth trying.'

Mrs Proctor re-bundled the baby more tightly. She knew a good idea when she heard one. It had been an awful night, what with the terrible cold and losing the mother. She could push her bicycle home presently. Useless for her to take the baby to her place since she had neither milk nor bottles. She had not been able to find any in the room when she looked round, either. All sorts of sewing stuffs and needles and pins, but nothing for a baby. It really was as if the poor child had decided to ignore the pregnancy, pretend it wasn't happening, for there was nothing here to say she had been expecting it, not even a size one baby vest.

'I agree with you, doctor. Let's try and find someone to look after it just until the weather turns, until we can make arrangements.'

Dr Bailey picked up his new black leather bag with its discreet gold initialling, and together they went downstairs, Mrs Proctor still carrying the baby in the shoe box.

Outside in the stone-cold corridor, with its Victorian tiled floor and fine plasterwork that told of former warm and colourful days when the house was a family home, they knocked on Mrs Mac's unlocked front door. It swung to and fro a little in the draught as they waited politely for an answer and listened to the sounds from within, a tap running, a baby crying fitfully, a child calling out for a glass of water.

Out of the darkness of the small hall a large handsome

red-haired woman appeared in a flowered apron of a too-thin material that was obviously doubling as a dress, underneath which she had tightly buttoned a much-mended wool cardigan for warmth. It was to this affable person with her warm presence and her reassuringly kind grey eyes that Mrs Proctor quickly explained the problem. Mrs Mac appeared to listen but Dr Bailey noticed that all the while Mrs Proctor was talking the woman had eyes only for the baby wrapped in the towelling and propped in its box.

'Well now, who is this so?' was all she finally said, as if Mrs Proctor had not just finished telling her.

This time it was Dr Bailey who explained their plight as plainly as he could, worrying that he was really asking too much from the obviously overburdened mother standing in front of him, for even as he was speaking he could hear sounds of children still awake and wanting her, despite the hour. But Mrs Mac did not appear in the least interested in his apologies for disturbing her, and before he had finished she had her hands stretched out for this so-recent arrival.

'Just you stop your worrying now, doctor, and Mrs Proctor too, for haven't you come to just the right door? I have everything here for a dozen babies and more, if you were to only know it. And ask anyone around, babies is my speciality, newborn babies in particular, I love them more than my own life.'

Dr Bailey smiled at Mrs Proctor for the first time that evening, momentarily delighted. This was the best bit of news they had heard the whole miserable night. They both knew that the unfortunate baby, born into such dreadful circumstances, might now have some sort of chance during its first few hours on earth.

'Well, if you're quite sure you're sure, just until morning. Until Mrs Proctor can make arrangements, and so on,' Dr Bailey said, backing off a little way down the corridor, suddenly aware that he must smell of whisky. 'I mean, if you're quite sure?'

16

'When it comes to babies, I'm not quite sure, doctor, I'm completely sure. Even our old doctor always said, "Mrs O'Flaherty, you know more about babies than I'll ever even begin to know."' Mrs Mac tossed back her thick plait of long red hair, and took the baby in the box from Mrs Proctor. 'Now off yous go. Put the baby in hospital, what are you thinking of, both of you?' she asked them, smiling. 'Hospital's the most dangerous place you can put a baby, everyone knows that, nothing but bugs and diseases. Don't you give it another thought, it'll be quite safe here with us at Number Four, and that's all there is to it. Pick it up any time you want,' she added, already turning away as if she was afraid they might change their minds and decide that her flat was an unsuitable place to leave the baby.

'Pick her up. Her. She's a girl. It's a girl,' Mrs Proctor told her, turning back quickly, suddenly realizing that kind though she knew Mrs Mac to be she might now refuse to take the baby in, seeing that so many women had no interest in girl babies, nor any liking for them either, only really wanting sons, which was strange when you thought about it, what with so many killed in two world wars.

'A girl, is she?' Mrs Mac's eyes softened. 'Well, aren't I the lucky one?'

'And I'm sorry about the shoe box,' Dr Bailey called back, already by the front door that led to the street. 'That's all we could find to put her in.'

'Get on with you, doctor,' said Mrs Mac, and she gave a rich laugh at the very idea of apologizing for the shoe box. 'Didn't you know that anything to do with shoes is lucky, for does it not mean that the Little People brought her to us?'

The next day the snow was so thick that it seemed London was entirely deserted except for children walking to school, or a pony and cart passing with a call for 'old iron, any old iron'. And so it continued for some days, days during which the new baby was fed and looked after by Mrs Mac, becoming the centre of the family's attention if only because of her sex, and as the snowdrifts piled up outside no-one came to remove the dead body of the mother from the room above, let alone to check up on the baby.

In the end it was nearly a week before Mrs Proctor herself was able to reappear at Number Four Porchester Crescent, and when she did eventually manage to visit the once gracious old house where she and the young locum had left the baby that cold dark night she was appalled to find that the poor dead girl was still lying upstairs.

'What a thing to happen!' she said, hurrying out to the street once more to use the public telephone box. 'I don't know what they're all coming to!'

'They'll give her a good Catholic funeral, I hope?' Mrs Mac called after her. 'For I'm sure I saw the poor girl once or twice at early morning Mass.'

'Never mind the funeral rites, Mrs Mac,' Mrs Proctor sighed, clicking her tongue. She stopped and turned. 'Have you any idea of her name? I can find nothing in her room except these few pasted-up pictures. Did she not have any friends around here? Mrs Burgess—'

Mrs Mac said a little too quickly, 'Mrs Burgess used her for sewing and that but there would not be a hope of her knowing who she was, believe me, Mrs Proctor, not a hope. Ask anyone round here. Young girls coming to London, they call themselves all sorts of names to avoid being found by their parents, or – well, all sorts and shapes of reasons. You can't blame them. Why don't you step in for some tea now? Wait till you see the weight our little angel's put on for us,' she went on, all too anxious to change the subject. 'What a wonderful thing you did the other night, Mrs Proctor, for this is surely just a little angel sent to visit us all, wouldn't you say?'

'She's a very pretty baby all right,' Mrs Proctor agreed,

as Mrs Mac made the tea and she stared into the straw basket with protective feelings mingling with reverence for a new life. After a pause she said, 'I'll be truthful with you, I don't like to think of her being handed over to the Council, I don't like it at all, Mrs Mac. She'd be much better off with you, here, wouldn't she?' She looked around the poorly furnished but scrupulously clean kitchen in which they were sitting. 'Much better off. They never do well, babies that are put in municipal care, I don't think. Particularly during a harsh winter like this. There's always some bug, and we're all still locked out of the hospital, you know, whole wards closed down because of the outbreak.'

'She might have died so, the baby might have died had you not left her in with me?' said Mrs Mac with evident satisfaction.

'She still might die if she goes there, and then all our efforts would be for nothing, just wasted.'

'Dead like her mother,' Mrs Mac went on. 'What a waste of our little flower's life,' she continued, hammering home the point. Mrs Proctor didn't seem to notice this but only stared thoughtfully into Mrs Mac's handsome face with its white skin and freckles which were so prolific it would be hard to find a space between them.

'If she goes to the Council she'll be up for adoption and maybe sent into the wrong hands. Some of these adoption families, I don't know. Not suitable at all. They adopt and then they send them back after a few months. It's pathetic, the things I've seen, you can imagine. No, perhaps you can't imagine, Mrs Mac, being so kind, but believe me, it is pathetic.' Mrs Proctor stared down once again at the little face lying peacefully asleep in the basket. 'Well, I couldn't tell you.'

'She would be better off here so, with us,' Mrs Mac agreed, and taking the baby from her crib she placed her in Mrs Proctor's arms. 'There now, put your finger into her hand and feel the strength of her.'

Mrs Proctor put her index finger into the baby's palm, and then she looked up at Mrs Mac and shook her head disbelievingly at the power that seemed to be coming from the tiny hand. No council could ever give her the love and care that Mrs Mac could give her, and that was the truth. There was only one course to take now, and she was convinced of it, the one that would be best for the baby.

'Supposing – just supposing that the poor baby had died with the mother? I mean no-one hereabouts knows she was born alive, except us and the doctor – and if we told the hospital and the undertaker she must have died and the girl disposed of her, no-one will know better, will they, Mrs Mac?' she said, dropping her voice despite the fact that they were quite alone. 'And what with all the bad weather there's enough going on for them not to even bother to ask. There's the death certificate saying the mother died of a haemorrhage, of course, but nothing else to say exactly what happened, and what with the mother being such an unfortunate creature—'

'Well now, I don't suppose they would know there *was* a live baby,' Mrs Mac interrupted quickly, her voice too at its lowest level as she looked up from her tea, all innocence. 'No-one would know but us, and that young locum. But he's gone off. He was hardly here more than a minute that night, as I remember it. Not likely to return either. You know locums, Mrs Proctor, they can't wait to shake the dust from their feet. Too much like work, London, you know?'

'There *is* only the death certificate signed by the doctor,' Mrs Proctor repeated, more to reassure herself than Mrs Mac. 'That's all there is. Dr Bailey thought I would come back for the baby, but he was gone the next day so there was no-one to make sure.'

'Nor would they care if they did know about the baby, Mrs Proctor, saving your presence, you being a medical person – not with the shortage of staff, and one thing and another. Sure the baby could have been thrown dead into a dustbin by the mother before she crawled up onto that bed upstairs and died, for all the rest of the world knows or cares, when you come to think about it, wouldn't you say? Or I could have given birth to the baby myself, could I not now, for all they know? And as for my boys, they believe what I tell them, if they know what's good for them, particularly since their father left for America and I'm doing all the raising of them.'

'So. No-one knows about her, not really, except you and I.'

The two women stared at each other for a few seconds, each knowing what they meant without having to say anything. Mrs Proctor felt a satisfying surge of relief at the idea that the baby might not have to be handed over to the authorities.

More than that, she felt a great deal less guilty.

This way at least the baby would be adopted into the kind of home the poor dead girl would have liked, and kept in the place where she herself, after all, had lived. Like this the child would be raised with other children, and by a kind and loving mother. It could not be better, really. Much better probably than if the mother had lived, friendless and alone, struggling against the odds to keep her child.

'What have you decided to call her, Mrs Mac?' she asked, as if the whole matter had now been well and truly settled and there was nothing else to say.

'Sure my boys settled that long ago, Mrs Proctor.' Mrs Mac looked up, smiling. 'They've called her Ottilie – for wasn't it the name of the shoes on the side of the box you brought her in?'

Two

1954

Ottilie's day always began with climbing into bed to lie beside the woman she would always knows as 'Ma'. Here, with Ma's body in its clean but much-mended white cotton nightdress warming her, and the pleasant smell of the early morning tea Ma was sipping, she was certain that she had once again awoken to her own safe little world, a world where Ottilie was the star.

Here too, lying beneath the old faded flowered quilt, her blissful sense of being loved and wanted was emphasized by the distant sounds of all her brothers leaving for school, Ma's radio playing, and the noise of the London buses pulling slowly past their flat window. All these outside disturbances only underlined Ottilie's feelings of contentment.

Sometimes she would slide right down beneath the sheets and blankets, almost to the bottom of the bed, pretending that she wasn't there, trying to avoid all her older brothers kissing her goodbye. Other times she would lie against the thin old pillows in their coarse hand-sewn cotton pillowcases waiting for the boys' farewells and their murmurs of 'Lucky thing, wish I was staying at home.' Always answered by Ma's saying, 'Get on with all of yous, best years of your life, school.'

This morning was different, though. Not that there were not shouts from the kitchen, and Lorcan the eldest as always bringing Ma her cup of tea with 'There you are, Ma' as Ma listened to *Housewives' Choice* on the grand old mahogany radio that occupied pride of place in the corner of their bedroom. This morning was different because the boys were up and shouting not because they were going to school, but because they were all moving to the country.

It had finally all seemed to happen so quickly. First a letter from Da in America and talk of money's being sent, finally Ma giving a little scream and sitting down in the kitchen very suddenly as she opened a letter. And then instead of just talk of getting out of London to what Ma always called 'a land of milk and honey' – now, all of a sudden, this was it, they really were moving, leaving Number Four and going far away into a foreign country that Ma and the boys called 'Cornwall'.

They were going somewhere where, Lorcan kept telling Ottilie, they could all learn to swim and fish, and there would be sandcastles and he would buy Ottilie a spade with which she could dig on those sandy beaches that she could see in some of the pictures on Ma's kitchen walls. In 'Cornwall', Lorcan told Ottilie, the sun always shone just like the pictures.

'But where 'xactly are we going, Ma?' Ottilie wanted to know, clinging hard to her mother's index finger as they walked down to MacDonagh's for the bread and potatoes. 'Where is Cornwall, 'xactly?'

Mrs Mac looked down at her youngest, and hearing the anxiety in Ottilie's voice she said, 'You know where Cornwall is, Ottilie pet, you've seen the pictures in the kitchen, that's Cornwall, dotie. Cows and fields, and little houses with thatched roofs where you can sit out in front of the door when the weather's fine, not like here with the smog and the buses going so close to the bedroom windows you could shake hands with the passengers. And we can take all our furniture. Sullivans is helping move us. You know, Mr Sullivan, the undertaker?' She stopped momentarily, frowning in remembrance of something, and then went on, 'You'll love where we're going, pet, you wait and see.'

But Ottilie still felt uneasy and strange about the idea of leaving Number Four, although when she stared at the pictures she could see that this place called Cornwall did look a great deal prettier than the main road outside Number Four where the rubbish lay listlessly in the gutters on a hot afternoon, or pieces of torn newspaper blew about under their feet on winter mornings, and all night long traffic moved past the window and babies cried. And yet, now that she knew they were really moving, going away from Number Four, she was only really happy under the kitchen table with her toys.

'Here.'

Ma bent down and for a moment her freckled face appeared upside down as she handed Ottilie an old post-card.

'That's where we're going to be near, dotie, just round the corner from that pretty place. Gorgeous, wouldn't you say?'

Ottilie turned over the postcard before looking at the picture on the front. There was no writing on it, but when she turned it back there was a picture of an old house with gardens running down to the sea. At six Ottilie's reading was not so perfect that she could understand all the words underneath the picture but she did understand 'The Grand', although the rest eluded her.

'That's right, pet, that's exactly it,' Ma said from above the table where she was making pastry and not really listening to Ottilie. 'It'll be grand, just grand, so it will. A home of our own, with our own front door, and summer coming, nothing could be more grand than that, I'd say. Away from streets and noise and dirty people, just flowers and fields, and air so clean you can hang your washing in it.'

Mr Sullivan gave them the loan of one of his oldest hearses to move themselves, and Lorcan's friend Charlie the young greengrocer on the corner offered to drive it for them because he said he could do with some sea air. Ottilie watched with interest as all the boys heaved and pushed everything they owned, and some things Ma joked she was sure they definitely should not own, into the back of the great black empty limousine.

'Now isn't that a fine sight if you like, pet?' Ma said, her usual deep optimism reflecting in her voice as she saw her proudest possession, the great old mahogany radiogram, being placed reverently beside the cardboard boxes of toys and books, old tea tins, towel rails and saucepans, all taped up with Mr Sullivan's special string and labels that said SULLIVAN across them. 'Have you Mrs Teddy safe, Ottilie pet? No you haven't? You've left Mrs Teddy? Well now, run back quickly before we all go without you. Imagine leaving Mrs Teddy, that's terrible for her, wouldn't you say? She'll cry her eyes out without yous.'

Quickly Ottilie ran back up the steps into the big dark hallway that had been the first place she had learned to recognize outside her own small world, back into the now empty flat, its door still swinging open as always, back to find Mrs Teddy.

There she was, in the corner of the boys' bedroom, a strangely forlorn sight, a small bear clothed in a blue dress and a hat sitting alone on the window sill. Ottilie snatched up her toy and then, feeling a little panic-struck at the sound of her sandals echoing on the stone floors, she ran into the kitchen searching for the dear familiar sights of her first home. But they were gone. Now there were no rows of green tea tins to stare up at, and no washing horse drying what Ma always called 'gansies' by the old gas stove, and when she peered into Ma's bedroom no mahogany radiogram, no bed, no piece of curtaining with small elephants on it to cover the window looking out onto the street where her family were patiently waiting for her to reappear. Clutching Mrs Teddy all the more tightly she bolted out into the street again. Whatever happened they must take her with them, they mustn't leave her behind at Number Four, because Number Four had quite gone.

'Just wait till you see the lovely green fields and feel the warmth of the sun on your face, pet,' Ma sighed, sitting back with her arm round Ottilie while in the front seat their neighbour Mrs Burgess gaily crashed through the gears of her new Morris Minor, doing her best to take off after Charlie in Mr Sullivan's hearse at a faster speed than was thoroughly normal for her.

Ottilie was sick seven times on the first leg of their great journey to Cornwall. She actually became quite proud of how many times, but after they had all stopped off to stay over at a pub called the Three Horseshoes, her sickness quite disappeared and she fell happily asleep with her ears full of the sounds of people laughing and talking in the bar below, her tummy at last having righted itself with a bowl of bread and milk and brown sugar. She only woke momentarily when Ma came in much later, rolled into her own bed under the window and fell asleep, soon snoring loudly as a result of drinking a great deal of her favourite stout.

It was only the next day, as they neared the village where Ma had bought their cottage with the money sent from America, that Ottilie started to feel the strangeness of the new country into which they had driven. To her childish eyes the hedges that shielded the little winding country roads appeared enormous, and the grass beyond them strangely uninteresting because of the lack of shops or lights. And the quiet, the very peace of it all, seemed so frightening that she found herself once more clinging to Ma's index finger.

'Well now, will you look at that, Mags Burgess?' Ma exclaimed as they pulled up behind the hearse in front of a cottage with a dark green front door. 'Will you look at what I've bought? It's even nicer than the man in the estate agent's promised, wouldn't you say?'

Mrs Burgess, a large woman with bright red lips and handbag and shoes to match, turned her equally bright blue-rimmed eyes on her friend.

'Never tell me this is the first time you've seen the place, love?'

'Of course not, Mags,' Ma replied, tossing her red plait behind her and pinning it up to the top of her head with a kirby grip as she always did in times of stress, 'sure didn't I see it all in the de*tails* that Lorcan and I sent for? And in the window of the agency? Of course it's not the first time I've seen it.'

'It's the first time you've seen it all right,' said Mrs Burgess, a triumphant look in her eyes. 'You had no idea until now *what* you had bought, did you?'

'I did too.'

'You did not.'

Without another word Ma opened the car door and stepped out into the midday sun. She strode up to the front door and opened it, Ottilie closely following. The two younger boys began to run wildly around the garden, shouting and yelling for no other reason than that they had arrived, while Lorcan and Charlie threw open the back of the hearse and started to unpack their few possessions.

'I did too know what it was like.' Ma stepped into the small flagstoned hall and turned to Mags Burgess who had followed her out of the car, inquisitive as always. 'See, it's lovely, isn't it?'

But that was before they stepped through into the other rooms. Water, damp, walls bulging, a tap dripping non-stop in the downstairs bathroom. There was a long silence as the three of them tiptoed gingerly through not just the darkness of the low-ceilinged rooms but the large pools on the old flagstoned floors. It was broken finally by Ma, who said with her customary good humour as she stared at all the water, 'Well now, isn't it just as well that the first thing the boys want to do is learn to swim?'

There was just one more second of silence, and then Mags Burgess and Ma started to laugh uproariously before turning back to the warmth outside, to the tall grass of the garden, to the unpacking of the hearse, and most important of all to the finding of the old brown teapot from Number Four. Once they had that everything would start to be right again, Ma said, while Mrs Burgess lit a cigarette and said, 'Well, you can always come back to London when you want, love, don't forget that. The landlord hasn't found anyone for Number Four yet.'

At which Ottilie's heart gave a little leap and she thought, 'Yes please let's all go back,' because secretly, deep down, that was what she wanted more than anything in the world, to go straight back to their safe life at Number Four with the noise of the traffic thrumming past the outside door and the half-open windows and everyone and everything that they knew so well, the manager who ran the pub and always slipped her chocolate, Mr North the manager of MacDonagh's who gave Ma the end-of-day loaves, Charlie's uncle in the greengrocery who set aside the cabbages. They were all her friends, and she knew now that she might never see them again, because of being in Cornwall, just because Ma wanted everything to be the way it had been when she herself was small and lived in somewhere called County Kerry.

'Ah, once we get the beds put up, and the water brushed out of the downstairs rooms, it'll be more like home than home, you'll see. At least the electric's on for us,' Ma said brightly to Ottilie after they'd managed to boil the kettle for some tea. 'All this place is in need of is a bit of a lick of paint, Ottie darlin', and some love. That's all this place needs, pet. Really. We'll have it like new in no time.' And she gave Ottilie a quick hug, as if she sensed the little girl needed reassuring.

It was the pitch-black darkness of it all. The deep, deep black of the night, no comforting street lighting, no feeling that outside there were human beings to whom you could run, recognizable people who walked or hurried towards shops and away from buses, or away from buses towards shops. Here on Ottilie's first night in this

29

place called 'the country' there was nothing but black.

Ottilie closed her eyes, terrified of the density of the darkness, only to find that it was black behind her eyes too and that shutting them against the dark did not send the fear away. All she wanted was to go back to Number Four where happiness was street lighting outside the window all night, and the gentle hum of the evening traffic soothing her to sleep only to wake her once more in the morning. She put her head under her pillow. She thought she was going to hate this place called Cornwall.

But in the morning everything was better. Ma laid out the old kitchen table in front of the cottage door, and although the grass was long and tufty in places Lorcan put stones under the legs and banged it down, and after a while it stopped wobbling. Then they all sat outside while Ma buttered bread and poured the milk she'd brought all the way from London into a blue and white striped jug, and set out a great slab of yellow butter, and what with the old brown teapot and their old nursery mugs to drink from, and being able to watch the birds come and feed when Lorcan threw the crumbs from their plates towards them, Cornwall suddenly seemed a great deal better to Ottilie than it had the night before.

'With a little help from God and the weather, we surely must be able to mend the roof and the plumbing before winter?' Ma asked of no-one, as the two younger boys started to climb trees and Ottilie wandered over to the little stream that ran between the cottage and the road. 'I should say so,' she finished, half to herself, as she walked to where Ottilie was trying to see past the weeds down to the stones where she thought there might be fish. 'Mind yourself now, pet. Just until you can swim.'

Ottilie turned to make sure Ma was watching, and then carefully removed her socks and shoes and stepped down the shallow bank into the stream. She wrinkled her face at the aching cold of the water and the feel of the sharp stones, but she did not attempt to climb out, so suddenly soothing was the sensation of real water in a real stream. With the sounds of the birds around, the smell of the fresh grass and the murmur of a bee busy somewhere near, she felt thoroughly happy.

She smiled back at Ma.

'You're bold, you are,' Ma murmured and left her to refill her enamelled mug with tea while Ottilie stared fascinated at the wildlife that was swimming past her feet and ankles. She saw a toad further up the bank, and a butterfly. Eventually, with Ma still gone, she stared up into the air around her, at the blue sky, the clouds, the birds, the sun which was already starting to warm her, and as she did so the picture that she saw above her, her picture, was suddenly filled with a red face, narrow eyes, bearded chin and a cap set on top of thick white ill-cut tufted hair.

'What you doin' here? That waater, that's not for 'ee to paddle in, not 't all. That waater goes t' troughs at top, 's not for 'ee t' put dirty feet in!'

Ottilie stared up at the angry face above her, and then turning quickly attempted to scramble up the steep sides of the bank down which she had slipped a few minutes earlier with such success. But now her bare, shoeless feet were so wet they slid uselessly, just as her hands proved useless when she tried to pull at the tufts of grass that grew what seemed yards above her on the steep sides of the stream. The man started to lean towards her, his own feet slip-sliding down the sides of the bank. Ottilie opened her mouth to call to someone but no sound came out. She wanted to shout for Lorcan and Ma, and Joseph, and Sean – for everyone, for them all, but she couldn't, even though she had opened her mouth wider and wider as he reached out and grabbed her, and anyway the sight of this large man slip-sliding down towards her froze her with fear. Finally a scream did emerge, but it was not hers. Ma was plunging down the bank towards the man.

'You leave her alone,' Ma screamed, just as it seemed

that the man's large red hands had reached out to drag Ottilie towards him.

'She be paddlin' in our waater – tedden right. Paddlin's for sea, not for our waater. That waater serves all o' us in these cribs.'

But the old man's angry words of justification were wasted on Ma. All she could see was the stranger's hands on Ottilie's shoulders, pulling her towards him. Without a moment's hesitation she hurtled forward, and reaching up she punched him as hard as she could. He stepped back, his eyes registering astonishment at the woman's primitive fury, but as he did so his old wellington boots slipped suddenly out from under him on the watery base of the stream, and he staggered backwards before falling with a sudden, frightening force.

Ottilie watched with fascination from behind Ma as he just lay there while Ma looked down in amazement at his extraordinary and very prompt state of unconsciousness, as visibly astonished as he had been when she had punched him in the shoulder with such force.

Ottilie, realizing that she was the cause of all the trouble, promptly stuck her thumb in her mouth as Ma let out another great scream, this time for someone to come and help her drag the old man up the bank before he 'drowned in the water, God help him'.

'I think you've killed him, Ma,' Lorcan announced when he joined his mother in the stream, watched closely by Mrs Burgess and the other two boys from the bank above them. 'Hey. Someone help me, will ya?'

Between them all they dragged the old man as best they could from the stream and up the bank, until they finally placed him on the grass. Mrs Burgess ran inside for a jug of cold water from the kitchen to throw over him.

'It's ice cold, anyway,' she cried, running back out again. 'It hurts to put your hand in it.'

The water must indeed have been cold, because within seconds the old man was starting to sit up, and then cursing and swearing and holding the back of his head, not to mention his sodden cap, while Lorcan and Joseph and Mrs Burgess fussed over him and apologized what seemed to Ottilie to be a hundred times for the accident.

Thoroughly conscious now but still furious, he backed away from them, wanting nothing of their brushings down and offers of cups of tea.

'I shaan't forget whaat 'ee done,' he shouted, and still cursing and holding his head he staggered off down the road, his clothes leaving a wet trail on the hard uneven surface.

'Ah, Ma, what did you want to go and do that for?' Lorcan groaned, and he shook his head disbelievingly at his mother as the rest of them watched the angry old figure disappearing into the distance, the sound of his footsteps still reverberating in the quiet air long after he had become a far and distant figure. 'I mean, what in heaven's name possessed you? You've made an enemy before we've even hung up our trousers on the bed rail.'

'Sure 'twasn't my fault the silly old man fell over, Lorcan, and never say I've made an enemy,' Ma said without much conviction, still looking after the damp figure staggering down the hill. 'Any man touches my children I give them what's coming to them, Lorcan, you know that. Didn't he have his hands on Ottilie's little shoulders? One second later and she could have been taken from us and we would never have seen her again. I've known that to happen before. Tinkers and gypsies and old men of no fixed abode, they steal children to help them with their own stealing. And didn't my own father used to say that you have to swat them like flies as soon as they land near you?'

Lorcan sighed and shook his head. 'We're not in Ireland now, Ma, we're not even at Number Four. That man is not a tinker or a gypsy, he's probably some local character. And he's not likely to take this lying down, I tell you. The postman warned us, people round these parts are very

33

clannish, St Elcombe particularly. The postman said we're foreigners here, as much as if we'd come from abroad, and that's the truth, Ma. That's why we've got to be careful, because of being foreigners in St Elcombe.'

As Lorcan spoke the whole family listened, silent and suddenly worried. Lorcan was after all the eldest. Lorcan was the most sensible too. He was in Da's place, and they all knew it. Ma looked across at him, shamefaced, knowing that he was speaking the truth. She never liked upsetting Lorcan, the quiet one, the good one. Lorcan was a shoulder to lean on, a man already in his mother's eyes.

'You must be careful, Ma. We don't know anyone here and there's no-one likely to be on our side,' he reminded his mother more gently, before starting back towards Charlie and the hearse to resume the unpacking. As he went he tried to shrug his shoulders, but his face still reflected his worried state of mind.

'I'm sorry, Lorcan, really. My temper just got the better of me,' Ma called after him.

'Ah, you did what you did, and what you did you did for the best reasons, Ma, and nothing at all to be done now. Let's just hope that the man is not some sort of great huge power in the village, because then our goose will be well and truly cooked. And eaten for that matter.'

'If he's a power anywhere except in his own mind, I personally would be flabberstruck. I mean, an old man like that, he's no more than just a local nobody, surely?' Ma looked round for reassurance.

But as they were all soon to discover, there was no such thing as a nobody in St Elcombe.

Three

A magical discovery was made by Ottilie over the next weeks. Ladybirds would sometimes land on her out-stretched arms if she stood still enough, and they could be put into a jam jar with a lid which her second brother Joseph had pierced with his treasured penknife. The insects made fascinating viewing as they climbed about the grass inside the jar before being released when evening came. And this was only one of many entertainments, for there were spiders' webs to be watched and nests to be made from straw and grass for ungrateful wild birds who never seemed to be tempted to use them. These delights soon became more than adequate compensation for the darkly frightening nights that Cornwall had brought to Ottilie's life.

Just lying in the grass and listening to what seemed to her fanciful imagination to be armies of ants in hobnailed boots marching towards her was happiness itself. And the sky above her that first summer, it was always, always blue, so blue that because it was reflected in the sea Ottilie came to think that blue was the sea's natural colour and it would always stay like that, little realizing that when the sky turned grey, so too would the sea.

There was so much to do at the cottage it was just as well that the early summer weather continued hot and cloud-less. Even Mrs Burgess was reluctant to go back to London, although she finally did.

She had hardly departed before Lorcan and Joseph, with the aid of books borrowed from the St Elcombe library, started on the rebuilding of the cottage, Sean acting as an unwilling builder's mate. And so it was that a new routine established itself, a routine that seemed to make Ma look younger and happier with each day that passed, and as the days turned to weeks it seemed that the move from Number Four could only be deemed a success.

For Ottilie there were still more unlooked-for joys in keeping watch for field mice, in seeing her feet and legs, day by happy day, turning a richer and deeper brown – a colour which at evening she noticed was gloriously emphasized by the white marks made by her bathing suit – in the seemingly endless golden afternoons during which, while the boys worked on the cottage, Ma would take her down to the sea to paddle. It was not so far to the shore that they could not walk the whole way, Ma strolling in the sunshine, her hips swaying comfortably, Ottilie beside her carrying her newest most precious possessions which were a tin bucket and a small plastic spade that Ma had bought for her at the shop near the beach.

Most days Ma and she took their tea in a basket so that Ottilie's skill in building some new and even more elaborate sandcastle was rewarded by sitting back and biting into mildly gritty teatime sandwiches and sponge cakes whose icing ran a little from being in the sun. Then Ottilie watched with satisfying contentment the incoming tide slowly flood first her castle's moat, then its inner courtyards, before eventually drowning the whole edifice, a signal for her and Ma to turn for home, the cottage and the boys.

'It's too hot for sandwiches. We'll go up to the shop and buy you a cornet.' Ma pulled Ottilie to her one afternoon and retied her sun bonnet before kissing her and coaxing her feet into her beach shoes with their long shoelaces that tied round and round her ankles. 'Come, pet, take Ma's finger, and we'll go on up. We may not be millionaires, darlin', but we can afford to buy you a cornet today, and maybe take a block in some newspaper back to the boys, for they've been slaving on the cottage so they have and they deserve a little treat.'

Ottilie did not notice the silence in the shop when Ma and she walked in that afternoon, but she did notice the bright shiny beach balls hung in nets above her, blown up ready to be played with on the beach. She gazed at them mesmerized as Ma went to the counter and asked for a cornet. The ice cream had to be scooped out with a special spoon from a big container. Ottilie longed for a beach ball, but knew, without being told, there was no money for such a thing.

'Shall we'm put ice creaam block in newspaper for 'ee, ma'am?'

'That's kind of you, I'd say.'

The woman took down a cardboard box for carrying their purchases as Ma carefully counted out the money from her old red leather purse, exactly the right amount for the ice creams in pennies and halfpennies. Ottilie remembered that, because Ma had such a thing about change. Once the boys had found a shiny new shilling on the road. They wanted to keep it, but Ma would not let them, although she stared at it with reverence as if imagining just how nice that little shilling turned into a fresh-baked loaf might taste. But no, they had to leave it on the wall beside the road, in case the person who owned it came back looking for it and was in greater need than they. The boys had found that hard, a whole shilling was after all a whole shilling, and they would have dearly loved to buy some sweets with that money, but what Ma said went, so the shilling stayed.

That was why Ottilie remembered how carefully Ma had counted out the money, because of the business of the shilling those many months before.

This afternoon there were no such lucky finds, just Ma taking the wrapped ice cream that the lady behind the counter handed to her all tucked up neatly in an old grocery box, and then they were outside the shop, and Ma had just leaned down to wipe Ottilie's mouth with the corner of her small flowered handkerchief, saying in a low voice, 'One day that woman will think to smile at me while I'm spending my hard-earned in there.'

She had hardly finished speaking when the woman who had sold her the ice cream and the extra wafers for the boys came out of the shop, closely followed by her daughter and one of the other customers.

''Ere, you cum 'ere, madam, you cum 'ere 'twonce. We'm mun ask to see what's en your box, please?'

Ma straightened up and looked in bewilderment first at the cardboard box in her arms and then at the women.

'Sure there's not a thing in my box except what the lady gave me. Why would there be?'

They stood round her and Ottilie, very close so that Ottilie could smell a faint scent of onions on them, while Ma as if in a trance handed back the still closed cardboard box into which the woman had put the ice cream wrapped in newspaper and the extra wafers for the boys.

'Whaat be this then, my dear?'

The shop owner, a small woman in a flowered apron, stared accusingly from Ma to the small cardboard box as she lifted out not just the newspaper parcel but a small packet of biscuits and a packet of tea.

'You ben stealin' my goods again you ben, and we'm all seen 'ee this time. Seen 'ee with our own eyes we'm did! And 'tes not the first tem, 'tes not, we'm noticed you afore!'

As soon as she saw those items, items that she would never buy, Ma knew they must have been deliberately put there by the shop owner.

'Those have been put in there by mistake,' she said in a voice that Ottilie recognized was strangely constricted and yet determinedly calm. 'We – we don't drink that kind of tea, and I always bake our own biscuits of a Sunday, so I do.'

''Tes stealin' all th' same, my dear, whether 'tes your kind o' tea or not. If 's not ben paid for, 'tes thievin'.'

'I tell yous I would not steal from yous, madam, not if I was starvin' and my childer too, but if you want payin' for these t'ings I'll pay, and there'll be an end to the whole unfortunate matter.'

'We'm poor folk round 'ere, but we'm honest folk, not like 'ee,' one of the other witnesses said, adding, 'You ben stealin' from 'ere regular, we'm thinking.'

'I haven't been into the shop more than a dozen times all the time we've been at St Elcombe, and we've brought our own tea with us to the beach most days we've come,' Ma said, her voice now starting to tremble. 'As God is my witness, I'd no more steal from anyone than cut the throat of one of my own childer.'

'You'm Irish. Irish's always thievin', 'tes what we'm heard, an' 'tes true. We'm heard you'm like Irish lempet-pickers from the old time, they wus allus stealin'.'

'We'm goin' to take 'ee down to station and we'm goin' to tell constable, we'm going to tell police.'

Ottilie did not know quite what was going on but she knew about policemen all right, from living at Number Four. No-one who lived at the flats liked policemen, and no-one ever called one or took anyone else down to a station, so that long before Ma said, her voice still trembling, 'Don't be frightened, Ottilie pet, just hold on to Ma's finger and we'll soon sort all this out,' she knew that something terrible must be happening, more awful even than when Ma had pushed the man over when Ottilie was playing in the stream.

'If only we knew where there was a telephone or we had one our own selves I could call Lorcan and he would come down and he would know what to do,' Ma went on, as Ottilie trotted beside her, clutching her index finger for dear life. 'Mebbe the policeman will let us call the neighbour to tell Lorcan, Ottilie pet. Say a prayer, dotie. Why do they think we're like the lempet-pickers? We've no business with lempets, no and never would. This is all such a terrible mistake.'

Ma made a sound that was something between a sob and a sigh, but the women did not seem to hear her, and certainly showed no pity for her. Within minutes, they had shepherded Ma and Ottilie up the steps of St Elcombe police station.

Clinging to her mother's index finger Ottilie prayed with all her heart for Lorcan to arrive. His handsome young face and tall figure would be such a blessing at this point, and his measured manner, always so comforting to everyone, but most especially when Ma was in what Lorcan always called 'one of her stews' as she was now, telling the policeman over and over again in her soft Irish voice, 'But tell me why should I do such a thing when I have plenty of money to pay and plenty of tea at home in the tin?' as the women all crowded round explaining what they had seen and putting the packet of tea and the biscuits too in front of the constable.

Ottilie sat down on a chair and stared at the picture on her tin bucket. She had never seen Ma in such a state. It was frightening for Ottilie to notice that Ma's normally composed face had turned all blotchy, and her hand clutching the red leather purse shook and shook as if she was suddenly old and needed a stick to support her. Ottilie had rather not look at her, just wait for Lorcan to arrive. Once Lorcan arrived everything would all be all right, because it always was all right when Lorcan was there.

'Would you like to get in touch with a solicitor, once you've been charged?' asked the policeman at one point, in answer to which Ma shook her head, hardly able to frame an answer to his question because her lips were trembling so much.

'Sure I've no business with a solicitor, how would a woman like me have a solicitor? It's my son Lorcan I want to talk to, he'll know what to do. These women – they know as well as I do that I never stole from them,

Constable. On my life I – I would rather die than steal from them. I'm a woman alone, my husband in America, and who would there be to look after me childer, Constable, if I'm to be charged and I might end in prison, and no-one to speak for me?'

After some more of such talk, with the policeman's voice becoming more and more measured as Ma grew more and more hysterical and Ottilie concentrating on the picture of the children playing on the side of her bucket, the policeman indicated to Ma that since there was no telephone at their cottage he would send someone on a bicycle to fetch Lorcan.

'These people must really hate us, Ottie darling,' Ma murmured over and over again as they waited for Lorcan to arrive. It seemed to be hours later that he eventually appeared, dressed in a clean white shirt and a dark tie, his hair brushed tidy and flat as if he was about to go to church. 'Oh, Lorcan, at last you're here! Lorcan, these women, they say I've taken tea and biscuits from their shop. Tell them I would never do such a thing, tell them.'

Lorcan put out his strong hands and attempted to steady his pleading mother.

'Don't say anything more, Ma. Of course it's a mistake, just don't say any more.'

'But Lorcan,' Ma wailed, clutching at him with her roughened hands, 'I didn't take anything – you know well I always bake our own biscuits.'

'And a right load of old jaw-crackers *they* usually turn out to be,' Lorcan agreed, trying to joke. 'Come on, Ma, don't cry, please. We'll go home and think of something, like we always do.'

But Ma could not help herself, what with the relief at seeing Lorcan and the awful fear brought on from being in a police station accused of something that she had obviously not done. Ottilie turned away at the sound of her mother's sobs, her eyes filling with tears, the sound of her happy mother crying bringing a lump to her throat so large that it was as if she was trying to swallow away one of those jaw-cracking biscuits about which Lorcan and the boys were always teasing Ma.

Ma continued to sob while Lorcan tried hard to stay calm and listen to what the policeman was saying. Ottilie, hardly able to contain her fear at seeing her mother so distressed, also strained to hear. Words like 'first offence' and 'magistrates' court' and 'bound over', and then at last there was the fresh cold air of outside and Ma had stopped crying and they were all walking home together, heading for the cottage, where Ottilie imagined they would all be safe once more.

It was only as they reached the freshly painted green door that Ma suddenly gasped, 'Oh, Lorcan, dotie, imagine.' She started to cry again. 'After all that, after all that, I've only gone and left your ice cream in the police station.'

Joseph had his theories about the people in the shop and Sean agreed with him. They were obviously relatives or friends of the old man Ma had pushed over by mistake that first day. He had gone back and told them all about the nasty woman who had punched him in the shoulder, as a consequence of which they had waited and waited until that hot afternoon to plant the tea and the biscuits among Ma's shopping.

'I mean you know Ma, she doesn't usually need a box but they gave her one that afternoon and she took it because of wrapping the ice cream in the newspaper to get it home, see? They must have thought it was Christmas. All those weeks waiting for Ma, and then – bang, they had her!'

The idea of such a wicked conspiracy in the town would have been thrilling to the two younger boys had it not been their mother who was the innocent victim. There was no doubt in the minds of Joseph and Sean that had Ma not pushed the old man in the stream over that day all would have been well, and no-one would have planted the tea or the biscuits in her box. Only Lorcan felt differently.

'I don't know,' was all he would say whenever the subject came up at night, and then he would take himself off to study more books on building and plumbing. 'I just don't know.'

Cornwall, St Elcombe, the cottage, even walking to the seaside with her bucket and spade, it all changed after that and became dull and sad. Once more Ottilie found herself longing to be back at Number Four where no-one had ever pushed anyone, and everyone in the neighbourhood loved Ma, and she had not taken to suddenly bursting into tears as she did now whenever they went walking all alone along the beach, saying 'I've too much on my mind, pet' to want to build castles with Ottilie any more. Worse than that, she no longer wanted Ottilie to paddle or run about while she sat on the sands watching her. All she wanted now was to walk and walk, and walk, until eventually they were so tired that when they returned home they had hardly enough energy to eat their tea and put themselves to bed.

And when the day came that Ma had to go up in front of the magistrates in Branhaven the boys joked and laughed too noisily in the station taxi all the way there, because they were so frightened that Ma would be taken away from them. And there again, once they were in the magistrates' court, as Lorcan said afterwards on the cab-ride home, 'She might as well have whistled as plead not guilty. I mean, you could see the magistrates looking up and seeing Ma's flaming red hair and thinking that no shopkeeper *wouldn't* spot her taking something. And they certainly couldn't muddle her up with someone else, not at all. I mean red hair. It's a dead giveaway. Never mind – could have been worse, Ma. A great deal worse.'

Lorcan patted his mother's hand happily. Like all of them he was just glad she had not gone to prison, but she snatched it from under his.

43

'That solicitor. He was worse than useless. A bucket with a hole would have held more water than the case he made out for me. And it could not be worse, Lorcan, and well you know it,' Ma muttered as she stared out of the window into the gathering dusk. 'It could not have been worse if the wretched woman in the shop had murdered me. Never mind the ten-pound fine and the humiliation, what about my reputation? Where am I now in a place like St Elcombe, unable to go shopping for anything without everyone staring? Places like this, they never forget what they think you've done, not if you live to be a hundred. Where am I now, a woman alone and without a reputation?'

'You'll still have a reputation, Ma, of course you will. Everyone who knows you already won't believe you took those things, will they, Mr Martin?' he asked the taxi driver. 'No-one will believe you would be bothered to take a packet of tea you never drink and biscuits you never eat. People are a great deal nicer than that, aren't they, Mr Martin?'

The taxi driver glanced at Lorcan in his driving mirror and nodded. Mr Martin was the postman's brother, and already the postman had proved more than friendly to Lorcan and the boys, helping them out with tip-offs as to where to find cheap or second-hand building materials for the cottage.

'We'm very friendly folk at St Elcombe, ma'am, very friendly.'

Lorcan smiled across at Ma.

'See? What did I tell you? People are much nicer than we give them credit for, Ma.'

The boys and Ottilie all smiled with relief at Mr Martin in his driving mirror. At least he was all right, at least he was not against them.

And so the children arrived back at the cottage in a much more cheerful mood than they had imagined possible, which was more than could be said of Ma, who continued to stare out of the taxi window a sullen and forbidding expression on her face. When they all tumbled out of the car thrilled to be home once more, she merely gave Lorcan the door key from her coat pocket and sat down on an old chair on the grass outside, saying, without any of her usual grace and kindness, 'Just don't bother me for a while, will you?'

'OK, Ma. But you know, cheer up. Really. It could have been worse.'

'Cheer up? Didn't you see that reporter creature in there? Taking it all down? Cheer up indeed!'

'Yes, but he won't necessarily put it in the paper, now will he, Lorcan? They don't print everything they write down.'

'Just leave me alone for a while, Joseph, will you?'

'Yes, come on, Joe.' Lorcan gave his middle brother a tug on his arm. 'Leave Ma in peace. Come on, Ottilie, I'll give you a piggy back.'

Lorcan swung his young sister behind him, and making horse sounds he trotted her up to the front door. But the moment the door creaked open in response to the large old-fashioned key with its three great teeth, and long before Lorcan had put a light on or even stepped into the hall, he knew something was wrong.

It was the smell. It was the awful overpowering sickening smell. And when he put Ottilie down and she ran past him and slipped and fell on something dark and damp and Lorcan heard an unmistakable snorting sound, he knew exactly why there was such a stench. He put on the sitting room light and saw the reason standing in front of them, a piece of wool hanging out of its mouth, looking twice its normal size due to the low ceiling and the cramped room.

Joseph, crowding behind, stared first at the pig and then at his brothers as Sean started to laugh.

'Don't be an eejit, Sean, laughing like that. Will you just look at what it's done to all our fine work?'

45

Lorcan gestured round at the freshly painted walls in despair before they all dashed into the next room where the precious old radiogram stood, to see if what they now dreaded was really true. It was. The place had been wrecked. There was dung everywhere, or mess of one kind or another. It would take hours just to scrub the place down, let alone redecorate. Even Ma's knitting had not escaped unscathed.

Ottilie climbed out of the way as her brothers shooed the pig out of the cottage and down the road and Ma, half laughing and half crying from the shock of it all, as always went into the kitchen to make a cup of tea. Ma's answer to everything that happened, in sunshine or in shadow, was a cup of tea so strong and dark that it could have been mistaken for gravy.

But she could hardly have been in the kitchen for more than a second when she came straight out again, shouting for the boys to come and see what she had just seen, her face red with fury and her mouth working to get out the words.

'Who would do something like this?' Sean demanded of no-one when he returned with his brothers, and he pummelled his head with his fist. 'I mean who would write that on the walls of someone's kitchen?'

'Who'd you think?' Ma asked, once more seated on the old kitchen chair in front of the cottage. 'Who else but one of the friendly local people such as the postman and his brother, or the friendly farmer down the way, all these nice friendly souls we're surrounded by – the ones Lorcan's always telling us are so nice and kind? That's who did this.'

'Hang on, Ma, the pig didn't come from the farm, they only keep cattle and sheep. Even so they're going to hold on to it and try to find out where it does belong. They were really very kind, Ma. Most upset for us. I mean they really had no idea of who would do such a thing.'

'Ah, what does it matter, Lorcan? What does it matter

now who did it? For aren't we ruined anyway?'

'Never say so, Ma. Come on, Joseph, Sean – Ottilie too, you can help. Empty your bucket of those shells and bring it in. We'll show Ma just what a good job we can make of the cleaning up. The place will look like a painting before the night is out we'll have it that clean.'

Ma turned back briefly as the children trooped into the cottage.

'Just remember the one thing a person can't do is clean up their reputation, Lorcan. Once you're guilty in a court of law you're guilty for ever and no amount of scrubbing will take away from that. No carbolic, no cleaner, nothing. Once your reputation goes that's it, for ever and ever, amen.'

'Yes, Ma.'

Lorcan answered dutifully enough but once they were all inside and he was directing the clean-up operations, and they were beginning to sweep out the breakages from the side tables in the sitting room that the pig had charged into in its fear, not to mention the droppings everywhere on the flagstones, he said to Joseph and Sean in a low voice, 'Never mind Ma, she's only got this thing because of Da, you know? She's never forgotten the business with the police planting that money in his car and his having to go to America. But this time it was only a fine, not prison, that and the solicitor's fee, and if we put our shoulders to the wheel I reckon we'll all earn that back soon enough.'

'Of course we will,' Joseph agreed, nudging Sean. 'We've plans all right, haven't we, Sean? Plans to earn money any way we can to help Ma and you, and Ottilie,' he added, picking her up and giving her a twirl. 'Even Ottilie who was sent to us by the Little People.'

After that the children all set to at once with the cleaning, cheered as always by their elder brother's commitment.

But when Ottilie asked what was written on the wall Lorcan would not tell her.

Only when Joseph and she were alone in the kitchen and she asked him over and over, 'Please, please, please tell me, I won't tell Lorcan you told, please, please tell me, Joseph. What did it say, Joseph, please tell me?' did Joseph, who was already tired out from helping to paint out the writing, finally look down from his stepladder and give in at last, thinking that really he would do anything for a quiet life.

'Oh, Ottie, if you really want to know, it said "Irish Pigs Go Home",' he told her, carefully dipping his brush in the white paint they were busy putting up all over the cottage. 'But don't you worry about it, because we're not going to,' he finished, frowning at the daub he had just made on the wall with more than usual vigour.

'Are we really not going back to Number Four? Are you sure we can't, just for a little while, Joseph?'

'No,' Joseph said, not really listening. 'We're not going home. We're staying here in Cornwall. It's better for us, Ottie.'

Ottilie turned away. She could not tell Joseph how much she longed for the old days at Number Four, those days she remembered as golden and warm, now gone. She would give anything to swap the singing of the birds for the sound of buses pulling slowly past the windows of the flat. Sometimes she would lie awake in the darkness of the countryside imagining she could hear the sounds of other children playing in the street, laughing and happy as they tore up and down on their fairy bicycles, narrowly avoiding pedestrians who stepped aside with tolerant expertise as they all raced each other to some lamp post in the distance, or set off for the park with their roller skates hanging from their handlebars. In contrast Cornwall seemed peopled by enemies, making them unhappy, telling them to go home.

Four

Lorcan had decided to go out to work. After all, he argued, now he was nearly seventeen it was surely high time he left school and helped out with the finances? Ma, who had always been against the idea, seemed suddenly uninterested whether or not Lorcan went on studying, or took up an apprenticeship in building, or anything else for that matter.

'What does it matter, Lorcan, dotie?' she would ask, sighing, whenever the matter was raised. 'In the scheme of things what does it matter, when you come to think of it?' Gone were all her usual cheerful family catchphrases such as 'Let's give it some gumption now, shall we?' and 'Nothing stops the O'Flahertys except heaven's gates', all said in her soft Western Irish voice.

So Lorcan went out to work, and Ottilie went to school.

Although she went to a very different school from Joseph and Sean, a small convent run by a nun and a priest, Ottilie hated lessons quite as heartily as the boys, and longed to be free like Lorcan to go to work in the morning, to come back with some money to give Ma.

Maybe if she could give Ma some money she would love Ottilie the way she used to, and maybe she would smile and laugh the way she had always done until that dreadful day in the shop when both of them had to go to the police station and Ma had cried so awfully after Lorcan arrived wearing his best white shirt, his head of thick curly hair all tidied.

'What you doing there, Ottie?' Lorcan came into the

kitchen, his handsome face dark and tanned now from being outside all day so that the colour of his blue-grey eyes stood out in a most startling way from the brown of his face. It was now deep winter and their little cottage was being rocked by the winter winds, and when you walked down to the beach at St Elcombe the sound of the waves pounding the beach was so loud that not even the crying of the seagulls could be heard above it, nor Ma walking along the beach every afternoon as she did now, whatever the weather, talking to herself. 'You're not to upset Ma by making a mess.'

'Not making a mess, Lorcan, making jam tarts,' Ottilie told him, standing on a kitchen stool to mix the flour and the margarine for the pastry while Joseph, his dark head bent over his homework, sat studying opposite her at the table.

'You don't know how to make jam tarts, Ottie.'

'I do, I do, I do!' Ottilie raised her voice in indignation.

'Oh, you do so? So how do you?'

'You take eight ounces of flour and half as much of fat and then you add the water little by little, and you roll it out with a rolling pin. See? I know because we did it at school.'

Lorcan nodded solemnly. He had no idea whether or not Ottilie was right but when he looked down into the bowl he had to admit the mixture did look like raw pastry. He went out, saying, 'Well, as long as Joseph's watching you.'

'Don't worry, Lorcan, I'll put the jam in the pies, and the tray in the oven for her. I won't let her burn herself.'

Joseph helped as he had promised and Ottilie watched the clock as if it was ticking away her last minutes on earth. Finally there were the tarts looking as good as anything. Ottilie picked up a plate and a cup of water and went through to Ma who was asleep in the tiny sitting room before an unlit fire.

'I've made you a jam tart and some tea, Ma,' she said,

and she pushed her arm gently. Ma did not stir, so Ottilie pushed her some more. Still she did not stir, so Ottilie, having carefully placed the jam tart and the cup on a side table, climbed onto her lap and rocked her face between her hands. 'Please, please wake up, Ma, please?'

Lorcan must have heard her because he came through from the hall where he was mending a lamp. Seeing Ottilie rocking Ma's face between her small plump hands he caught her up and took her out, saying, 'It's no good, Ottie. When Ma's like that nothing will wake her, pet, nothing at all. You'll just have to wait to give her your jam tart, you understand? Just wait till she wakes of her own accord, OK?'

Ottilie nodded, confused and worried, but she ran off back to the kitchen.

'Ma sleeping it off, is she?' Joseph looked up from his book as she came back in. 'Sleeping off the gin. Gin. The big sleep drink,' Joseph went on, giving a fair imitation of an American accent.

'Why does she have gin, Joseph?' Ottilie wondered, transferring her kitchen stool to the sink so that she could wash up.

'She has gin because she's upset still, you know? Because of the incident with the old man that day in the stream, remember? Well, since then, all the local people – well, not all of them, but some of them – they've been out to get Ma. That old man. Well. See, he's related to practically everyone in St Elcombe. And it seems Cornish people don't like Irish people because of what's on the news, Lorcan says. But Ma should never have punched him like that. It was asking for it. But then you should never have got into the stream that feeds into the troughs. That water's very sacred to people round here, you know, like in church? Everything that's happened, it's all your fault, Ottie,' Joseph added, meaning to tease her.

But even though she knew that Joseph was really only teasing Ottilie had to swallow hard to stop herself crying, because although Joseph did not mean what he'd said about its being all her fault that Ma had changed so much she knew it was true. It *was* all her fault. If she had not climbed into the stream that day the man would never have put his hands on her shoulders and Ma would never have defended her and the people in the grocery shop would never have pretended that she stole their tea and biscuits.

Every day after that Ottilie brought Ma a gift, something she had made or something she had drawn or painted, or a piece of fruit given to her by the greengrocer on her way home from school. Much as she wanted to eat the apple or the banana, she always kept it in her satchel for Ma. But when she ran into the cottage hoping against hope that today she would find her old Ma, the one who was always so happy and kind, she would stop at the sitting room door the moment she heard the sound of Ma snoring, and not bother to go any further into the room, knowing straight away that the old Ma was still not back, that she was lost to them for another day.

One day Lorcan came back full of news. The builder was so pleased with his work he was to get a pay rise, another two pounds a week, but better than that Mr Hulton's firm had been asked to renovate the old Grand Hotel on the seafront.

'You know, the one that looks like a crumbling sandcastle?' he told the other children. 'I reckon we'll be there for years and years. Mr Hulton says there's enough work there to carry us into the next century.'

Lorcan was so thrilled with his news that he even tried to wake Ma, but as usual Ma was sleeping so heavily that not even he could wake her properly.

'I just wish I could get her to stop being like this, just once,' he said, turning away from her in sudden and uncharacteristic despair. 'I wonder should I go and see the doctor? Should I tell him she's not well most days now?'

'Don't be daft. You can't tell anyone anything, not here

in St Elcombe,' said Joseph. 'Please, Lorcan. Just leave Ma alone. She'll soon go back to being like she was before. One of these days she'll stop falling asleep, she will, really. I expect it's just what Ma herself was always going on about, just a – what was it? – oh yes, just a *phase*.'

'If only they hadn't put that thing in the paper,' Sean sighed. 'It was when she saw that – "St Elcombe Woman Fined" – that she got really bad. Such a fuss. They spelt her name wrong anyway – "O'Flannery" – and it was only a small item at the bottom of a silly page of news, after all, nothing to write home about.'

'Not to her, Sean,' Lorcan told him sadly. 'To Ma that piece in the local paper was as big as a message put up in neon lights in Piccadilly itself. She won't ever shop in St Elcombe now, not ever, even if she was dying. No, it has to be over the cliffs to Branhaven. As if anyone would try a thing like that twice. And as if they don't know of her in Branhaven as well as St Elcombe. But no-one can tell her. Da always said they never could, mind.'

The strange thing was, Ottilie noticed, that when Ma returned from walking over the cliffs to Branhaven, which she did most days no matter what happened, she never brought very much back with her. Just a packet of soap powder, or sometimes a tin of apricots or a jar of Marmite. It seemed an awfully long way to go for so very little. Meanwhile the winter crept into early spring and the spring tides were fierce, so fierce that Lorcan warned Ma again and again not to walk over to Branhaven unless she knew the weather forecast.

'People have been blown off those cliffs you know, Ma. You must take care of yourself, particularly in those old shoes of yours with the laces always coming untied.'

'I know what I'm about, Lorcan. I'm still the woman of the house, think what you may. And I'll thank you not to tell me how to go on, dotie darling, for all that I'm sure you mean well.'

'I'm not telling you how to behave, Ma,' Lorcan told her, trying to take her hands in his to make her look at him. 'I wouldn't do that, Ma, ever. I just don't want you having an accident, none of us do. And of course you're still the woman of the house, and always will be.'

Ma looked up at her eldest son, her eyelids swollen and her face plump now from the water retention caused by alcohol. She said nothing, but Ottilie could see that as she turned away her lips were trembling from the effort of not crying. She thundered from the room, her new much fatter figure making her seem clumsy where once she had been so graceful. Even her hair was no longer as lustrous as it had been, but flat and unkempt, and the long plait was not now anchored firmly on top of her head with a kirby grip in moments of crisis or decision but left to hang down around her face.

Ottilie already knew what would happen next. Lorcan would have to watch helplessly as Ma once more escaped from the cottage, perhaps to walk yet again down to the beach or across the cliffs to Branhaven, and the usual feeling of inadequacy would sweep over him, the feeling that he might as well not be there for all the use that he, her eldest son, was to her. He loved his mother, but only she could stop herself from being destroyed, only she could pull herself back from the state into which her own hurt pride had sunk her. Ottilie knew all this because she loved Lorcan with all her heart, and because she loved him she would see the hurt in his eyes, and the look that was so much older than his years – the shoulders already a little stooped from anxiety, the hands already roughened from manual work, everything telling of the old young man that he was, the fated eldest son so often required by absent fathers to throw away their precious youth so that Da could be free.

'Are you ready for school, Ottie?' he asked, looking down at her.

Ottilie nodded, silent as always at these moments when

she knew that Lorcan and she were feeling just the same even though he was seventeen and she was seven. Nowadays Lorcan might work all the time at the Grand Hotel on the front, but Ottilie was sure that she was fast catching him up in cleverness. She could make pastry, write her name and tie her own shoelaces, but what neither of them could do was bring their beloved Ma back to be with them the way she had always been.

Sister Raphael said to pray to God for things that you really wanted, and He would know all about what was truly in your heart. But to Ottilie praying meant just saying over and over again 'Please make Ma better' and squeezing her hands together so hard that they hurt, so strongly that they ached when she finally stopped begging God, besieging Him, to make Ma better soon.

Lorcan and the boys always walked Ottilie to school together. It meant leaving as early as seven thirty because Lorcan had to be on site by eight o'clock. It also meant that Ottilie was left alone each day in the school hall for nearly an hour. Nowadays she would spend the time kneeling in front of the statue of the Sacred Heart of Jesus, absorbed in prayer for Ma and mesmerized by the sight of the statue's golden heart with all the rays of love coming out of it.

Today Ottilie prayed so hard for Ma to be the way she had been before she was accused of taking the tea and the biscuits from the shop that for the rest of the morning, even when she was writing her alphabet or reading aloud from her Early Learning Book, she still felt as if she was praying, as if she was elevated in some way, watching herself from above and seeing everything that was happening in the classroom, but not being really there.

So intense was her experience that when all the other children went out into the playground to skip, if they were lucky enough to own a skipping rope, or to practise netball, Ottilie stayed behind to pray in front of the statue, and it was there, as she was praying perhaps harder than she had ever prayed before, that she felt a firm hand suddenly fall upon her shoulder.

So elevated was she, so much apart, that she almost passed out from the fright of that hand on her shoulder. So it was that when she turned to look up at the nun standing behind her, Ottilie's face had already lost most of its colour.

It was to lose even more by the time Sister Raphael had finished telling Ottilie that her mother had 'met with an accident'.

Now it was Lorcan who was speaking, confirming what Sister Raphael had said in her clipped English voice, her eyes always so stern, her thin lips pressed together as if even her words must be subjected to the vow of holy poverty. Lorcan was using the same words that Sister Raphael had used. Ma had 'met with an accident', as if an accident was someone to whom a person had to be introduced, a polite procedure that was followed by death.

Lorcan walked along talking all the time, thinking perhaps that by keeping going he could make sense of everything to her, but most of all to himself.

'It's not that surprising really, Ottie, now we come to think of it, is it? I mean I've been expecting something like this, and so has Joseph, we all have. It's not as if we haven't been warning her, and the way things have been – well, even you must have noticed, Ottie. Ma has not been herself for a good long while, not since being in the paper.

'And Joseph and I, you know – we couldn't stop her going over those cliffs to Branhaven any more than we ever could stop her doing anything she wanted. We did try, Ottie, all of us, but sometimes no-one can stop another person from doing what they want, they will just go on in their own way. That's how Ma has been these last months, going on in her own way, so it's not our fault what happened. She just must have slipped and fallen the way we all feared she might. But she didn't suffer. She must have died instantly. The police said so, and they know all about that kind of accident, Mr Hulton says. He told me, you see, he came and told me that Ma had fallen off the cliffs and her body had been seen by another lady walking her dog.'

Lorcan stopped, and Ottilie stood still too and stared up at him. Quite suddenly her eldest brother appeared even older than he had seemed when he dropped her off at school earlier. He seemed taller too, more like a real man than ever, perhaps because he had been called away from the Grand before he'd had time to change from the work clothes that made him look like other men they passed, all of them wearing overalls.

'Will Da come back to us now, Lorcan? Will he come and take us back to Number Four?' Ottilie wanted to know. Not that she knew Da, not even what he looked like, but she thought she just ought to say something quickly, there and then, in case she cried. Being brought up with boys she knew never to cry or they laughed at you.

'Oh, Da hasn't been near us in years, Ottie. I doubt if Ma ever heard from him again, after he sent her the money for the cottage that time. I think she knew it was a kind of pay-off, you know, that he would not be seeing us or her again for a good long while, if at all.'

Lorcan paused, thinking to himself and then speaking out loud as if hearing the words rather than just thinking them was reassuring, calming.

'I think that's why she moved us like that, you know? To be away from any memories of Da at Number Four. They were very happy until the police and that came for him. And of course, Ma being a country girl, she liked the idea of going back to fields and meadows. Remember those pictures she was always picking up and staring at in Number Four? The ones of the fields and the sea? That's why she brought us here. That was how she remembered Ireland, when she was a child, and that's why she wanted to come here. She thought it would be like Ireland.' Lorcan stopped pacing up and down the road, and kneeling to Ottilie's level he looked at her very seriously. 'I'm sure Da is around somewhere, of course, I doubt that he's dead or anything, but there was nothing at Christmas from him, you know, not even a card, so there's no way of reaching him in America and telling him Ma's had an accident. He travels around so, for the work, and to keep ahead of the Green Card thing.'

Lorcan could not bring himself to say that his mother was dead.

In his mind even as he voiced his thoughts Ma had still only 'met with an accident'. Fallen over the cliffs. Tripped on her shoelaces. Broken her neck. She was not dead so much as not alive. And she was simply not alive because she had done what he and Joseph had kept begging her not to do, walked over the cliffs to Branhaven just for a bit of a shop in windy weather.

'Fact is, Ottie, Da could be anywhere and America's a very big place. Look, I've gotta go now. You're a good girl. Be brave now, and try hard at your books. Don't let me down.'

Lorcan reached down and hugged Ottilie and as always Ottilie swallowed hard, her nails pressed into her small hands, trying not to let Lorcan see that there were tears in her eyes, trying not to show Lorcan just how frightened she was at the idea of not having Ma with them any more. What would it be like not to find her sitting on her chair outside the cottage, or even sleeping in the sitting room, what would it be like not to hear her say 'Come here while I give you a kiss, dotie'?

'I've to go and see the others, and then back to the site. Mr Hulton said I must go straight back once I've told you all about the accident because I'm a professional and it wouldn't do in front of the other men to have too much time off because then they'd all want it, you know? I'll pick you up at tea as usual. Stay until we come. Don't move now, whatever happens, after the bell rings, just wait for us.'

Ottilie turned back towards the school. Back into the dark panelled hall, and back past the small altar with its statue of the Sacred Heart before which she had prayed so hard that morning, begging God with His big golden heart with all its golden rays to turn Ma back into a happy person again, to stop her sleeping, to make her, please, please, please, like the way she had been before, the way Ottilie always thought of her, laughing and singing and making little jokes and always looking on the best side no matter what, being the Ma she remembered from Number Four. She so wanted her to be back with them again just how she was before they came to this foreign country called Cornwall, before Ottilie had sinned by paddling in the stream that day and making the old man angry, before God punished her and Ma had her name in the paper as 'St Elcombe Woman Fined'.

As she passed the statue on its plinth Ottilie stopped and stared at it as if she had never seen it before, which in a way she felt she never had, for now she looked at it, now she knew that Ma was dead, she realized that the statue was not God with a big golden heart, someone full of love for small children, but just something painted by a man, and the man with the big heart – he was just something painted too, nothing to do with God or being kind.

'I hate you,' she said silently to the Sacred Heart before returning to her class.

'You can't come to the funeral, Ottie. You're too young!'

Sean was taking advantage of them all, pushing home his point, making sure that Ottilie felt that she was yards younger than the rest of them, too young for this, too young for that.

'I'm coming, I'm coming, I'm coming!' Ottilie bent her head down low. 'I want to come.'

'You can't come. You're too young, and you're a girl.'

Lorcan appeared wearing a black tie and a white shirt and a suit that Mr Hulton had given him from his attic, which had once belonged to Mr Hulton's son.

'Of course Ottilie's coming, Sean, and that's that. Ma was her mother too, the only one she has known.'

Sean shook his head of red curls towards his sister, his green eyes taking in her appearance. 'But she's not got a black dress, Lorcan. Everyone will talk.'

Lorcan disappeared back into the cottage and then reappeared with the black lace mantilla veil that Ma always wore for church, which he placed gently over Ottilie's dark hair. 'There,' he told her, 'you're as smart as paint now.'

Carrying their missals, they all walked up in a file to the tiny modern Catholic church with the corrugated iron roof where they had worshipped so many times with Ma, whom Ottilie fully expected to see seated at the back of the church saying her rosary, or slowly reading her way through one or other of the Catholic newspapers on sale outside the door. Or sighing gently through most of the service, as if the priest was keeping her from something far more important.

But Ma was not there, she was in the wooden box with the single red rose on it, and Lorcan's hand holding Ottilie's tightened as they all walked towards it.

'Please help Lorcan not to cry,' Ottilie could not help praying. It would be terrible if Lorcan, who had always been so tall and so old and a father to them all, it would be terrible if he started to cry because that would mean that they really were truly alone.

Lorcan did not cry. He conducted himself as perfectly as a man should, and although Ma had not known many people in St Elcombe there were others in the church, whom Lorcan had shaken hands with when the service was over, and they had followed the coffin to the churchyard and thrown the earth upon the wooden lid. Lorcan now asked them back to tea at the cottage. Mr

Hulton and his wife, and two people whom Ottilie did not know at all, Mr and Mrs Cartaret, a handsome dark-haired couple who Ottilie was told by Joseph 'might be going to look after you'.

'And you. They want to look after you and Sean and Lorcan too, don't they?'

'No,' Joseph said, running ahead to the cottage door at which he jumped with flattened hands before turning to look at Ottilie, his dark eyes thoughtful and concerned. 'They don't want me or Sean but they'll let me help with the building work on their hotel once I'm sixteen, and they'll look after you. Mr Hulton told Lorcan they don't want boys, they want a girl because Mrs Cartaret lost a little girl in the sea years ago, and now you could be a new daughter for her and she could bring you up, but you'll have to be called Cartaret like them, not O'Flaherty, but since the Little People brought you that doesn't matter, does it, Ottie?'

'I don't want to be called Ottilie Carter-let. I want to go on being me.'

'Shsh.' Joseph nudged her, and pulled her into the kitchen away from the other mourners and shut the door. 'Listen. It's good they want you, Ottie. They'll give you new shoes and clothes and you'll have lots to eat because of its being a hotel where they live, and when you grow up Lorcan says you'll learn to arrange flowers and answer the telephone like a lady, and there will be lots of money. Always. Think of that, Ottie, you'll always have something to eat.'

'But I don't want to do flowers, I want to be here with you and Lorcan and Sean.'

'Shsh,' Joseph said angrily, and he widened his large dark grey eyes with their thick black lashes dramatically, at the same time jerking his head in the direction of the door which was now opening to reveal Lorcan. 'Shsh, Ottie, or you'll spoil everything for all of us, do you hear?' He squeezed her arm hard and with intent, the way he would do sometimes when Ottilie wriggled too much while he was watching television. 'They're Mr Hulton's friends, these Cartarets, and they're going to help us all. Tell her, Lorcan, tell her how lucky she is that Mr and Mrs Cartaret want her to go and live with them.'

But neither Joseph's words nor his arm-squeezing made any difference to Ottilie.

'Please don't make me go and live with Mr Hulton's friends, Lorcan,' she cried, and she threw herself at her eldest brother and clasped his knees to her face. 'Please, please, don't let me go and live anywhere except with you. I just want to be with you and Joseph and Sean. Oh please, Lorcan. I'll be so good. I won't make jam tarts or anything again, not ever, not if you don't want it, oh please don't send me away.'

'Shut the door, Joseph, for God's sake, before they all hear her.'

Lorcan unclasped Ottilie's arms from around his lower half and lifting her up quite easily he placed her on a tall, wooden kitchen stool, the one from which she always used to wash up, the one she was ready never ever to make tarts from again, if only Lorcan would not send her away.

'Now stop this, Ottie, do you hear? Ma's dead and we have to make the best of everything, see? Mr and Mrs Hulton, well, they've been very kind to us, being that they're Catholics and all that, and they've found you a place in a proper home where you can be a proper girl, and grow up to be a lady in a pretty dress, and have all those things Ma would have wanted for you, but couldn't give you.'

'I don't want anything, I just want to be here, always,' Ottilie sobbed. 'Please, please don't send me away, Lorcan.'

'You will go away and like it.'

Lorcan's face was suddenly furious and he shook Ottilie.

'You will go away and like it, do you hear? And you're

not to cry or they won't want to take you, they don't want a little girl with a blotchy face and untidy clothes. They want you same as you were in church just now, see? Looking like a little angel in black lace and being good. That's why they came to Ma's funeral, to see you, and because Mr Hulton told them you were a nice little girl who needed a home. You're lucky, Ottilie, we all are. Ma was a thief, and most people don't want anything to do with the children of a thief.'

'Ma was not a thief! How dare you, Lorcan!'

Joseph sprang at Lorcan ready to hit him, but his eldest brother fended him off with one hand, determinedly speaking in a low voice for he was terrified of being heard by the other mourners.

'She was, Joseph. Ma was a thief all right. A good thief I'll warrant you, but a thief all the same. All those trips over the cliffs to Branhaven, all those tins of peaches and that, they were all stolen. Every single one of them. You didn't know, none of you knew, but I knew. She didn't take that tea and those biscuits from the St Elcombe shop, but she took a hell of a lot of other things. Ah, for goodness sakes, Joseph, she even took the bucket and spade she gave to Ottilie here.'

Joseph and Ottilie stared at Lorcan, completely silenced. Realizing he had their attention now Lorcan continued with one eye on the still shut kitchen door.

'It all began in London, when Da left her, see? She started to take in children and look after them for people who didn't feed them enough and didn't have money. That's why she was called "Mrs Mac" never "Mrs O'Flaherty" while we were at Number Four. MacDonagh's was where she took all the things, see? She stole food for us and the other children she looked after. Don't ask me what went on in her head for her to think that she could, don't ask me, please. But at Number Four it didn't matter, because the manager of Macs always turned a blind eye and of course the story in the neighbourhood was

63

that Ma went there at the end of the day just so she could buy all the cheap foods, and that's why they – you know, the neighbours – they called her "Mrs Mac". As a matter of fact, in the end I think even Ma came to believe that story herself, that she was actually paying, just getting everything cheap, not stealing it.'

Lorcan paused.

'It was all right when we were back there, all that time we were at Number Four, but then we came down here, and of course it wasn't the same, for why would it be? There was no kind manager and no Macs or anything like that, no greenies on Saturday from Charlie's uncle, just Ma and her big coat pockets and her paper bags waiting to be filled up with things she hadn't paid for.'

Lorcan paused as he looked at the shocked faces of the two younger children and for a second he felt for them, but he also knew it was better that it was he who was doing the telling and not someone else. It had to be said, especially now that Ma was dead. They had to understand, all of them, that their mother was a human being, that they had not lost an angel or a saint.

'The three of you, you thought it was some sort of con-spiracy, that the shop people were just getting back at her because of her getting punchy with that fellow who was ticking Ottilie off the first day here, but of course it was nothing of the sort. He's just a poor old gombeen, queer in the head and simple at that. The poor people who owned that shop, when they put the things into the box to catch Ma – which I am sure, quite sure, they definitely did do – you have to feel for them, for weren't they all at the end of their tether because they knew her pockets had been filled with their stuff on so many occasions? All those times Ma was meant to be watching Ottilie on the sand, she was in and out of there when they were at their busiest, taking things. You couldn't blame them for wanting to catch her, really you couldn't, it's their livelihood too, you know.'

'But Ma always said she'd put my hand in the fire if she caught me stealing.'

'That's it, Joseph, that's just it, and she would have done exactly that. She didn't want us to grow up the way she was. But for herself she – well, you see, she never thought what she was doing was wrong, she didn't see it that way. I reckon she was so much in the habit of doing what she did, I reckon she just thought she was feeding us, helping us, the way a mother bird brings back the worms, you know? That's why I think she took to the drink the way she did, after it was in the paper about her being fined. She drank not because she wanted to *stop* taking the things, because she didn't, but because she just couldn't understand being *caught*. That's different, isn't it? She still went on going over the cliffs, still went back to the same old ways. Only in Branhaven she started to steal gin as well, which she'd never done before – she never stole for herself before – and then she'd drink it on her way home. The police told me that they found the path where she walked was littered with the half-bottles that she'd thrown down towards the sea. It was inevitable that one day she would fall. And shall I tell you something?'

Ottilie and Joseph stared up at him.

'It was far better that she did. Better for her to be dead than locked up in some six foot by nine foot prison cell with only a lavatory for company.' Lorcan looked directly at Joseph, excluding Ottilie. 'She was a wild bird, our mother, she would have just battered her poor wings against the prison bars. As it is she's gone before us, and sleeps the sleep of peace, God rest her.'

Lorcan turned and looked into Ottilie's eyes, his own beautiful grey ones as sad and solemn as Ottilie had ever seen them.

'So now you know, Ottie,' he told her, still speaking in a hushed and urgent manner, 'why you're so very lucky that Mrs Cartaret has decided to take you in as she has done. God help you, being taken on by Mrs Cartaret, you must be the luckiest little girl in the whole world. And do you know something? Do you know that from now on, for ever and ever, you will never want for anything? Imagine that, Ottie, imagine being that lucky? You will never need to take things from a shop to feed your children, you will never believe that you have to do those things to help your babies. You will always have shoes for your feet, as they say in Ireland.'

Ottilie turned away from Lorcan, a helpless despair descending on her. From now on she was quite sure that for her the sun would never shine again, the flowers would never flower again and she would never again lie in the grass listening for the sound of grasshoppers or ants on the march.

If she had known that in all her life she would never feel sadder than she did at that moment she might have been comforted, but as it was all she knew was that from now on she was completely alone.

Part Two

To mourn a mischief that is past and gone
Is the next way to draw new mischief on.

Shakespeare, *Othello*

Five

Cornwall, 1958

Ottilie was upstairs, high up in the top of the hotel, but if she stretched herself enough, holding on to the sturdy iron bars that protected the window, and turned her head sideways, she could just see Lorcan, far below, painting the black railings that bordered the private frontage of the Grand Hotel, St Elcombe.

The reason she was so anxious to make sure that Lorcan was below her window was because at last the great day had come, the day upon which the hotel staff had spent all week remarking, namely her tenth birthday, and despite Melanie's having asked ten children around Ottilie's age to a real birthday tea, with cake and candles, all Ottilie could think about was that her beloved Lorcan had promised to join them.

'Do get down, Miss Ottilie. Oh for heaven's sakes would you look at you, and in your party dress!' Edith, one of the staff, tut-tutted at her, fussing as always, her great round face looking as worried as if she thought Ottilie was about to try to jump from the window, not just look down at Lorcan. 'There.' She straightened Ottilie, pulling down the child's long black velvet party dress with its old lace collar and cuffs, while at the same time whipping a hairbrush from the window sill and beginning once more to brush Ottilie's long dark hair away from her face and down her back, rearranging her black pearl-studded Alice band and the small strand of coral beads round her neck. 'Mrs Cartaret will tell me off something awful she will, if she sees you perched up there. Anyway, who was you lookin' at, might I ask? Not got an admirer already, have we now?'

Edith drew in a mighty breath and her large bosom responded in kind to the intake of air.

'Oh, Edith,' Ottilie said, and she raised her large brown-flecked grey eyes to Edith's face before sighing and saying with a patronizing air, 'You really must try not to be so terribly esoteric.'

She had no idea what 'esoteric' meant, but she had heard it on Blackie the hall porter's radio that morning very early and thought it might apply to Edith, that it might somehow suit her. Edith looked as if she just might be 'esoteric' with her old-fashioned hair and her cameo brooch in the middle of her white uniform collar.

'Don't be personal, Miss Ottilie,' Edith reproved, trying to look stern but failing. 'You and your long words. You've more words to your bow than most people have hot dinners. I don't know where you get it all from, I'm sure I don't. Still, now you're in double figures I dare say someone will give you a grown-up dictionary and that way you might start to understand half the things you come out with, because I'm sure I don't, really I am. But who were you looking at down there, anyway?' She stared at Ottilie for a second.

Ottilie turned away, lifting up her head and gesturing grandly. 'Don't worry about my safety, my dear old nurse—'

'You and those old pictures you keep making me take you to at that fleapit cinema. Really, Miss Ottilie. I am not your old nurse, and what's more you know it.'

Ottilie looked up at Edith who was smiling and patting her crisp, tightly permed hair, and looking as if she was trying to decide whether being an old nurse to Ottilie was worse or better than being an old maid at the Grand. Not that it mattered which conclusion Edith came to, and they both knew it. Ever since seeing *Romeo and Juliet* at the cinema in Branhaven Ottilie had found it impossible

70

not to turn poor Edith into an old nurse. At that particular moment, though, all that really mattered was that Ottilie had successfully avoided answering Edith.

Although she could not say exactly why, Ottilie was quite certain that Edith must not be told that she had asked Lorcan to her birthday party, because if she were Ottilie felt she would be sure to try to discourage him. Ottilie did not know why exactly Edith would try to stop Lorcan coming to her birthday party, she just knew she would. But no-one was going to stop Lorcan coming to her party, and Ottilie had already been downstairs and written his name on a card and put it on a plate next to her own, for it was no exaggeration to say that if she wanted nothing else for her birthday, Ottilie wanted Lorcan to come to her tea party. Her heart actually ached just seeing him so far down below, painting all those railings day after day. She so wanted him to know that she had watched him every day, working his way round. That was why she wanted him to come to her party, so that he would know that she still loved him, and watched him from above, and to give him a piece of her birthday cake. Chef had baked it and it was quite grown-up, chocolate with black cherries and lots of fresh whipped Cornish cream, and ten candles on it.

'Ah, there you are.' Melanie Cartaret paused in the doorway looking vaguely surprised as she always did on seeing Ottilie, as if she was still amazed at herself for taking the orphaned girl in, for adopting her, for bringing her up. Yet the expression in her eyes was very proud when she saw how pretty Ottilie was looking in her new dress. 'My dear, you look all of ten years old suddenly,' Melanie went on admiringly. 'Really, I am pleased with myself for thinking of putting you in black velvet. It is *very* flattering for your skin, Ottilie dear, truly.' She rearranged Ottilie's coral beads to lie more tidily in the lace collar of the dress and then, taking her hand, she walked down the main stairs of the hotel with her.

Sometimes Ottilie wished that Mum and Dad were not so very proud of her. On the other hand she knew it was very little to pay in return for living at the Grand and having so many friends in the new staff that came every year, and very often in some of the older guests who came to stay too. She was lucky in every way. She was lucky in being able to use the swimming pool any day of the summer, and in having pretty clothes and food and all those things that everyone everywhere must want. So being polite and nice was really a very small thing. It was just that sometimes she wished that she could be more herself with Mum and Dad, and not the person that they thought she was, or ought to be. On the other hand she also dreaded that they might discover just what a bad person she could be, because if they did they might get rid of her as quickly as they had adopted her. That person, the person they had not adopted, could only be let out once the door of her bedroom was shut in the evening and everyone was downstairs in the large, old-fashioned dining room. Then Ottilie could lie in bed and in her imagination be as wicked as she liked.

She would fantasize about going down into the dining room of the hotel wearing only her bathing suit and jumping out from under the pudding table and frightening all the old ladies in their evening dresses and diamond brooches. Or she would imagine putting an old hat under the silver meat dishes so that when Gianni, the head waiter, removed the silver dome with his usual flourish, instead of a magnificent fillet of beef there would be Mum's best hat with the veiling, or the hotel cat. Sometimes she would laugh so much at these ideas that she would have to go to her bathroom and splash her face to stop herself from laughing until she was sick.

'There now.' Melanie looked proudly from her husband's face hovering just behind them both to the scene below, down the steps into the great dining room of the

Grand. 'There now, isn't that lovely, Alfred darling, isn't that just something?'

Melanie nodded towards the central table round which were sitting ten carefully selected children, all of them dressed in one or another version of a theme on black and white. The staff had set the table with black and white napkins and flowers dyed specially, and black and white candles, and right in the middle the famous chocolate cake with an outer icing of black and white and a lucky black cat on the top. And of course the staff themselves, Edith and everyone, were in black and white as well, because they always were in black and white.

'Isn't that just charming, darling?' Melanie asked her husband. He darted forward to photograph his wife and Ottilie on the grand semi-circular staircase coming down to the dining room, and after that their arrival at the birthday table, before taking another of the cake and the table with the staff standing behind the chairs of the small guests who were now applauding the birthday girl.

But while Ottilie was going from guest to guest and shaking hands, all she could think of was that Lorcan would be arriving soon. She hoped that he would not feel shy and embarrassed from not being in black and white too. In between opening presents and talking to the guests Ottilie found herself fantasizing that Lorcan might arrive wearing his white overalls, the ones he was wearing all morning to paint the railings. She wished he would, because it would look so funny in the grand dining room, and it would mean that they could laugh together the way they had always used to do in the old days before she came to live at the hotel.

She had not seen Lorcan close to for a long time, not since before Christmas when he and Joseph and Sean came to lunch with her in her apartment on the top floor of the hotel, and then they had all been so hungry that they could not wait to tuck their napkins into the collars of their best

73

white shirts and eat as if they were sure they were never going to eat again. It had seemed to Ottilie that there had been hardly any time to hear how they were or what had been happening to them, before the two eldest had to go back to work, and Sean back to school.

Ottilie had been longing to see them all and to give them their presents, things that she had spent practically all year making them, a felt pig for Sean, a long scarf knitted on big needles for Joseph, and a book of funny drawings for Lorcan who said how funny they were without even looking at them, so great a hurry was he in to get through all five courses and back to work before Mr Hulton discovered that he was gone.

'It's all right, everyone knows you're here,' Ottilie had kept saying once the waiters had served them, because the boys didn't seem to understand that it didn't matter the three of them being there with her, that no-one would mind, that the Cartarets had truly laid on the lunch for them all especially, so that Ottilie could see them before Christmas was upon them and she was needed at the hotel to be charming to all the elderly guests who booked in every year at the Grand for the festivities. But the boys, besides eating as fast as they could swallow every course that was put in front of them, seemed to have spent their precious time with her looking uneasily around at everything, the paintings, the cut glass on the table, the silver forks engraved with the hotel crest, as if a policeman was going to arrive at any moment and accuse them of breaking and entering. Joseph had said when he was leaving, 'I envy you all this, Ottie,' and although Ottilie had smiled up at him to cover her embarrassment she had been grateful to him too because, all in all, she realized that perhaps it was better said than not.

Seated at her birthday table Ottilie looked round at the faces of all the invited children as she herself sat down and pulled at her starched napkin to put it on her knee. She knew everyone who had come to her party because they were all children who had come to the hotel at some time or another with their parents, or their grandparents, or were connected to the Grand in some other way. All except for Philip and Constantia Granville who had never come to the hotel before, whom Melanie had invited because she had just met their mother at a cocktail party. The Granvilles were one of the fifty oldest families in Cornwall. Ottilie knew this because Edith had told her. Ottilie was not terribly interested in people's families, unless they were guests at the hotel, but looking at them she thought the Granvilles looked quite gentle and polite, unlike some of the children. They were both tall and blond, as tall and blond as Ottilie was petite and dark.

'Do you like parties?' she asked Philip Granville.

'Not really, no. I prefer staying at home with my tame hare as a matter of fact.'

The seriousness of young Philip's manner impressed Ottilie, and she couldn't help agreeing with him that staying at home with a tame hare would be much more interesting than going to a tea party because someone happened to be ten that day.

'Do you like going to the cinema?'

'Not really, no,' Philip answered, and he looked at Ottilie, his blue eyes very serious. 'I only really like animals and being outside.'

'Where does your hare live?'

'In my room. With me. I rescued him.'

Ottilie gave a small sigh of admiration but before she could ask Philip Granville more about his hare she saw Lorcan arriving in his best tweed suit, his hair smoothed down, his white collar as stiff as anything, his tie just so. She wanted to get up and run across to him and fling her arms around his neck but Melanie, who was standing behind her chair, leaned forward and gently but firmly pushed Ottilie back into her seat again as soon as she started to rise to greet her eldest brother.

'It's all right, darling, I'll deal with this.'

75

Before Lorcan had finished walking slowly and self-consciously, his best shoes squeaking, down the great semicircular staircase that led into the dining room, Mrs Cartaret had hurried up to him.

Ottilie tried not to look, but finally all she could do was look – as Lorcan, the dearest of all her three brothers, smiled shyly and awkwardly at Mrs Cartaret coming towards him wearing her best cocktail party smile. Although she could only see the back of her head Ottilie knew that Melanie would be smiling at Lorcan the way she smiled at the hotel guests, and trying to take the small present Lorcan was holding from him before he had even finished speaking, thereby making it plain that she did not expect him to do more than leave the present with her and then take himself off.

Watching anxiously from the other side of the dining room Ottilie swallowed hard, wondering how much it had cost Lorcan to take time off work to come to the party to which she had invited him so many weeks before. It must have cost him money that he dearly needed to save for all the books he was studying at night so that he could go to some religious college that he had tried to tell her about at Christmas. Ottilie had not really wanted to hear about it, because she had hated going to the convent and enjoyed going to church even less.

She could see Melanie talking to Lorcan as if he was a hotel guest, laughing and smiling but blocking his progress to the birthday table all the same. She would not be able to imagine, as Ottilie could imagine, how much trouble it would have been for Lorcan to come here today. Her mum could not see in her mind what Ottilie could see – Lorcan returning home in the middle of the day and carefully bathing and changing his clothes, ironing his own shirt, brushing his hair, putting the bicycle clips on the bottom of his clean trousers, bicycling back to the hotel, chaining his bicycle to those railings that he had not yet finished painting, walking into the foyer of the hotel, talking his way past the staff who knew him only as one of the builders, and then summoning up the courage to come into the dining room in his best suit. Worst of all, Mum could not imagine, as Ottilie could imagine, just how much he would have looked forward to the party, only to be turned away by Mrs Cartaret as he was now being, politely but firmly, charmingly and sweetly turned away, and not allowed to join Ottilie and her friends.

Back he would have to go, not just up the staircase, this time feeling even more awkward, but across the foyer, back to his bicycle where he would put on his clips again, and all the way back to the cottage where he would have to take everything off once more, the specially starched shirt, the neatly pressed suit, the black polished shoes, the tie that was normally only taken out for church.

And tomorrow morning, at work, what would he say to Mr Hulton about all the time he had taken off work – the best part of an afternoon, just to come into the hotel by the front doors and leave a present and go away again? What would he say? Ottilie's legs under the birthday table wrapped themselves tightly round each other at the thought of how embarrassed he would feel, and knowing the other men working on the hotel she could imagine just how they would tease him and call him a snob for wanting to take Ottilie a present himself, because Ottilie suddenly knew that was how it would look to his mates at work, just as though Lorcan had wanted to join in with the snobs at her tea party, to push himself forward where he was not wanted, whereas the truth was that Lorcan would not have dreamed of coming to the party had not Ottilie asked him so particularly.

'Lorcan!'

Ottilie pushed her chair back and ran as fast as she could after him. Lorcan was halfway up the stairs. He turned and looked down at her.

'Come back, please, Lorcan! Please, please, please!

77

Come back and sit beside me and watch me cut the cake, please?'

Lorcan looked first at Ottilie's pleading face and then across the room at Melanie and the formal group over at the table.

'There's no place laid for me, Ottie,' he said, his face half smiling and half rueful.

'Oh but there is, Lorcan, I laid one specially, and wrote your name.' She nodded towards the table. 'Please come!'

Melanie's smile had now become more fixed than ever, but Ottilie pulled on Lorcan's hand, and now his own smile had lost its hesitancy and he murmured, taking her hand, 'Very well, Ottie, if you have laid for me.'

Ottilie pulled out Lorcan's chair and smiled round at her young guests.

'This is my brother, Lorcan,' she told them all proudly.

Mrs Cartaret leaned over Ottilie's chair and for a second the smell of Chanel No 5 overwhelmed her adopted daughter as she said, 'Really, Ottilie, I don't think Lorcan wants to sit with all you children.'

'On the contrary, Mrs Cartaret,' Lorcan replied, 'I am greatly honoured.'

'This is Philip Granville, Lorcan,' Ottilie said, introducing the young fair-haired boy who shook hands with the dark-haired young Irishman. 'Lorcan's a painter,' Ottilie went on proudly.

'A painter?' Philip Granville looked impressed.

'Yes, he paints railings.'

Lorcan smiled suddenly at Ottilie's obvious pride in him and then placed the small packet he'd brought with him beside Ottilie's plate.

This belonged to your mother. Ottilie stared at the words written in Lorcan's careful hand as Philip Granville leaned over to look at the contents of the small old-fashioned cardboard box, a beautifully wrought bracelet.

'Rather pretty, isn't it? One of my aunts has jewellery just like this.'

Philip took the bracelet from Ottilie and held it up, staring at the insets of tiny sapphires and diamonds.

'I know Ma wanted you to have it, Ottie,' Lorcan murmured to her alone, and his eyes softened as Ottilie put it on her wrist, slipping it over her hand without unfastening the catch because it was still much too big for a child.

Philip Granville looked across at Melanie in her Balmain dress and pearls.

'Your mother is a very pretty woman.'

At which Ottilie turned and smiled mischievously at Lorcan. Her smile said, there really was no point in explaining, was there? Lorcan's answering smile confirmed that there truly was not. But then Ottilie looked down once more at the bracelet and an awful thought passed through her mind. If this beautiful bracelet had belonged to Ma, was it perhaps stolen?

Following her birthday party Philip Granville asked Ottilie over to Tredegar, his family home. Edith was most impressed. Just to take Ottilie and pick her up in one of the hotel cars Edith wore her best brooch, the one with the yellow stone in the centre, and her best grey macintosh, dark grey with a belt that still buckled, albeit the buckle was becoming a little worn, Ottilie noticed, although that was almost all she did notice that afternoon. She was certainly far too excited about the prospect of meeting Philip's tame hare to notice much about Tredegar.

Later, in the kitchens of the hotel, she heard Edith extolling Tredegar's exotic flower arrangements set in immense silver and crystal vases and the vast kitchen with its centuries-old flagstoned floors and its kitchen range that dated from a hundred years ago, but Ottilie herself was not interested in these things. She only noticed the Great Danes the colour of gunmetal with their strange yellow eyes, who sat silent and still in front of the warmth of the immense fire that burned in the dark panelled hall, as if hoping that by remaining so still they would be mistaken for stone. Yet fascinated by the dogs as she was, she was more than happy to run up the stairs after Philip to his suite of rooms and meet his tame hare.

'This is Ludlow.'

'He's beautiful.'

This was a rare moment. Ottilie, who was hardly ever silenced, was overcome by the sight of a tame hare seated on an old sofa. For once, she could think of nothing whatsoever to say as the animal sat quite still and allowed her to stroke his head, watched by his proud owner.

'Do your mum and dad mind him being here, inside with you? I can't have animals because of being in a hotel.'

'No, mine don't mind, they're divorced. Divorced people don't mind what you do, at least not if you're their children, I find. They don't come here very often. Most of the time there's just Constantia and me. And the staff, of course. They look after us. Mamma and Pappa, they just argue about everything if they come here, so it's better just to have staff. Besides, they're much nicer to you than parents, actually. Come on, I'll show you my soldiers if you like.'

Ottilie suspected that soldiers were not going to be very interesting, but because of always being on show at the hotel she knew very well that she had exquisite manners even though she was only ten, and so she said nothing but followed the slender figure of Philip Granville through the connecting doors into another of his large rooms. If he wanted to play with his soldiers then she was perfectly prepared to watch him. But when she saw what he meant by 'soldiers' Ottilie was amazed.

What Philip had laid out was a whole great battle, and what he called 'soldiers' were truly elegant lead figures of men in uniform, on foot or on horse, or riding gun beside carriages, endless lines of them, each piece of their uniform picked out in still brilliant colours. The plumes, the gold, the scarlet, the regimental colours, everything that had been the mighty spectacle of war before the reality of death, was laid out in meticulous lines, and it was beautiful, as beautiful as the sea, even though what was to come was so terrible. Ottilie thought of the sound of the gunfire, of the terror of the horses, of the beautiful uniforms stained with blood, of the poor boys dead in the mud.

'I'm in the middle of the Crimea, actually,' Philip told her. 'It's pretty good fun. Do you know anything about the Crimea?'

'I certainly do.' As Philip looked pleased but quite definitely surprised, Ottilie said by way of explanation, 'There's an old gentleman who comes to the hotel every year and he tells me all about battles, but although he's a general he hasn't any soldiers any more. He only has books and maps which he shows me, and medals that he wears in the evening. This is much more interesting, though,' she continued at her usual conversational gallop. 'Because you see this old general, well, he really only knows about the Second World War, North Africa, Italy and so on, and by then there were no horses. Do you want me to help you with your battle? I can if you like.'

Philip frowned. The idea of a girl helping him stage a battle was obviously pretty startling to him.

'I tell you what,' Ottilie went on, seeing the doubt in his eyes. 'I'll stand by in case – because you look a bit wobbly about that.'

Philip laughed at that. 'I suppose I did,' he admitted. 'It's just that one time a friend of Constantia's helped when I was staging Waterloo and she lost some rather good figures, ran off with them into the garden or something and we never did find them.'

'OK. I'll just watch you, then.'

Ottilie smiled reassuringly across at Philip who she saw was shy but determined not to give on this point. Living in a hotel meant she was really quite used to people not wanting you to do things sometimes and at other times wanting you very much to do things, and straight away.

But soon after, only a matter of minutes as it happened, they were both too involved in arranging the battle of Balaklava for Philip to remember Constantia's friend, and Ottilie was moving soldiers into battle order with matched concentration.

Tea was a very relaxed affair. Philip handed round scones and toast with something he called 'Gent's Relish' on it with gay abandon and pulled faces the moment the Portuguese maid who had served it left them to cake and their own devices. They both talked non-stop and halfway through tea Ottilie realized that she had at last found a friend of the kind that she had only really dreamed of until then, not just someone she could chatter to as she chattered all day to the old ladies and gentlemen who stayed at the hotel, but someone whom she could talk with on equal terms. Not like her brothers, who she remembered now were always stopping and sighing, and saying in tired voices, 'Well, Ottie, what is it now?'

'Philip, can I ask you something?'

'If you want.'

'Do you — well, do you really like Elvis Presley records and rock and roll and that sort of thing?'

When Ottilie finally screwed up enough courage to ask this question they were both still seated at the tea table contemplating a second slice of the quite delicious chocolate cake. Knowing that so much ran on Philip's reply Ottilie stared at the lace insets in the tablecloth rather than at him, but she soon looked up as Philip fixed his clear blue eyes on her and, having helped her to a fresh piece of cake, shook his head slowly.

'No,' he told her, raising his voice slightly as if his determination to be truthful made him nervous. 'No I do not. I don't like anything like that. I just like being out of doors and riding, and playing with soldiers and reading books like *Beau Geste* and that sort of thing. Constantia says I'm going to grow up stuffy like our father, just liking the outdoors and not going to the theatre or cinemas.'

Ottilie looked at Philip with relief.

'Well then so am I, because I don't like that sort of thing either. I'm ever so glad that you don't, because – well, because I thought I was like that because I'm always having to sit with the older guests at the hotel and they only play old gramophone records of Noel Coward singing "I'll See You Again" and they don't know who Grace Kelly is or Frank Sinatra or anyone like that. They never go to cinemas and they only really know the conjuror who comes at Christmas.'

'In that case you must be just a bit old-fashioned, like me. Don't worry, lots of people are, it's just how it is. I get teased at school for it, but I take no notice and I'm older than you.'

Philip smiled suddenly at Ottilie.

'Come on, let's go and see Ludlow and play with him.'

When it was time to leave, and Ottilie was just about to start explaining away Edith to the Tredegar housekeeper with 'I'm just about to be collected by my sort of old nurse person', because if she was honest she was more than a little embarrassed by Edith's macintosh and funny hat and was in a positive fury of inner embarrassment in case the Tredegar staff thought Edith was her mother, Philip smiled at her most particularly.

She was so grateful for that smile, which was directed right at her. It was as if he understood exactly, as if he knew just what it was like to be picked up by people who are not your real mum or dad. His smile said that he knew only too well how Ottilie felt. It was as if he really understood people like Edith coming to fetch you, and that he had had an 'Edith' too, so that as Ottilie was driven back to the Grand, agonizingly slowly, and with a great lack of smoothness and comfort due to the constant screech of Edith's gear-changing, she found herself staring out into the darkness of the late February day and hoping that

Philip and she could go on being friends until they were quite grown up.

What seemed like half a century later, due to her creepy crawly driving, Edith dropped Ottilie at the bottom of the great sweep of steps that led into the foyer of the hotel. Looking up at the impressive white mock Gothic façade Ottilie felt as she always did when she looked up at the hotel that was now her home, both pleasantly surprised and strangely excited. The hotel, living and being at the hotel all the time, was the part of being 'little Miss Cartaret' that Ottilie really loved.

And never more so than this evening after returning from Tredegar.

There everything, although beautiful and gracious, had seemed strangely empty. At Tredegar footsteps rang out on the stone floors of the halls and the wood of the stairs, the heels of the softest leather shoes sounding as if they were metal-tipped so much did sounds echo. At Tredegar, besides herself and Philip and the staff there had seemed to be no human beings, just sculptures in alcoves and niches, and paintings, and everyone in those paintings so very dead and gone.

Whereas now, from the moment Ottilie walked back up into the hotel, there were no empty spaces, and no sound of her shoes ringing out and echoing in the cold air as there had been when she had walked round Tredegar with Philip, Ottilie all the time imagining that they might already themselves be ghosts, or a boy and a girl stepped down from one of the paintings hanging darkly in halls and corridors, so different was it from the Grand where there were people everywhere. The page boys calling for people who weren't there or people who should be there, guests treading across the acres of red carpet to make a telephone call, or to go to the cocktail lounge, or to dinner. People of all ages and all types, some dressed for dinner, some for arrival, and all there at the Grand for different reasons. Love affairs, anniversaries, birthdays, holidays,

84

reunions, honeymoons, rest, recuperation, any and every reason brought people to a hotel such as the Grand at St Elcombe, even off season.

To Alfred Cartaret the guests at the Grand were there to be entertained. 'We're in show business too, you know,' he would tell the new staff every season. 'We're here to please as much as anyone singing and dancing with the Roller Coasters down at the Theatre Royal. Only unlike the Roller Coasters, or even the Queen, we're on show twenty-four hours a day. They may have time off but for us, here at the Grand, there is no time off. If an eccentric millionaire wants to call down for teacakes at two in the morning we must see he has them. If a star from the films wants only white roses and Bollinger champagne, that's what we supply, day and night and whenever he wants them. For us there is no backstage, no time off, no putting our feet up. That is part of the job, to be always on call, so to speak, all the year round, and what a pleasure it is, you will find, when you see the joy people take in coming back here, time and again, to find it just the same dear, impeccable old Grand as it was last year, a real joy for them and a source of pride to us.'

Alfred always made the same speech, but it was a good one, and although the old staff knew it by heart the season's new intake never did, and they would look impressed, as if they were joining something that mattered, which the Grand at St Elcombe did to Alfred, and ever more increasingly to Ottilie.

Melanie was quite different. She enjoyed the Grand as if she was yet another of its guests, to her mind the most important of its guests. The Grand was her backdrop. She had once been an actress, for a very short period before her marriage, but long enough for her to learn how to wear her clothes and walk into a room as if she was walking on stage. Her greatest enjoyment, once she was dressed in one of her many beautiful evening gowns, was to walk down the steps of the great gold staircase, her blond hair coiffured into her favourite Marlene Dietrich style, the sequins on her evening dress glittering, and the jewellery at her throat and ears glowing. Descending the gold staircase at the Grand was an art that she knew all about and enjoyed to the hilt.

'My dance and drama teacher always said, "Melanie, never, ever look down. Look straight ahead when you walk down a staircase. Everyone looks at you, you know, if you look straight ahead, and smile."'

And that was what she would do every evening. Melanie would stare straight ahead as she descended the stairs, not once allowing her head to bend to see what her elegant feet in their evening shoes were doing, not once allowing her lips to do anything but smile.

Halfway down the stairs she would always pause to allow that night's diners to look up and note the beautiful Mrs Cartaret's evening dress and elegant figure before proceeding into the restaurant where the waiters, all of whom Ottilie always thought had a crush on her, fell over themselves to pull out her chair, place her napkin on her knee, present her with the menu, or merely look up at her as she paused on the stairs and sigh with reverence at her elegance and beauty. The hotel was Melanie's theatre and she was without doubt the star of its nightly production.

'Your mum is one of the great attractions in this place,' Alfred would tell Ottilie. 'There are men who come here for dinner every month just to catch sight of her. She is a great asset, Ottilie, your mother – a great, great asset.'

Ottilie knew that Dad worshipped Mum and everyone else knew it, but not everyone agreed with him that 'Madame', as Melanie always insisted on being called by the staff, was an asset to the hotel. Sometimes Edith could be heard murmuring about the expense of Madame's clothes.

'Something new every night. Hardly a week goes by but Madame's sending for something from Knightsbridge or Harrods or somewhere. And as for the hairdressing salon, she's never out of it. Sometimes it seems to me that it was put into the hotel just for her, really it does. But then Madame must have what Madame must have.'

This last was only too true, as everyone at the Grand was well aware. Madame did not approve of the St Elcombe schools, finding them 'common and horrid', so Ottilie's schooling had ceased the moment Dad and Mum had privately adopted her. Mum did not approve of sending children to convent schools and said so. She also said that she would not dream of adopting a child and then sending her away to a private school.

'There is no law in England to say that a child has to go to school, Ottilie darling. There is only one rule and that is that a child must be educated, so we will hire tutors and teachers for you,' Ottilie's new mother had told her very grandly on the little girl's second night at the hotel, as she pulled the old linen sheets around Ottilie and tucked her in. 'I don't want you mixing any more with St Elcombe children. It will do you no good at all if you are to live here and be an asset to the hotel.'

But as time went by and no-one ever seemed to remember to hire tutors or teachers for her, it was finally left to Ottilie to educate herself from the hotel library.

Edith had bought her a small Oxford dictionary for her birthday, but Ottilie was far too impatient to look up any words that she did not understand, so she was always using them all wrong, and of course once she discovered that that made people laugh she had even less reason to look up their proper meaning. All this was part of the Ottilie Cartaret who lived at the Grand and nothing to do with the Ottilie O'Flaherty who had been born in Notting Hill and lived there until she was six.

But although not going to school was so much nicer than having to look serious and wear a grey jumper and skirt and attend church all the time, it also meant that her whole life was at the hotel, and there were hardly ever children staying. When Philip and Constantia went back to their boarding schools Ottilie's mind turned once more to her beloved brothers. She missed them all, but somewhat to her surprise she missed Sean the most, because he had sometimes played games with her or read to her, before Ma had died and Ottilie had been given away to the Cartarets.

Out in the town for their afternoon walk Ottilie fell into the habit of nagging Edith to be allowed to walk past Sean's school when the children were coming out, in the hope of catching sight of him, which they finally did. As soon as she saw her brother Ottilie's face became pink with excitement and she let go Edith's hand and ran towards him.

'Sean! Sean!' she called out, jumping up and down in her lace-up fur-lined boots, her heart leaping when she saw how he had grown into looking like Joseph had just finished looking. 'Sean!' She ignored the stares of the children passing her, swinging their satchels, their faces already determined by life at home, by their parents, by not being rich as Ottilie was now she was living at the Grand with so many people to wait on her.

At last Sean saw her, and once again Ottilie's heart jumped with the excitement of it. Here she was, Ottilie, the youngest, and there was Sean, her next brother whom she loved so much. But at the sight of his sister coming towards him Sean looked so appalled Ottilie might as well have been naked. He looked frightened, too, and Ottilie suddenly realized that he was probably afraid she might fling her arms round his neck and kiss him or something, in front of his friends.

'Don't come here, Ottie. Really. Don't come here no more, d'ye hear? 'S bad enough without yer comin' 'ere and makin' things much wuss. All right?' Sean pushed Ottilie on the arm. 'Really, go away, all right?' he called to her angrily, his Cornish accent more emphatic than ever, and he ran off as fast as he could.

Ottilie's eyes filled with tears and she looked away from Edith, quickly wiping her clean white gloves across her eyes. He hadn't meant it, of course. That was just Sean, he always had been a bit shy.

'Come on, Miss Ottilie,' Edith said quietly, having given Ottilie time to swallow away the lump in her throat as they both watched Sean disappear round the bottom of the main street, his satchel bobbing about on his back, his socks around his ankles, his red hair bright against the grey of the buildings. 'Time to go home to tea.'

Home to the cheerful sound of the reception bell being ting-ting-tinged for the page boys. Home to the arrival of new guests. Ottilie ran back up the steps of the Grand and thought, 'Yes, this is home now.' She never again asked to go and see Sean or Joseph, and Edith never offered to take her, as if they both accepted that trying to meet up with Sean had been a failure, as if they both knew that nowadays Ottilie in her smart pale blue or grey Hayward's coats or navy blue jackets with brass buttons and expensive Scotch House kilts looked just too different from the poorer children streaming past them back to their cottages and flats, too different to be able to pass herself off once again as one of them.

'I don't think it's ever wise to go back into the dim and distant past, Miss Ottilie,' Edith said later, as Ottilie, her tea uneaten, retired to bed early without so much as a word or a joke. 'You take my mother, now, she's still keeping wool against the war being on again and rationing her butter and being sensible with the marmalade when she could be enjoying herself same as the rest of us. No, you want to keep to the present, Miss Ottilie, really you do. Nothing else is healthy to my mind.'

But when she was left alone Ottilie found it difficult to accept Edith's advice about the past, particularly now she was ten and Lorcan had given her Ma's precious bracelet, which Edith had taken and put 'somewhere safe'.

Six

There was a special feeling to the start of each season at the Grand. Even before Ottilie had become so much part of the place that regular guests would look for her within minutes of their arrival, she could sense it. She could sense it before Blackie, the Grand's ageing porter, had puffed and panted and staggered with the first luggage to the lift. Before the sea had stopped raging and the winds whipping around the newly painted exterior of the Grand, Ottilie would know without even looking in the hotel diary that the first day of the season was upon them.

It was a sixth sense that came from living all the time in the hotel, knowing its rhythms, its heartbeat, its sense of its own fitness. As if on the exact day given in the guide books, the hotel was like an actor viewing itself in the mirror to the side of the stage, checking its appearance and adjusting its costume most precisely, before saying 'Now!' and sweeping on into the full glare of the summer season.

'Mrs Le Martine is arriving at four o'clock today,' Ottilie heard Edith being told by Mrs Tomber the senior housekeeper. 'Shall we have a last check of her suite?'

'I'll go,' Ottilie said before Edith could put down her duster and turn to answer Mrs Tomber. 'You stay, Edith, and I'll go. You know how much she likes me!'

Neither of the staff could argue with her. Mrs Le Martine and Ottilie had been confidantes for three or four seasons now.

Mrs Le Martine always asked for Ottilie within minutes of her arrival. Mum said it was because she had no children and was a widow and that it was 'rather pathetic really', but Ottilie found Mrs Le Martine fascinating and not at all pathetic. Just seeing her expensive luggage, heavy leather with deep gold initialling and a trunk that opened outwards like a wardrobe so that all her clothes could be taken straight out of it on their own hangers, was thrilling. And then to put her heavy glass scent bottles on her dressing table and place her silver brushes beside them, and help the maid hang the clothes or put away the satin handkerchief sachet and the matching nightdress case, was a magical ritual which made Ottilie feel as if she was helping to serve at a religious ceremony.

All Mrs Le Martine's clothes had discreet labels in them and, unlike Mum who boasted that she could dress in five minutes, Mrs Le Martine never dressed without the help of one of the hotel maids. She rang down when she was ready, and they came up and helped her. Ottilie was sometimes allowed to watch the last stages of her dressing in the evening. She especially liked the moment when Mrs Le Martine opened the small safe in her suite and took out one or two of the many leather boxes with her initials on them. She would view their contents and plump for one or another of the necklaces and matching earrings that she so liked to wear.

'The amethysts tonight,' she would say. Or, 'No, Edith, how many times must I tell you? *En parure*, you silly creature. Pearls with black, always. Pearls with black, most especially black velvet.'

Mrs Le Martine liked white flowers in her suite, but never chrysanthemums which she said were 'funeral flowers'. She also liked a box of rich tea biscuits by her bed, but only the finger-sized ones, not the ordinary round ones. And she liked pot pourri but never, ever a mix with any lavender in it because, she said, 'It reminds me of my hated governess who used to hit my hands night and morning so that I would never grow up and marry, because I would be too crippled to play the piano or hold hands with a man. But there you are, I grew up to do both, so there really was not much point to all that cruelty, was there? Except it did put iron in my soul.'

Treading across the deep blue carpet to the wardrobes Ottilie stared into their depths to make sure that the hangers Mrs Le Martine liked so particularly were waiting there in readiness. It was exciting to think that the strong, polished mahogany ones would soon be supporting Mrs Le Martine's size eight suits with their silk-lined skirts, and the soft padded ones, with their small lavender bags removed in deference to her hatred of lavender, her blouses and evening tops. And the white and gold Louis-Quatorze chests of drawers would soon have cashmere twinsets and silk crêpe nightdresses arranged in their flowered paper-lined drawers in such a way that Ottilie would find herself secretly stroking them when Mrs Le Martine was too busy bossing the maids to notice.

From her first season at the Grand onwards Mrs Le Martine had warmed to Ottilie, and said so to her face.

'I took to you the moment you came in with that bunch of exquisite flowers that you had picked from the hotel hothouse and smuggled up to me, you naughty girl,' she would remind Ottilie, laughing, because unlike the rest of the world Mrs Le Martine was not fooled by Ottilie. She knew that Ottilie was naughty and mischievous, and she liked her for it, which was why it was always such a relief to be with Mrs Le Martine, and why Ottilie looked forward with such intense excitement to her arrival, to hearing her lovely rippling laughter in the downstairs foyer, to her satisfied sigh when she saw her suite and turned to tell Ottilie that she had 'got everything just right'.

Because as far as Ottilie and Mr Cartaret were concerned it was Ottilie's duty, her prized duty as it happened, to get everything completely right for Mrs Le Martine's arrival each year.

'She is a great star,' Alfred would say of Mrs Le

93

Martine, sighing with appreciative approval, although never within his wife's hearing. 'Really a great star. She could have been a great actress, you know, but of course she is too refined for such a life, too sensitive. Plucked from the firmament they are, wonderful women like Mrs Le Martine, Ottilie, plucked from the Milky Way and sent down to enchant us mortals. We are indeed privileged.'

After these words Alfred would give a deep sigh which had within it more than a vein of melancholy, and Ottilie could sense that he too was looking forward to Mrs Le Martine's arriving, eager to meet her demands, loving to please her as much as Ottilie did, as they all did, longing to hear her say in her slightly husky voice, 'But this is charming!' so that each person felt, as never before, that they and they alone had filled Mrs Le Martine's eyes with delight and set her small, elegant hands aflutter with appreciation simply and solely because of what they had done for her.

First, and long before they saw her, they would hear her low gurgling laugh with its entrancing mixture of merriment and complicity. Next they would smell her scent – 'Never perfume, Ottilie dearest' – and this again it always seemed to Ottilie would be long before they saw her. 'Enchantée' was the name of Mrs Le Martine's scent. (Edith always said, 'I never did see such large bottles of perfume, Miss Ottilie, not nowhere. I think she must have had them made up special in La France before the war, really I do.') And then at last Mrs Le Martine herself. Not tall like Melanie, but small and petite like Ottilie, but so exquisitely made that it seemed to Ottilie who was already nearly her height that Mrs Le Martine was really just as tall as Mum, so finely made were her legs and arms, so small and white her hands.

This day, as always on her arrival, Ottilie met her by the reception desk.

First, as always, came the embrace. Ottilie had rapidly

become used to the fact that one of her many duties as the 'hotel child' was to submit not only to letting herself be talked about – 'My, you have grown this last winter' – but also to being kissed by the ladies and patted on the head by old gentlemen who smelt strongly of either camphor or moth balls.

But being kissed by Mrs Le Martine was not a duty at all. In fact Ottilie found she longed for it, because not to be kissed by Mrs Le Martine would be to miss out not just on the smell of her famous scent but on the feel of her cool hands either side of your face, on being close to the softness of her lace or chiffon blouse and her lingering look of appreciation as she held you away from her and murmured to Dad, 'But this is a young lady, Mr Cartaret. Your daughter has grown into a young lady this winter past.'

After this little ceremony they were off, the whole of her team, willing and eager, all smiles, all keenness.

First Blackie, sweating and puffing, the buttons on his old uniform looking fit to burst due to a long winter of indulgence in steamed puddings. Then the Grand's team of page boys, long past their thirtieth birthdays but small like jockeys so they could still pose as young, trooping after Blackie. After them came Ottilie, usually in a brand new dress with a starched *broderie anglaise* pinafore over the top and tied in a big sash at the back, and finally Mrs Le Martine herself, walking gracefully and elegantly, smiling at members of the old staff who would have made some excuse to leave their duties and greet her on her arrival and carefully nodding at new members who had yet to be put under her spell.

Once outside her suite Blackie and the 'boys' would stand aside as Ottilie put the key into the lock and flung open the double doors and Mrs Le Martine and she floated in together, each appreciating the immaculate scene before them in quite different ways. The furniture set just as Mrs Le Martine liked it, the flowers in tall vases – if possible white lilac somewhere in the arrangements. The champagne in a bucket, even though she never touched it, just liked it to be there on show, and finally the picture of her late husband which she always sent on ahead to be put beside her bed, just in front of the biscuits and the water carafe.

Unpacking was always left to the maids. So first, before the solemn business of setting out her clothes was begun, there was welcoming sherry, a small glass for Mrs Le Martine, and a glass of barley water for Ottilie, after a sip or two of which, having safely seen to the departure of Blackie and the boys, Mrs Le Martine would turn to Ottilie and in a conspiratorial voice say, 'Well, has *she* arrived yet?'

It was hardly necessary for Mrs Le Martine to ask, for they both knew that for the person in question not to have arrived would be like the sun refusing to rise in the morning, or the tides outside the windows stopping for ever.

Neither Ottilie nor Mrs Le Martine ever had to say any more than 'she', because being conspirators they both knew whom they meant by *she*.

She was the lady who always took the top suite and never left her room. *She* was the lady who after her arrival never dined downstairs and was seen only by the maids who took up her trays in response to orders for room service. *She* was the lady who came, the older staff loved to tell Ottilie when she herself had first arrived at the Grand, year after year at the same time, ever since spending her honeymoon in that same top suite. The suite which, once arrived, she never left. *She* was the mysterious lady who always stayed at the same time as Mrs Le Martine but never appeared in lounge or foyer, in dining room or garden, but could be seen in all weathers sitting on her balcony gazing out to sea as if she was waiting for someone to arrive at any minute, and longing only for that.

'Her name is Mrs Ballantyne,' Ottilie had told Mrs Le

Martine when she first became intrigued by her mysterious fellow guest, 'but downstairs they call her Blue Lady. They say that she honeymooned here in the top suite but that her husband, who was much older, died while they were making a little trip to the Italian Lodge near Wychetty Bay in Devon. And do you know what? Chef says she nearly went mad from the grief of it all. And that is why she comes back here every year, and always will perhaps, for ever more.'

'Oh the fascination of it.' Mrs Le Martine had clasped her hands together in delight as Ottilie finished speaking. 'And the way you tell it, Miss Ottilie. Too delightful. Mad with grief indeed! Where do you get your expressions from, I would dearly like to know? But. What a business. We must find out more, or we will faint from the excitement of not knowing, surely?'

Mrs Le Martine always called Ottilie 'Miss', it was one of her peculiarities. Ottilie loved this almost most of anything about her, that Mrs Le Martine never let anything pass her by without changing its name – very effectively sometimes – to something else or adopting some new or different style of address.

So Ottilie was always 'Miss Ottilie' and Edith was 'Droopy Dolly', and Blackie the hall porter was 'Taresome Ted' and even Mum and Dad were 'Her Majesty' and 'His Majesty' behind their backs.

But sometimes Mrs Le Martine said 'Oh Miss Ottilie' in a voice that was suddenly just a little *too* like Edith's, which would make Ottilie feel uncomfortable and cause her to look round to make quite sure that poor Edith was not there. But having found that she was not, she would feel safe to laugh, and once more a delicious feeling of relief would flow through her that when she was with Mrs Le Martine, as with no-one else, she could allow her naughty self to be seen, and that despite this, Mrs Le Martine still seemed to like her.

So not only did the start of the season bring with it its

own excitements, new staff joining the few old regulars, occasionally to go very soon afterwards and be rapidly replaced, but more important to Ottilie, after the long winters of storms and rain and high seas, it brought with it Mrs Le Martine and Blue Lady.

'You see far too much of that woman,' Melanie would say to Ottilie at regular and monotonous intervals during the whole month of Mrs Le Martine's annual stay, at which Ottilie would open her eyes wide, assume her most innocent expression, and instead of protesting, which would be useless – because everyone knew that Ottilie danced attendance on Mrs Le Martine from the moment she arrived until the moment she left – she would be sure to murmur, 'Can I help you with anything, Mum? The flowers, the telephone – I've finished helping Mrs Tomber.'

Ottilie was always sure that even though her mother was all too well aware that she was distracting her from the main issue, nevertheless Melanie was so terribly lazy that she could not help availing herself of any offer of assistance, and this despite the fact that, as far as Ottilie knew, she never actually did anything in the hotel anyway except appear in the dining room and be charming to everyone once she had walked down the stairs, observing her dramatic ritual of looking straight ahead and not down at her feet.

One particular day Ottilie had only just finished saying 'Can I help you with anything?' when she noticed that Melanie was looking more than a little apprehensive, not at all her usual superior self, not at all the person that Ottilie was always so careful to be good and well behaved around.

'You see far too much of that woman, Ottilie. She will tire of you and turn on you, really she will. You must be careful not to foist yourself upon guests,' she repeated mechanically, several times, but without her usual command.

'Yes, Mum,' Ottilie agreed.

'Also, I think you should stop calling me Mum and call me Ma, now that you are older. I think it would be more fitting if you were to call me Ma, and Dad should be Pa. Better in front of the guests, too. I thought I saw someone looking at you the other day as you said Mum, as if they did not think it either suitable or fitting for me, and I do not think it is.'

Ottilie frowned. This was going to be difficult. And it was no good making one of her jokes as she would if she was with Edith or Philip Granville, or being cheeky as she would if she was with Mrs Le Martine. She had noticed that Alfred Cartaret would always say to Mrs Tomber or his secretary, when he was faced with a problem, 'You deal with this', but Ottilie was not a man, she could not turn to someone else and tell them to 'deal with this'. Instead she opened her mouth, and then closed it again, quickly realizing that for once she truly did not know in the very least how to answer this new edict from Her Majesty.

It would be so difficult to try to explain to Mum that Ma had been Ma. Ma was Number Four and the fun and the warmth and wearing sandals without socks and knowing people like Charlie on the corner, people that Mum and Edith would now never dream of letting Ottilie know. And Mum was Melanie, the Queen of the Grand, all perfume and silk, and if she tried to swap them round it might be a bit confusing.

'I think of you especially as Mum, now,' was how she finally put it, carefully leaving out all the feelings of pain and confusion that just hearing the name of Ma brought into her heart, all the agony of that day in the police station when Ottilie had stared at the picture on her stolen tin bucket rather than look up at the policemen in their uniforms or listen to the sound of Ma protesting her innocence to Lorcan.

How could she call Mrs Cartaret Ma? Ma had been a

thief, and really – as Joseph had said afterwards so bitterly – 'should by all that is right have been in gaol', whereas Mum was a beautiful woman who had come into Ottilie's life and adopted her, lifted her out of her poor existence at the cottage and made her grand and rich.

Mum had taken away Ottilie O'Flaherty and replaced her with Miss Ottilie Cartaret, given her a beautiful room and books and toys and expensive clothes and as much food as she wanted whenever she wanted it. She had made her into Miss Ottilie whom all the staff at the hotel spoilt. She had made her into a princess who was asked to places like Tredegar by boys like Philip Granville whom other boys like her brothers Joseph and Sean called snobs.

'Yes, I really think from now on, Ottilie, since you are older, you should call me Ma and your father Pa.'

Please don't make me, please, please, please, please God help her not make me call her Ma.

'I tell you what,' Ottilie said, her eyes over-wide, 'why don't you let me call you Mamma and Pappa? The older guests would like that ever so much, wouldn't they?'

'Don't say "ever so much", Ottilie, it's common. Have you been watching the television in the staff room? I hate you to pick up expressions from the television, you know that.'

'No, Mum – I mean *Mamma* – I never watch television. Sorry, Mamma.'

There was a small pause, and Ottilie, who had long ago learned never to let Melanie know just what she was thinking, opened her eyes even wider and smiled although she actually felt like crying, for some reason that she could not understand, crying the way she had cried when she had been left on the steps of the hotel the evening of Ma's funeral.

'Oh very well, Mamma it must be, if you think you like that better, if that makes you happy.' Melanie put down her silver-backed hairbrush and looked suddenly bored by the whole idea and at the same time peculiarly restless and unhappy too. 'But please don't argue all the time with me about everything, Ottilie. Terribly tiring, you know. Now to other things. I do hope and think you are old enough to be someone I can entrust with a secret?'

She paused and looked at her adopted daughter.

'You mean you want to tell me something that I should keep under my hat?'

Melanie continued to look across at Ottilie, and for one second Ottilie could see that she was really rather surprised by what Ottilie had just said, as if she had suddenly guessed that Ottilie had secrets with other people, secrets that she knew nothing about, and perhaps never would.

'Yes,' she agreed slowly, as if suddenly seeing Ottilie for the first time, 'I certainly do want you to keep this under your hat.'

Ottilie nodded. She knew all about keeping things under her hat from Mrs Le Martine. It was an expression that she always used, particularly when they were trying to find things out about Blue Lady and why she came back to the hotel every year – well, they knew why, but not *quite* why – not really, really why.

Certainly it was to do with Blue Lady's husband's dying so tragically when they were still on honeymoon, and his being such a loss to her, and his being so terribly rich. But they both wanted to know much more than that, and yet in the three whole years that Ottilie had been living at the Grand, in the seven years that Mrs Le Martine had been arriving for the opening month of the season, they had not found out anything more, except that she always wore the same clothes, which Mrs Tomber the housekeeper said to Ottilie were now beginning to look 'old hat'.

Fleetingly Ottilie observed to herself that hats seemed to feature a great deal in grown-ups' conversations.

Melanie stood up and walked with her usual graceful sloping walk, hips forward, hair brushed back from her face, to the central table of her large, ornate bedroom with its elaborate fittings and what always seemed to Ottilie to be miles of fitted wardrobes. 'Madame's closets', as Mrs Tomber always reverently referred to them, were each lit from within by special lighting so that when Madame opened a cupboard she could see all her clothes illuminated. One glance at each wooden drawer or shelf showed her all the rainbow colours of her cashmere twinsets, all the beauty of her hand-embroidered Italian blouses, all the Chinese silk shawls, all the delicacy of her nightwear and her underwear made specially for her by Roses in Knightsbridge, all her shoes – pink, blue, red, two-tone, suede, shoes of every description – and that was all before the cupboard for her hats was opened, because Melanie's hats were so many and various they took up not one closet but two.

And they were nothing compared to the closets for her evening clothes, the long sequin-studded evening gowns, the short slipper satin evening dresses with matching coats. If Alfred ever dared to comment upon the arrival of some new parcel from London containing yet another garment, his wife always said in ringing tones, 'I must have these things, Alfred. You cannot possibly expect me to be of any use to either you or this place if I am to be clothed in rags.'

The very idea of Melanie appearing in rags was quite impossible to imagine, and certainly Madame's clothes, Madame's nightly descent of the semicircular staircase, Madame's grand sweep into the dining room past openly admiring diners did give the hotel a certain class and glamour, no-one could deny that, and no-one did deny it. Melanie was not only a feature of the hotel, she was its centre, a personality in a way that her husband could never be, but as Ottilie was to discover, it was at a price.

'Ottilie,' Melanie said, sighing a little as if she was about to tell her about someone else other than herself, 'Ottilie, darling. I have to tell you the most annoying thing I have ever heard.'

Ottilie waited. She had a feeling that she was going to be told something she did not want to hear because of the way Melanie was fiddling about with her cigarette lighter, turning the smart gold object over and over, over and over, over and over, again and again. There was something about her doing that and her way of smoking in rapid inhalations that was making Ottilie uneasy, as if she was seeing a side of Mamma that she had never seen before.

'Yes,' Melanie continued. 'The most annoying thing I ever heard,' she repeated. 'I don't know how it is, but it surely is, and that is that I am more than certainly in trouble with my bank manager. I cannot tell Dad – I cannot tell Pappa, as you want to call him, because he already gives me what he thinks is such a large allowance for my clothes and things, and he just doesn't realize that I can hardly manage, if I am to look presentable at all, on what he does give me, the little that he does give me – even though it might seem quite large to him. If you understand me?'

Ottilie did not quite understand in the first instance, but then it took only a glance round Melanie's bedroom with its miles of cupboards for Ottilie to understand that it might be perfectly possible, however rich you were, not to have enough money to pay for all the clothes presently illuminated in Madame's cupboards.

'Now,' Melanie continued, having stubbed out one cigarette and begun another immediately which she lit once more with the gold lighter. 'You're such friends with Mrs Le Martine, are you not? I wonder if you could just find out for me, that's all you have to do, just find out, in a roundabout sort of way, if she would like to buy any of my clothes? You can tell her that I am having a grand clear-out. Make it seem as if you haven't talked to me about it though, and then we can see if we cannot sell her some things, mmm? She loves clothes – all those trunks just for a month, and we are the same size, if not the same height.'

Ottilie blushed scarlet. In fact her cheeks became so red

that she thought if she held her hands in front of them they would become as warm as hot crumpets. What an agony of embarrassment for her to be asked to deceive her greatest friend in order to take money from her. What on earth would Mrs Le Martine say?

'And Mrs Ballantyne, the woman you call Blue Lady? You could do the same thing with her, could you not? I could easily arrange for you to take up her tea one afternoon instead of Mary. I mean it's only fun. Women love buying things that they think are a bargain, and after all, Ottilie, most of my clothes are scarcely worn. And they're all beautifully cut, you know. I mean they'll probably end up baying for bargains from you, but just don't tell them I know you're trying to hook them. Just drop a hint, a light mention, that's all, and wait for them to take you up on it, make a bite. That's always the best way.'

Melanie had resumed her pacing of her large bedroom.

'You could even say that I don't want to sell anyone in the hotel anything because I don't like people being seen in the same things as me, which is quite true. You can tell them that my clothes normally go away to be sold secondhand in Knightsbridge, which they all do, normally – except the place for some reason closed down at the end of last year. I mean, usually they are falling over themselves to buy my hardly worn clothes at secondhand prices, which leaves me with quite enough left over to settle with the wretched bank, but not now.'

Ottilie's colour had subsided and she had just started to think that what Melanie was asking of her was not so very terrible after all, that it would not be so difficult to drop a hint here, a hint there to Mrs Le Martine or Blue Lady – and what was more, she thought, with a sudden growing sense of excitement, she would now have every excuse to make *friends* with Blue Lady – when Mrs Cartaret raised a new issue.

'And there's something else, Ottilie. I want you to take

104

these, and once you have, remember – I haven't seen you, and I don't know anything more about them.'

Melanie stopped her pacing suddenly and dropped a pair of something small and heavy into Ottilie's hand. She did it so casually and with such a lack of any sort of ceremony that the small items could have been something that she had just picked up off the carpet and wanted Ottilie to throw away. As it happened they were something that she wanted Ottilie to throw away, as she explained, but when Ottilie opened her hand and saw what the small but surprisingly heavy objects were, she knew that Melanie certainly could not have picked a pair of diamond earrings up from the carpet.

'When we have finished talking, as soon as you can, I want you to go for a long walk with Edith and throw them away. Down a drain is a good place, any old drain in the town. Just let Edith go on ahead and then drop them down the drain, Ottilie. This will help me. This will really help your mamma a great deal, and after all I have done for you, Ottilie, you do want to help me, don't you?'

Melanie turned her eyes outlined with her favourite bright blue shadow on Ottilie, and very suddenly, indeed without hesitation, Ottilie knew, as always, that *of course* she wanted to help her.

What else could Ottilie say? The woman standing in front of her had adopted her, changed her life, given her a hotel that was just like a palace to live in, everything. Ottilie put the earrings in her pocket. She did so swiftly, and without saying a word, as if she had done just such a thing before, and she saw that for once Melanie was surprised by her silence, and by the grave look on her face.

'They are worth over a thousand pounds on the last valuation,' Melanie went on, talking quickly. 'I can settle my debts with that. But to keep the wretched bank manager happy until the insurance company pays out, I *must* have some small sum to float at him, anything, just anything, or your father will be furious. That's why you have to sell some of my clothes to the guests if you can, Ottilie. It is vital, you do realize? In my position I simply cannot do such a thing.'

There was a short silence during which Ottilie stared up at Melanie wondering, as always at these moments, what sort of person she was, and why she would not just go and ask her husband for the money and that would be that.

'If you don't,' Melanie said, staring down at Ottilie so that her beautiful dark eyes seemed to her adopted daughter to be intent on burning into her own grey ones as she spoke, 'if you don't do everything I ask I will not just punish you the way you most hate, but something terrible will happen to you, Ottilie, something really terrible. Don't forget that.'

She walked over to the drinks tray and poured herself a gin and tonic.

'You know I don't like punishing you, but it has to be done sometimes, we both know that.'

Ottilie's heart sank and panic filled her eyes and her ears until she thought her body was melting. For the next hours all she could think of was that word 'punish'.

She never knew whether it was the earrings themselves or the knowledge that they were worth so much money that weighed more heavily as she walked beside Edith to the shops that afternoon. Certainly the implications of the worth of the earrings were quite terrifying, but the act of throwing away such valuable objects was awful, more awful even than what had happened to Ma that afternoon when she was found to have the tea and the biscuits in her carrier bag.

'You look a bit sick, Miss Ottilie. You feeling all right?'

Edith bent down and stared at Ottilie, her face at its most concerned.

'I am all right, thank you, Edith. But thank you for being sententious about me, all the same.'

'Sententious? Whatever will you come out with next!'

Edith breathed in the ozone on the sea breeze and her blue eyes narrowed with amusement.

With her gloved right hand around the diamond earrings in the bottom of her pocket Ottilie could not help suddenly thinking that was particularly funny. If Edith knew just what Ottilie had *come out with* she would die from the shock of it. But such moments were only a few seconds of relief in the overall tension that was over-shadowing their normally boring and uneventful walk.

Telling someone to throw away your earrings was one thing, but doing it was quite another. It was not in the least bit easy to throw away the earrings without anyone seeing. Everywhere, even so early in the summer season, there were people, people, people. People walking and looking, drifting and hesitating, crossing roads, stopping by traffic lights. To throw away even two such small objects as earrings would take the greatest ingenuity and suddenly it seemed to Ottilie that she might not be in possession of such powers.

Apart from anything else, Edith would keep looking down at her every few seconds, checking on her, remark-ing every now and then that she was 'definitely looking a bit peaky' while all the time, as always, holding Ottilie's hand as if she was afraid that someone might suddenly come along and kidnap her charge, or her charge might herself suddenly run off never to be seen again.

As they walked determinedly on, a wind sprang up from nowhere and whipped round the corner of the cliffs, tearing round the sides and bursting into the safety of the bay into which St Elcombe fitted so neatly. Edith bent her head against its force, holding on to her hat with her gloved hand. Ottilie did the same, knowing with a sinking heart that any minute now Edith would turn for home, and they would be returning along the front and up into the hotel once more, with the earrings still lying a ghastly secret in the bottom of Ottilie's coat pocket.

'Oh, look. How awful, Edith, look . . .' In a desperate

attempt to gain some time Ottilie allowed one of her gloves to be carried off on the wind, and then watched in a sort of detached fascination Edith running after it, down the steps of the hotel out towards the pink road that led to the iron gates and so once more to the sea front and the palm trees of St Elcombe. As the poor woman dashed after her white glove Ottilie looked round in desperation for a drain, anything into which she could drop the two earrings, but there was nothing, and then Edith was back, laughing and smiling, carrying the glove, holding her own hat in place, and generally continuing to be the worst kind of companion for the criminal Ottilie now knew that she was. More even than Ma when she was her whole life, the centre of everything that was wonderful at Number Four, Edith appeared at that second to Ottilie to be a shining saint compared to her own awfulness.

'Skippety skippety up to tea we go,' Edith chanted, as she always did, and she took Ottilie's left hand once more as they walked together up the broad steps towards the welcoming bustle of the Grand, only to find Mamma waiting for them in reception.

She took Edith aside at once.

'The most ghastly thing has happened, Edith,' she murmured, ignoring Ottilie completely. 'My diamond earrings have been stolen. The police are here. They are insured, of course, but let's face it, they've been in the family for so long, no-one can make up for that. No money can compensate for the sentimental value.'

Police. Edith's face became chalk white – after all, if something went missing all the staff felt implicated, under a cloud. 'Diamond earrings. How terrible, Madame, how perfectly terrible for you.'

'It is terrible, Edith, it is too terrible for words. More terrible than I can tell you, and I am afraid that I have to ask you to go to the staff sitting room where the police will interview you.'

Ottilie watched as Edith, now more green with fright

than white or grey, removed her poor macintosh and hat in a hurried sort of way. She patted and reassured Ottilie and then went off towards the staff sitting room to confront her worst of all nightmares, a policeman in a uniform.

'Ottilie, you can go to your room. This is all most unpleasant, and I want you kept out of it.' Again Melanie's blue-shadowed eyes seemed to be burning into Ottilie's own, saying, 'Behave yourself, do as you're told, or you will be punished, remember?'

Nevertheless, remembering only too well how Ma had cried at the police station that day, for once Ottilie defied Melanie's burning glance and ran after Edith. Reaching up to her, she kissed her cheek and hugged her.

'It's all right, Edith, really it is. Everyone knows no-one here took them, really they do.'

Edith nodded, but her blue eyes were full of fear. With the earrings still in the bottom of her pocket, Ottilie knew just how she felt, just how her knees must have gone to complete water, her heart be throbbing in her throat, her hands running with sweat.

'To your suite, Ottilie, please. Until this matter is cleared up, to your suite, please.'

Melanie nodded sharply at Ottilie and she turned and headed for the staircase, her mind in a turmoil of childlike anxiety.

Ottilie stared out at the early evening. The earrings were still in her Hayward's coat, still lying heavy in the pocket of that coat that was now hanging in the pretty hand-painted cupboard next door to her own private sitting toom. Supposing the police came into her room and searched her cupboard? Supposing she threw them out of the window? They might search the garden and find her finger prints on them.

Supposing she put them down the plughole in the bath-room? That would be easy, except once when an old guest dropped his gold tooth down the plumber came right back up with it. Apparently they were searching all the staff rooms, looking through all their clothes, supposing they searched the drains? That day at the police station Ottilie had seen a young boy, just her age now, and he was being what Lorcan had called 'had up' and he was later found, 'poor gossoon, hanging from his belt in the police cell'.

Lorcan. Of course. He would know what to do. To run back home to the cottage would be the answer to everything. No-one at the hotel would miss her at this hour, and she could tell Lorcan everything, and maybe he would think of something, or maybe he would throw the earrings away for her somewhere where no-one would ever think of throwing them, somewhere where they could never be found, not ever. Whatever happened, Lorcan would surely tell her what to do, or Joseph, or Sean. Someone at the cottage would tell her what to do.

Ottilie would never forget jumping out of that window and the feel of the soft earth as it seemed to rise and meet the bottom of her sandals. It didn't matter now that she had dirtied her always immaculate white socks, that she had fallen once or twice as she escaped from the back of the hotel and out towards the straggle of cottages that lay behind it, and onto the hard, high-hedged but winding road that led up, up and away into the countryside, where lay, not the enclosed fascinations of hotel life, but fields and cows and wild birds and flowers, and a breeze that sprang up from over the top of the tall hedges, a breeze which seemed to be less salty, more mellow.

All the time Ottilie was running and running towards the cottage she had forgotten that Ma would not be there when she arrived. She knew she was dead, of course, but even so she did not expect her not to be there when she eventually arrived. Her rich laugh, her long thick red plait of hair, her lively voice overlaid with the soft Irish tone, everything that was Ma was what Ottilie was really running towards. The smell of her lavender scent, the early morning tea rituals, that was what she was racing towards, the pure love of Ma who had made Ottilie the centre of her life, her own little star, whom Ottilie loved more than anyone else in the world.

There at last was the door, but behind it was not the smell of lavender, nor the sound of the rich, gurgling laugh, nor the glimpse of the flowery frocks that she wore, but the sound of a tinny transistor radio playing, and as Ottilie burst into the cottage there was not the smell of polish, and tea on the stove, the brown pot ready to be filled with bubbling water beside the blue patterned mugs, but the strong smell of old boots flung across the door and tobacco, strong cigarette tobacco, not the kind that Mum smoked in her sitting room at the hotel, but another kind, acrid and unpleasantly real, and Lorcan was not sitting studying at the kitchen table, as she had somehow thought that he might be going to be, and Sean was not there doing his homework. Only Joseph was there, smoking a tipless cigarette, a dull look to his already mature gaze, his hair longer than it had used to be, and a tattoo on his arm.

'Ottie!' Joseph seemed unpleasantly surprised to see her, as if he had been expecting someone else, as if she was the very last person he wanted to see. 'Aren't you meant to be at the hotel?' he went on, frowning, and already walking her back towards the cottage front door.

'Where's Lorcan?' Ottilie managed to get out, .even though she had a stitch in her side from running, and could hardly breathe.

Joseph looked down at the unusual sight of Ottilie's muddied white socks, dirty shoes, and her coat which was now edged with mud.

'What have you been doing, Ottie? What have you been up to? Coming bursting into the place like this, whatever are you doing back here? You don't belong here now, you know, you belong to the hotel now, you know that. Do they know you're here, Ottie? Have you done something wrong?' he added at last, noticing the tension in her young face.

Ottilie looked up at Joseph.

'Yes,' she heard herself say. 'I've done something terribly wrong, and now the police are there, and I don't know what will happen if I don't get rid of these like I said I would, but there's always someone, so I can't. I have to get rid of these earrings the way Mamma wanted but I can't because Edith's always there and now the police are there I can't because someone will see me, and they might search the whole countryside and find them, but I must throw them away or something terrible will happen to me. Oh, and I so hate it when she punishes me.'

Ottilie heard herself sobbing and sobbing and then felt Joseph's hand on her shoulder reminding her, as if she needed it, that this was possibly how she was going to feel when the police did come for her. She would feel the sudden weight, her shoulder would suddenly be pressed down by a roughened hand.

'Ah come on now, Ottie, stop your crying and howling. There's no need for it. Give me the earbobs or whatever they are, I'll throw them away for you. For God's sake, you're carrying on as if you've stolen a car, not a pair of old earbobs.' He put out his hand for them. 'Give them to me, Ottie pet, and I'll throw the wretched things out the window for you. Lord, you've got yourself in a right old state now, haven't you?'

Ottilie could not wait to give them to someone else. She delved into her wretched pocket and put the heavy drop diamond earrings into Joseph's hand that was already so rough and coarse due to the building work at Hultons. Now they were out of her keeping, somewhere other than her coat pocket, it was as if she had been terribly hot with a fever and now was cool and calm, and the sobbing stopped quite suddenly with a big shudder that shook her body, and inwardly she sighed with relief as she saw Joseph's large hand take the wretched things and zip them inside his mock leather jacket pocket.

'There now. All gone. See? And never been here either.

112

Stop your sobbing and go home now, I'll throw them away for you. You always did get yourself in a fine old state, right since you were a bit of a thing at Number Four. If you were in one of your states, Ma always said, there was no dealing with you. There's not much to throwing away a pair of old earbobs, you know? You just *throw* them away! Even so, never mind, eh? I'll get rid of them for you in, as they say, a twinkling of an eye, all right?'

He smiled down at her.

'Just tell me one thing, though, Ottie. Why in heaven's name did you take them if you were going to get so upset about them?'

Ottilie stared up at her middle brother, who was actually laughing at her.

'But I didn't take them, really I didn't, Joseph. I don't like earrings. No, they were from Mamma to throw away because—' She stopped as she remembered Melanie's eyes boring into hers and her words 'something terrible will happen to you'. If she told Joseph the real truth maybe something terrible would happen to him too, to both of them. 'I didn't take them, Joseph, really I didn't,' she finished.

Joseph nodded, not believing her and not really listening either, turning away to light an untipped cigarette from the one he was already smoking, the way he would never have done if Ma were alive.

'I don't suppose they're worth more than a shilling or two, are they? The earbobs, not worth more than a few shillings, I don't suppose?' he asked casually, still seeming not to be really interested in anything except his cigarettes, which he now turned round and round in his mouth as he sucked in the smoke and blew it up into the cold, stale, dusty air of the cottage.

'Oh but they are, Joseph. Those earrings are worth pounds and pounds. That's why the police are there looking for them, that's why they might even search the pipes the way they did when old Mr Pepper lost his gold tooth and it had to be found whatever happened because it cost him over a hundred pounds.'

'Oh yes, and how many pounds would it be that these are worth, then?'

'A thousand pounds.'

There, it was out.

Joseph gave a short laugh after a second's astonishment.

'A thousand pounds, eh? Is that all? In that case we had better send them off to our favourite charity so?' he said, half to himself. A pause, and then: 'Right. OK. Now. Ottie, this really is strictly between you and me. Look. Ottilie. You don't want something bad to happen to you, now do you?'

Ottilie was sure that she did not want anything bad to happen to her, of that at least she was quite, quite sure. 'You mean, you want me to keep something under my hat?' she volunteered for the second time that day.

'Exactly, Ottie. You should keep this under your hat, if you were wearing one,' he added, joking. 'Now, first. You mustn't tell anyone you've been here, and if you don't, well then neither shall I, all right? Look. Remember that time I knew what it was they had written in the kitchen even though Ma and Lorcan had told me not to tell you? Well, this – it's just like that time, really. This is strictly between you and me, Ottie, and no-one else. You know, like when you go to confession and the priest never tells out? Think of me like that priest, you know, you've told me something, but I will never tell out. It doesn't matter that you took these earbobs, really it doesn't—'

'But I didn't take them—'

'Doesn't matter, Ottie. Forget about it. It doesn't matter. Really. Mrs Cartaret will get the insurance and I will get rid of them for you. Now all *you* have to do is to go home, clean up, and forget all about it. OK? It's just a bad dream, and now it's stopped. Just forget all about it. No-one knows you've been here now, do they? You're quite sure?'

'No-one, no, I swear it, Joseph.'

'Good, well then off with you, and not another word.'

He opened the cottage door suddenly, but not very wide, as if Ottilie was a cat or a dog he was putting out at dusk, and Ottilie shot through the narrow opening and started once more to bolt towards the little road, the high hedges, and another world.

Oh the relief of running and running and knowing that she was free of those dreadful objects. She would always hate jewellery now, for ever and ever afterwards. She would never like jewellery, or diamonds, or anything to do with earrings, or anything at all like that. They would always make her feel sick.

The sea breeze was now strolling not whipping round the corner of the hotel but it cooled her hot cheeks as she slipped back into the empty reading room and crept up the back stairs to the sanctuary of her own suite once more.

Soon Edith would come to her, and everything would be all right. Ottilie would joke with her and everything would be like it was. But first she must wash her socks, and clean her shoes, and brush the mud from her coat. No-one must find out where she had been. Only Joseph knew, and he would never tell. He would throw away the earrings for her, probably in the bottom of the cement mixer that Mr Hulton and his men used, or in the stream that ran past the cottage where the old man had shouted at her that first day.

Except they would show up in the clear water, just as they would be sure to be found by someone local in a hedge or a field, their brightness catching the sun, or someone's boot overturning them, or their spade. No, Joseph would find somewhere else to throw them. Perhaps he would take a bus ride and then throw them away? But the worst of it was, as Ottilie knew only too well, all that time God would be looking at him, and at her, and He would know.

Hardly minutes after Ottilie had cleaned up her clothes

as best she could – the mud appearing to her frantic guilty eyes to be more like blood – Edith returned to her suite, quietly relieved that the police had searched the staff quarters and nothing had been found.

'Leaves a nasty taste for all of us, though,' she told Ottilie. 'Really it does, Miss Ottilie. I just don't understand who could have done such a thing to Mrs Cartaret. She was in tears, she was that upset by the end.'

Ottilie's eyes strayed to the cupboard. She had hung the now damp-edged coat to the back of the wardrobe. She had placed the still damp shoes at the back of the many rows of shoes that she owned. She had washed out her white knee socks and wrapped them round and round the towel rail underneath her bath towel to dry them. All traces of the real criminal had been washed off, or wiped off. No-one could find out that it was her now, no-one.

'Would you like me to read you a story tonight? You look too washed out to read to yourself. You know your trouble, Miss Ottilie? You have a skin too few. I reckon you've suffered for us all today, just as if it was you that was the thief.'

Ottilie nodded and closed her eyes. The words from the favourite chapter of her favourite book offered Ottilie nothing but consolation after the hell of the day that had been, and Edith's voice was so warm and kind.

'*Home! That was what they meant, those caressing appeals, those soft touches wafted through the air, those invisible little hands pulling and tugging, all one way! Why, it must be quite close by him at that moment, his old home that he had hurriedly forsaken and never sought again, that day when he first found the river!*'

Against the sound of Edith's voice reading, Ottilie thought – home! She had tried to go home not just to get rid of the earrings but to find Ma and her old happy ways, to find Number Four and the dear golden days that had always seemed so full of sunlight and laughter when

116

Lorcan, Joseph and Sean had loved her, and played with her, and not wanted her to go away from them.

'Poor Mole stood alone in the road, his heart torn asunder, and a big sob gathering, gathering, gathering, somewhere low down inside him, to leap up to the surface presently, he knew, in passionate escape.'

Edith stopped as Ottilie turned away, her eyes straying to the old-fashioned thick chintz curtains hanging at her windows, rows of decorative bobbles adorning their swagged pelmets and running down the long edges until they ended at the carpet where they lay an inch or two beyond the floorline in extravagant spills. She had not been 'home' very long, but it had been long enough for her to notice that there were no such pelmets at the cottage, no extravagant spills of curtains thickly lined, no soft carpets, no kind eyes like Edith's looking down at her with concern as they were now, only Joseph looking at Ottilie as if she was someone he now hardly knew.

'Are you all right, Miss Ottilie?'

'Oh yes, Edith, quite all right, thank you.'

'Well, that's all right then,' said Edith. 'It has been quite a day, I'm afraid, Miss Ottilie, but all's well that ends well. And no more to be said.'

Edith continued to read.

'Meanwhile, the wafts from his old home pleaded, whispered, conjured, and finally claimed him imperiously. He dared not tarry longer within their magic circle. With a wrench that tore his very heartstrings he set his face down the road and followed submissively in the track of the Rat, while faint, thin little smells, still dogging his retreating nose, reproached him for his new friendships and his callous forgetfulness.'

One last great shuddering sigh escaped from Ottilie, and then she was asleep.

Seven

Mrs Le Martine was almost as excited as Ottilie at the thought that Ottilie might be actually going to have tea with Blue Lady. But first, for her mother's sake, Ottilie must try to hint to Mrs Le Martine that she had prior knowledge about Mamma's designer clothes going to London to be sold. After the horrors of her experience with the diamond earrings, dropping hints to Mrs Le Martine seemed as easy as helping to give a tea party for lonely, bored children on a rainy day at the hotel.

Ottilie began with flattery, though she knew that Mrs Le Martine would not believe a word. Even so she knew she would enjoy it, that they both would, just like playing a familiar card game, or going for a walk each step of which you knew but which you could pretend that you did not, stopping and exclaiming at each turn at a view, or a statue, or a perfectly planted garden as if you had never seen it before.

'I love your lavender coat and skirt, but I think I like you best of all in pink.'

Mrs Le Martine was quite used to Ottilie threading her way through all the clothes in her cupboards, and sighing and making appreciative remarks. As a matter of fact Ottilie always thought that she must rather like it, because as Ottilie did so she would stare at her own reflection in her silver hand mirror and turn her head to and fro, watching her reflection intently as Ottilie's words came floating back to her across the deep-carpeted room.

'Do you know, Mrs Le Martine, my mother has a pink

Chanel suit, quite new, but she has been seen in it just one time too often in the hotel, so it must go back to the secondhand shop in Knightsbridge to be sold hardly worn. Such a pretty pink. I wrapped it for her this morning . . .'

'Which shop in Knightsbridge?'

All Mrs Le Martine's clothes were wrapped in some form of tissue paper or box with one of many Knightsbridge names printed in silver or gold across it. Ottilie often felt that Mrs Le Martine might even own this place called 'Knightsbridge'.

'Oh, it's just a little shop where all her clothes must go once she's finished with them because of being seen too often at the hotel, and of course she can't give them to staff or anyone in the town because they might turn up here wearing them, and then where would she be?'

'Well, quite. Your mother could not have that, I do see.'

There was a slight pause while Mrs Le Martine continued to stare at herself in her hand mirror, and then Ottilie offered, 'Of course, I want her to keep them for me, but she won't because they won't be at all fashionable by the time I grow up.'

'No, I don't suppose they will, Miss Ottilie.' At last Mrs Le Martine turned from the hand mirror and, head on one side, looked across at Ottilie who was now busy trying on some of her shoes. 'I might be interested. Would you like to show me the Shah-nelle? I missed going to the Collections in Paris this year, and, as you know, I have always been interested in collecting Shah-nelle.'

This was another pretence that they both kept up, that Mrs Le Martine always went to Paris to the Collections and never bought her clothes secondhand from the shop in London which was just about, according to Mrs Cartaret, so sadly to close. Ottilie had long ago realized the truth because of the cleaning tickets that still adhered to the so-called 'new' clothes that Mrs Le Martine arrived with every year.

But that was another thing that she and Mrs Le Martine

shared, their pretence. That's why they laughed so much, because they both enjoyed pretending so much, and it didn't matter that not very much was true. All that mattered was that they laughed and enjoyed themselves during the month that she sayed at the start of the summer season every year.

Later Mrs Le Martine said, staring at the pristine Chanel suit in its beautiful white box that Ottilie had raced to find in her mother's rooms and returned with at equal speed, 'Of course it will be very expensive, I expect, perhaps too expensive, don't you think?'

'It will be less if you buy it now, here,' Ottilie found herself saying with a certain urgency, remembering the look in her mother's eyes what now seemed like a lifetime away, but was really only two days.

'Would Mrs Cartaret accept forty pounds for the coat and skirt, do you think?'

'Oh yes.'

'In that case, ring for Edith, Miss Ottilie, and I shall try it on.'

Edith must be rung for, and then Mrs Le Martine dressed in the suit, but not before she had negotiated a full change of lingerie and Edith had done up her silk stockings with the suspenders that she so favoured – silk-lined, and tiny as if, Ottilie always thought, made for the Little People in whom Ma had believed so fervently.

'Did you know that in Ireland there is a shoe two inches long, made of mouse skin, and yet the heel of it is quite worn down, and the sole a little too, so it must have been worn by one of the busiest of the Little People?'

Ma had told Ottilie that often, as the start of a story designed to soothe her to sleep. Often the shoe had been lost by a little girl running away from her wicked stepmother to find the Land that Always Will. Sometimes it would be worn by a mischievous leprechaun searching to steal the Big People's shoes when they were bathing in the sea. Now Mrs Le Martine looked across at Ottilie.

'My dear Miss Ottilie, how fascinating,' she murmured, not actually very interested at all, as she turned and turned in front of the dressing mirror before the fascinated eyes of Edith and Ottilie. 'Oh yes, I think this is quite a fit, although it is a little long. But how particularly lucky that Her Majesty and I are both size eight, how most particularly lucky.'

'You look ever so elegant in that, Mrs Le Martine,' Edith murmured. Despite this flattery Mrs Le Martine waited until Edith had gone, which meant that she had to wait for Edith to stop hanging about removing fluff from the carpet and pretending that there was something she had forgotten so that she could listen to their talk, and then quickly found some crisply clean money and gave it to Ottilie.

'There, dear, give this to you-know-who and tell her I am most grateful for the opportunity to buy Shah-nelle, but be sure to reassure that I shall not wear it until I return to London, never in the hotel. We could not have that, of course.'

If Ottilie thought that Melanie would be grateful when she passed on that first money for her secondhand clothes, she was very much mistaken. She simply took it from her as if she was a little late in arriving with it, and said, 'Did I tell you, everything is fixed? Mrs Ballantyne is expecting you for tea tomorrow, at four o'clock. Do be on your very best, won't you?'

Ottilie nodded, not wanting to catch Melanie's eye, and then with much relief she effected her escape from the suite, and bolted off back to Mrs Le Martine with the news that tomorrow, only twenty hours away from now, she would at last be meeting Blue Lady.

This time Mrs Le Martine must come to Ottilie's suite to help her choose her dress, and to watch Edith brush and comb her hair and tie the sides of it up in a beautiful bow at the top of her head while brushing the rest down her back in a thick and shining and satisfying fall of hair.

'Most decorative, Edith,' Mrs Le Martine purred as Edith turned Ottilie towards her. Tartan dress, broad white lace collar, wide sash, long white socks, black patent leather shoes, and a full petticoat beneath edged with lace just a little of which, as was currently the fashion, was allowed to show. 'Oh yes, Edith, most satisfactory. Come here, pet.'

Mrs Le Martine leaned forward and pecked Ottilie on the cheek, giving Ottilie a wonderfully satisfactory inhalation of 'Enchantée'.

'Good luck, Miss Ottilie,' she murmured in her husky voice, 'and don't forget the details, all the details. I want to know everything, please, right down to the last little jot or tittle.'

No need for Edith to take her upstairs, for during the last three years Ottilie had spent much time playing in the Great Suite on rainy days. She knew the way very well. She actually loved the grandness of it, the loneliness of it, the strange sense of its always waiting to be occupied by the very rich. The moment the double doors opened to admit the visitor the sea did not just come into view, it rose up from outside the French windows ahead and slapped them in the face.

Mrs Tomber always said, with great satisfaction, 'We never have had any trouble in the Great Suite', and if this was so it might be because the view of the sea and the rocks was so spectacular that the occupants of the rooms were constantly reminded that do what they might they were as important as sandhoppers compared to the sea outside.

In the long lonely winters when the hotel was shut Ottilie loved to people the rooms with exotic characters, polo-playing princes and grand ladies, brilliant painters, Chinese empresses and American film stars, the kind of people that never seemed to come to the Grand at St Elcombe.

But despite this particular suite's being such an old friend, Ottilie had absolutely no idea of what to expect when she pushed open the double doors of the Great Suite. It was all very well for Mrs Le Martine and herself to imagine that they knew just what Blue Lady looked like, but they only knew her from afar, from their surreptitious daily glances up towards her balcony as they wondered over and over what she was doing there, so still, staring out to sea at the waves and the rocks on either side of the bay.

And no good asking the staff, Edith or anyone, because they were all so vague, having no powers of description unless there was something really out of the ordinary about someone that they could seize on – such as a broken arm, or a great white beard. But if the person in question did not have some special peculiarity they would reply to Ottilie's curious questions in a vaguely impatient voice as if the very idea of answering her was a colossal effort, 'Well, I wouldn't know, really, Miss Ottilie. Well, all right. I'll tell you. Quite pretty, she is, I suppose, for her age that is, but a bit old-fashioned now, see? But always quite polite, I would say, but as I say, definitely old-fashioned. Now I really must get on.'

They nearly always ended their poor efforts at description with 'Now I really must get on' as if Ottilie had embarrassed them with her questions. Perhaps because of this Ottilie had already formed the opinion that Blue Lady would be really quite old, not old as Mrs Le Martine was old but really, really old, because from afar, right above them on her private balcony, Mrs Ballantyne – which Ottilie kept having to remember was actually Blue Lady's real name – always looked as if she was going to be old, tiny and frail, sitting in her dark glasses with a hat pulled down, and nearly always with a rug on her knees and sewing on her lap.

The shock to Ottilie therefore of seeing her on the other side of the elegant sitting room, beside the French windows of the Great Suite, was astounding. It was as much of a shock as expecting someone quite young and then finding them to be very old. It was as much of a shock as seeing how Joseph had seemed so suddenly to have changed into someone Ottilie simply did not know, tall, and handsome, but sort of grim, and with a tattoo on his arm, just like any other man that might be working on a building site for Mr Hulton, not like the Joseph she remembered even from Christmas last. It was as much of a shock as finding out how difficult it was to throw earrings away when you knew that God was watching you and Edith would be sure to notice. It was a bucket of cold water of a shock to see that Mrs Ballantyne was anything but old.

Not only that, but as Ottilie edged into the room with her tea tray, quietly shutting the door behind her with a push of her rear, she was instantly aware of the change in the atmosphere of the rooms. The Great Suite was no longer a furnished and carpeted, richly curtained blank canvas for an active imagination, the kind of imagination that Ottilie possessed, it was no longer a great toy box for her to open so that she could play with its contents, but a changed and most positive place filled with alien possessions.

It was only on giving a quick surreptitious look round that Ottilie remembered that Mrs Ballantyne's arrival was always preceded by the delivery of innumerable personal belongings, and that she herself always arrived last, late at night and alone, hurrying up the stairs as if she was terrified that someone might see her, as if for the Great Suite to retain its magical, ghostly hold on her no human eye must behold her for longer than a few seconds, for if it did she herself might melt and disappear.

Outside the long windows it was an afternoon of dark grey clouds, and a dark grey sea rose and fell, pushing up the white tips of each new wave ever higher, so that at times it would seem they were vying to be taller and more imposing than the unmoving rocks on either side, or playing some game of touching the ceiling of the lowering sky that so exactly matched the sea. Even the palm trees that grew closer to the shielding comfort of the hotel seemed to be bending just slightly to the will of the wind, and certainly despite the late spring no-one was about outside, either below the balcony or beyond the window at which the lady now sat sewing steadily, her head bent over her needlework.

'Put the tea tray on the round table,' she called out in a pretty if strangely mechanical voice. 'Leave it just there, and put two teaspoons of Lapsang Souchong from the silver caddy that you will notice in front of you into the strainer in the teapot, pour on the hot water from your jug and leave for one minute by the clock that you can see on the other side of the table, take it out, and then place a slice of lemon in each cup, pour on the tea and set one beside me and one beside the chair opposite, please.'

Ottilie, despite considerable previous experience of helping out with teas, felt more nervous at the sound of these instructions than she could possibly have imagined. To calm herself she thought of the kitchens from which she had just come. Down there, way below them, the staff would be laughing and joking as they set cream teas for one, or toasted muffins for two and put them in the old-fashioned muffin dishes. Down there the chefs would just be coming back on duty, stubbing out their untipped cigarettes by the back doors, waiting to swing into action as the evening star started to climb the weather-dark skies outside the windows and their wives and girlfriends settled back to watch the evening news on small black and white televisions, or listen to the shipping forecasts on their radios.

Mrs Ballantyne had never once raised her head from her sewing frame as she issued her instructions, and so, as Ottilie obediently poured hot water onto the closed straining spoon filled with Lapsang Souchong and waited an exact minute by the small, round mahogany clock in its special case by the caddy, it was still impossible for the inexperienced young waitress to see very precisely the face of the lady for whom she was making this delicately flavoured tea.

And besides, she was too intent on getting the tea right to permit herself to stare across the darkening room, unlit as yet by any of the large Chinese porcelain lamps, and illuminated only by that little amount of light that the weather and the time of year permitted.

Obedient to Mrs Ballantyne's so-precise instructions she set a cup of tea first beside her, and then beside the empty chair.

Mrs Ballantyne must have finished the stitch upon which she was concentrating so hard, because at last she did look up just as Ottilie was looking down and for a second she stared into Ottilie's eyes.

'Who are you?' she asked, but only after it seemed to Ottilie that she had given a little start and her eyes had, for a fleeting moment, lit up, as if she had found herself staring into the eyes of an old friend whom she really loved and had not seen for years. But it was only a second and then the brown eyes, rimmed with a faint green eye-shadow, seemed to once more glaze over, to become indifferent.

'I am Ottilie, Mrs Ballantyne. Ottilie Cartaret.'

There was a slight pause as Mrs Ballantyne placed her sewing frame to the side of her chair and picked up the fine china teacup that had been put beside her, sipping at it delicately and almost without a sound.

'People have such peculiar names nowadays,' she remarked. 'Such peculiar names.'

''parently it's actually short for Odelia, Mamma says, but I'm never called Odelia, only Ottilie.'

'Good heavens, imagine, did you ever hear the like of that?'

Mrs Ballantyne raised her head slightly as if she was

talking to someone in the room, someone whom Ottilie certainly could not see but she now saw she had set a cup of tea for beside their chair.

Ottilie nodded at the empty chair which Mrs Ballantyne had addressed, because she felt so awkward and could think of nothing else that she could do. It would seem quite silly to say anything more, because of course had Ottilie thought the origin of her name *un*interesting she would not have told Mrs Ballantyne about it.

'Myself I like a name to have an old-fashioned ring to it, rather than a peculiar or quaint ring,' Blue Lady went on, picking up her sewing frame once more but glancing, with a fleeting, loving smile, at the empty chair opposite her.

At this Ottilie could not help having a quite searching look round the room for this unseen person who had not yet attempted to drink the cup of tea set out so precisely for them. But there was definitely no-one else in the room, and so Ottilie stood on in an agony of embarrassment, not knowing what to say to these remarks that were not being made to her, pulling awkwardly at her *broderie anglaise* apron and wishing for perhaps a fiftieth time that Melanie had not been so terribly extravagant with her clothes money, and wondering how soon she could make good her escape. Above all she hoped that Mrs Ballantyne would tell her to go, because now she was here, in the Great Suite, only a few feet from her, Ottilie could see just how wrong she and Mrs Le Martine had got Blue Lady. For someone who, like Ottilie, had been looking to see an old lady with a lace collar and a cameo brooch, and if possible a great chignon of white hair, being so close to Mrs Ballantyne was certainly a great disappointment.

For a start she could hardly be more than thirty years of age, or something around that (Ottilie was not very good at ages), yet at the same time there was something very un-modern and not at all up to date about her. It was not just that she did not wear modern clothes, or that nowhere about her was there any evidence of the shirtwaisters and stiff petticoats that were currently so fashionable. It was not just that her suit had a nipped-in jacket, and a skirt that fell in an unfashionably long length to her ankles in a style that Mrs Le Martine had told Ottilie when they were talking 'fashion', which was practically every day, was 'New Look 1948', nor that her shoes were what Ottilie knew used to be called 'peep-toed' or that her make-up was unfashionable in that it emphasized her lips, so that they looked red and full. It was something about her whole being, as if she, despite not being old at all, was set as much in the jelly with which Chef always surrounded his *oeufs en gelée* as one of the softly poached eggs themselves.

And although Ottilie could see that she was very pretty, and that like Mrs Le Martine she was just the size to fit into one of her mother's coat-and-skirts or one of the evening dresses that Mrs Cartaret was so intent on selling, she could also see that Mrs Ballantyne would never buy anything modern and up to date from either Mrs Cartaret or anyone else, for the very good reason that Mrs Ballantyne was quite obviously a person from the past. She was a person from another era, haunting the Great Suite in clothes which could now only be found in some magazine that not even the Grand would still have lying about on some dusty shelf. She looked as strange and old-fashioned as any of the old ladies who stayed at the Grand at Christmas, with their long crêpe evening dresses, their shingled hair and their delicate little reticules hanging from silver and gold chains from which they would from time to time remove their gold or silver powder compacts and pat their noses between dinner courses, discreetly turning to one side so that no-one would have cause to notice them.

'It is a very dark day today,' the voice from the chair went on, addressing that same empty chair opposite her, while at the same time holding out the fragile fine china teacup, part of the special tea service that was reserved especially for the Great Suite. 'It is a very dark day indeed.

129

And *I* will have another cup of tea, please, young lady.'

Just at that moment Ottilie had been hoping to bolt out of the door and down the stairs back to the fun of the kitchens, back to friendly faces and steam and bustle, but instead she silently stepped forward to do as bidden, leaving the other cup undrunk beside its chair.

She stared at the little mahogany clock as she minutely observed the tea ritual for a second time. This must be the reason why none of the staff liked even talking to her about Mrs Ballantyne. This must be the reason why none of them really liked taking trays up to her in answer to her calls for room service, the ghostly undrunk cup of tea.

This must be the reason, because of how she was, because of the frightening atmosphere that she brought into the room and which lingered about her, making Ottilie feel shivery at the sound of her mechanical tones, her strange way of speaking. The staff did not want to talk about Mrs Ballantyne, because Mrs Ballantyne was a ghost.

Yet unlike most ghosts she spoke, and her voice was the most upsetting aspect of Mrs Ballantyne, because it was a voice from which all expectation had quite gone. A voice which reflected some deep inner misery which was frightening, and at the same time unreachable. Having watched Ottilie place the teacup on the table beside her, she once more turned back to sewing in front of the fast-darkening backdrop outside the window where the storm clouds appeared to be dominating everything. But as she turned the large solitaire diamond on her finger appeared to catch what remained of the disappearing light, so that Ottilie, whose head was always full of romantic notions, imagined for a fraction of a second that its light might be acting as a secret signal to some boat being thrown about in the wrangling seas beyond the windows.

'I love the sea when the sky is darkening.'

At this Ottilie could not help nodding, even though by now she knew that the remark was most certainly not meant for her, and that she was in reality nodding in place of someone she could not see, because Mrs Ballantyne looked up and stared across at the empty chair opposite hers.

'The sea is at its best when in dark and lowering mood.'

Ottilie, silent as always, nodded yet again to the back of the chair, at the back of Mrs Ballantyne's elaborate but severe chignon, at the sea in front of both of them, at the boats on the horizon, but actually to someone whom she could not see but who was none the less, it seemed to her, as real to Mrs Ballantyne as to Ottilie herself.

Downstairs the soups would be gently simmering, the bread rolls warming up, the butter curls glistening, and people would have begun dashing in and out of the service doors. There would be lights and the dessert trolley would be about to be wheeled into position, jellies and trifles shimmering, miniature eclairs glowing in their dark chocolate sauce. Everything would be such a contrast to this dark and gloomy room and its strange occupant with her long painted fingernails, her sculpted Dior clothes, and her heavy rings that seemed to be pushing her small, slender hands down towards her needlework, at the same time making it difficult for her to hold her needle except with almost straightened fingers, in a sewing style that old ladies in the lounges downstairs always used.

'Yes, and perhaps there will be thunder. That would be exciting, wouldn't it, darling?'

Mrs Ballantyne smiled at the empty chair and then gazed out at the sea ahead as if she was following someone else's gaze rather than her own, as if she had heard someone say, 'Oh, do look at that.'

Gradually, step by step, like a sort of reverse Grand-mother's Footsteps, Ottilie found herself backing towards the double doors, and then slowly, so slowly, she managed to turn one of the old-fashioned pointed handles. Then, quickly, she bolted out of the door, shut it and fled down the stairs again, without the tea tray, without having even

131

mentioned her mother's clothes, without anything, but above all without Mrs Ballantyne and her invisible guest.

'What on earth can you mean, Ottilie?'

Melanie turned with evident reluctance from her hand mirror and placed it face down on the glass top of her much beribboned dressing table with its underskirts of shell-pink satin, and its overskirts of muslin draped in decorative swags and caught up at the sides by bunches of beautifully made artificial roses.

'Please explain what you mean.'

Long before she opened her mouth to announce to Melanie that, unlike Mrs Le Martine, Mrs Ballantyne could have no possible interest in Mrs Cartaret's model clothes, Ottilie had determined that she would tell Mamma that she no longer wanted to have anything to do with passing off her old clothes onto hotel guests.

'Mrs Ballantyne only likes very old clothes, she told me so herself.'

'That, Ottilie Cartaret, is a barefaced lie. I happen to know it is a barefaced lie, because Mrs Ballantyne is quite mad and has been for years. You could not possibly know that she is only interested in old clothes, because once she gets up into the Great Suite she never makes the slightest shred of sense.' Mrs Cartaret paused to throw a pill down her throat and at the same time took a sip of her gin and tonic. 'That is a lie!'

Ottilie turned scarlet at this and at the same time found herself wondering why her mother had sent her up to take tea to the woman if she knew all along that she would not be in the slightest bit interested in her cast-off clothes? Nevertheless, as always when she made something up, she could not give in, and anyway she knew what would happen if she was caught in a lie. It was the rule. Everyone at the Grand knew what happened when Ottilie was caught in one of the lies in which she believed so heartily. However well meant, they were always punished. 'What I

132

mean, Mamma,' Ottilie went on, trying not to let her growing sense of desperation creep into her voice, 'what I meant was, well, that Mrs Ballantyne only wears old clothes, so there didn't seem much point in asking her, see? I mean did there? See?'

'Don't say "see" like that, Ottilie, it's vulgar. And don't wriggle your feet. Keep still when I'm talking to you. So, there didn't seem much point in talking to Mrs Ballantyne, did there? Well, perhaps you will think there is some point when I tell you that unless we get rid of some of these clothes, and soon, there will be no pocket money for you for the next six months, at least!'

Mrs Cartaret's sudden tempers, coming from nowhere, were something to which Ottilie had been forced to become used when she first came to live at the Grand. Sometimes she would even stamp her foot, or throw something at her mirror. Edith always murmured under her breath, if she was an unfortunate witness of one of her sudden squalls, 'Take no notice, Miss Ottilie, just take no notice. Whatever happens, just take no notice.'

But Ottilie found it difficult to take no notice, particularly if, like now, she was trying to save up all her hard-earned pocket money to buy Lorcan a fishing rod for his birthday.

'I could ask Mrs Le Martine if she has a friend who would like something. How would that be, Mamma?'

'Mrs Le Martine! You and Mrs Le Martine, you make me sick both of you, thick as thieves and always gossiping and carrying on. Mrs Le Martine tells lies just like you do. You both tell lies. She is nothing but a liar, pretending to be something she is not. And so are you. You're a liar.'

Mrs Cartaret sprang up from her dressing table stool and ran at Ottilie in sudden fury, her hairbrush in one hand.

'I'm going to beat you for telling lies, and then I'm going to lock you in that cupboard, you horrid little girl,' she shouted. 'I'm going to lock you up until you promise never to tell me lies again!'

Ottilie froze. It was such a very long time since Mrs Cartaret had last beaten her, she had quite hoped that she never would again. The last time was when the sauce chef had left without warning and Ottilie had tried to help out in the kitchens and dropped a whole tray of plates. She had been marched from the kitchens, in front of the whole staff, and beaten and locked in a cupboard. She so hated that word 'beat'. *I am going to beat you.* She would never say that word when she grew up, not ever. She would never say 'beat'. She would never beat anyone either, as Mamma was trying to beat her now.

'Please, Mum – Mamma – please, don't beat me. I'm sorry for telling you a lie, really I am.' Mr Cartaret appeared at his wife's bedroom door as Ottilie started to plead with Mrs Cartaret. 'Please, please, please don't beat me, please, Mamma. I didn't mean to tell you a lie, really I didn't!'

'In for a beating, are you?' Ottilie heard him ask. But he went away before Ottilie started to cry out. And later he said to her as he passed her in the corridor when Edith had let her out of the cupboard, 'We all have to go through it, you know. I was beaten. Did me no harm, really it didn't. Besides, being in a dark cupboard's nothing to complain about. Quite good for you, I understand.'

What he did not say to Ottilie was why it was good for you. Nor did he tell her the real reason why Mrs Cartaret had flown into such a particularly bad temper that afternoon.

Ottilie had managed to dry her tears long before a welcome ray of light illuminated her lonely and terrifying sojourn locked among Mrs Cartaret's heavily scented clothes and Edith, creeping silently in once Madame had gone to make her entrance down the golden staircase, was able to let Ottilie out and take her back to her own suite where she bathed her in silence, both of them avoiding looking at the red marks or into each other's eyes.

If Edith and Ottilie had met each other's eyes they would have been unable to avoid telling each other the truth, which was: 'Mrs Cartaret is mad.'

So they did not look into each other's eyes, and while Ottilie listened to Edith reading to her from yet another chapter of her favourite book her mind went back to the old days when she was the centre of Ma's life, her little star, and she lay beside her basking in the warmth of their early mornings together, while Ma sipped her morning tea and music played from her pride and joy, the great grand mahogany radiogram.

One day soon perhaps Ottilie would be able, somehow, to go back to what she still found herself longing for so heartily, would feel herself once more trotting beside Ma heading for Number Four and all its warmth, but as it was now there was just Edith. Yet at least that was something, at least she was lucky in Edith.

'Edith?'

'Yes, pet?'

Edith stopped, placing her finger under the word she was about to read, which she always did most precisely.

'Now I won't be having pocket money for six months I shan't be able to give Lorcan a birthday present, will I?'

'No, pet, I don't suppose you will.'

Edith looked grave. It was grave. Very grave. The whole thing was extraordinarily grave. After all, as they both knew, in six months Lorcan would be twenty-one years of age, and as Edith always said, there was no birthday more important than that, surely?

'Perhaps I could do a paper round, like Chef's daughter does?'

'Oh no, pet, that wouldn't be allowed. Never. Not for you, Miss Ottilie.'

'What could I do, then?'

'Just try and be good, and hope for the best.'

135

'I do try and be good, but it doesn't seem to work, does it, Edith? So there doesn't seem much point in hoping for the best.'

'It does do good sometimes,' Edith said, her eyes quickly returning to the book. 'I often hope for the best, Miss Ottilie.'

Ottilie closed her own eyes with one of her particularly deep and shuddering sighs. If only she understood more about everything maybe it would make it easier to be good. In the morning, long before Mrs Cartaret was up and about, she would go and see Mrs Le Martine and they would laugh and talk and maybe some of those things in her life that she so loved would be all right again.

But in the morning when Ottilie crept down to see Mrs Le Martine she had checked out of her suite, leaving only an envelope addressed to Ottilie by her dressing table mirror. Inside the envelope there was a card. The words were printed very carefully on the card.

For you, Miss Ottilie, to spend as you wish.

Inside the envelope there was a great deal of money, a frightening amount. So much that Ottilie ran back to her own suite and Edith, unable to face counting it herself, quite terrified at just the sight of it.

'Why did she want to give me all this, Edith? Quick. Hide it. Or Mamma will think I have stolen it, won't she?'

Ottilie practically threw the envelope at Edith, and Edith, sort of knowing at once why neither of them must say anything to anyone about it, that it was a terrible secret between them, immediately stashed the envelope and the money in the side pocket of her uniform as if she was afraid the door would suddenly be flung open and they would both be accused of having stolen it, and it would be taken from them.

'You mustn't say, Miss Ottilie, and I wasn't going to tell you, but it appears that Mrs Le Martine heard all about what happened to you – you know, being punished – and she wouldn't stay here after that. Not a minute longer. She wanted to say goodbye to you, but you were fast asleep, and she was that upset she wouldn't stay until morning, took a hire car and left. There was a terrible row between her and Madame, at dinner. Everyone was very shocked in the dining room, I hear, and several regulars left early. But you were asleep by then, thank goodness, because it was not nice, as I understand it, not nice at all.'

Colour flooded Ottilie's face and she could feel not just the pain but the terrible humiliation of the beating the previous day. 'Oh, but I didn't want her to hear about that, really I didn't.' Ottilie started to cry. 'I didn't want Mrs Le Martine to hear about that at all.'

Edith bent down to Ottilie and put her arms awkwardly around her, because although they were always together they did not usually hug each other.

'You must feel proud, really, Miss Ottilie, because Mrs Le Martine really went for Madame when she heard from someone on the staff that she'd been beating you. She said you were the nicest little girl she'd ever met and she wasn't staying a minute longer. She blamed her something terrible, blamed Madame in front of everyone. Mrs Tomber said she heard from Chef who heard from Thierry the head waiter that it was terrible to hear how Mrs Le Martine went for Madame, but of course they were in Mrs Le Martine's corner, although they can't say so, because of their jobs.'

Ottilie tried to stop crying but she could not, because she knew now that she would never again be able to pretend to Mrs Le Martine that she was a cheerful, mischievous little girl. Now Mrs Le Martine would know all about her mother, and about Ottilie's not really being cheerful at all. The two of them would not be able to pretend any more, would not be able to tease each other and make believe. It was all over, for ever and ever, just as Joseph and Sean were all over, not wanting to see Ottilie any more, and perhaps even Lorcan too because of not being able to save up for the fishing rod, because of no pocket money, because of everything.

As Ottilie dried her eyes, Edith went on, 'I know all about what she's been on at you for. Mrs Le Martine told me everything, Miss Ottilie. Trouble with Madame is she has clothes mania, begging your pardon, Miss Ottilie, but truly that's what she has. They'll be the death of her, one day, they will really, those clothes of hers. Never content, never happy, enough is not enough for her. Sending you round to people like Mrs Le Martine, making you ask them if they want to buy her old clothes indeed. She's just punishing you because she's bored and cross. She doesn't really need the money at all, not like my mother needs money. It's as if she wanted to humiliate you because of her own poor little girl drowning in the sea when she was lunching and not paying attention. Now look, see. I'll keep this money for you. No-one knows about it except you and me, and we aren't telling, are we? We'll keep it under our hats. And I'll buy that fishing rod you want to give Mr Lorcan for his birthday, when the times comes, so I will, and I'll wrap it for you, and all that. You just leave it to me and I'll do everything. And not a word to anyone, mind? Mrs Le Martine will be back next year, course she will, as right as rain and twice as wonderful, as they say. She'll be back. You see if she isn't, mark my words. And then you can thank her for everything, quite quiet, when no-one's around, and that's that. No more to be said.'

But there was something more to be said. Ottilie looked up at Edith, her eyes dry of tears now, but even so she had to speak slowly so as not to be upset again.

'Edith?'

'Yes, pet?'

'Can I ask you something?'

'Course, pet.'

Edith adopted her most mature expression and waited for the inevitable question.

'Will I ever grow up?'

Part Three

Come, fill the Cup, and in the Fire of Spring
  The Winter Garment of Repentance fling:
The Bird of Time has but a little way
  To Fly – and Lo! the bird is on the Wing.

Rubáiyát of Omar Khayyám

Eight

1964

By the time Ottilie was sixteen most of the Grand's regular visitors had died. All the old ladies with their fur stoles and their reticules, their long dining dresses and their vague aroma of camphor, had gone, quietly and elegantly departing for another life, making way for a new and very different age where no-one stood for the National Anthem, revered the Church, or cared to know what it was to use *papiers poudres* to lessen the shine on their noses, and the Beatles were widely thought to be more famous than Jesus Christ.

Of course it was inevitable, it was bound to happen and everyone said so. It was only to be expected that with change came change, but knowing this did not make it any easier. Particularly for the Cartarets, and most especially Alfred Cartaret, for Alfred did not like change, to put it mildly. In fact he abhorred it. He still wore black tie and embroidered slippers for dining in the evenings even if he and Melanie were dining alone in their rooms, and he would raise his hat in greeting to everyone along the sea front outside the hotel, although it sometimes meant that by doing so in a force ten he risked seeing his precious hat from the specialist hatter in Savile Row blow off into the sea.

Observing the steady decline in the Grand's bookings as the Sixties approached and then overtook them, Alfred had taken on less and less staff as each new season began. Those few workers that he had taken on had been foreign, but when they found it too hard to bear the low wages and the cold English winters, while the countries they had come from could offer holidaymakers air flights and a week's break for what it cost for just a few nights at the Grand, he had been reduced to using only his hard core of local staff from the town. 'That's what a good hotel depends on, after all, its old timers, both behind the reception desk and in front of it. Regulars will always finally come back to regulars, you know,' he would say, as if he had planned this all along, as if he really wanted to manage with only a quarter of his original staff.

But despite the regular staff at the Grand, despite the same Swiss chef, Blackie the porter and Thierry the head waiter, now a grandfather – despite everything's staying reassuringly the same, with the old regular visitors dying off one by one it seemed that all Alfred's optimism was purely and simply talk.

Nowadays no young people wanted to stay in a great old-fashioned seaside hotel with thick white linen cloths in the dining room, and thick white linen sheets in the best suites, and a staff who would not dream of presenting a newspaper on a breakfast tray without its having first been ironed. Outside the slow life at the Grand no real fires were being burned in hotel grates any more, and no-one cared to be offered three different vegetables in their own sauces with seven tablespoons of butter added to the creamed potatoes, and pancakes were no longer *flambées* at table in front of admiring guests who watched through lorgnettes and sighed with delighted appreciation.

Of course the reluctant knowledge of the Cartarets' new difficulties did not dawn upon Ottilie suddenly. It came to her little by very little as she was maturing, and it was actually the very personal things which she started to notice first, beginning with her mother's entrances down the great gold staircase.

Melanie's long-awaited entrance into the dining room, of which Ottilie had used to be so proud, and everyone had used to like to talk about, was among the first of the

142

changes she noticed, because it was no longer watched by all her mother's old gentlemen admirers with their military moustaches and short-back-and-sides haircuts, but by embarrassed young waiters waiting, all too often, to serve only the proprietor and his family of two.

At first Melanie no longer bothered to dress up and come down at the beginning of the week, because even she must have realized that she had started to look just a little foolish sweeping down the stairs to an empty restaurant. Then, gradually, bit by bit, she stopped appearing at all on weekdays, until finally her grand entrance was limited to Saturday nights only, and even then only if Edith could reassure her that at least half the tables were full, otherwise she would stay in her room and talk back to the newscasters on her small Bush television, loudly denouncing the Labour government for encouraging cheap foreign holidays at the expense of the British tourist trade, her glass of gin beside her chair, her bottles of pills comfortingly near in the bathroom.

'I don't know what to do, I just don't know what to do,' Ottilie overheard Alfred saying out loud to himself one day at the start of winter. 'I just don't know what to do, really I don't.'

Ottilie knew that he must be alone and talking to himself because his voice sounded so low and worried and he never sounded like that in front of anyone else. She could hear him opening his desk drawer and pouring something into a glass, and she knew that he would be staring at the accounts books in his office trying hard, hoping against hope, to make them add up to more than they could possibly ever do in these dark times when not even Americans would come to England.

As she heard him saying 'I just don't know what to do' yet again, and as she imagined him, his grizzled head bent over the accounts books, trying to convince himself that he would be able to make ends meet very soon, that soon the telephone would be ringing and all the old timers would be flooding back to stay with them and there would be an orchestra playing on Saturday nights, Ottilie flattened herself against the corridor wall outside his office. For some reason which she really could not understand, despite its being autumn and the hotel's being eighty-five per cent empty she had hoped to find him in a more buoyant mood than he had been in of late.

'What do you know about anything, anyway?' That was all Melanie ever said to Ottilie nowadays if she made any suggestions for improvements at the hotel, and then as Ottilie turned away, knowing that it was useless to argue with a woman who took pills and drank gin at the same time, she would add, 'I'm just sorry we took you on, really I am, just so sorry we adopted you. I know your father isn't sorry, but I am. You've been nothing but a drain on us from the very beginning, a constant drain, and there's no two ways about that. All those clothes I bought you, all those toys – I could do with that money now, you know.'

Ottilie never bothered to anwer her when she was in that sort of mood, which was practically every day now – none of the staff did. The long-suffering hotel housekeeper, Mrs Tomber, would merely raise her eyes to heaven, and even the saintly Edith would purse her lips, and then they would all carry on as they had been, trying to make up to Mr Cartaret for his wife being as she was, all well aware that they took on twice as much work nowadays because they wanted so much to get the Grand through the present very difficult times until eventually, somehow or another, the old days would come romping back and people would appreciate the 'old-style' grand hotel once more.

'You want to what?'

Mr Cartaret stared at Ottilie over the top of his half-moon glasses, his eyes round and melancholy. His gaze did not upset Ottilie in the least. If it had been his wife staring at her it would have been different, because what with the pills and the gin and the onset of late middle age Mrs Cartaret's expression had become more and more sour, and the look in her eyes more coldly indifferent, more filled with dislike for herself, for everyone, most of all, it sometimes seemed to her adopted daughter, for Ottilie.

'I want to go to Paris, to a cooking school there, just for a few weeks, just for a month.'

'I don't think it's possible.'

Ottilie knew that this was Mr Cartaret's way of saying that he could not afford to send her. She also knew that he was worrying as to who would take Ottilie's place helping out at the hotel, if only for a few weeks, that, although he never said so, he was all too aware that she dusted and cleaned and stood in for just about everyone on every floor, and that Mrs Tomber might well crumple into a heap of exhaustion at the very idea of managing without her.

'I know it's difficult. I wonder – I wonder if you could listen to my plan?'

'I am listening, Ottilie.'

'Mrs Tomber and I have arranged to take on two temporaries, young girls, Spanish, very nice, and they will do my work—'

'You're too young to go abroad on your own, and besides, I don't like Spanish staff, you know that. It's never been successful for us to have Spanish staff.'

'No, listen, really, please!'

Ottilie always spoke in an over-cheerful manner to her father as if she was talking to someone who was not very well. She wanted to cheer him up, make everything all right for him, bring back the old days with lots of visitors coming to the hotel instead of just poor Blue Lady for her one month every year, but otherwise none of the old guard, none of the old courteous couples with their hired chauffeurs and their pathetic pretences that their personal maids were 'unfortunately unwell' rather than long dead.

'No, listen, Pappa. This Spanish girl is coming with her cousin, and they don't mind in the least working hard, they're really very used to it because they've been working at the Angel Inn these last weeks, and since the Clover House group took them over—'

'They slave them there, I do know that.'

'Exactly. And as for the rest . . .' Ottilie knew the bit about the money was going to be awkward, but she pressed on with her usual over-hurried way of talking, the words falling over themselves. 'Well, you see, Mrs Le Martine sent me a cheque and I've saved and saved. Actually, it was her idea. She thinks I should. She thinks I would be of more use to you if I went to cooking school and learned a bit of French so that I could be more of a help instead of running around after everyone all day.'

'Mrs Le Martine should mind her own business. You know your mother has no time for that woman. And besides, I don't approve of you taking money from her. She's no relation of yours.'

'She might be.'

Nowadays Ottilie made a joke of her adoption by the Cartarets, she found it best. Alfred looked up at her and started to say something, but then seeing the logic in her reply he stopped, hesitated, began to say something else instead, thought better of that too, and finally said, 'Well, as a matter of fact, she might. Could well be a relative of the O'Flahertys, couldn't she? By the way – how are all those brothers of yours?'

Because she was asking something of Alfred, because her father knew he was going to have to answer her directly rather than go in for his usual evasions, Ottilie had steeled herself for this question, or one like it. She had already anticipated that he would be sure to ask her something calculated to delay the moment when he would have to respond. Alfred always did find some remark to make her feel suddenly vulnerable, stupid or lacking in some way (sometimes if she had just washed her hair he would murmur 'Our cat has got a long tail' as he passed her in the corridor, or on another day if she was trying to justify something he would say 'Oh, clever dicks, they are a plague').

Ottilie knew that fond as he might be of her (and she thought he was quite) nevertheless now that she was grown up his overriding wish seemed to be to make her feel uncomfortable for some reason. In this instance he knew, all too well, that 'all those brothers' of hers had long ago left St Elcombe, and with the exception of Lorcan she never heard from them, not even a card at Christmas, nothing.

As soon after he had left school as was possible, Sean had gone to Australia on an assisted passage, and Joseph – well, they all tried never to give a thought to Joseph now, it was too painful. As for Lorcan, he was training for the priesthood, which although surprising was not that extraordinary considering what a wonderful father he had been to them all when they were growing up.

'Oh, please, Pappa,' Ottilie continued, ignoring as she always did Alfred's ability to refer to her roots at the most inopportune times, his funny little waspish streak that always seemed so anxious to remind her of her brothers' defection. 'Please let me go. It's only for a few weeks, and I'm to stay in the business apartment of the family of one of Mrs Le Martine's old friends on the Left Bank, and there's a cooking school there called the Parisian School of Cookery—'

'Original name—'

'And I will come back with new ideas and be much more of a help in the kitchens and everywhere, I promise. Mrs Le Martine has even arranged for someone to take me round the kitchens in the Paris Ritz. Another old friend of hers works there, it seems. I will come back much better, really I will.' Even as she pleaded with Alfred, the words bumper to bumper, trying to make him see just how much a few weeks in Paris would mean to her, Ottilie was utterly certain that it could only happen if her mother did not hear about it until it was a *fait accompli*, as Mrs Le Martine would call it, and Ottilie was gone.

'Very well, but on one condition. You are not to tell your mother.'

Now it was Ottilie who tried not to look astonished.

It was the first time she had ever heard her father suggest that she should deceive, or admit publicly that he was capable of even suggesting deceit. 'Nowadays your mother gets very upset about all sorts of things, and Mrs Le Martine is one of them. You know Mrs Le Martine never came back here after that dreadful night six years ago? She stays at the Angel Inn of all places?' Of course Ottilie knew, she looked forward to her old friend's visit all year. 'Your mother has never forgiven her for her dreadful outburst that night in front of all the staff and so many of the guests, Ottilie. It was most uncalled for, I must say.'

Ottilie did not like to say so, nor would she, but she knew all about this, because from the moment that Mrs Le Martine had left that night in such a blind fury at what had happened to Ottilie they had kept in touch. Ottilie had written to her at fortnightly intervals, via Edith's home address.

First she had, naturally, written to thank her for the money she had left in the envelope that day, and then she had written to her about what had happened at the hotel, and about saving for Lorcan's fishing rod, and how the money Mrs Le Martine had left meant that she did not have to save for it at all, and how there was still some left and that she was saving *that* to buy Mrs Le Martine a Christmas present. And how Melanie had gone back to being nice to her. And not to worry because Edith had said that her mother was taking pills and going through a 'trying time'. After that the writing of the letters, the sometimes rather one-sided correspondence (Mrs Le Martine was not a natural letter writer) had become a habit for Ottilie, something to which she looked forward, as if the act of writing the letter was a form of meeting Mrs Le Martine for tea in her suite, the way they had always done in previous years.

Thank heavens Mrs Le Martine was not like a mother to

her (Ottilie realized that she had already had too many mother figures in her life) yet Ottilie had become a little like a niece, or perhaps a goddaughter to her, and she thought that this was perhaps because Mrs Le Martine had no other young people in her life, in spite of knowing so many people.

Ottilie knew that Mrs Le Martine hated her having to be what she called 'an unpaid servant' at the Grand, that she wanted something better for her and that was why she was always trying to think of ways to help her, and why she sent her clothes and money via Edith. She knew, as well, that Edith liked her role of 'safe house' for all this postal love and attention, and that Edith too, like Mrs Le Martine, wanted Ottilie to be a lady and grow up to have a better life than she had ever had.

'You don't want to be like me, Miss Ottilie, really you don't. Just dancing attendance on your mother all your life, and when she goes, which she will very soon believe me, left with nothing but your memories and too old for marriage.'

Much as she loved her, Ottilie found that she could only agree with Edith. She did not want to grow up like her, but life was difficult like that, particularly at the moment, particularly at the Grand.

As with a woman who wants to hide her age, it was her hands that had given Ottilie away. For when, on the first day of her annual visit to St Elcombe – but now in summer, and to the Angel Inn – Mrs Le Martine had taken them in her own, she had recoiled as if they had given her an electric shock.

'Miss Ottilie! What *have* you been doing? Scrubbing floors and baths without gloves! Your palms are becoming like pumice stone, not at all attractive, really not at all. Oh my dear, you will never marry a gentleman, really you won't, not if this goes on.'

Although their relationship had changed so profoundly over the years, and although Ottilie was no longer able to

149

make her heroine laugh quite so readily as she once had because Mrs Le Martine *knew* now about everything, and her wonderful old brown eyes now looked at Ottilie with compassion and pity where once they had sparkled with amusement at Ottilie's cheek, there was one aspect in which Ottilie was quite certain Mrs Le Martine would never change, namely in her determination that when she grew up Ottilie should become a lady.

She had been the first person to assess Ottilie's maturing looks for her.

'You have nice hair, very nice hair, thick and brown. You have beautiful eyes, large and expressive, you are very well made, your hands and feet are excellent, and provided you stay slim all should be well. However, your profile is not all that we would wish because your nose is too heavy, but your chin is small and your voice undoubtedly an asset. All this means that, if you take care to work hard on yourself, you will sweep men off their feet and break great numbers of hearts. Personally I will be most disappointed if you do not make a very great marriage indeed.'

Ottilie did not dare to tell her guiding light – the person to whom she could always turn for advice, the only person to whom she could really talk or write about her feelings – she could not tell her the perfectly dreadful truth about herself, something not even Edith knew about her and to which Ottilie could never admit.

Ottilie did not want to marry.

Paris had changed. Ottilie knew this because Mrs Le Martine had told her so, often and often. Although this did not stop her wanting Ottilie to go there for a 'little polish', she nevertheless spent a great deal of time moaning to Ottilie about the way Paris had changed so dreadfully, and, naturally, for the worse, not at all like when *she* had known it in the early Fifties.

Ottilie did not mind hearing that Paris had changed so much. It did not prevent her from longing to get to know this much worse Paris for herself, if only for a few weeks. As a matter of fact Ottilie was so used to being warned that life was about to be a disappointment, something to which she should undoubtedly inure herself, that she really hardly noticed how frequently Mrs Le Martine reminded her of the destruction of the old Paris, its loss of elegance, the decline of its restaurants, the lack of money to run the great private houses, or 'hôtels' as they were called there.

Everyone Ottilie had ever known at the hotel, every older guest who had ever stayed had always said to her about everything – even sometimes about the Grand itself – 'Oh, but it's not at all like it used to be'.

This phrase had been said so often to her that Ottilie found she had developed a form of double vision, so that she could never pause to admire anything, not a sparkling sea, not a beautiful bowl of fruit, not a tree in blossom outside the window, without also reminding herself some few seconds later that it could not of course be quite as beautiful as she thought it. No apple was really as crisp, no dress really as pretty, no-one as beautiful or as kind as 'before the war', because she had been told this so often by so many of the older guests at the hotel that she had actually come to believe it.

But then came Paris.

And as she stepped off the train at the Gare St Lazare, as the crowds hurried around her, as she picked up both her suitcases and determined on taking the Métro or the autobus, and the smell of *abroad* swam towards her, and the excitement of being alone and unknown in a great city washed over her, together with the knowledge that she was free for the first time in her life to do as she wished when she wished and that not even Edith knew where she was, Ottilie realized that she simply did not care if Paris was not like it used to be. She did not care how it had been, nor what she was missing from that time of 'used to be'. For the first time in her life all she cared about was now, and here, and already within a minute of her arrival she knew

151

deep down in her deepest heart that *now* was wonderful, and magical, and to hell with how it used to be. First she needed somewhere to stay.

As she had told Alfred quite truthfully Mrs Le Martine had arranged for her to lodge, free of charge, in the business apartment of an old family friend. Having taken a taxi cab and proudly worked out the correct fare and a generous tip, Ottilie now faced the great broad steps running up to the door, but she could only see them, not reach them, for there were two great locked wrought-iron gates in front of her, while beside her the large red face of someone whom she at once took to be the concierge peered at her with more than a little interest.

'*Ah, MADEMOISELLE!*'

From now on Ottilie would have to get used to the extreme enthusiasm of the Gallic race, their inability to wash out a cardigan, buy a potato, or walk their dogs to a lamppost without reacting in the kind of way that not even the rescue of a drowning man off St Elcombe Point would have evoked in someone English.

'*Mais ENFIN! Vous êtes attendue, VOUS! Mais vouz avez voyagé LOIN, enfin!*'

Ottilie did not understand a word of the concierge's welcome, but she very well understood the gates opening to allow her into the prettiest courtyard garden set about with statuary, and the beaming smile of the fat concierge, whose offer to carry one of her suitcases certainly did not go amiss.

The apartment door eased itself open, and Ottilie edged her way into a front hall set about with large, dark oak chests, a marble bust and a vast vase of dried flowers. She looked with some admiration at everything, knowing all at once that she was standing in a hall that had been decorated by a man. The choice of dark red Pompeiian walls, and navy checked rugs, and the smell of expensive cigarettes long extinguished but greatly enjoyed, had nothing to do with the feminine sex.

As it happened she had not bothered to ask Mrs Le Martine anything about the friend to whom the apartment belonged. She had merely accepted her offer with embarrassing eagerness, persuaded her father to let her off from being the unpaid under-housekeeper at the hotel, and bolted onto a boat heading for France so fast that by the time Alfred Cartaret had turned round, Ottilie was gone. And what was even better about her timing was that her mother, back from staying with a friend in Switzerland, had missed her opportunity to cancel Ottilie's plans and tell her father that the hotel could not go on for a minute without her. She had missed having to make it her painful duty to tell Ottilie that she did not deserve any sort of rest from her life at the Grand, because nowadays she should be paying them back for everything they had done for her, and would do for her, not least giving Ottilie their *name*.

And now it was too late. Ottilie was gone and not even Melanie could bring her back. Edith had packed her suitcases for her so beautifully that Ottilie feared she might feel homesick when she saw just how starched and fresh Edith had made all her old clothes look, because there was no question of Ottilie being able to go abroad dressed in the latest fashions, no Jackie Kennedy-style coats and dresses for her, just old shirtwaisters and flat little ballet-style pumps, and her dark brown hair worn daily either in a pony tail or loose about her shoulders in a page-boy hairstyle held back by an Alice band of black velvet.

Not that madame la concierge in her flowered dress and with her steely little hair curlers still nestling under an old cotton scarf seemed to mind, because she carried on beaming at Ottilie despite the steep flight of stairs up to the apartment door and despite the suitcase with which she was intent on helping Ottilie.

'*Vous avez les clefs, ENFIN! Voilà, Mademoiselle, voilà! Vous allez apprendre la cuisine française? Mais c'est merveil-LEUSE, ça! C'est MAGNIFIQUE! A plus tard,*

Mademoiselle!' she cried, having unlocked the apartment door with a series of keys and handed Ottilie her own set.

The concierge was gone, and for a second Ottilie stood alone and quite still in the chicly decorated hall listening to the sound of her footsteps retreating down the stone staircase to the lower floors until eventually she reached the courtyard outside. Ottilie watched her from above, waddling across the cobbled stones of the central part of the courtyard garden until she reached the little door in the wall from where she doubtless observed the rest of the world coming and going and probably not realizing that pretty soon their business would be her business.

Once she had seen the concierge retreat to her little house in the wall Ottilie felt it was all right to explore the apartment. If she had not been so used to the strangeness of rooms just left, or rooms about to be occupied, she might have felt intrusive, but as it was she felt perfectly at liberty to open and shut those doors that had been left unlocked for her use, and peer into cupboards or look for a coffee maker in the kitchen without feeling that she was in some way trespassing.

From the first she could sense that the owner of the apartment must be very rich indeed, not just because the furnishings were so understated, the materials at the windows and on the beds, the linen sheets, the coffee machine, the navy blue and white china – everything in the flat was so perfectly, acceptably rich, and out of the reach of most people except the very rich – but because it *smelt* rich.

When she was growing up at the Grand Hotel Ottilie had always told Edith and Mrs Tomber, the housekeeper, that long before a guest arrived and she saw their suitcases, long before they rang down for room service or left out their shoes to be cleaned, or sent their chauffeur or their secretary ahead to check out their rooms – long before this happened she could smell riches.

'I always know when someone rich is about to arrive

long before they're here!' she would boast loudly and childishly, to Edith's intense embarrassment and Mrs Tomber's incredulity, but now, here in Paris, she was certain that had not the concierge led her up to Apartment E and let her in, Ottilie's nose for wealth could have brought her to it quite on its own.

She imagined to herself as she wandered down the corridors in a sort of haze of delight that it might even have been just the smell of a rich man that would have brought her to the apartment door, the smell of tobacco, expensive aftershave and clean laundry. And following this thought came another, that with his impeccable taste, and the indefinable aroma that swathed the rooms, should they ever meet she would be quite unsurprised by the sight of him, in fact she would know him immediately.

She was sure that he would have a perfect haircut done by a barber who had known him since he was a little boy, and that his clothes would include an expensive cashmere or wool overcoat, under it a shirt or a cashmere sweater so little worn that the creases were still detectable down the sides. He would wear shoe leather that never creaked and carry hand luggage and a wallet that looked light but felt heavy, because they were old, and they would be discreetly initialled.

This was the man who owned the apartment in which Ottilie now stood, she was sure of it, just as she was sure that he would be older, not very, very old, but older, with a slight grey at his temple, and although tall, not so tall that he would have to bend down too far to kiss a woman's hand, or put his cheek against hers while he danced with her. He would be all these things, she thought, and more, because judging from the many paintings and drawings of what must be his beautiful wife, he loved her extravagantly.

The kitchen of the apartment was pulsatingly up to date and austere, glistening with modernity, and had tall stools of which Ottilie, who was by now feeling more than a little hungry if not ravenous, took immediate advantage, sitting on one of them first to drink coffee and eat one of the croissants that she had managed to buy at the station, and then to dream, to pretend to herself that from now on her life would always be like this, that one day she would be able to be cool, and alone like this, whenever she wanted.

Soon it would be time to go out and explore the tiny winding streets around the Left Bank quarter, time to attempt to order her first meal in real French rather than 'Menu French', time to be surprised by the structure of real French menus. (It would be very different, she was sure, from the kind of food that Chef back at the Grand at St Elcombe *imagined* what he always called *les français* were eating.) Soon she would do all those things. Now, however, she would do nothing at all but run water in the bathroom next to the only bedroom that remained unlocked and ready for her arrival into a large old-fashioned bath, water that ran with tremendous, gushing enthusiasm from a great broad central chrome tap, and climb with difficulty over the side into the great claw-footed iron tub which she had previously scented with some bath essence given to her by the always loving Edith.

As the water closed over her limbs and the bubbles clustered around her nipples in decorative rings, Ottilie surveyed her form for the first time not as something to dress, but as a perfect young body, watching it relax in the water as someone might watch a flower that opened only at evening.

She could not let go of this overwhelming, intense joy that being alone was giving her, the knowledge that for the next few weeks no-one would telephone her, or fling open her sitting room door unasked and call for her to run down and help in the kitchens, or run up and help with bed-making for a late arrival, or an unexpected booking. In fact she had left St Elcombe in such a determined hurry that really no-one, anywhere, except Mrs Le Martine, really knew where she was, nor she imagined would they care very much, not with two Spanish girls taking her place, and life being so quiet at the Grand at the end of the season. She sighed first of all with the whole incredible thought of it, the strangeness of it, and then it seemed to her that her heart, or her soul, whichever was most sensitive and alive to life, was leaving her body and floating above the water in which she lay, rising, rising and rising until it was looking down at her lying in the great iron bath, noting her smile, her dampened hair, her utter happiness.

Dinner in the *quartier* was even more exciting than everything that had previously happened. The early October evening air was balmy, and she was able to stroll out across the courtyard, leave her keys with the concierge and walk the narrow streets in a dark green twin-set and plaid skirt with no jacket or coat.

As she made her way down the narrow winding streets, on the concierge's instructions, past the great church of Ste Geneviève and on to share a corner seat of a table next to a clutch of arguing students at the famous Deux Magots café-restaurant, Ottilie could sense the optimism and the enthusiasm of the young people she passed. Strolling by her, always in groups of two or three, after the mostly middle-aged inhabitants of St Elcombe they seemed to her to be ravishingly beautiful; and since they were students, naturally intelligent and clever.

As Ottilie observed them she realized that she did not *want* to see them like this, she did not yearn for them to be like this, but quite simply saw them as they actually *were* at that moment. In a few years, of course, they would doubtless be dowdy, serious, resentful and dull, but at this moment, on this warm October evening, they knew they were, as she knew they were, as she knew *she* was, intelligent, beautiful and optimistic, but most of all full of the best reason for living which is, quite simply, living.

157

They all knew, as she knew, that for this short time in their lives they could argue and accept, tolerate and disagree with everything that the world had ever written, sung or depicted, but to be young and in Paris, to be a student and living on the old Left Bank in 1964, was to know for the rest of your life what joy and just *being* was all about.

Ottilie ate alone, omelette and salad, coffee and an ice cream, and then walked home as slowly as possible, stopping every few yards to gaze at the interiors of the tiny old shops with their artful window displays.

Here were no crowded windows where no-one could possibly understand what they should be looking at, as in St Elcombe, no goods so diverse that someone would be hard put to discover what the shop was trying to sell. Here there was only ever one book, one piece of velvet, one hat, nothing too much, nothing too little. At last, she felt she was witnessing taste, and it was like an electric charge to her senses, it shot through her and made her dizzy with the sheer sensuality and wonder of it. If she had known how, she would have made love to it.

Up early to go to the Parisian School of Cookery and Ottilie was all too conscious of her real ignorance of classical French cooking. All the way there, a tourist guide in one hand, her American traveller's cheques in the other, she wondered at her courage in going to a French cooking school where she would surely be a subject of extreme mockery, having never made so much as a *sauce béarnaise* or even a *mayonnaise* in her life, although she had witnessed the making of hundreds from an early age, the kitchens of the Grand having always been one of her favourite places, where she had been tolerated from the moment she had arrived as the newly adopted daughter of the old hotel.

But now, as she walked down the narrow streets towards the address in her hand, Ottilie felt an unaccustomed nervous tension, for ahead of her, in her imagination, she saw a great team of bewilderingly expert fellow pupils all clothed in white aprons, their hair held back by chef's caps, their nails short, their eyes full of the messianic gleam that was usually only associated with religion. What a revelation, therefore, to round the corner of yet another private little courtyard set about with the kind of chairs and tables that were normally associated with small pavement cafés, and see a number of blue-rinsed middle-aged ladies with pronounced American accents eagerly heading in the same direction as herself, all inevitably clutching the same familiar books of traveller's cheques.

'Looks as if you're going to be the youngest by about thirty years, dear!' one of them joked to Ottilie.

Ottilie, who was now sixteen and three-quarters but, given the hard work that had been required of her the previous few years, felt at least twenty-five, smiled, and tried to think of something to say. Looking down the little queue of grey- and blue-haired women she could hardly deny that it did indeed look as if she was going to be the only student much below the age of fifty.

'I'm much older than I look, I promise you. I'm actually a grandmother,' she joked back. It was something she sometimes said to hotel guests, and said lightly it always passed the moment off, because at the Grand so many of the guests were always bemoaning their ages to her, or saying, 'But you wouldn't remember that, now, dear, would you, you're far too young.'

Finally, when they had all signed the old, buff, barely legible cooking forms and paid their traveller's cheques to the *Parisian School of Cookery*, Ottilie reflected to herself with some humour that it was just her luck to be gifted a cooking course in a neighbourhood filled with beautiful young people and find that the average age of the students she would be seeing every day was probably going to be forty-nine and a half.

The ground rules for the cooking course were explained

in broken English by the proprietress of the school, and in broken French by an American woman. They were all to be given, each day, a little recipe to make, or part of a recipe. For instance if they were to have a *tarte tatin* for the dessert then one pupil would be required to make *la pâte* – the pastry – and some other pupil the actual ingredients for the tart. When they had all finished making their various recipes for the morning, the food would be taken downstairs and eaten for lunch, for *déjeuner*.

The mood that Ottilie was in, just the word *déjeuner* was exciting, and saying *la pâte* instead of dull old *pastry* gave her a birthday feeling.

The silence at the start of that morning was, despite the very mature appearance of the eager students of the little school, profound. It was as Ottilie had first imagined it would be when she had been walking along with her guide in her hand – church-like in atmosphere, and yet at one moment, when she found herself looking round the large, airy, light room, she became unexpectedly moved by the sight of these undoubtedly redoubtable ladies from the East Coast, or Middle West, or wherever, of America, with their wedding rings removed, and their pinafores tied tight, struggling with such sincerity to attain that most difficult of all arts, a cooking skill.

Ottilie's particular recipe that first day was unexpectedly easy to make, *oeufs persillés*. Eggs, hard boiled, cut in two, the centres removed and then mixed with mayonnaise and finely chopped parsley before being carefully replaced in the centre of the whites. Quite simple, but when they sat down to eat them as part of the hors d'oeuvres, like most classical mixtures they all agreed the result was light, or as Mrs Blandorf from Connecticut, of the especially blue rinse and the humorous eyes, said to Ottilie, 'makes you want Easter to come round quick!'

Not all the results were so good. Mrs Blandorf's pastry was, as she herself admitted, to huge laughter, 'about as light as Mr Blandorf's humour'.

The course stopped on the dot of half past two o'clock, and so, by some unseen agreement, Ottilie was taken off by Mrs Blandorf and her friends 'to see the Art, dear'. As a matter of fact, as Ottilie readily admitted to herself, it was they who were *dear*, solicitous and charming, and full of the kindly acceptance of life that Ottilie had so often observed in the older women who lunched or dined at the Grand. As if life, having thrown itself at them, having allowed them to survive childbirth, husbands, the domestic grind, and their own natures, was now, in these short years left before the real burden of age was upon them, allowing them a little time at last to relax and enjoy themselves in a way that they perhaps had not done since they were teenagers, or perhaps had never done.

Their gaiety was infectious, and their enthusiasm undeniable. It did not matter if they were all hopping on and off the Métro, or an autobus, or just walking, to them everything was enjoyable, despite their ages, or because of them perhaps. Ottilie sensed that they, like her, had stepped out of the normal day-to-day routine of their lives and were enjoying the lack of daily grind to the hilt, up to and possibly well above the actual experience, because there was no-one to reprove them or make fun of their sincerity, no member of their family ready to cut them down to size and sigh 'oh *Mother*'. No-one to tell them to 'be their age'. Most of all, for a few weeks anyway, there were no housewifely duties to weigh them down, or in Ottilie's case no hotel visitors or staff to keep them on the hop with their demands.

Ottilie called them 'the girls'. They seemed to love that. 'Come on, girls,' she'd call, 'time to go to the Louvre.' Or 'Come on, girls, time to head back.'

'I can't think when I last enjoyed myself this much,' Mrs Blandorf sighed during the second week of their course. 'I keep saying to myself "Jeannette Blandorf, just imagine if you had missed out on all this."'

There was a small silence as all of them, comfortably

161

seated at their café tables and watching the world strolling by, imagined between sips of strong French coffee that they had not seen the advertisement in the magazine or newspaper, imagined that they had not in a moment of determined independence had the courage to write off for details, face their husbands or their old mothers or their bossy, demanding children and say gaily, 'Just off for a cooking course to Paris, dear!'

'I don't know about you, but it's going to be a bit different facing Ludgrove over dinner after this,' Mrs Blandorf continued. 'And as for bridge on a Wednesday, what will they say when I hand round my *tartelettes au jambon en chemise*?'

'Perfection! Just so long as you get me to do the pastry,' Ottilie murmured, at which of course they were all off again, laughing about absolutely nothing really, laughing not because Ottilie's oblique reference to Mrs Blandorf's terrible hand at pastry had been particularly funny, but because they felt happy, which after all, Ottilie thought, as she walked slowly back to the apartment, leaving them all to return to their hotel, was surely the best form of laughter?

But back at the apartment there was a letter waiting for her, and as soon as Ottilie saw that it was addressed in her father's writing she knew that she did not want to open it.

Ottilie stared at Alfred's handwriting. The writer was careful, intelligent, and literate, the handwriting told her. Out loud she said to the silent flat, 'I don't want to open this!' and her heart started to beat really rather fast, as if she had been running. Just seeing her father's handwriting brought her present happiness and freedom into terrible contrast with that other existence. It was as if she was once more set to watch her own life on television, only now in black and white, not in colour, and the sound would be turned down so low that she would miss every other word, so much was she in love with Paris, with the flat, with the narrow little streets, with the cooking course, the cafés, the art galleries, the sound of French.

'I'm not going to read it,' she went on, still aloud to the flat. 'Not only am I not going to read it, but it has never arrived.' She knew it would be full of *I am afraid your mother is right, you should have told* her *of your plans to take a month off long before you left,* or *The Spanish girls, as I predicted, are less than satisfactory and we really must consider the possibility of your returning early.*

As soon as she saw the letter Ottilie knew that if she read it she might as well just pack up and leave for St Elcombe that minute. Reading it would mean that the spell was broken. Paris would be over and with it all the laughter, and all the gaiety. Mrs Blandorf's pastry would no longer be funny, and the 'girls' with their blue rinses and their good humour and their ability to laugh at themselves would never be the same again. And, as with a holiday photograph containing the smiling faces of long-forgotten people who had once seemed so glamorous, but now in a cheap snapshot could be seen to be all too ordinary, Ottilie would be hard put to it to remember why it had all seemed so magical.

'You're not going to do this to me!' she called to Alfred back in St Elcombe as she saw him in her mind's eye staring hopelessly at his ledger books, and taking the letter she tore it up and threw it in the wastepaper basket.

Whatever happened she was going to have her month in Paris, quite alone. Whatever happened no-one, but no-one, was going to take these few weeks away from her. She would have them no matter what and no matter who.

Tonight she and the 'girls' had planned to revisit a little club called L'Abbaye which was tucked behind the church of St Germain des Pres. There they would once more listen to the singing, once more become saddened or delighted by the songs. Nothing in that letter torn into tiny pieces and left in the chic wastepaper basket was going to stop that.

Nine

Ottilie, Mrs Blandorf and her friends were having their last luncheon together at the Parisian School of Cookery. They had all tried their best with the menu, and it had to be said, in celebration of their last meal together, that the result had been very satisfactory, if only to them. If the proprietress and her assistant assumed their usual polite if studied expressions as they ate their *navarin de mouton*, or discussed the amount of oil in the salad, there was no such problem for their pupils, who were now, in their own imaginations at least, experts on French food. And if husbands, so gaily referred to in the previous fortnight – Ludgrove Blandorf, or Pip Bartlett, or Tom Zeigler, in Connecticut, Ohio, or Los Angeles, did not and never would like French cuisine, it was evident that their wives had been and seen and conquered, and that as far as they were concerned this meant that they had fought through the cooking and eating equivalent of the Korean War. They were heroines in their own and each other's eyes. They would write to each other, of course, they would never forget each other, naturally.

Ottilie could have hugged all of them to her, so endearing did she find their conversation, and so much did she want them to be returning home to men who would listen to their anecdotes and at least try to share their enthusiasm for Paris, French food, and holidays in Europe. That they would very probably not be doing so she already knew from the determined gaiety with which they enjoyed their last self-cooked luncheon together.

Although they were flying off home with new ideas that could, if they were allowed, add so much colour to their lives and interest to their existence, Ottilie knew that their accounts of their fortnight in Paris would be met with stony stares and 'What's this?' expressions, and that soon all they would have would be their letters to each other, and their photographs of themselves in front of well-known Parisian buildings or monuments.

Ottilie knew all this because of having grown up at the Grand. She knew all about the fleeting nature of holiday friendships and the formality of the exchanging of addresses. She knew all about wives asking for recipes, and husbands trying to get away from their conversations to play what they always called in martyred voices 'some quiet golf', as if being on holiday was a penance from which a man could, once in a while, be allowed to have some time off, time off from his wife who, it always seemed to Ottilie, had spent most of her life waiting for a holiday with her husband, so that she might talk to him.

'Trouble with you living here at the Grand, you've seen too much and know too little,' Edith would admonish Ottilie, now that she was older.

And although Edith only ever said it in a laughing kind of way Ottilie knew that it was true. By the time she became a teenager Ottilie *had* seen too much, though not of the kind of harsh backstreet behaviour that Edith sometimes hinted at – gangs with knives, near-escapes from rape, nothing like that.

What Ottilie had seen were the terrible silences of married people, the hatred underneath the polite conversation, the narrowed eyes as one or other of a couple left a room, the mocking laughter of the staff as they retold their experiences with guests at the end-of-season staff dinner.

By the time she was a teenager Ottilie knew all about couples who tried to make love in front of the waiters or waitresses when they took up their breakfast on a tray, and other couples who were not married but pretending to be,

166

and yet others who had, the waiters always hinted, 'strange tastes'. She knew to hang about in the corridor if she heard Mrs Tomber's disapproving command, 'Don't go in there until I've done the bed, Miss Ottilie!' She knew too how to tell a married woman from a mistress, or a husband from a lover (different size suitcases, different expression, different way of signing the register – lovers always smiled too much and looked far too 'natural', the receptionists had told her, and it was not long before Ottilie was able to realize the truth of this).

But most of all Ottilie knew that the golden rule was never, whatever happened, to *start* a conversation. Rather, by being of service she had learnt to encourage guests to talk to her, not the other way round. Never to tell one guest of the previous visit of another (in case they were meant to be somewhere else at the time), never to refer in any way to anyone who had stayed at the hotel before. Discretion was the key to everything, because as Mrs Tomber often said, her eyes dramatically narrowed, 'You would be surprised, really you would, Miss Ottilie, the complications that can occur in even the nicest establishments.'

'I will come to the airport to see you all off,' Ottilie said to Mrs Blandorf as with sighs of delight and sighs of contentment, and still more sighs of 'If only we were at the start of this instead of the finish', she and her friends the 'girls' finally walked away from the Parisian School of Cookery for the last time, under the archway of vines, and off down the narrow little street that led once more to the busy boulevards and life as it is normally lived from day to day, filled with ordinary little tasks and not enough laughter.

'You don't want to come to the airport, honey!'

Ottilie did not, but she smiled and said she did because it somehow seemed the right thing to do, and anyway she suddenly felt lonely at the thought of staying on in Paris without the girls, of going to the cooking school for the second part of her course with new versions of them, or an entirely different set of them.

They flew off with much waving of handkerchiefs, leaving Ottilie with a number of addresses in America where she could contact them, either written in largish handwriting on small notepads in black ink, or printed in smallish letters that looked like handwriting on large cards with frilly edges, and put in envelopes that had coloured tissue paper on the inside.

'Here, have these, honey.' Mrs Zeigler had handed Ottilie a smart carrier bag which said 'Rue Rivoli' printed very small in gold on one side and was filled with international magazines. 'No point in taking them back to Los Angeles with me when I've read them.'

Back at the flat and trying to pretend that she was not feeling momentarily rather flat because the second part of her cooking course did not begin until the following Monday and she faced spending the weekend entirely in her own company, Ottilie ran a bath as she had often done when she was small back at the hotel, just for want of anything else to do.

As the great tub filled with pleasantly warm water she flicked open one of the magazines donated to her by Mrs Zeigler, only to find herself staring at a face she had once known but was now only just able to recognize.

A young man – the article stated that he was 'under twenty-five' and 'compellingly handsome' with 'dark hair and dark grey eyes and a slight Southern accent'. The confident but wary look in the eyes, the determined set to the looks, they were unmistakable. She was looking at a photograph of her brother Joseph.

But if Ottilie was not any longer 'O'Flaherty', nor it seemed was Joseph.

Open-mouthed, Ottilie read that her middle brother was now named Joseph *Maximus*, and he was not the second son of three boys and a girl, but the eldest son of a Mr Maximus and born into the hotel trade. Originally from England, he had emigrated to America and was now one of the managers, at what must be the youngest age ever, of the flagship of an international hotel group.

Before she read on, Ottilie sat down on the stool in the bathroom, her hair curling in the steam. No-one in the family had heard from Joseph since that terrible night when Ottilie had given him the wretched earrings to throw away for her. Ottilie only knew many days later that he had left home the following day, to Lorcan's hurt and Sean's desolation, leaving only a letter to say that he was going because there was nothing more for him in St Elcombe.

Ottilie stared at the picture, holding it too close to her eyes as if by doing so she could make quite sure that it really was Joseph whom she was seeing, as the water continued to rush and gush into the great iron bath. It was as if by staring at his photograph she could understand Joseph and his going better. But most of all it was as if by staring at the photograph, at his expression of confidence in himself and his future, she could fully grasp what it meant to her that he was, after all, at least alive.

In her innocence that night, Ottilie had honestly thought that Joseph would simply throw away the earrings for her. It had been stupid of her really, because knowing Joseph and his often voiced determination to free himself of what he saw as the confines of his family she ought to have guessed that he would be incapable of ridding himself of something that could provide the means of his escape from St Elcombe.

Yet, being only ten years old at the time, she had sincerely believed that he would throw the earrings away, and that would be that. She had really imagined that, as Joseph had said that night, he would be like the priest in confession, and that Ottilie, having confessed to taking the earrings and promising to throw them away for Melanie, would then be able to run away and forget about the whole wretched business, that she would have been absolved for her part in Melanie's deception of the insurance company.

But such had not been the case, and could never have been really, not if she thought about it. Indeed, as she stared grimly through the bathroom steam at Joseph's photograph, Ottilie agonized yet again over how she could ever have been so foolish. Joseph had been the middle boy. Not the oldest one like poor Lorcan, not the one forced to replace Da in Ma's life, compelled by circumstances to be a 'pretend husband' to his own mother.

Nor had he been the youngest like Sean – easily forgiven for a great deal, spoilt by the attention of two older brothers – no, Joseph had been the middle one. The one who was at neither extreme of his mother's love, the one who had been conveniently there to be a companion for both the elder and the younger boy and because of this was in effect cut in half. Someone so divided could only become whole on his own. In other words, out of all of them, Joseph had been the loner.

He had lied to Ottilie about being able to trust in him, but bad as that could be, hurtful as that could be, it had not been as hurtful as his disappearance. Whatever anyone said or did, beating you or cutting you in two with their words as Alfred sometimes liked to do, nothing could be as bad as simply disappearing. And no amount of prayers (and *how* Ottilie had prayed) and no amount of poor Lorcan's saying endless novenas, no amount of making sacrifices to Our Lady to speed Joseph's return, had brought him back. Indeed, if prayers could have returned Joseph to his family he would have been back within the month, but as it was it seemed that heaven was deaf to his family's entreaties, until Sean, who had always been a religious boy, finally stopped going to Mass altogether, as a bribe to God.

'I shaan't go back till God has sent Joseph back to *us*, all right?' was how he put it to Lorcan in his Cornish accent.

For weeks after his disappearance, from afar, and in an

agony of guilt, Ottilie had watched Lorcan turning up daily for work at the Grand, looking older and older as the time went by and they heard nothing. He grew so thin that finally Mr Hulton noticed and sent him to see a doctor at his own expense, but the doctor had said it was just shock. *Just shock*. Edith said *just shock* could kill you. Edith said that calling what Lorcan was suffering from *just shock* was just what a *man* would do, and that the trouble with most doctors was that they certainly did not understand that the person inside was as important as the person on the outside, and that until they did they would never be able to help people suffering from *just shock*.

It was from this time onwards that Ottilie had started to work so hard for her parents in the hotel. Every time she ran upstairs when she did not need to, every time she ran downstairs when she did not have to, every time she stood in for the telephonist or the receptionist (she could say 'Grand Hotel reception speaking' as well as anyone) it seemed to her that God might just be watching her hundredth willing errand and forgive her the trespass of giving Joseph those wretched earrings that evening. That being so, He would, out of the kindness of His heart, send Joseph back, not to her but to Lorcan and young Sean who were missing him so much, who imagined even now that, like Ma, he might have been swept over the cliffs into the sea.

But it seemed that God was not watching, and nor it seemed did He appear to care in the least, and eventually Ottilie found that she was simply running errand after errand for the sake of it. At first she did it to take her mind off imagining Joseph dead and it being all her fault, but after that, as she grew older, she did it to help her parents out, and after *that* because the hotel was doing so badly.

God, Joseph, how could you? I mean really how could you? How could you have left us all in such agony all this time? Not knowing if you were alive or dead? Changing your name so

171

that we could not find you. Getting rich on the money you must have made from my mother's diamond earrings. Becoming rich and now, it seems from this magazine, even a little famous, and still not letting us know? It doesn't seem possible. Could you not once have sent Lorcan just a little card to say you were alive? For heaven's sake, did you not know that after your disappearance everything would change for ever?

Because of your disappearance the family just broke up – Sean went to Australia, and Lorcan to train for the priesthood. After that day you disappeared Lorcan became obsessed by the idea that it was all his fault. He thought if he had kept a better eye on you, been a better brother to you, you would never have gone. He thought you felt unloved, without parents. He kept saying to me, 'If only I'd been a better brother to him, not let him just drift on.'

But Lorcan was a wonderful brother to you, Joseph. No-one could have had a better brother. He even learned to cook for you and Sean, Joseph. Don't you remember how after Ma died he learned to cook beautiful omelettes and home-made pies for you, and puddings the way Ma always used to make them, and how you told me he would even wash up on his own so that you and Sean could get on with your homework?

That's how much he loved you both and tried to make up to you for what had happened, with Ma dying and us all being left, and yet all you could do was disappear and never send a word! I can hardly believe that all the time we were crying ourselves to sleep at night there you were, all safe and sound in America, all the time knowing – you must have known – that we were all in St Elcombe praying for your safety?

Ottilie would never know how long she sat on the bathroom stool staring at the picture in Mrs Zeigler's magazine and making that pathetically indignant speech over and over again in her head to her middle brother, but eventually she rose to her feet, and having bathed and tied a towel around herself, and another around her still damp hair, twisting it into a turban on top of her head, she

172

stepped out of the bathroom door and down the long corridor, straight into the arms of a tall Frenchman with dark hair, immaculately cut, greying at the sides, and wearing one of those soft sports coats that Englishmen never care to wear – which is to say a jacket that fitted beautifully, in a soft cashmere.

Ottilie knew it was soft cashmere because she actually walked right into it, and for one fleeting moment she could feel that softness that only cashmere gives against her own soft skin. It was surprisingly sensual, and she sensed immediately, although her thoughts had been anywhere except where she was, that the man was French because he smelt so appealingly of Gauloise cigarettes and a recent cup of coffee, and rarely scented aftershave. Also he had on a soft-collared shirt with a thin tie, which again was not something which Englishmen, anyway in St Elcombe, ever wore.

Before she even looked up Ottilie knew that she had walked straight into the arms of the rich man who owned the apartment, he of the impeccable taste and the beautiful wife.

'Ah, but I know who you are – Ottilie Cartaret, no?'

Ottilie jumped backwards as soon as she heard his voice, but as she did so she made sure to put her hand around the top of her towel to reassure herself that it was knotted quite tight. And yet she smiled at him, because just for a moment it seemed a pity not to allow herself a few seconds to enjoy the situation. He, an older, handsome, distinguished man, she a much younger woman, just out of girlhood. He very much clothed, and she without a shred on despite the thickness of the towel – his towel, the towel belonging to the flat.

'Yes, I am Ottilie Cartaret.'

He was tall, quite a lot more than fifty possibly, urbane of course, suntanned, with eyes of a startling hazel green. Ottilie knew at once as she stared across the space between them that whatever his age – perhaps because of it, she

173

would not know since she herself was not yet seventeen – she knew immediately that he was far too attractive for his age, and hers.

'I knew I would know you,' Ottilie heard herself saying, which she realized just too late sounded really rather provocative.

'You knew that, did you?' he asked in a French-accented English which was really more American than British, while his eyes took in her standing there in a towel, her hair in a turban on the top of her head, her feet and legs dry, but also suntanned and bare.

'Yes,' Ottilie nodded, determined to carry on the conversation as if she was fully clothed. 'I'm afraid it is from being in this flat. And I knew just what you would look like, even though there were no pictures of you. It's just that feeling that one gets living in someone else's apartment. What I mean is— What I should say, rather, is it was very kind of you to say to Mrs Le Martine that I could stay here,' she added a little hastily, remembering her manners rather too late. 'And . . . Are you sure it's still all right? I mean if you want to be here too? If you would rather be on your own, I will quite understand. I prefer to be on my own myself, I find, quite a lot of the time.' Too many words said too quickly as usual, but there – they were out, and that was that.

A look came into Monsieur's eyes at just the mention of Mrs Le Martine's name that was difficult to understand. It was as if just hearing Mrs Le Martine's name brought back something that Monsieur (as the concierge always called him) would rather not remember. But he said in a firm, loyal tone, 'I would do anything for Madame Le Martine. And of course you can here stay, my Gahd, but of course! I am old enough to be your grandfazzer, and you are *une jeune fille très bien elevée, n'est-ce pas?* This *appartement* is very big, even fer two, and my son he may be 'ere soon, so I will stay in case, because with him about you may need a chaperon, you know. Sons!'

174

He shrugged and laughed, waved his hand in an elegant gesture, and, turning towards the corridor from which Ottilie had so suddenly appeared in her bath towel, he disappeared towards his own suite of rooms, singing all too appropriately, it seemed to his admiring audience of one, '*La Vie en Rose*'.

Ottilie closed her bedroom door and lay against it the way she had once seen Ingrid Bergman doing in a very old film to which Edith had taken her at the St Elcombe fleapit. She was on her own in a stylish apartment in Paris with a Frenchman with an American accent who was far too attractive for his own good. How Mrs Le Martine would laugh if she told her and say, 'Whatever next, Miss Ottilie!'

After that first encounter with Monsieur, by which name his lodger always thought of him, there was added electricity in the Parisian air for Ottilie, and she could not help recognizing it. Every morning when she slipped out of bed – making sure not to run her bath in what she now realized was his bathroom, but to use the shower room next to her own – she chose her clothes with ever greater care. And every afternoon when her cooking lessons finished, leaving her new set of American friends at the cooking school to discover the Louvre on their own, unable to help herself, Ottilie returned to the apartment, somehow drawn back to that electricity that an attractive man can create around him, that feeling that any minute now *something* would happen, although quite what she hardly knew.

'Monsieur' might be how Ottilie thought of him, and yet she had not so much as glimpsed him again since that first meeting when she had only been in a bath towel, and somehow she thought if she did meet him again she would never dare to ask him what she really wanted to know, which was if he was Monsieur, where was Madame?

Where was the beautiful woman in all the paintings and

drawings around the flat? Where was the mother of his son, seen posing so elegantly with her new baby in her arms? Where was the smiling young woman in the drawing that Ottilie thought was so beautiful? A slender beautiful young woman having her hair brushed by a little dark-haired boy dressed in a Tyrolean suit?

In other words, where was the love of Monsieur's life?

Without realizing it, and in between enjoying the riot of the new intake of more good-natured and gloriously carefree ladies from Texas and Ohio, all intent on having themselves what they called 'a ball' at the Parisian School of Cookery, Ottilie began to fantasize about her 'Monsieur'.

This was yet another legacy of growing up at the Grand Hotel, St Elcombe. Ottilie was almost physically incapable of meeting someone and not compulsively making up some story around them. A childhood and early adolescence spent watching new arrivals and wondering about them, wondering why they were coming to the hotel, what they would be doing while they were there, and what their lives were like at home, meant that with each new face came a new story waiting to be invented.

But fantasize as Ottilie might about the man who was allowing her to reside in his beautiful apartment, after that first evening Ottilie never did encounter Monsieur again, and wilfully the last days of her last fortnight in Paris raced by, each day seeming determined to increase its speed to such an extent that Ottilie started to dread waking in the mornings, hating to see daylight once more, because each new autumn morning meant one day less, and one day less meant that soon she would be back to everyday life at St Elcombe, and nothing would ever be the same again.

I would be charm if you would come to dinner with me on your last night.

The plain card with the French-style rick-rack border was pushed under her bedroom door.

Monsieur wanted her to dine with him!

But how did he know that she had only one night left in Paris, and why did he want to take her out to dinner when he hardly knew her? Not that Ottilie really cared in the least to know the answer to these two questions, or indeed any others.

That morning she chose to wear her navy blue travelling outfit with the stiff white collar, and so dressed, stylishly and impeccably in a suit that had once belonged to her mother, which Edith had altered especially for Paris, Ottilie left a note on the hall table for Monsieur.

J'aime bien dîner avec vous, Monsieur, ce soir.

She did not think this was at all the correct French for a formal acceptance, although she did know enough to put 'vous'. At the same time she signed herself not 'Mlle Cartaret' but, after some deliberation, 'Ottilie Cartaret', and then she skipped off towards the cookery school, running past the concierge's little house and calling '*bonjour, madame!*' and feeling in a fury of excitement at the idea of having dinner with Monsieur despite its being her last night in Paris.

It was also her last day at the cookery school. And at half past two o'clock it was time to walk for what she knew had to be the last time under the little archway wreathed in vines, and onto the narrow street outside with a feeling of *must remember this,* a feeling of *don't ever forget,* a feeling of *whatever happens no-one can ever take these four weeks away from you, not ever.*

'Are you feeling as sad as I am, honey?'

One of the American ladies squeezed Ottilie's hand as together they looked back at the archway that led to the little courtyard filled with tables and chairs where they had all dutifully eaten their way through each other's cooking.

'Yes.'

Ottilie was feeling sad. She had to admit to that. What she could not, however, also admit to was a feeling of intense excitement, as if something wonderful was going to happen to her that evening, as if her whole world was suddenly going to change, which indeed it was, although it would be some years before she discovered why, or just how completely.

Monsieur stared at Ottilie in amazement and seemed just about to smile, or even laugh, but then he appeared to check himself and think better of it, and instead he put his head to one side and made an '*ah!*' sound with a flat 'a' not an 'aaah'. So it was not exactly, Ottilie quickly noted, an appreciative sound but rather an abrupt 'Let's think again' sound, the kind of sound a person makes when they have suddenly thought of something they had not thought of before, or changed their minds about something completely.

If Ottilie could have seen what he was actually thinking she thought perhaps she might not like it at all, but happily for her she could not, so she waited in the doorway, looking at him where he stood by the collection of drinks at the further end of the *salon*, shyly wondering why it was that when a Frenchman looked at you, any Frenchman anywhere, on the Métro, by the bus stop, if you were English you always had the feeling that he was smiling *at* you rather than *with* you.

'Mademoiselle Cartaret – Ottilie – if I may? Yes, 'ow can I tell you? We are going to Tour d'Argent for dinner, yes? So. You must look wunnerful becoz there will be many wunnerfully chic women there, *le tout Paris, enfin!* I cannot – I cannot take you to Tour d'Argent dress as an armchair!'

Ottilie looked down at her flowered cotton summer evening dress. It was an 'Edith special', cut down from one of Melanie's dresses long ago. Ottilie had worn it many times in the hotel restaurant and for staff birthdays. It was meant to be a classic, or what Edith always called a 'classic'.

'I am afraid I will have to go dressed as an armchair,

Monsieur, or not at all, because I only have this dress,' Ottilie explained haughtily, determinedly resolute on the exterior, head held high, while inside she melted at the very idea of how terrible a flower-printed dress with a ribbon under the bust must look to a rich, chic, Frenchman who had silk mills and a historic factory which, Mrs Le Martine had told her in impressed tones, produced some of the finest and most beautiful fabrics for the top Italian and French designers.

'May I dress you, please?'

Ottilie thought 'Why not?' for she was not so naive as not to notice that his eyes had already undressed her.

'But of course,' Ottilie readily agreed, as always suddenly feeling liberated in his company. 'I do look terrible, don't I?' she confided to him, suddenly unable to keep up her haughty façade, and yet wide-eyed at this immediate intimacy that they had achieved.

'Awful!' he agreed, walking ahead of her and indicating for her to follow him. 'So Ingleesh, so awful!' he told her, turning back. 'This dress, you poor darling – my Ghad, she is so badly made! Perhaps all right for an old couch, *n'est-ce pas?* But you don't want people at Tour d'Argent to sit on you, *ma petite, enfin,* do you? *Look* at you, but not sit on you, I think!'

At this Ottilie completely lost the remains of her assumed *hauteur* and started to laugh, and the more she laughed the more Monsieur did too, until they were both quite helpless.

'This is my mother's, cut down,' Ottilie explained eventually, wiping her eyes, her sides aching, while at the same time she marvelled at this sense of being quite at ease, in a way that she had never felt with anyone else.

'My Ghad, Ottilie! Promise me. Never ever wear Ingleesh clothes again, will you? You are too petite, too *fine*, you know? You must always wear European clothes, and sometime maybe some of the new American younger designers, but not Ingleesh. You are not tall enough,

179

although you 'ave a good little figure and that is great.'

Monsieur's Americanized French was entrancing, giving everything he said a dashing appeal, each sentence reminiscent of some sort of stylish beefburger, but served with a *sauce béarnaise* on the side.

'Come with me. My factory 'as made some beautiful silks for many beautiful couturiers, and when they are finished they often send me back something, an original for my museum of costume near Lyon. Sometime I like, sometime I do not and I give it to a woman friend, but yesterday something very new and beautiful arrive. It is not quite original enough for my museum, but it is *ravissant*, and I hope you will be ravished by it.'

He looked down at her thoughtfully for a second, and Ottilie smiled. It was her last night and frankly she could not wait to be ravished by his choice of dress and to hell with the conventions, if there were any.

She followed him down a long dark corridor into an unoccupied but obviously once very feminine room. Going to a great dark oak cupboard, he opened it and took the dress, with reverential and minutely artistic care, from underneath its cocoon of cotton covers, unwrapping it piece by piece, many, many times, because such is the fear of daylight, he explained to Ottilie, that when an original and beautiful garment is finished it must be wrapped over and over in only the best cotton for fear of sunlight harming it.

Finally there it was, the dress he had chosen to unveil for her, and he stood back, holding it up against her. They both viewed what could be about to be a fine result in the long looking glasses that decorated the end wall of the elegant, old-fashioned *boudoir* in which they stood.

'Mademoiselle Ottilie, I do not wish to embarrass you, but do you 'ave any underpinnings for such a dress?'

At this remark, which seemed to shatter the awestruck silence that had fallen as they both looked at Ottilie and the dress in the mirrors, Ottilie blushed, because, she suddenly realized, no man had ever spoken to her about her underwear before.

'Only a little!'

'A little is great, a little is all you must wear with such a dress, Mademoiselle Ottilie, you know? And when you step in, let me tell you not to worry yourself because you will find it is all built in, *n'est-ce pas?* All very tight. It will embrace you inside, *n'est-ce pas?* And just some sheer on the legs, mmm, stockin' very sheer, yes? Much smoother. And shoes, let me see?'

He went to a cupboard and opened a door. Inside Ottilie could see literally dozens of pairs of shoes, most of them hardly worn.

'All samples, you know? We are sent samples of so much, my Gahd! And zen I send zem to my nieces, to their friends, to the charities for the ladies' causes, you know? 'Ere, these will be very pretty, ravishing. I think I have your size quite right. I have the eye, you know, for the female size. I have many, many sisters, and I the only boy.'

Ottilie tried on one tiny sandal, so little leather, but the heels so incredibly high that even she could see that it made the length of the dress seem quite conventional.

'I not only have many sisters, I have great taste, *n'est-ce pas?*'

Monsieur nodded at his reflection in the mirror almost affectionately. As for Ottilie, she could hardly wait to tear off the dress she was wearing, which she too now thought of as an old chair cover, and throw it out of the window down to the place where the concierge kept the dustbins, because that was where it quite obviously belonged.

Bedroom door firmly locked, she struggled into the dress which Monsieur had chosen for her. All the time she was struggling out of the chintz dress and into the model dress she did not dare to look at herself in her mirror, because just seeing the beauty of the dress and how it was made filled her with dread that she was not going to look

181

very nice in this ravishing garment, that beautiful though it was it was not going to suit her, or she it. But when she turned to face herself in the wall mirror she saw how very wrong she was.

She saw what now seemed to be a much taller and more slender dark-haired girl, a girl with a solemn awestruck expression, a girl who looked as if she was always meant to grow into someone out of the ordinary, someone she would not have known from a few minutes before. Could just a dress make such a difference to her? It was as if she had never seen herself before, as if with the putting on of just one dress she was a butterfly finally emerged from the chrysalis of childhood.

Off the dress had certainly looked lovely, but on it seemed to her that the dress was almost *too* beautiful. Made of gold iridescent silk with a high Medici collar that framed her face behind her head, it had a pleated train and skin-tight sleeves. It was not only a beautiful dress now, Ottilie realized, it was a dress for all time, fashion at its most *haut* and *couture* at its most arresting, but at the same time owing everything to yesterday.

The collar that framed the face, the train, the skin-tight sleeves, everything about it said 'the past is present in me'. And because Monsieur had cleverly chosen such high-heeled shoes for Ottilie's small, slender feet, when she walked up and down she found the length of the dress seemed quite perfect, and that her slim, not quite seventeen-year-old figure was also perfect for its exaggeratedly tight figure-hugging lines.

Ottilie unlocked her bedroom door. As she walked slowly down the corridor towards the double doors of the *salon* she found her greatest difficulty was not to smile. Outside the room, within which she knew Monsieur would now be waiting for her with some impatience, one eye on the great gold clock, she tried to assume her most serious expression. She tried to think of cold, blue, sad, bad things, and having done so she put her hand over the

182

old handle of one half of the double doors and turned it.

Because she had been at such pains not to smile foolishly, like some sort of stupid naive girl wearing her first real evening dress, she put her hand up to her face and bit on her thumb.

'My Gahd, that is beautiFOOL, but please remove your finger from your mouth, Ottilie. You are not a girl scoot, *enfin*, you are a beautiFOOL girl. BeautiFOOL girls do not *mangent leur doigts!*'

Monsieur frowned and walked towards Ottilie, one hand by his side, the other poised to adjust whatever he thought needed adjusting. The collar – twitch. The skirt – twitch. The tiny train – he spread it out a little before standing back and then walking all round her. Finally he stretched out his hands and pulled back her long dark hair in a manner that was as detached and disinterested as a hairdresser's.

Ottilie stood quite still as he did so, for this was the first time a man she hardly knew had touched her hair.

'I think you must knot it into your neck. You know what I mean by that? A knot? Brush under and then knot, very tight, it will set off ze collar much better.'

Back once more to her bedroom, and having done as he instructed with the aid of a few fine hairpins, Ottilie once more reappeared in front of Monsieur and received a nod of approval.

'Good.'

He smiled suddenly and picked up his beautiful, red-silk-lined evening coat and nodded for her to precede him. For a second, as he handed her an evening cloak and helped her put it round her shoulders, Ottilie felt terrified. How would she survive all evening with an older man, walking ahead of him into hotels or restaurants? Then, remembering Melanie making her nightly descent down the steps of the gold staircase at the Grand, she pretended that she was doing the same. Staring straight ahead of her, head held high, hips slightly forward, eyes blank, lips smiling just slightly, she started to walk elegantly forward, and it was in this way that she entered what seemed to her to be the great arena of the Tour d'Argent.

On their way to the restaurant in his chauffeur-driven Citroën Monsieur had appeared to suddenly bow to a whim and stop off at the Georges Cinq to 'show you off to my old American friends there. My Gahd! Why should the Tour d'Argent 'ave all the fun?'

Ottilie was solemnly introduced, as prearranged with her, and by agreement, as 'my English goddaughter'.

All the eyes on her in her figure-hugging dress said 'Oh yes?' but in truth all the time she was sipping her grenadine through a straw, and he was sipping his dry martini – without a straw – Monsieur treated her with such courtly detachment, and yet looked so proud of her appearance – head held high, dark hair caught into the nape of her neck, no make-up except for a little touch of lipstick – that after only a few minutes not only had he convinced his acquaintances of his godfatherly status, he had somehow managed to convince Ottilie that she was indeed his goddaughter.

At the Tour d'Argent it was quite different. Here the waiters looked her up and down with outward appreciation, but, as they pulled her chair back for her and spread her heavy linen napkin over the precious dress, Ottilie had the feeling that the expression in their eyes definitely said '*cocotte*'. And she herself felt that Monsieur had, for many evenings, long ago, or perhaps even just recently, brought the beautiful woman from the paintings and drawings to this very table, but she was too discreet, too well trained from her childhood at the Grand, to ask him anything, or indeed to do more than look forward to listening to him, to lighting his cigar, and look as decorative and sophisticated as it was possible to be when you are still only sixteen and dining in perhaps the greatest restaurant in Europe.

*　　*　　*

What will happen when we go back to the apartment? This thought would keep recurring. The trouble was, Ottilie had never had to think ahead for herself because at the Grand there was always someone she could talk to, or someone to whom she could turn. From the moment she stepped out of her bed to the moment she went back to it at night she was never alone, and although nowadays Alfred looked permanently worried, and Melanie rarely left her suite except on Saturday nights, nevertheless everything that happened was taken care of by them and the staff, and all that was required of Ottilie was that she should be what they always called *of use*.

It was very different now that she was alone in a restaurant with an older sophisticated man, and for a few seconds, as she contemplated this thought that 'something might happen' when they returned to the apartment, it seemed to her that she really should begin to learn to think ahead a little. Yet even though she was indeed afraid of that thought, even though she felt a sense of foreboding, the truth was that dangerous though her situation was, or might be, she still somehow could not find it in herself to care so much that she would allow it to dominate the evening. From the moment that she had seen Monsieur looking exactly as she had always wanted an older man to look, tall, tanned, dark hair greying at the sides, slim, elegant, and displaying a very evident enjoyment in her youth and beauty, she had only wanted to continue to live from minute to minute, as she had been doing for the past four weeks, because that, it seemed to her, was what real happiness was all about.

It was all about now, catching hold of the moment and not letting it slip away. Now was the colour of the coral-pink lobster against the plate, now was the woman dressed in black at another table with a violet-coloured sash and a little evening hat with a veil in the same colour.

'You really love *couleur*, do you not, Ottilie?'

Ottilie smiled and she herself coloured a little as she

realized that perhaps a too-long silence had elapsed while she had selfishly allowed herself too much time to look, however surreptitiously, around at the other diners, at the other women, at the evening, at the darkened skies and the stars beyond the windows, at everything except Monsieur who was after all her host, her godfather for the evening.

He seemed to understand though, because he smiled and nodded at her as if he had always known her, as if he could appreciate and share her fascination with other people.

'I too love *couleur*. That is why – my Gahd, that is why I am so *fortunate* in my business. Silk is all about *couleur*. And you know, when they unroll those *couleurs* in front of my eyes, sometime, sometime I think I am the luckiest man on zis earth. To be living and working with what to me is sacred – to be living and working with *couleur*, well, you can appreciate, Ottilie, it is so sensual. You know? So – 'ow can I say? – well yes, if you will forgive the vulgarity, it is *sexy*!'

There, it was out, and it lay between them as if he had spilt some wine on the tablecloth. SEXY. In Ottilie's mind it was capitalized, it was emphasized, it was neon-lit.

'Ah, now I see I have shocked you a little bit, Ottilie! But you know, my muzzer she was americaine so I am partly a little New World, and also I was at Harvard for three years, so I am allowed these *petites libertés* from the New World, no?'

'No, no, at least yes, no, not at all, I quite understand. As a matter of fact I think you're right, as a matter of fact. It is sexy, colour *is* sexy, it is just that I never thought of it like that before, and that is pretty strange when you come to think of it, considering I live by the sea and the sea is all about changing colour, and in a hotel, and people are all about colour, and so yes, of course it is sexy, and that other word – sensual. And you're right, I am in love with colour.'

186

The words had tumbled over themselves – Ottilie even spoke what little French she had managed to master too quickly – but now they were out and lying about the table, and Monsieur seemed to like them, because he appeared to be picking over them before replying.

'I will advise you in your life tonight, my little Ottilie.'

She was *his* now, and she did not care in the least.

'You are a beautiful young girl, and now I will help you because that is what an older man is for. But first I will begin with the best advice in the world.'

He hesitated, and so Ottilie leaned forward and asked, 'Which is?'

'Never eat cheese at night!'

If Monsieur knew everything about dining and wining, if he knew on which side of which hill a grape had been grown, if every waiter in the room appeared to know him, and more than that, if everyone in the restaurant did too, and stopped by their table to talk and smile, and appreciate the sight of this handsome older man dining in company with his English goddaughter, and if the men murmured their appreciation of Ottilie's beauty to Monsieur, and if he seemed to want to share their pleasure in her appearance, in her youth, in the delight of the evening, the glamour of the occasion, Ottilie at least knew how to make people talk.

People were what growing up at the Grand had been all about, and not just old or lonely people without friends but all people, and so it was, without realizing it, that Ottilie had mastered the ability to watch people when they were not talking, and listen to them when they were silent.

So now, as they were served coffee and Monsieur rolled a cigar between his fingers and then held it out for Ottilie to light, she remembered the expression in his eyes that first evening when he had arrived in the apartment, when he had stood looking at her, wrapped only in one of his own chic navy blue bath towels with the dull purple edge.

187

'How did you actually meet Mrs Le Martine, Monsieur?'

The cigar smoke smelt delicious and the shape the smoke was making seemed to curl its way around Ottilie's words.

'Ha! You may well ask that question, Ottilie. How did I meet 'er? I met 'er because long after the war, because my parents have this so great respect for 'er. She has come over here from England under cover many, many times. Mrs Le Martine she go straight ahead and she volunteer for this work, because she know all these people because her husband had a French fazzer. That is why she is so good for the undercover work, not just that she speaks French without any accent, but her name is French, *enfin*! If the Gestapo shout "Arrêtez, Le Martine!" and you do not turn, in those day you are dead, *mort*, believe me. You have two second, maybe less, you can imagine, *n'est-ce pas?* You have two, maybe three second and then bang, you are dead because everyone only turn, *comme ça* – he snapped his fingers – 'when they hear their name shouted *if* it is their name. She was "Le Martine" already ten years, so – no problems for her.

'You know, every time I see *un général*, no matter who he is, with all these *médailles* – medals – I think of those days. It was Mrs Le Martine, and she has no medals, it was small people like her who had the *courage*. Fifteen times she was dropped into France. Once she walk into an 'otel and she put something quite small into the pocket of this Gestapo general, and it was a revolving door where she pass him, nice smile, beautiful clothes, you know? So he smile and he follow her into this revolving door thinking of making a "pick-up" for himself. This man – *c'est un diable* – he was famous for hanging children, you understand? So. She walk off, the door she jam, the explosion happen, and no-one think this young woman with her beautiful clothes has put an explosive in his pocket and jam the door. All they see is this woman, very pretty, very nice, and she walk off, slowly, slowly round the corner, then the general blow up and no-one understand how it happen!'

Ottilie always loved stories, but she particularly loved stories that were true – growing up at the Grand she had heard so many from the old ladies and the gentlemen. It was not difficult for her to imagine a younger Mrs Le Martine, always so well dressed, even during the war, her slender figure swaying on slightly too high a heel in front of the Gestapo general, her smile, even her entrancing laugh, and how she would walk ahead, and how he would follow her not realizing what she had slipped into his greatcoat pocket, not realizing that she was his angel of death, sent perhaps by the little children he had murdered to do to him what they could not do to him themselves.

'She is a wonderful woman, Mrs Le Martine. I would do anything for her, you know?'

'Yes, even have an English girl to stay in your flat?'

'Yes, even that. But you know – *merci, oui, encore un café!*' as the waiter leaned over to offer them more coffee. 'I tell you 'ow many times that woman come to France? So many times, and after so many times she must have become *more* frightened. My Gahd, you know how it is, you do something once' – Monsieur shrugged his elegant shoulders – 'and it is all right, you do it twice, a little bit more frightened, *n'est-ce pas?* You do it three, four, fourteen times, you must know *terror*! Always thinking this time it must be the last, but always with Mrs Le Martine, she is always thinking, she told me, "Just one more time, one more time to kill someone who has killed so many innocents, to stop him killing more."'

'How did she know so many French people, though?'

Ottilie frowned. Up until that moment she had not thought of Mrs Le Martine, despite her name, as having had so many international relations that she could slip in and out of wartime France with such confidence, knowing that she would always know someone.

Monsieur looked round the restaurant, at the diners, at

the waiters, at the chic and beautiful women, the immaculately dressed gentlemen.

'My dear Ottilie, if you think that *le tout Paris – le gratin* as we call it in France – if you think that we know many, many people I do assure you that we do not. We are as nothing compared to the waiters, the chefs, the concierges. The people who know everyone are the people who work in these places, the restaurants, the hotels.

'They know us, of course, but they also know each other, so they know *double* what we know, what you and I know. Mrs Le Martine she had been first a waitress at the Georges Cinq 'otel, and then she was a lady's maid to the Comtesse de la Chard de Corbonne. A beautiFOOL woman! A woman who everyone has love. And she has love everyone! Many, many men, but all her secrets they are with Mrs Le Martine. No-one but Mrs Le Martine know who has loved her mistress. She is discreet, always, Mrs Le Martine, but she know everyone. The lovers they all have valets and lady's maids, and *they* 'ave 'usbands and wives, and so—' Monsieur shrugged his shoulders. 'And so Mrs Le Martine she is someone who know *everyone*!'

Ottilie was amazed, yet somehow unsurprised as well, because after all everything Monsieur had just said made sense of everything that Mrs Le Martine was, and everything that she was quite definitely *not*. Her adoration of everything that was fine and beautifully made from clothes to furnishings. Her ability to cheer Ottilie and pull her out of her occasional adolescent self-pity, her staunch support of her young friend over the years, from the dreadful night when she had left the Grand in such a furious hurry once she learned of Ottilie's having been beaten by her mother. Everything made sense, given her previous occupation of a lady's maid. Now she thought about it Ottilie realized that Mrs Le Martine was too carefully elegant to be real, too insistent on standards to be like Philip and Constantia Granville. Everything about her was really rather too much the Countess, and too little the maid.

Seeing that her large eyes had never left his face, and Ottilie had remained quite silent, Monsieur obviously felt it was safe to continue his story without fear of boring his young companion.

'And so, most sadly, the poor young Countess she died young, of something that young girls still die from in those days before we have penicillin, huh? But in her maid, in Mrs Le Martine, she made sure that she lived on because – Mrs Le Martine became her!' Ottilie's eyes widened as Monsieur went on to explain. 'Everything, everything we think of as our Mrs Le Martine, every strong characteristic – that is not her originally, originally that is the Comtesse de la Chard de Corbonne come to life. I know this because I have spoke with many, many people, and they are old friends of this famous young woman, and they all say when they have met Mrs Le Martine with me, but it is Marie-Thérèse to the life! The laugh, the walk, the clothes – *everything* is her mistress come to life. Of course that is why she became so good for this work against the Gestapo, when she become this beautiful woman in place of the maid, you know? She become *la Comtesse*. She is a – how you can say, a *doppelgänger*? Of course it happen many times, you know, the secretary become like her boss, the valet become like his master, but maybe never quite so well, I am told, as Mrs Le Martine and the beautiful Comtesse de la Chard de Corbonne. Here, I will show you.'

Monsieur took an old crocodile-skin wallet from his evening jacket and from the side, after removing many small photos, he produced one now faded to a sepia tint.

'This is her, no? This is the woman who rescued my fazzer and my muzzer and me – yes?'

Ottilie took the photograph and stared at it. It was indeed Mrs Le Martine. There was her mysterious smile, there her elegance, there her beautiful clothes, the scarf knotted just so, everything perfect, the angle of the hat, the long elegant legs.

'But you see, Ottilie, this is not Mrs Le Martine. This is the Countess.'

Ottilie gave Monsieur back the photograph. She could not say so to this man, but quite a large part of her was now suffering a sense of disappointment, of being let down. If Mrs Le Martine was only a replica of someone else long dead, if she was most definitely not herself, if she was only a maid imitating a Countess, she seemed somehow a little lessened in Ottilie's eyes. She suddenly felt as if she had been tricked. Perhaps Monsieur sensed what Ottilie was thinking because he said, 'Of course, you know, it does not matter if she is a maid or a Countess, she is a great woman, and a very brave woman,' and he replaced the photograph in his wallet. 'I like to think of you, Ottilie, as always having a friend such as her. So. Alas, now this beautiful evening must end, I must return to Lyon, you must go back to England. I hope you will always remember what I have said to you, all the wise advice I have given you, yes? Please repeat to me like a good pupil.'

Ottilie repeated obediently in an approximation of his accent, 'Never salt the meat before cooking. Scent yourself before you dress, but most of all never eat cheese at night!'

There. It was all over. The glorious evening was over, and to Ottilie the realization was like a bucket of cold water, because all of a sudden, without more than a few minutes' warning, he was leaving the restaurant and she was walking in front of him. He was handing her into the chauffeur-driven car and all her worries about what was going to happen when they returned to the flat were over, and although Ottilie knew that she should feel relieved for some strange reason all she was actually feeling was disappointment. So much so that when they arrived at the station where he was to take his train and Monsieur leaned across and gave her a large envelope with her name on it, she even forgot to thank him.

'*Au revoir*, Ottilie, and don't forget this little advice I give you—'

'How could I? Never eat cheese at night!'

They both laughed and then he was gone, walking quickly away, a small expensive suitcase in one hand, towards the train, towards the manufacturing of his beautiful silks, towards his colours, his other life about which Ottilie knew nothing, and now did not want to know any more. It did not matter that he was too old and Ottilie too young, all that mattered was that tonight, this one evening, they had shared something that perhaps neither of them would ever forget, something which added to and did not subtract from the beauty of the city, like the light rain on the road glittering in the car's headlights, the few people loitering around the station waiting perhaps for their lovers, or their friends.

The night outside the car window was as smooth and dark and as beautiful as any night in Paris, and along the black and wondrous waters of the river *bateaux mouches* made their leisurely coloured way, great barges of inviting pleasure set about with joyous little lights of different hues.

'Thank you,' she called to the chauffeur. 'Thank you,' she called to the concierge. 'Thank you,' she called to the stars, and it was only when she tripped up the stairs and back into the arms, the warm dark embrace, of the apartment that she thought to open the large brown envelope carefully inset with cardboard which Monsieur had handed her so quickly at the station. And although, happily for her, it would be some months before Monsieur's gift to her brought about misery as great as the happiness she had recently known, the impact on her of first seeing Monsieur's surprise gift was very far from miserable.

She stared at it, and first she laughed out loud in amazement, and then she leaned back against her bedroom door and sighed at the inscription on the back – *Don't ever lose that innocent expression, ma petite!*

Part Four

'It isn't a quite dead garden,' she cried out softly to herself. 'Even if the roses are dead, there are other things alive.'

Frances Hodgson Burnett, *The Secret Garden*

Ten

It was the dull, grey, leaden atmosphere that Ottilie walked into that late afternoon of her return from Paris that warned her she should have read the letter Mr Cartaret had sent to her. It was the way the staff, from the reception desk onwards, smiled at first with delight at her, and then quickly looked away, as if suddenly remembering that they should not be doing so, as if they knew that just by smiling they might invite trouble. It was the way that Blackie, the old hall porter, walked by her with his old nose in the air, as if he now despised her, as if they had never been friends.

Ottilie was in trouble. She knew it. They all knew it.

On the way up the stairs to the Cartarets' suite Ottilie had to stop and remind herself that no-one could now beat her. She was too old. She could run way. No-one could lock her in a cupboard. No-one could make her go and sell their clothes to guests for them, or throw away their jewellery to help pay their debts. That part of her life was over and done with and they could no longer force her to do things that she did not want.

Of course, when she thought 'they' she was really thinking of Mrs Cartaret. She could be unkind and say bad things, she could make Ottilie work in the hotel all the hours that God had given, but she could no longer beat or humiliate her the way she used to.

What she could do, however, was tell her that Edith was dead.

Eleven

Of course Ottilie had known death before, when she was a small child. She had seen Ma's coffin before the boys gave her away to the Cartarets, and she had known what it was like for someone she loved not to be there when she wanted her so much, when she had run back to the cottage that time, with the earrings in her pocket, expecting Ma somehow to be around, with her rich laugh and her thick red plait of hair, but then she had been young, six years old, now she was older, and death, she found, had changed for her, particularly Edith's death. Nowadays death came hand in hand not with just sorrow, but with the feeling that she should have done something, that she could easily have done something, to prevent Edith dying, that somehow if she had not been so selfish, if she had read that letter, she could have come back from Paris and Edith would not have had her heart attack.

Matters might have been a little easier for her if Melanie, who after all still drank far too much gin, and had been prescribed tranquillizers for 'her nerves', had been so out of control that she was not aware of what was going on. Unfortunately, with her looks slipping away from her, it was as if Melanie was quite determined to make all around her appear as ugly as she now felt herself becoming.

'I cannot understand why you were so selfish, *so* selfish as to think that it was all right to simply stay on in Paris not getting in touch, not telephoning. It did not seem to me to be *possible*. With all that you *meant* to Edith, all that you *owed* poor Edith, how could you just stay on in Paris *ignoring* the whole thing? I could not believe that anyone could be that selfish. What an appallingly selfish view of the world you must have, Ottilie, appallingly. Thank God, if the rest of the world is to be like you, thank God that your father and I will not live to see it. A world peopled by such selfishness does not seem possible. Not possible. It will be an appalling place. Edith asked for you, you know, she asked for you many times, and I just had to tell her, "Edith, Miss Ottilie is in France and I am afraid she just does not *want* to come back. We have told her you are gravely ill, Edith, but she will not come back to see you." We had to say that. There was nothing more we *could* say. We had to tell her the truth.'

Happily for her, over the nearly ten years of her adoption, Ottilie had been able to develop a way of mentally sidestepping what happened to her, a way of pushing the hurt aside, so that it stayed pulled back like a curtain, while she strained every effort to concentrate only on the light ahead through the windows to the side of that curtain which was so often patterned with misery and guilt.

And so now to stand back from Melanie's constant torrent of sadistic words, her enjoyment, her revelling in the misery of Ottilie's supposed guilt, Ottilie imagined what Edith would say if she heard Melanie *at* her. (Edith would always use that expression, 'Been *at* you again, has she, Miss Ottilie?')

With that kind of remembrance Ottilie found would come reason, and light, and even a little colour, imagining Edith with her calm eyes, her close-permed crisp hair, her cameo brooch at the neck of her uniform dress, standing composedly in Ottilie's suite and saying something ordinary and calming so that neither the words nor the beatings would hurt quite so much, knowing that only ordinariness could restore the kind of calm that was necessary for a child to be able to face another day.

'*Take no notice of her, Miss Ottilie, she's in one of her bad moods, just take no notice. Mrs Tomber and I, we just ignore her, and she soon comes round, really she does.'*

Ottilie and Edith had been very close. Edith and Mrs Cartaret had not been really close even though Edith had worked at the Grand for so many years, which was probably why Melanie had not gone to the funeral or even sent a daisy. Ottilie knew this from Mrs Tomber, who whispered it, her eyes narrowed with shock and dislike, while they were making up beds together.

'You would have thought, Miss Ottilie,' the housekeeper muttered, 'you would have thought that after all this time she would have had the common decency to go to poor Edith's funeral, but no. She sent Blackie and myself and Mr Cartaret, while she just sat at home with her gin and her television. What a thing!'

But her mother's apparent dislike of Ottilie was nothing compared to the open distaste now displayed by the staff at the Grand. It seemed that they were determined as one to stand behind Mrs Cartaret, 'Madame' as they still called her, in their open hostility to Ottilie when she returned from Paris.

This open disapproval was made all too evident at every hour of the working day, as they turned silently away from Ottilie when she spoke to them, or kept their eyes averted as she passed them, or moved pointedly away when they saw her approaching. It was difficult for them not to speak to her sometimes, since nowadays she was in charge of most of their activities, but they kept what they had to say to a minimum, and every sudden silence that fell as she approached signalled to Ottilie the one word – Coventry.

She had seen this form of punishment before, seen it happening to other people, new maids if they flirted too much with Chef or upset Mrs Tomber, or failed to give Blackie the attention he so craved, and she had been unable to prevent it. She had seen the misery it caused the victim but she had never imagined that it could happen to her, to 'Miss Ottilie' the spoilt daughter of the Grand Hotel, St Elcombe.

Of course it only gradually dawned on her what was happening, as day after day her sudden entry into the kitchens or the lobby or the reception rooms of the hotel would be greeted with an equally sudden silence, and then, eerily, laughter and talk would resume the moment she left, the sound following her through the swing doors and up the service stairs until with relief she reached the ground floors and the prospect of the sea beyond the old glass doors.

At one particularly low point Ottilie found herself digging her fingers into her hand and realized that her knuckles must be turning white in the effort not to beg the maids not to turn away when she addressed them so that she ended up speaking to the backs of their heads. On other days it was all she could do to stop herself imploring Blackie to stop whistling in her face when he was spoken to about the filthy state of his shoes. Or Chef just to look at her when she discussed the next day's menus with him – menus which Ottilie, after her month in Paris, had seen needed to be considerably revised. But somehow hearing the flat, uninterested tone he used with her, and watching how he, like the rest of the staff, appeared to have mastered the technique of looking anywhere except at her, Ottilie always stopped just in time. Life with Melanie had taught her the hard lessons early. You did not beg, you did not cry, you smiled and got on with it.

Or as Edith would say, quietly and prosaically in her calm voice, 'As long as you've got your health and strength, Miss Ottilie, that's all that matters in this life.'

Late at night, alone in her room, Ottilie could not avoid realizing how miserable her life was, but back out there, in the hotel, moving up and down the stairs, back and front, she carried on, determined to find an answer to the deadlock while wondering, night after night as she lay gazing at the darkness, what she actually could do? She

202

knew that she had to win against the staff somehow or her position would become untenable, but how?

And then it came to her, and it was the words of that dear old major general who used to come to the hotel for August which came back to her, for in between describing those battles that made the very name of England and the English so invincible, he would stop and murmur some phrase of sweet old-fashioned advice.

'My dear, never forget, if you want to stop a bolting horse, put your thumb in its neck and then pull, use its own strength against it.'

The moment Ottilie walked into the kitchens that morning she sensed that they all knew something had changed.

'People are like that,' she thought, looking round, knowing that the way she walked, the look in her eyes, everything about her must have altered so substantially that a silence fell at the moment of her entry, but not the old sullen silence, not the 'here she comes, let's bait her, boys' silence, a quite different sort of silence.

'Right. Now, Chef,' Ottilie said, smiling, 'I should like your attention, please. To begin with the escargots last night. They were far too salty. I heard Lady Saltrim complain of it, and when I tasted one down here I must say I agreed with her. Make a note, please.' She handed him a small notebook and pencil, which because he had been wrong-footed Chef took, in spite of himself. Ottilie then turned to the young pastry chef, a new cheeky so-and-so with a Beatle haircut and an identity bracelet. 'No jewellery in the kitchen, Dean, please. And the *petits fours* that you made yesterday, much, much too big. *Trop grands*, if you understand French, which you should if you want to cook better. Guests only want something to pop into their mouths, they do not want to have to plough through sweetmeats, really they don't.' She turned back to Chef who was now reddening in fury. 'No more pastry around the fillet, please, Chef. I know it is fashionable but

203

I find it heavy. In future the fillet is to be presented individually, if you would, in the classic manner – lightly fried in butter and olive oil and served on a piece of rounded bread fried in the same juices. Here at the Grand we must try to avoid fashion fads and stick to the classical. It can never fail us.'

Some of what Ottilie had just said was parroted straight from her cooking classes in Paris, but none of the staff would know that. She turned her attention to the kitchen now. It was way below what it should be in terms of cleanliness. She had known this for some time, but had not had the courage or given herself the authority to say what had to be said, but since neither Alfred nor Melanie ever came down to the kitchens a decline in standards was inevitable. She started to pull out saucepans and cooking pots from cupboards and turn them over, all the time talking, talking, saying over and over, 'Oh no, no, this will not do, no and not this either.'

When she had finished, most of the contents of the kitchen were on the stone-tiled floor. Ottilie stood back to survey her handiwork.

'Good. Well, that is something to be getting on with, anyway.'

She smiled round at them, very sweetly.

'I'll be back to inspect your work in a couple of hours.'

She turned to go, still smiling. How right the old general had been. Since they had sent her to Coventry, there was now not a thing they could say, because to do so would be to break their own code of silence. Effectively she had used their own strength against them.

Having mentally dusted herself down, she fetched her winter coat from the cloakroom and went to visit Edith.

Ottilie walked out to the graveyard alone, determined to talk to Edith by herself. The church was some way out of St Elcombe, a tiny Saxon place of worship some two miles away. Normally its atmosphere of Anglo-Saxon sanctity brought about a feeling of peace, but today was different and Ottilie shivered as she stood on the edge of the old churchyard, looking for a freshly dug grave. Perhaps it was the fact that it was such a dark grey day, the sort that makes the sound of trees moving in the wind, waiting for the rain, seem like people, waving and sighing and waiting for death, but she wished herself once more back on the road and heading for the cluster of white cottages which led eventually down to the town.

'I'm very sorry I didn't come back from Paris, Edith, really I am. I didn't know that you had suffered a heart attack. I'm afraid I threw away the letter telling me because I wanted to stay and I didn't want to come back. I hope God punishes me for not coming back to see you when you had had a heart attack, but I want you to know that I truly would have done if I had known.'

After she had finished her speech, said aloud as if Edith was standing in front of her, Ottilie put her flowers on the grave. They looked rather odd because there was as yet no tombstone, but nevertheless she knew from Mrs Tomber that Edith was lying in the ground underneath the earth all right, because Edith always had said that she would prefer a nice old-fashioned burial and no new-fangled crematorium, nothing like that, that was not her style at all. As she walked back towards the road she raised her eyes up to the frowning sky and knew for certain, and she could not have said why, that Edith was watching her. No matter what Melanie said or did in the next years or months, or weeks or days, nothing would take away from Ottilie's feeling that Edith was quite definitely watching her, and smiling.

'I'll live my life for you, Edith,' Ottilie said, looking up to the sky. 'Just you see if I won't.'

Visiting Edith's grave and making the speech to her was one of the brave moments, for once back in the hotel Ottilie remained as unpopular as ever.

'Madame put it about that you knew Edith was ill from the first, that you knew all about her heart attack, and didn't bother to come back, because you were having too nice a time of it in Paris,' Mrs Tomber kept saying, as if reminding Ottilie of why she was being ostracized made any difference at all.

But if Ottilie was effectively now placed in Coventry by all those people who she had once thought were her friends, she still had to work as hard as ever in the hotel, stepping in and substituting at the last minute for anyone who happened to have a cold, or a cough, or some disaster at home that prevented them from coming to work. And it did not stop Melanie treating her as her personal maid and calling for her at any time of the day or night, sometimes as late as midnight, and sometimes as early as five in the morning if she could not sleep and wanted someone to bring her tea.

'Your mother will never get over your betrayal of Edith, not coming back to see her in the last hours, you know that,' Alfred told Ottilie factually, at least once or twice a week, usually when he was about to hand her one of his neatly written lists of things to do.

Great Suite needs preparing for Mrs Ballantyne.

China in the drawing room cabinets needs washing, full complement of Victorian matching dinner plates, very valuable, be extra careful please and do not enlist any of the other maids to help you as they are liable to be careless.

So although Ottilie had been effectively frozen out by the staff she was still expected to deal with all the diplomatic problems concerning the running of them, those delicate, embarrassing problems with which Alfred did not care to deal, and Melanie could not be left to deal.

As Mrs Tomber, who couldn't care less who talked to whom just so long as the hotel was running along smooth lines, often remarked ruefully, 'For someone who was once a great beauty Mrs Cartaret has a tongue like a viper, and that's for sure, Miss Ottilie.'

After a while the silence started to become oppressive, so oppressive and finally so miserable that sometimes Ottilie would stop on the stairs leading up to the Great Suite – which during these dark days was hardly ever occupied except once a year by poor, mad Mrs Ballantyne in her strange-looking New Look 1948 clothes – and having paused for a minute, she would stare ahead to the sea, suddenly and crazily attracted to the idea of running down to the beach and throwing herself into the waves. With all the power of her imagination she would feel the waves closing over her, the dreadful cold reality of it, the weight of the water in her clothes, and then feel herself sinking into the dark water, feel the seaweed entangling her and finally see herself dragged out to sea, and oblivion, her body to be eaten by fishes, her soul committed for ever to dark despair.

But then she would remember her debt to the Cartarets for adopting her and bringing her to the Grand, her nursery specially done, her childhood filled with old people who spoilt her, Edith always helping her get over things, the staff in nicer days before Paris, when they did not disapprove of her, when they all laughed and joked with her, when they still liked her, and it would seem unfair to leave the Grand so suddenly, leave them all in the lurch. Most of all Edith would not approve, and Ottilie could imagine her shaking her head and saying, 'You don't want to cause misery, Miss Ottilie, do you?'

She still wrote to Mrs Le Martine, of course, but nowadays for some reason she heard even more rarely from her old friend. It was almost as if, Ottilie having written to tell her she had met Monsieur in Paris, Mrs Le Martine knew she could no longer pretend to be someone else in front of Ottilie, that now they both knew too much about each other to be able to have the jokes and the fun any more, that not even talking about 'Shah-nelle' suits and the newest fashions would be very amusing to either of them.

Yet Ottilie kept on writing to her mentor, keeping the tone as cheerful as Ottilie herself nowadays never seemed to feel, and holding all the while to the idea that the Grand was still its old self. That pretence too Ottilie kept up, even though she realized that Mrs Le Martine could not really believe in such a romantic notion any more.

As time crept by Paris seemed a century ago, and Ottilie could never hear a French accent or hear a street accordion or watch a French film without a depth of nostalgia which was not really in keeping with having spent only four weeks there. Again, to cure herself of her homesickness for those few weeks she took to writing letters to her acquaintances from that time. But, unlike Mrs Le Martine, Ottilie's American friends from the Parisian School of Cookery actually wrote back.

Their replies were so prompt, and so enthusiastic, Ottilie knew at once that they too felt the same nostalgia for those few carefree weeks they had spent together trying to master the secret of the omelette, trying to find out why a teaspoon of sugar in a vinaigrette dressing made all the difference to the taste of that same dressing.

Mrs Blandorf always ended her letters, 'Now you take care of yourself, dear, do you hear?'

'Sounds kind of oldish for a young girl at that hotel of yours, Ottilie!' Mrs Zeiger kept insisting in her letters, in between graphic descriptions in large black writing of how her *navarin de mouton* had gone down 'about as well as fried buffalo' with her guests at a recent winter dinner party.

Over the next eighteen months Ottilie began to realize that Mrs Zeigler was all too right. It *was* oldish at the Grand, and sometimes it seemed to Ottilie even a little macabre, what with Blackie going by in his uniform, now far too small, with his middle-aged face and his old-fashioned way of saluting, and his pillbox hat more suited to the page boy of nineteen he had been than to the venerable hall porter he had become.

Ottilie had never been to school and made friends of her own age. She had stayed in Paris in a middle-aged man's flat, she had been adopted by a couple who were already well into middle age, and now she was working alongside a staff most of whom were nearing retirement. As the months went by she sometimes felt so desperate to talk to someone nearer her own age it was difficult to stop herself rushing out into the street and collaring the nearest boy or girl and dragging them into the Grand for coffee or a drink. Lorcan she never saw except at Christmas. Sean she never heard from. Joseph she had seen in the magazine, but would never, she supposed, hear from again either. It was as if the early part of her life had never existed, as if she had never had brothers.

She went to bed with hands and feet throbbing from the work she had undertaken during the day. Sometimes she would wake up in the night, her heart beating too rapidly, and know that she was putting herself under too much strain, but be quite unable to work out how she could alter anything. If she did not do the work, who would? If she was not there to answer Melanie's calls for tea or coffee or a gin and tonic at all times the task would fall to Alfred, and he did not have his old energy any more. Sometimes just hearing him sigh so deeply was enough to send Ottilie scurrying away to try to work harder and longer than ever, just to try to make up to him for the sadness of the times, for the life that had departed from the hotel, for the twentieth century speeding by too quickly for him, for everything that he had known and loved going, for the old days disappearing never to come back.

And then suddenly it happened, or at least not 'it' but Philip.

If Blackie or Mrs Tomber had suggested to Ottilie that as she watched Philip walking into the foyer that morning she was watching a knight strolling into her life she would have believed them. For with his tall, blond, patrician looks, his just right faded sports jacket worn with a newly fashionable denim shirt and faded corduroys, his slip-on shoes, and his greatcoat with the military buttons that had once belonged to a great-uncle, he seemed no less.

'Philip.'

Ottilie said his name as factually as possible in case he had not come to look for her. He was actually leaning on the reception desk, his blond, thick, curly hair brushed back, laughing and teasing the receptionist who wore butterfly glasses with silver pieces set into them and was obviously becoming pink and flustered under the pressure of his attentions, but although Ottilie could see at once that he was a man as her eyes took him in all she could really see was the young boy after whom she had used to run through the woods as he attempted to call down owls, or who sat on her legs as she tried to tickle trout.

'Philip.'

As Philip heard her voice, he turned.

'Miss Ottilie Cartaret, I do declare.' Despite spending so much of their growing up times together, walking and fishing in the warm Cornish springs and summers, or, on rainy days, what Philip called 'mucking about in the house,' she had not seen Philip for several years. And now he was in the Army.

'You're home on leave.'

Philip looked behind him jokingly, pretending that he thought she was addressing someone else, and then turned back to Ottilie, saying, 'So I am.'

'It's really nice to see you again.'

She could not help sounding formal, but she felt so happy to see him it was difficult not to get what he in the old days of their childhood would have called 'soppy', and it did not seem to matter either if it was only for a few minutes before he went off to meet someone else in the restaurant, or the cocktail bar, because just seeing him was a burst of sunshine in her otherwise dreary day-in-day-out existence.

'I would hardly have known you,' Philip told her,

drawing her over to the other side of the foyer, well away from the receptionist. 'Are you well?'

As Ottilie looked at Philip she remembered that they had always enjoyed an unspoken closeness when they were growing up, as if in each other's company they could find solace against the pain they had both experienced. Whether it was playing with Ludlow, his tame hare, or sadly burying him, or arranging military battles with his old lead soldiers together, they had always been at ease, not needing to say very much, just understanding each other and being happy. So now it was not very surprising for Ottilie to see that Philip's eyes were full of concern. But he did not say 'My God you're so thin' or 'You look twenty-five not eighteen', he just looked down at her, and once he put his hand on her arm as if to steady her.

The words that he was thinking went, as always with Philip, unsaid, but what he actually did say was, 'Care to come to a party, Miss O? Constantia's back at Tredegar for all of two minutes, and after four seconds finds herself as bored as an unpicked raspberry. Needs must we give a party, needs must we ask the whole neighbourhood. She has a list as long as the kitchen table, which is very long indeed. I have a list as short as what Nurse used to call my pinkie and on it is only one name. Yours.'

If she had not known it would be such a dreadful thing to do, Ottilie would have burst into tears there and then. A party. People of her own age. Music. Dresses. Laughter.

'I should love to come to a party, Philip. If I can, but I'm not sure I'll be able to.'

'Of course you can come to a party, Cinders. You're not telling me you're previously engaged, or married with seven children already, are you?'

'Oh no, nothing like that,' Ottilie agreed hastily. 'Good heavens, no. What it is . . . What it is – it's here. It's sometimes very difficult to get time off from here.'

'Time off from here?' Philip looked round the empty foyer with feigned amazement and a patrician mockery.

'Time off from here,' he repeated. 'You're not a night nurse, or a surgeon needed for a brain operation. Of course you can have time off from catering to pampered guests. All the old trouts can do without you for one night, surely?'

'It's a bit difficult at the moment, particularly if it's a Saturday. Is it a Saturday, your party?'

'Yes, Ottilie, it is a Saturday, Ottilie, because that is the night when everyone from London is usually down, I think you'll find, Ottilie. Mondays are not good for parties, nor are Sundays. Saturdays we find fit the bill and then we can snore through the sermon in Sunday church, wop our roast beef, and fall into yet another recovery sleep.'

Philip's conversation mirrored a warm normality, reflecting as it did the basic acceptance that life could be fun, that behaving just slightly badly was good for you, that youth was for being young. Yet although his words were light and flippant they filled Ottilie with sadness, contrasting as they did so starkly with the kind of dialogue that was her everyday fare.

'*You are such a deep disappointment to me. When I think about it, really it was after you arrived that everything started to go so wrong. You were a mistake, I'm afraid. We should have left you where you were at that dingy little cottage with those brothers of yours.*'

'If it is a Saturday then you will never be allowed off, is that what you're saying?'

She had not actually said anything.

'It's very difficult,' Ottilie finally volunteered, dropping her voice, and quietly indicating for him to follow her out to the green sward in front of the hotel. 'You see, my mother, Mrs Cartaret, she is really very ill at times nowadays, with her nervous depressions, and my father is getting quite old, looking after her, the strain of this place. You know the sort of thing? And so it's very difficult for me to get away.'

212

Philip took Ottilie's hands in a very grown-up sort of way, in a way that made her realize at once that he must have already made love to girls. But having taken her hands he now looked down at them.

'Tut, tut, Miss Ottilie, what would Edith say to these? Not the hands of a lady, are they? Have we been leaving off our hand cream at night?'

The very idea of having enough time to put on hand cream at night made Ottilie smile suddenly, but looking up into Philip's eyes and remembering the happiness of running all over Tredegar with the Great Danes and pretending to be characters from some old book they were both reading, she heard herself say in a calm, accepting way, 'Edith's dead, you know, Philip. She died of a heart attack while I was in Paris. She had one, and then she had another, and then she died.'

'Well she would do, probably, after two,' Philip said, using his reasonable, unemotional and considered voice, the one he had always used when something not very nice, or very sad, had happened, but also when he wanted to make people laugh, or cheer them up.

Ottilie suddenly started to laugh, at the same time putting her hand over her mouth, feeling the sudden roughness of it, knowing that her eyes were underlined with tiredness, black patches which must make her laughing seem a little hysterical to an onlooker.

'Oh, Philip, you always were like that,' she gasped, half bent double. 'Edith loved you for it. She used to say "Mr Philip's so naughty with his gallows humour, really he is."'

'Listen, let's cut the cackle and face this thing head on, Carruthers. It's your mother who's going to be a pill about this, isn't it? She's the one who's going to be putting up the objections. So why don't I go to her and say "Mrs Cartaret, I know you want to do your best by us boys who are about to be posted abroad, and I happen to be one of them, so stop being such an old bag and let your daughter go to a party on a Saturday night for once." How about that? Should do the trick I should have thought.'

For one glorious moment Ottilie imagined the scene. She imagined Mrs Cartaret, gin glass in one hand, cigarette in the other. She imagined the tall, patrician figure of Philip Granville standing so tall and handsome in her sitting room, bringing a much needed breath of fresh air into it, making it seem as stuffy and as claustrophobic as it absolutely was, and it was wonderful. Then she remembered something else.

'It *would* be lovely, Philip, really it would, but it's impossible. You see if you go and ask her, she'll say yes, of course she will, but then she will throw a fit when the night comes, and I won't be able to leave anyway, so it's better to be realistic about it, really. And then there's my father. She takes it out of him so dreadfully if I do something I want to – when I went to Paris it was hell on wheels here, I believe. She even accused him of trying to get off with one of the Spanish girls. You know, she'll go that far, she really will.'

'In that case,' Philip said, after a short pause during which he frowned and gazed out to sea, 'in that case there is nothing for it but go AWOL.'

'Sorry?'

'Come to the party and to hell with the consequences. Spike your mother's drink, put too much gin in her martini, stick a sleeping pill in her Horlicks, do something, but come to the party. Or else.'

He started to walk off towards his car.

'Or else?' Ottilie called after his tall, fair-haired figure, his dark old-fashioned guards officer's coat with the wonderful swagger to the back. 'Or else?'

'Or else I will never speak to you again.'

'Really?'

'Really. You're dining with us first, by the way. We haven't farmed you out, don't worry. And Constantia says if you haven't a dress, she'll lend you one.'

214

'Oh, I have a dress, all right,' Ottilie called after him.

That was the one thing she did have, a dress, and what a dress.

Before she could resurrect the dress from where it was hidden at the back of her cupboard, carefully preserved like an Egyptian mummy in yards and yards of white cotton, Ottilie had to plan her escape. It was not easy, not on a Saturday night when even the Grand at St Elcombe attracted at least a dozen diners, and when her mother was quite likely to suddenly decide to make one of her rare appearances in the dining room, and when her father would pick himself up from his invoices and his receipts, from his carefully annotated accounts books, and put on winged collar and bow tie and descend to the dining room with measured tread, as in the old days when, it now seemed to Ottilie, an orchestra had always seemed to be playing and life had been one long party for the Cartarets and their staff.

She planned her Saturday night deception most carefully, and like a good criminal she based her plans most securely on the character of her victim. Her mother was currently what Philip would call 'screwy' in that she could not be relied upon for anything except to drive Ottilie and the staff as mad as herself. But if Ottilie could manage to persuade Melanie to dress up in one of her old dinner gowns and accompany Alfred to the dining room for dinner it would mean that for once she could be counted upon not to be at the other end of her extension line summoning Ottilie every few minutes until late into the evening.

'I'm too tired. Really, I don't feel like it, Ottilie,' Melanie moaned. Ottilie knew that she was by no means too tired, and it was far more likely that she would prefer to stay upstairs so that she could drink more than was possible if she was in the public rooms. She had put on a great deal of weight lately, but still looked very handsome, as handsome as a woman half her age. Ottilie had persuaded her father to buy her a new evening dress and present it as a surprise, a dress in her new, rounder size, but nevertheless a very expensive dress.

'Not too tired to open the parcel that has just arrived for you, surely?'

Ottilie knew that it was always best to use a soft coaxing voice with her when she was on her second or third gin of the morning. Anything more would bring on tantrums or one of those quick switches of mood that came from nowhere and so terrified even the oldest members of the staff.

The dress in the parcel was obviously expensive, but Melanie's expression as she took it out of its fresh tissue paper was that of a child torn between two moods. Part of her wanted to love it, because it was expensive and because Alfred had obviously chosen it with great care – new sizing, perfect cut, beautiful deep maroon which set off her blonde looks so well. The other part of her wanted to find fault with it, wanted to say 'It won't fit, it's the wrong colour, and besides Capucci is not really my designer' so that she could stay behind upstairs with her gin and not accompany her husband down for dinner, which would mean making an effort, thinking of someone else beside herself.

Somehow, by *not* asking her to try it on, by merely pointing out its beautiful cut, the loveliness of the colour, Ottilie was able to persuade her to try it on, so that when her mother finally emerged wearing it, it did seem for a few seconds to both of them that the old days had come back. She looked magnificent, and standing in front of the long mirror in her bedroom even Melanie was forced to recognize this.

'Shall I wear my diamond earrings with it?' she asked Ottilie that evening while Alfred, in white tie and tails, moved in and out of their suite.

'Oh, yes, your diamond earrings – they would be fine.'

Ottilie could hardly bring herself to say the words, or look at the costume jewellery to which Melanie was referring, hardly keep her eyes from straying towards anything else rather than watch her mother clipping on a pair of paste earrings, which nevertheless looked very fine on her.

'Are you ready, dear?'

Alfred was calling, and Melanie smiled at the sound of his voice, and her own lifted for the first time for years, and she called back, 'Yes, Alfred, I am coming, as soon as may be, darling.'

'They're playing our song, Melanie.'

This was an old joke of theirs and one that Ottilie remembered from the time when she had first arrived at the Grand, when she had first climbed what had then seemed to be so many very steep stairs to Melanie's suite, holding Edith's hand, and preparing to say 'goodnight and God bless' to her new mother and father.

But now it seemed to Ottilie, looking at them, that she would always remember them tonight, how handsome they both looked, and how devoted they seemed, with Alfred holding out his arm in the old way, and Melanie taking it with practised elegance, and the two of them making their way, slowly, oh so slowly, down the stairs as if they were stepping out to some music that only they could hear.

'And you, Ottilie, would you please follow?'

'I am afraid I have a terrible migraine. I must go and lie down.'

Alfred nodded. He didn't seem to care in the least.

'Oh, very well. How sad. It would have been nice. But still.'

They continued down the stairs, and Ottilie plunged off in the direction of her own suite, thinking only of how many minutes it would take her to dress, lock up, climb down the back stairs and thence onto the fire escape, and into her old Deux Chevaux to drive out to Tredegar in time for dinner.

She had already put on her nail varnish, toes and fingernails both, donned her undies and her sheer stockings and made up her face (but *not* put on her lipstick in case Melanie, who did not approve of her wearing it, noticed it) so that her transformation was practically instantaneous when she returned to her suite.

Just before she turned to see herself in the mirror, kicking the short train of the dress behind her, it occurred to Ottilie that she might no longer look as she remembered herself looking the night she went out with Monsieur to the Tour d'Argent, that although her hair was freshly washed and knotted in the classical manner in the nape of her neck, that although she had been careful to go to bed early the night before and to take a long bath, after all the long hours of labour she had been putting in, the dress might look ridiculous. She knew she had lost weight and that her appearance in the drab dress of her uniform, in flat shoes and black stockings, had actually shocked Philip, who only remembered her from the days when she was little Ottilie Cartaret, the pampered young girl who belonged to a successful hotel.

Certainly the dress did not cling with quite the same confidence as it had clung to her that wonderful night in Paris, but it was still the same exquisite cut, and although it might now be a little less tight-fitted it was still made up of the same iridescent silk, the Medici collar still framed her face, setting off her dark hair as precisely as a frame to a picture, and the train still whispered and swayed behind her as she rehearsed walking in the tall, high-heeled delicate evening sandals that Monsieur had chosen for her that memorable evening when it had seemed to both of them the whole restaurant was about to applaud as Ottilie swayed confidently towards their table watched admiringly by what seemed to be the whole of fashionable Paris.

Confident that she could still manage both the train and

218

the high-heeled shoes, Ottilie slipped them into a shoe bag and herself back into her flat work shoes and started for the door of her suite. Just in time she heard voices and knew that one of them belonged to Mrs Tomber. With second sight, and before the housekeeper had even started to put her pass key in the door, Ottilie fled back to her bathroom, and flung herself inside.

'Are you all right, Miss Ottilie?'

Ottilie acted out a groaning sound.

'Just a migraine, making me feel a bit sick, Mrs Tomber.'

'Madame wanted to know if you were all right. She wanted you downstairs with them, but I'll tell her you're still poorly.'

Seconds later she was gone, and happily it was Saturday night and she would soon be driving off in the opposite direction to that which Ottilie would be taking to Tredegar, off to stay with her sister for the weekend as she always did. To be safe Ottilie waited and listened, and then finally, heart in mouth, shoes in hand, she slipped out into the empty hotel corridor, and down the back stairs as planned until finally she climbed carefully down the outside fire escape and ran towards her second-hand, brown Deux Chevaux.

Of course it would not start, would it?

'*Come on, Oscar,*' she prayed as with each turn of the key the engine spluttered into life only to shudder back into silence. '*Come on, Oscar, come on!*' Finally she closed her eyes and for the first time for years, and to her immense shame because it would seem so trivial to someone else, she prayed, to Edith, to God, to Ma, far above her. '*Please!*'

They must have heard her for seconds later, with what seemed to Ottilie to be a Gallic shrug, Oscar her beloved but temperamental little convertible shuddered into life and lurched forward towards Tredegar, towards dinner, towards what seemed suddenly to be life and love.

219

Unaccountably, just for a second, when she at last arrived at Tredegar Ottilie's confidence ran out and she became a prey to nerves. She had never before been to a grand occasion, and she suddenly felt not excited but nervous, cold and shivery and wondering if she could possibly go through with an evening spent with the fashionable and the beautiful.

She felt too nervous to join the other women and their black-tie evening-dressed partners who were even now following each other down the wide path leading to the great front door. For Ottilie, unlike all the confident figures walking ahead of her, was without a partner, and for a moment it seemed to her that she always would be, and that the women walking ahead of their men with that slow solemn walk that derives from coping with the length of one's evening dress would all ignore her. Doubtless the men would too. Having at last arrived, against all the odds, at Tredegar all Ottilie could now visualize was passing the dinner party that lay ahead of the dance ignored and in silence. She saw that she was likely to be some sort of pathetic wallflower decorating the sides of the ballroom while everyone else danced the night away in the company of people who, while they might be all too well known to them, would be completely unknown to Miss Ottilie Cartaret.

That she should experience such feelings was not really very surprising, particularly since she had not visited Tredegar for such an age. In fact, now that she was here at last it seemed to her that she had hardly known it, she had forgotten so much. Forgotten that there were two large eagles with spread wings at the gates, and that the drive was over a mile long but not dark and overcrowded with rhododendrons as were so many Cornish drives. The loveliness of Tredegar's Elizabethan façade was easily seen long before the visitor started to tread the long path that led up to the old oak door, which meant that Ottilie, along with the evening's other visitors, could see just how beautiful Tredegar was long before they arrived. Set in perfectly rolled green lawns and surrounded by walled gardens with terraces that reached down to the same sea that ran up below her window at the Grand, Tredegar was the very image of the perfect English country house to which an Englishman dreams of returning when abroad.

As she parked her car, straightened her dress, and wrapped herself around in an old Twenties evening cloak that she had discovered in the attic of the Grand, Ottilie had not been able to stop herself from thinking how strange it was that despite the fact that she was now grown up, the house should succeed in actually looking larger than when she was last there, when she herself had been considerably younger. It should seem smaller, as childhood places do when a person grows up.

Or it might be that having only visited Tredegar in order to play soldiers or feed Ludlow dinner carrots smuggled from the kitchens at the Grand she had quite simply not truly noticed its contained beauty, its quiet grandeur. Perhaps also she had always been too busy looking forward to seeing Philip, or fretting that Edith was driving too slowly so that the all too precious minutes of playtime would soon be gone and Edith would be returning with her to the hotel long before Ottilie had time to tell Philip everything that she knew he would like to hear. About the old general in Room Six who on hearing from Ottilie of Philip's military interests was planning to send him a whole other set of Victorian lead soldiers. About Blue Lady in her strange New Look 1948 clothes back on her annual visit and still talking to the empty chair. About Blackie's new friend who had taught Ottilie to whistle through her fingers. Philip had always loved to hear about all their eccentric guests. He had particularly loved to encourage Ottilie to mimic them, saying over and over again, 'Oh, but that's brilliant' and sometimes, she remembered him sitting doubled over with laughter at

Ottilie's efforts to entertain him with her imitations of people at the Grand.

Now Ottilie paused on the threshold of the old house. Ahead lay the great reception hall filling up with guests, behind her lay the past when she had used to love to fling herself through the doors to find the Great Danes with their strange yellow eyes. For a second it seemed to her that she was looking backward, and then she turned and looked forward and there was Philip, and the moment he saw Ottilie his face lit up just as it had used to do when she would arrive in her dresses with the lace collars and the smocking that Edith spent all summer sewing. But this evening they were separated from each other by the crowd of other arrivals and anyway Constantia was walking towards Ottilie, her hand held out in greeting.

'See you back down here,' Philip called up to Ottilie as she followed his sister up the old polished wooden stairs from above which his elegant ancestors looked calmly from their portraits. Ottilie just had time to smile down at him before turning the corner of the staircase.

As Ottilie followed Constantia up to her bedroom to leave her cloak she could see Philip chatting animatedly below her to some new and stylish arrival, and suddenly it seemed to her that every girl in the room was looking more beautiful than she herself could possibly look and that Philip would want to sit next to them rather than her, and she could not blame him in the least.

'Ottilie Cartaret.'

Constantia, who was now a tall, slender blonde with the face of an angel but blue eyes that looked out at the world with the hard stare of an eagle, smiled at Ottilie in her dressing mirror, and then lit a cigarette.

'How dare you?' she murmured. 'How dare you look better than the rest of us, Ottilie Cartaret, and whom may I ask did you persuade to buy you that dress? St Laurent, is it?'

Ottilie, who had spent the previous forty-eight hours

222

rubbing cream into her hands and practising putting up her hair so that it did not look what Mrs Cartaret always called 'provincial', turned and without thinking said, 'Oh no, not St Laurent – Balenciaga. It was given to me by a Frenchman in Paris. He supplied the silk to make it.'

'My, my,' Constantia said, drawing on her cigarette, 'and what on earth did you do to get him to give you that, may I ask? No, don't tell me, just follow me downstairs, and in my turn I will not say a word to Philip, I promise.'

Two seconds later and Ottilie realized that it was already too late, much too late to see that as soon as she could possibly do so, Constantia would go straight to Philip and tell him that Ottilie was wearing a couture dress bought for her by 'some strange Frenchman'.

But since what was done was done, Ottilie tried to put this thought from her and concentrate instead on walking down the slippery polished wooden stairs with her head held high and her hips pushed forward a little in the way that Monsieur had approved that evening in Paris. ('All the models walk this way, Ottilie, a little exaggerating, you know? It makes the dress move better, huh?')

But as she followed Constantia into the great hall below the thought persisted, and she just knew from the haughty look that Constantia's eagle eyes had given her that she had made a really terrible mistake in telling Philip's sister that she had been given the dress by a Frenchman in Paris. Unwittingly she had made herself sound as if she was what Edith would sometimes murmur when reading about someone in a newspaper, that they were 'used goods', and nothing she could now say could make up for it.

Once downstairs, perhaps because he came straight to her side, Ottilie suddenly understood that the party was really being given by Philip for her, so that they would meet again, and had nothing whatsoever to do with Constantia's being bored at the weekend. The moment she walked towards Philip, the high Medici collar of her shimmering tight silk dress framing her face, was a

223

moment that she would always remember, and she knew that somehow she could not put a foot wrong, and that every man in the room was looking at her and mentally making a note to dance with her later, and that Edith would be proud of how she looked.

Dinner was laid in the cellars of the house, so that, freeing the main reception hall and drawing rooms for the band and the dancing later, the guests descended to cellars lit only by candles and set about with three large dark purple clothed tables and pink flowers. While waiters in knee breeches served the food and the wines, a trio of violins and a cello played while the guests ate and talked.

Ottilie knew all too well about the complications that could arise from the placing of guests at dinner, the sometimes insuperable difficulties of pleasing everyone at once. Tonight the mixture of guests were a few from well-known local families and many others from the kind of London circle that would not take kindly to being placed down the table, so when Philip passed her murmuring, 'You're beside me, Miss Cartaret,' Ottilie was hard put to it not to turn and say, 'That's not quite right.'

Nevertheless she gave him a questioning look which was countered by the laughing expression in his eyes as he personally pulled out her chair, looking across at Constantia with one of his raised-eyebrowed looks which said, 'You're surely not thinking of going to do something about this, are you?'

All at once from their exchange of looks as she sat down on his right Ottilie realized that Philip had changed the names on the dinner cards in front of them, and that Constantia would be furious. Suddenly they were not children in any way at all any more, and Tredegar was not a game of Monopoly where Philip and Constantia would inevitably end up throwing the board at each other. Philip was a man, and a man at ease in his ancestral home. It was his house, and not Constantia's, and by putting Ottilie on his right, he had asserted his ownership.

As he sat down beside her Ottilie smiled mischievously, and in a second she recognized that they were still both running away from Constantia, as they had always used to do, because she only ever seemed to want to play whist or canasta even on the hottest days, while Philip and Ottilie wanted to play imaginary games where they dressed up. Games like 'King Arthur' who was said to come from Cornwall and about whom they were both obsessed, or best of all a game they just called 'Beau Geste' which was joyous because it took so long and involved playing with things of which Edith would never approve like matches and swords taken from Tredegar's walls and smuggled out to the garden.

From that moment on, although she could see that all the other girls at their table were pretty – some of them to her mind a great deal prettier than she was herself – nevertheless Ottilie knew that Philip was only thinking about her, and that he might be talking to someone else but in reality he was looking at Ottilie's dark hair and the way the line of the dress showed off her figure, and the silk of the dress that shimmered and moved in the light of the candles. What she had not anticipated, would never have thought to expect of Philip, was that at the end of dinner, as the ladies left the table to follow Constantia out of the room in the traditional British way, he would slip her a note.

Before the ever marshalling Constantia could see it, Ottilie had slipped the note up the sleeve of her dress. Upstairs, while all the other girls powdered their noses and talked about things she knew nothing about – like going to a Beatles concert, and London, and hunting with the Beaufort – Ottilie turned and looked at the scrap of paper.

Meet me by the boat when the lights go down and the candles are lit.

Ottilie smiled. She knew just where the boat was, by the little lake where they had loved to play, Ottilie pushing Philip laid out in Arthurian clothes, while carefully holding on to a rope, herself dressed as Guinevere, a sword set in the middle of the lake, tied to an old stick.

'I don't know what you did to get that dress, Ottilie, but it is certainly the hit of the evening,' Constantia murmured, as once more brushed and repowdered, the girls made their way down the old polished oak staircase.

She said this just as Ottilie saw Philip coming towards her across the reception hall, but as the music started and they began to dance, it was some long while before Ottilie could let go of the feeling that Constantia had reached out and scratched a nail down the side of her cheek.

'Is something the matter?'

Ottilie smiled and shook her head. How could there be anything the matter? She was dancing with Philip at Tredegar on a beautiful evening and soon they would be meeting, just like in the old days, by the boat, but this time under cover of darkness, as the moon crept up, and the clear Cornish skies sparkled with far-flung stars.

As they danced she knew for certain that they were suddenly and obviously no longer pals, but passionately and urgently in love, and in the kind of way that makes just waiting for the music to start so that you can touch each other seem to take a century, and walking towards the dining room together for a glass of wine the most intimate act of your life. It was impossible to ignore. Ottilie knew now what she had probably known from the moment she saw Philip standing in the foyer of the hotel, that she was in love with him and that it was quite possible that he was in love with her.

She knew it from the way that Philip was not looking at her, and from the way that she was not looking at him. And suddenly and frighteningly it seemed that nothing else in her life had mattered at all up until then.

'I must do my duty as host,' he murmured as they parted after one brief dance, knowing, excitedly, that they were soon to meet again by the boat, at the lakeside.

It might have seemed an age before they would meet

again, under the dark skies in a garden as brilliantly lit by the moon as any stage, but because Ottilie sensed joy to come she found that the time flew, and when eventually the lights dimmed and the music slowed to a blues number, and the farm workers from Tredegar solemnly dressed in their knee breeches bore the candelabra into the Great Hall, Ottilie knew that the time had come to slip away.

Finding her way across the garden to the sound of the sea in the distance was romantic in itself, and yet part of her wondered mischievously if any other couples might have made the same arrangement and she would find herself hurrying towards the wrong man, someone to whom she would call 'Is that you?' only to be answered by the wrong voice.

In the event it was he who arrived late, calling, 'Ottilie? Ottilie?'

To which she answered as she had always done, 'Have you remembered the matches?'

'You bet!'

Ottilie smiled as he half ran down to where she was standing. He was carrying a large packed basket.

'Let's go out in the boat.'

He stepped in first, tucking the basket under the seat, and she followed him carefully holding up the skirts of her precious dress. He rowed out to the island, and having dragged the boat a little way up the beach, he held out his hand to her.

'Cigarette?'

Ottilie looked at the packet and then up at Philip.

He had always smoked from when they were quite young and she never had, and nothing he had said could ever persuade her to try one, but now was different, now she was grown up.

'What a revolting taste! Ugh!'

She wrinkled her nose as he spread his evening jacket on the ground and they sat down on it for a few minutes,

227

Ottilie trying not to cough as she gallantly applied herself to the art of puffing on a tipped cigarette.

'If you persist, in the open air, after a while you'll find it makes you delightfully giddy,' Philip instructed her as he took the bottle of wine and two glasses that he had brought in the large basket together with a strange-looking plastic box and some records.

'Taken together with some of this you will feel quite fried!'

'Mmm.' Ottilie took a good sip of her wine to take away the taste of the cigarettes, and in no time at all she knew what he meant.

'Guess what I left here earlier?'

'Simply can't.'

Philip stood up and went to the base of a small weeping willow.

'Beau Geste? Remember our favourite game?'

He held out a package. Inside was a small wooden boat.

'Yes, but has it got a figure in it?'

Ottilie had always been anxious that everything to do with their games should be correct, and for a second she found that it was eight years ago and it mattered just as much as it always did that they should be burning the boat with a figure in it.

Philip held up a small figure. 'Satisfied?'

'OK.'

She stood up.

'Matches?'

She took them from him as he placed the boat on the water and then striking the match she handed it to him.

'You've cheated and put petrol in!' she accused him as the boat caught fire all too readily, bobbing up and down on the lake as Philip pushed it away from them. Philip nodded but did not smile. Instead, as they stood closer and closer together watching the little scene they had re-created, he took hold of her cool hand with his warm one and held it close, so close that after only a few seconds just holding hands became more intimate than any kisses, which when the time came made kissing each other even easier.

And how they kissed, but only after Philip had set out a small plastic portable gramophone, and an LP of Frank Sinatra songs to which they solemnly danced, cheek to cheek, round and round 'their island'.

'We've always loved each other, haven't we, Ottilie?'

Ottilie smiled. 'I suppose we have,' she agreed, letting go of him a little and smiling up at him, happy and relieved that she had liked being kissed. 'Oh, Philip, isn't it wonderful, just for a few hours to be able to forget about everything? The Army, guns, people, the hotel, everything, and just make love to music?'

'It's more wonderful than I could even imagine.'

'Let's always meet here and forget about everything and everyone, all our lives, do let's, Philip?' Ottilie asked, her voice suddenly urgent with the passion to escape, always.

'Of course! All our lives we will meet here, always, and forget everything!'

As they danced and started tentatively to touch each other between the kissing, in the excitement it was inevitable that Ottilie would forget that she had to be back in St Elcombe before the staff were up.

Twelve

It was dawn of an early, early summer morning which sometimes, if the air is cool enough, could almost be mistaken for late afternoon until warm toes touch cold grass, as Ottilie's did, and the shock of the wet, dewy, early damp around feet that have been dancing and walking all the long evening seemed to spring up into her head and clear her mind, and she suddenly knew that something was up.

There was not a great deal to go on, of course, just that strange feeling that she was being watched, but because it was late dawn there were no lights, and because there were no lights she couldn't be completely sure. The feeling was there though, and so strongly that even just looking up it seemed to her that she could feel eyes watching her. As she put her feet on the first rungs of the fire escape she realized that she had started to pray that she was wrong, but even as she prayed she knew that it was too late.

Silence she had been used to, silence as she walked into a room, silence as she picked up some required domestic item and then turned on her heel and walked out again. Silence as a couple of members of the staff saw her approaching, then the sound of conversation starting up once more, beginning always with a little conspiratorial laughter, but now as she retraced the route that she had taken earlier in the evening, she knew that something was wrong, that they were on to her, and it was simply a question of where they were, and where they were not.

They were not on the back stairs that led up from the

fire escape, they were not behind the pass doors that led into the main corridor of the hotel, and they were not in or around the reception areas that she trod through, evening shoes still for some reason in her hand, stockings tucked into her evening bag, her freshly made up lips tense with expectation, because she knew, she just knew that something was up.

All right, there were no lights and no sound of voices, and everything was exactly as it had been when she passed it on the way out to the party at Tredegar. The flower arrangements that she had done the previous day were still in place, and the carpets whose vacuuming she had supervised were still immaculate, yet she knew, absolutely, that they were around somewhere, and they were waiting for her. It was now just simply a question of where.

At last she saw the safety of her suite ahead. Its door closed, its lights still burning as she had left them to slip off to Tredegar, to laughter, to music, to dancing and to Philip. Seeing the door, and that thin seam of light under it, welcoming her, was reassuring. She had come this far without seeing anyone, perhaps after all she was wrong?

She relaxed. Her hand reached out for the door handle and she let out a quiet little sigh of relief, but before she could turn the handle it had turned for her and standing illuminated in front of her were her parents, and their faces were bleak with whitened fury, and her father although standing and holding on to the side of her sofa was swaying, looking to Ottilie's bewildered eyes puffed up with hatred at the sight of what was in front of him, a young woman with her evening shoes in one hand, beautiful silk dress shimmering, the Medici collar framing a freshly lipsticked face, eyes now over-large with fright.

'So.'

He could hardly speak, so great was his fury, and his fury was the more terrifying coming as it did from a man who prided himself on his sense of control. Anger was not something to which Ottilie had ever seen Alfred give in before.

'So. You are home at last.'

'No longer home, Alfred,' Melanie promptly interrupted him. 'No longer, not any more, not now. Remember what we said, Alfred.'

All at once it was the look that came into Melanie's eyes that told all, more than the triumph in her voice, more than the feeling that she could not wait to get rid of Ottilie now that she was grown up and wanted to go to parties and dance the night away with young men like Philip Granville.

The long days when only Mrs Tomber the housekeeper would speak to Ottilie. The campaign of silence continuing day after wretched day, week after relentless week, was at last all confirmed as Melanie's doing. Ottilie could see that now very clearly from the enjoyment reflected in her eyes. At last Ottilie knew for absolutely certain to whom she owed the torture of the last eighteen months. She owed it to the woman who had adopted her so enthusiastically, who had taken her in and given her a palace called the Grand Hotel in which to live, but who now loathed her for growing up and becoming an adult.

'Yes,' Alfred agreed, his own voice still trembling from emotion. 'Your mother is right, this cannot still be your home, not any longer. You can no longer call us your parents, not now.'

Ottilie could hear the sound of her heart beating, literally thumping in her ears, and in this raised state of extreme fright it seemed to her that she could see herself from above, as if she was her own ghost, watch herself in her evening gown standing at the door, and she could see her father and mother standing opposite her pale but magnificently virtuous in their fury, and yet she could not make any sense at all of what she saw. Not that is until her father threw a beautiful, hand-marbled cardboard folder towards her.

'I can explain everything,' Ottilie told them quietly as she realized that it was not the fact that she had deceived them to go dancing at Tredegar that had made them so furious, not fear for her safety that had brought them to this pitch of bitter anger, but what lay hidden in the folder. 'Really, I can.'

'There is nothing to explain, nothing at all. We can all see what you were up to in Paris now, we can all see how you spent your time, and since you made your choice there, you must allow us to make our choice here.'

'This was done from Monsieur's imagination, really it was.'

'Hah!'

Ottilie looked across at Melanie, momentarily amazed. She had never seriously imagined that anyone really did make sounds like 'Hah!' Sounds like that were so ridiculous.

'You posed for this. It is perfectly obvious that you posed for this,' Alfred stated, as a fact, and then, looking down at the folder, he sighed. After a few seconds the normally cool quality of his voice returned and he went on, 'You see, we cannot possibly continue keeping you here if this is how you go on. You must see that. It is really not at all possible. You will have to go.'

He was giving her the sack, dismissing her from her position as his daughter in much the same way that he would dismiss one of the maids.

'I – I don't understand.'

'You will,' said Melanie, and she appeared to be greatly relishing the grim nature of what she already knew her husband was about to say. 'Just listen to your father.'

'You will pack your bags, now.' Alfred turned and looked round the room. 'You may take only those things that belong to you, nothing else. And we never want to hear from you again, you understand? Never again.'

'But you must listen. Please, Pappa. Mamma . . .'

Ottilie heard herself begging and hated herself for it, because it was all so ridiculous.

'I – I did not pose for this. What happened was that Monsieur saw me one evening when he arrived unexpectedly at the apartment, from Lyon, and – and – and I was in a towel, two towels actually, my hair wrapped in one and my body in the other.'

Melanie turned her head away for a second in disgust at the word 'body'. She never liked words like that. Nevertheless Ottilie continued, determined to be brave, or if she wasn't particularly brave she must at least be honest.

'It was a matter of a few seconds, really. I didn't know that he was arriving in Paris that night. All that Mrs Le Martine had said was that I would have the apartment to myself because the family hardly ever used it – it was a business flat – and – and I could use it as I wished because the children were all grown up and in America, and the father lived in Lyon. So that's what I did. Even after I met him that once I never saw him again, because he was always up so early for business and then out all day until very late. So we didn't meet again until my last night, really, not at all, when he took me to dinner, and – he loaned and then gave me this dress, and these shoes, and that was it, really, until we parted when he gave me this drawing. He's a Sunday painter, you see, you know how so many Frenchmen are? And he had been so amused by our meeting, because I looked so surprised at seeing him I think, that he went away and did this drawing from memory. Except that he removed the towel from my bo— he drew me without the towel I had on, but really, I promise you, it was entirely from his imagination.'

'You see?' Melanie turned to her husband. 'You see? What did I tell you? She is incapable of telling the truth. And no good will come of her staying here in the hotel where she will be nothing but a bad influence on the staff. You have turned out to be no good at all, Ottilie. You must go. We cannot have you here any longer.'

'But I did not pose for this, I tell you, I really didn't.'

'Are you so stupid that you think I am that stupid?'

235

Alfred asked Ottilie, his voice starting to tremble with fury once more.

He picked up the marbled folder containing the drawing and with fingers that shook with the righteous indignation he was obviously feeling he undid the navy blue tapes that held it together. Carefully, his eyes narrowed with real dislike, he turned the beautiful drawing towards Ottilie and threw it on the table in front of her. 'Do you honestly imagine that I can believe you when you say that you never posed like that? Who do you think we imagined this is, or who are we supposed to think it is? Mrs Tomber? Imagination indeed. I might have forgiven you for posing for it more easily than I can forgive you for thinking me such a fool as to believe you did not.'

In the early morning light, the drawing suddenly looked, to Ottilie's eyes anyway, really beautiful, more beautiful than when she had first seen it in the early morning Parisian light, when she had laughed out loud when she realized what naughty Monsieur had done, how he must have remembered exactly how Ottilie looked the moment they first bumped into each other that evening when Ottilie had emerged from the bathroom completely unaware of his sudden arrival at the flat.

Now that Ottilie was faced with it so suddenly it occurred to her that he must have captured her expression of surprise most precisely, that this must have been exactly how she had looked to him when she had bounced out of the bathroom wrapped only in a towel. That was the genius of the drawing, really, the way he had contrasted the youthful firmness of her breasts and body with the surprise in her eyes. He had drawn the startled look from life and had added the confident nudity for contrast, and the effect was really very lovely because it gave the drawing an innocence, an enjoyment in the moment, the towel dropped behind, her body warm and rounded from its recent bath.

Standing opposite the contemptuous gaze of her

adopted parents Ottilie found that she could recall that delightful moment precisely, that it came back to her most vividly – Monsieur standing outside in the dark of the corridor, and Ottilie looking across at him, surprised but unafraid. And how they had both smiled, because it was one of those delightful and sensuous moments when a man and a young girl encounter each other, she without a stitch on under her bath towel, he fresh from the railway station still in his travelling clothes.

Ottilie looked up from the drawing, her eyes going first to Alfred's face with its five o'clock shadow and its tired middle-aged hue, and moving to Melanie's. Her lipstick had worn off and her hair, Ottilie noticed for the first time, was turning yellow in front from the smoke of her cigarettes.

'As a matter of fact,' she said slowly, 'although I did not pose for this, if I had posed for it – to be honest, I should be very proud. Because as a matter of fact I think this is a very beautiful drawing, and there surely can't be anything wrong in adding to the beauty of this world?'

There, it was out! Her other self, the one that she had used to let out when as a child she went upstairs and was sick with laughter in the bathroom after she had imagined putting an old hat under the lid of the big silver salver that normally held the roast beef, the one that imagined springing out and frightening old ladies as they helped themselves from the dessert trolley.

A short, stupefied silence followed Ottilie's statement, and then Alfred shook his head and sighed heavily, a sigh that said, 'You are beyond the pale, a lost soul, I cannot help you now.'

'See? I told you! I told you, didn't I?'

As his wife's words burst from her Alfred turned away, openly disgusted with Ottilie and obviously agreeing with his wife.

'No, really, I can't help you any more,' he said, walking towards the door, closely followed by his wife. 'I cannot

237

help you any more, even if I wanted to. There is nothing more we can do for you. Pack up your things and go, please. And make sure you are gone as soon as possible so as not to upset the staff.'

Melanie turned at the door. For some reason best known to herself she seemed to be enjoying the moment.

'I shall send Mrs Tomber to you to make sure that you pack only what is yours,' she told Ottilie, and for the first time Ottilie really felt the impact of her distrust. Now it seemed she did not even trust Ottilie not to steal.

A quarter of an hour or so later poor Mrs Tomber came hurrying in, still in her dressing gown. Her large eyes filled with tears when she saw that Ottilie had packed all her clothes and was already tying up the remains of her things in brown paper and string, that the wall was bare of her few small pictures, and the hairbrush and comb were gone from the top of the chest of drawers. Her teddy bear was no longer in the window and her summer straw was not hanging in its usual place on a hook above her bed but was tied to the side of her suitcase.

'Oh, Miss Ottilie, I never thought it would come to this,' she said, and she made a sound like a sob while pressing a fist to her mouth. 'I feel it's all my fault, really I do, for coming back early from my sister's. She had the 'flu, you see, and I didn't want to catch it because it always does go straight to my chest. So I was back in my room early and then I thought rather than just sit there watching telly I'd go downstairs and help. And Mrs Cartaret, and Mr Cartaret, they were downstairs all evening for once, laughing and smiling. They were in ever such a happy mood. But on the way up they met me, and they said, "Oh, Tomber, go along and fetch Miss Ottilie and tell her to come to our suite for a nightcap, would you?" Forgetting of course that you had a headache. But of course I didn't dare say anything to them, because you know your mother, she doesn't like people saying things to her that she doesn't want to hear.

'So anyway, I came along here, and – and I opened the door with my pass key, and in I came, and when I couldn't find you I'm afraid I raised the alarm, thinking something must have perhaps happened to you. And everyone came here – least Mr and Mrs C came, and they went through all your things, in case you had run off again to Paris or something. They opened everything. They even read your diary, not that it had much in it they said, but then, well, they found that thing – you know, that drawing – and, well, after that they insisted on staying here until you returned. They were set on it for some reason. Frankly, I told them that – that thing was probably just a sudent joke. I know our son had things like that when he was studying.

'They wanted to call the police, but I begged them not to. I said I thought you was probably just out dancing like any other girl your age – just a normal young girl – but once they found that drawing, well, that was it. They turned, they really turned, and they said things I never thought to hear respectable people saying, and it seemed to me that they were exaggerating for some sort of effect, you know the way people can once they've had too many drinks? But I never thought they'd go through with turning on you the way they have, never. This place won't be the same without you, Miss Ottilie, really it won't. Good heavens, you've worked your fingers to the bone here. I shall miss you so much!'

Ottilie nodded at the string for Mrs Tomber to put her finger on the middle so that she could tie a tight knot around the parcel she was making.

'As a matter of fact, Mrs Tomber,' she told the housekeeper, 'I think you're wrong. This place will be quite the same without me.' She looked round, giving the suite where she had grown up a last brave glance before she picked up both her brown paper parcels and placed the string round her neck so that they hung on either side of her shoulders. 'As a matter of fact I think you will find that this whole place, without any doubt at all, will be much better off without me.'

Mrs Tomber shook her head in disbelief, yet Ottilie could see that part of her disbelief was based on Ottilie's determined expression. Mrs Tomber could see from the look on Ottilie's face that not only did she now feel no regret at leaving, but nothing would stop her from going.

'Let's face it, Mrs Tomber, lately the Grand hasn't had much of an atmosphere – at least, not a happy one, not for me these last eighteen months, with no-one speaking to me, and all that sort of thing. Just think what a strain it must have been for them all, for all the staff, to shut up as soon as they saw me. Now they will be able to talk nineteen to the dozen as much as they like. No-one here really likes me, you know, I realize that now. Not really, not like a real friend. I can see now that all these years they just pretended, because I was young and because I was meant to be the daughter of the Cartarets, but they can't have really liked me or they wouldn't have sent me to Coventry for so long, would they?'

'Don't say that, Miss Ottilie, that's not true. Everyone liked you.'

'No, Mrs Tomber, I'm afraid they didn't,' Ottilie told her firmly. 'Take this last year. No-one's bothered to speak to me, no-one even gave me a card at Christmas. I pretended I didn't mind, but in the end you do, you know. I know it was wrong of me not to open that letter from my father saying that Edith had had a heart attack, of course it was, but I would have come back had I known Edith was ill, I really would.'

Mrs Tomber put out a hand, either to touch her arm or pat her back, Ottilie could not have said which, because she promptly stepped back, away from the housekeeper. She did not want sympathy any more, not Mrs Tomber's, not anyone's, she just wanted to get out of the hotel, through the old-fashioned glass doors and down the green sward in front of the hotel, and out onto the road, and away, for ever.

'Edith would not have wanted you to come back from abroad, Miss Ottilie, not if she was dying. She liked the idea of you being in Paris and dancing and having fun. Edith wanted you to have the life she never had. She wanted you to have gentlemen friends, and beautiful clothes and dancing and restaurants, and she told me so more than once, I can tell you. She thought it was wonderful, you being in Paris. It was only Mr and Mrs Cartaret who wanted you home, but not because of Edith, Miss Ottilie, because they missed you helping me run the place and because Mrs C was jealous of that Roseanna who stood in for you, thinking all the time that Mr Cartaret was giving her the eye, if you know what I mean, the way older women always do.'

Ottilie nodded. She did know what Mrs Tomber meant, but in the event it did not really matter. The fact was that she knew she was leaving the Grand for good, and the moment had come. She would once more be quite alone, just as she had been after Ma's funeral when Lorcan had told her that he was passing her on to the Cartarets, and she was lucky, and must not cry.

Ottilie put out her hand. Speaking in a formal voice such as she might use to someone whom they had just hired for the season, she said, 'Thank you very much, Mrs Tomber, for helping me pack, and for being the only person to talk to me these few months. If I had not had you to talk to I think I really might have killed myself—'

'Young people don't kill themselves, Miss Ottilie.'

'Oh but they do, Mrs Tomber. Anyway, your kindness saved me from doing anything too drastic all during these last dreary sad months,' she added, and she smiled.

Mrs Tomber seemed at first stunned by her honesty, and then uncertain as to what to do, but after a second she too put out her hand and slowly shook Ottilie's, pumping it up and down without saying anything, obviously afraid

241

to speak in case she became tearful. Ottilie understood this and shook her hand one extra time before letting it go.

'It will be all right,' she reassured the housekeeper. 'You'll see. In the end everything usually turns out all right, I find, if only because it stops.'

She headed for the front stairs, and right down the middle of them too, because this time she was not going to sneak out the back way and down the fire escape as she had a few hours earlier. She bumped and pushed her suitcases past all those same flower arrangements, down to the ground floor where she eventually passed Blackie who was up early as usual but still intent on ignoring Ottilie.

Ottilie struggled across the reception area, past his avoiding eyes as he bolted into his cubby hole with his plate of cakes and mug of tea, leaving her to bump her way, bit by wretched bit, suitcases in both hands, brown paper parcels hanging round her neck on a string, towards the glass doors which overlooked the green sward at the front of the hotel.

Poor old Blackie, Ottilie thought, as she puffed and panted towards the old-fashioned gold-decorated glass doors, and then she stopped, and pushed her suitcases through the doors into the clean, fresh air outside. Then she turned back into the hotel and trod swiftly back across the old-fashioned red carpet, beneath the large Edwardian glass chandelier, to where Blackie was reading his *Daily Mirror* in his cubby hole beside the lifts.

'Goodbye, Blackie. I've come to say goodbye to you. I'm leaving here after twelve years,' she said, curious as to what he might or might not deign to say to her. Whether after all these weeks of contemptuous silence he would now break his unyielding attitude and speak to her.

But Blackie said nothing, merely holding the newspaper in front of his face, pretending to read, as if she had not spoken, or mentioned that she was leaving. Ottilie waited a few long seconds and then reaching forward she pulled the wretched newspaper from his hands, holding it behind her back as she confronted him.

'Get to your feet!' she commanded, and now it was her eyes that were filled with fury. He stared at her in amazement. 'Get to your feet,' she said again. 'At once!' Being Blackie he did no such thing, of course, but Ottilie saw with some satisfaction that he was starting to pale under the impact of her rage. 'I have had quite enough of you and your nasty ways, you contemptible old bastard. All these years when I was growing up, what did you ever do for me? Nothing. And what did I do for you? Everything. All those times I covered for you when I was a little girl and you were round the corner ringing up to put a bet on when you should have been in your place, when I risked being beaten by my mother because I lied for you. And when my father wanted to sack you last year—'

'He never, Miss Ottilie—'

'Oh yes he did, he wanted to sack you all right. All that loyal service down the drain, Blackie. Imagine? He said you were too old. And too fat too, for front of hotel duties. But I put in a good word for you, Blackie, in fact I put in several good words for you, and that's why you're still here, putting on bets – and stealing cakes from the hotel kitchen,' Ottilie added with a look at the pile of Chef's home-made macaroons and madeleines that Blackie was in the middle of consuming. 'Well, it's the last time I ever do anything for you, Blackie, do you understand? The very last time, because you have not been thrown out this time, but I have, so from now on you won't have anyone to plead for you. No, nor cover up for you. From now on you're on your own, and here's a really good bet you should make, Blackie. The bet is – the bet is I bet you two to one on that without me to cover for you and make up for everything you don't do that you should, you'll be out of here by the end of the month. Want to take it, Blackie? Come on, take it – because it's a dead cert, I promise you.'

'You'll give me a co-ron-arary if you go on, Miss Ottilie!' Blackie gasped, putting a dramatic hand to his bulging chest.

'I won't, Blackie. You will.'

With that Ottilie turned and walked quickly back down the long red stretch of hotel carpet out into the air again. She carefully placed the parcel string round her neck and then, picking up her suitcases, she proceeded to struggle down the front steps until finally she was out into the road, where she paused, panting in the cool of the still early morning summer air, to rest and consider her future.

She had very little money, hardly more than thirty pounds in her bank account, thanks to having to work for her parents in return for her board and lodging and the use of her second-hand car. The car, of course! She still had the car that had been her seventeenth birthday present, that at least was a start. She could drive into St Elcombe, and although it was now the height of the season she felt sure she would be able to find work in one of the boarding houses, or in a pub on the edge of town somewhere. But first she must find lodgings.

It was white, it was neat, it was clean, and although there was no bath the basement flat she saw on that bright summer Sunday morning did at least have a basin and a lavatory en suite, and Ottilie reckoned that by standing in a washing-up bowl she could have a good scrub down, and no-one would be any the wiser.

'Well, there it is,' said the landlady, a tall respectable woman in a mock silk patterned dressing gown and pink feathered slippers. She looked Ottilie up and down, and perhaps since Ottilie had come looking for somewhere to stay at such an oddly early hour of the Lord's ordained day of rest, she added quickly, 'No gentlemen callers, no use of the telephone. Call box is on the corner of the street. No business to be conducted from the room at any time.'

'I understand.'

'Twenty pounds advance rent for the month,' she added and held out a hand for the money, but Ottilie only smiled at its lined palm and then looked up at her. 'I haven't had time to go to the bank, but if I may I will leave my things here, and go for some breakfast at the café by the station. On Monday I will go to the bank. Until then I can only give you five pounds on deposit, if that's all right with you?'

It obviously was not all right with her, but since the basement was obviously not something that everyone would want to rent the landlady finally nodded and turned on her heel. She closed the door behind her, and Ottilie listened attentively to the sound of her nylon slippers slip-slopping up the lino stairs to her own ground-floor rooms above.

'What a dreadful woman,' she told her suitcases as she humped them one by one into the bedroom area, which was behind a piece of cheap curtaining in the opposite corner of the room to where the basin and the lavatory stood. 'And how expensive!'

She sat down suddenly on the edge of the old iron bedstead. It was lucky she was slim and light because the mattress beneath her was as thin as she was. For a few seconds she leaned forward and rested her head in her hands, just to gain a bit of time, to pull herself together, to bat away the feeling of sudden despair that threatened to engulf her. After all, it was only a few hours earlier that she had been dancing in her beautiful dress with Philip at Tredegar, and now here she was, quite alone in the world, and seated on the edge of an old iron bedstead of the kind that most people throw out or drive to a rubbish dump.

For want of something to do, and because she knew that nothing except the pubs and the Station Café opened in St Elcombe on a Sunday, she started to unpack her teddy bear and her dressing gown from the brown paper packages that she and Mrs Tomber had so carefully parcelled up only a half hour before.

Ma had bought her the bear before they left Notting Hill. By coincidence he had been named 'Phil', his name coyly printed on one of those round pink and blue labels with which manufacturers sometimes decide to market their cuddly toys. Phil. Ottilie hugged him to her for a second, and then quickly put him down.

'My God. Phil.' Philip the man rather than Philip the bear was meant to be picking her up from the Grand and taking her out for a picnic lunch.

Ottilie pushed her suitcases under the bed and quickly washed her face, brushed her hair, and freshened herself generally. Then, leaping up the area steps two at a time, she started to bolt towards the telephone box on the corner. Luckily she had known Tredegar's telephone number off by heart since she was young and a privileged visitor. Unluckily, after the telephone had rung for some time, it was not Philip who answered it but Constantia.

As the money dropped, Ottilie knew at once that the last thing Constantia would want would be to pass on any message that she might wish to leave. In fact she was being so coldly polite it was quite obvious to both of them that she now hated Ottilie.

Unfortunately for Constantia, her manner was so chilling it served only to confirm what Ottilie had hoped but not been certain of until now, and that was that Philip really must be as much in love with her as Ottilie was with him. If that were not so Constantia would not be bothering to be so frigid and stand-offish. Consoling as this thought might be, it did not, on the other hand, help Ottilie to find Philip and tell him what had happened to her. She could not leave a message for him at the hotel either, unless she could get a message to Mrs Tomber by pretending to be her sister?

'Maureen – this is Joy.'

It was a passable imitation of Mrs Tomber's own voice and for a few seconds Ottilie could hear Mrs Tomber being taken in.

246

'How's the 'flu, love?'

'Mrs Tomber – actually, this is not Joy,' Ottilie quickly returned to her own voice, 'it's Ottilie. I wonder if you could do me one last favour. Could you get a message to Mr Philip Granville when he calls for me? Tell him I'll meet him at the Station Café at midday, if you don't mind?'

'I see. Yes. I see.'

She could hear Mrs Tomber's voice, nervous now, worried that just listening to Ottilie might get her the sack.

'You're feeling better, are you, love? Good. Well, bye-bye, Joy. See you next Saturday, love. 'Bye.'

The telephone box smelt of old cigarettes and there was torn newspaper wedged in the door, newspaper that caught at the heels of her shoes. Ottilie walked quickly back to the basement flat, to the view of the pavement and the start of the long wait until midday when she would hope to see Philip and tell him what had happened as a result of staying on the island too long, of finding out how much they liked kissing and touching each other, as a result of all of which Ottilie was now homeless.

'That is such an awful word,' Ottilie thought as she looked around her dismal surroundings. 'Homeless. I am homeless. I have no family. I have no-one now, no friends, nothing, except perhaps Philip, and I doubt if he will turn up because Mrs Tomber will be too frightened to hang around the hotel lobby when he is expected. Too frightened that if she is seen talking to him she will be spotted and everyone at the hotel will know that she is passing on a message from me and she will either be sacked or sent to Coventry. With only two years to go before she retires with full pension, that will be just what she doesn't want.'

Even so, on the off chance, she changed her clothes and brushed out her long dark hair and, feeling more than a little hopeless, set out for the Station Café to wait for Philip.

After all, what else was there to do? Until Monday morning came and she could go in search of a job, there was nothing.

As she entered the dismal café Ottilie found herself glancing up at the old mahogany-encased clock behind the glass counter wherein was displayed the most unappetizing food with which any traveller could be confronted. As she sat down with a cup of pale grey coffee poured to too near the top of the cup, Ottilie imagined Philip on any other Sunday strolling back from Tredegar's church in the grounds of his house, already, in his imagination, smelling the roast beef and Yorkshire pudding that, whatever the weather, their cook would have well under way because like so many men Philip only really liked a Sunday roast. He would stop and look down the wide path that led back to the little country road off which Tredegar was placed, and then he would turn happily back to his dogs and his lunch, already anticipating the crisp roast potatoes, the garden peas, and the blackberry and apple crumble and Cornish cream that would follow.

Philip still walked about Tredegar the way he had when he was a small boy, happy and confident because he belonged there. Tredegar was part of him the way the Grand had until a few hours ago been part of Ottilie. Yet unlike Ottilie, Philip could look up at Tredegar's inside walls and be reassured by the sight of his ancestors staring down at him. Men and women who three or four hundred years before had already become powerful and committed to the welfare of Cornwall. In time, after Army service, Philip would return to Tredegar and become Lord Lieutenant of the county and walk in a red and gold uniform behind the Queen when she came to Cornwall on a visit . . .

Ottilie stared at the pool of coffee on the table in front of her. Since it was Sunday there would be no-one in the café empowered to wipe the table clean until the following morning, so that everyone who came in after her would

248

have to face that same spill of coffee that she was facing. What a dreary thought. She looked up once more at the wooden-encased clock with its old-fashioned numerals. Five past twelve. She could not face pretending to drink another cup of coffee. She would wait until the hand reached seven minutes after the hour and then she would leave, walking as slowly as she could, her heart sinking at the prospect of waiting alone in her dingy basement room until dreary Monday morning came round and she could set out to look for work.

'Ah, there you are!'

Philip seemed to fill the dark brown café, with its slimy, grim, once cream walls, with the vibrancy of his presence, with his authority and his gaiety.

'Thank God! I thought you might have gone.'

He pulled her to her feet, kissing her spontaneously first on her cheek and then briefly on her lips.

'I thought you would have gone and I would have to send out a May Day for you. But what the hell has happened? Why are you here?'

Ottilie glanced round at the interested occupants of the other tables, and although she could not help smiling at the way Philip had pulled her to her feet, she felt too shy to answer. Besides, there might be someone seated at one of those tables who knew her. She was known in the town by relatives and friends of the staff, by gardeners' wives, by people who had worked at the hotel and now retired.

'I'm so sorry about all this,' she began, and then indicated with her eyes 'let's go outside', which Philip picked up straight away. They quickly left the café and started to walk up the hill towards his old Austin Healey.

'What's happened? Have your parents gone mad or something?' Spontaneously Philip took Ottilie's hands and kissed them and stroked her hair just the way he had done earlier in the morning when they had been on the island lying in each other's arms, quite alone, away from the dancing and the band. 'Come on, tell me.'

249

It was difficult for Ottilie to explain to Philip, who seemed at that moment to embody everything that was most especially life-enhancing, that because of a misunderstanding over a drawing she had been given by an elegant old Frenchman, she had been thrown out of her parents' hotel.

'Do you really want to know, Philip?' she asked him. 'I mean, do you honestly want to know the whole story? Or shall we drive off first and find somewhere for lunch, and then I'll tell you?'

'Lunch first,' Philip agreed quickly. 'Too uncertain for a picnic, I thought, so I booked at the Feathers. Constantia's furious because she laid on lunch for me and everyone else, but I told her too bad, this is the last day of my last leave and I need to be with the girl I love.'

Ottilie looked away. 'Oh, Philip, you should have stayed with Constantia.'

But when he had kissed her Ottilie quite changed her mind.

'I'm starving,' she told him, seconds after he had let go of her, which immediately made Philip laugh because he obviously was too, so they ran hand in hand to the car and drove off towards their table for two at the Feathers.

Ottilie stared out of the window at the green Cornish fields and the ripened yellow of the farm fields which were already being slowly harvested far beyond where they were sitting. Something most unusual had just happened. Philip had actually questioned her about her family – she had never mentioned her adoption to him and did not feel like doing so now – but even so, it was not at all like Philip to suddenly ask why everything had gone so dreadfully wrong between her and her parents, and Ottilie had told him.

For one second there was a long, disbelieving silence and then Philip started to laugh.

'Only you, Ottilie,' he said, eventually, as Ottilie, feeling mildly indignant, stared at the sight of him trying

250

to stop laughing and failing in spectacular fashion, 'only you could be thrown out of your parents' house because of a drawing by a painter to whom you didn't sit!'

'I know, I know. It's like being tortured for information you don't possess,' Ottilie agreed, pretending to look glum, but now, at last, beginning to see the funny side of it. 'Oh, but Philip, it is just like me, isn't it? I always was being caught and punished, even for things that the staff had done, wasn't I?'

'Always.'

'Actually, now I come to think of it, you're right. I suppose chucking me out was nothing to do with the drawing really, was it? Although I should not have cared a fig if I had sat for it, but I didn't.'

Ottilie frowned, still trying to make sense of everything despite Philip's having lightened her mood.

'Looking back I suppose it all started to go wrong when they saw that I was growing up. You know how it is, couples who have lost a child only think of adopting a daughter or son to replace the one who has died. They can't think beyond that, I suppose. They probably just didn't allow for me becoming an adult, because their own dead child never grew up, don't you think? To them she will always be a little girl in hair ribbons and a smocked dress, and that's really what I should have stayed if they were to go on loving me even a little, a young girl in a smocked dress.'

Ottilie stopped, remembering the photograph of the little girl with her teddy bear that Melanie always kept on her dressing table. No-one could ever mention the dead child, not even Edith. There was no real point in going on, not when she could see that Philip knew perfectly well what she was talking about, so she picked up her glass of bitter lemon and sipped at it.

Philip obviously understood because he said, 'So – they've chucked you out, and you have nowhere to go and no money either, presumably?'

'Oh, no, I have money. I shall be fine,' Ottilie lied, and she looked away, out of the window at the happy crowded tables outside the pub dining room, at the sunshine, at the blue sky. 'Aren't we lucky in England?' she went on, in an effort to distract Philip's attention away from her problems. 'Our fields never turn brown in summer like France or Italy, we always see green.'

'At this moment I am afraid I can only see red. I do not understand how your parents can do this to you. How can anyone do this to you? As a matter of fact how can anyone do it to anyone?'

'You're in the Army, you ought to know about people fighting each other,' Ottilie joked, but at that moment Philip put his hand up to her face to stroke it in a gesture which was so kind it made her warn him, 'Please, don't. Really, Philip, please don't be nice to me, I'll only get lachrymose.'

'God, that is so like you when you were young, Ottilie. Do you remember how you adored big words? I always got the feeling when you used one that you had no idea what it meant.'

'Too lazy to look them up in a dictionary—'

'The only girl I ever knew whom I could trust not to ruin a decent game of soldiers.'

'Blame all the old soldiers that came to stay in the hotel. They gave me an interest in battles.'

'I used to look forward so much to you coming, days before, planning everything, waiting for you by the front door.' Philip put his hand in hers despite the arrival of the lemon meringue pudding. 'Do you know, for the first time in my life I am actually dreading leave ending? I suppose it's because I have the feeling that I am actually going away from someone I would rather be with than not be with, rather than Tredegar which I know is always there and probably always will be. I don't know that with you, do I?'

'How long have we got?'

'Until five o'clock.'

Ottilie glanced up once more, this time at the old-fashioned pub clock. Five o'clock, and it was already half past one. The waitress put down a jug of cream for the pudding, and Philip poured some over both their plates and started to eat heartily. But Ottilie, who had been eating well until that moment, suddenly found that she had no appetite whatsoever. She had to find out all about Philip before he left.

'Why did you go into the Army, Philip?'

'Why do you think? To kill people,' he joked.

'No really, why did you? You hate killing things, at least you always used to.'

'It's a family occupation, going into the Army and then coming out again and returning to Cornwall to marry a nice girl and have children so that Tredegar echoes to the sound of happy laughter.'

Philip pulled a droll face while Ottilie thought she could imagine all too well the kind of nice girl that Philip might marry when he left the Army, someone most possibly just like his sister Constantia, a tall girl with blond hair and an eagle stare to her blue eyes.

'Do you hate the idea of coming home to Tredegar, of knowing exactly what is going to happen to you?'

'No, I love it. Tredegar means everything to me. Not my parents, but my grandfather, and all the animals, and the people who work there. It was the servants who used to look after us when we were growing up, and the luck of having my grandfather living to a ripe old age, that saved us from minding too much that the parents got divorced and had new babies. They stopped being interested in us at all, really. We might as well have been hunters swapped out at the end of the season. I tell you, when I have children I shan't let them out of my sight.'

Ottilie pretended to eat some more, and quickly changed the subject.

'Remember Ludlow?'

'How can I forget him?'

'I found a picture of him in my things just now.' She reached down into her handbag and brought out a small photograph of Philip as a boy holding the hare in his arms, taken by Edith with her box Brownie camera.

Philip stared at it, and then he cleared his throat and said, 'Let's get out of here and go for a long walk, shall we?' and this time it was he who pushed his food away and called for the bill.

They drove up to a favourite walk, well away from St Elcombe, somewhere where they could feel that the whole world not only could get lost, but had been lost, somewhere behind them, in the interior, away from the cliff paths and the sea.

'What are you going to do while I'm away? You must go to Tredegar and stay with Constantia until you find out what to do next. I insist that you do.'

Philip was holding Ottilie's hand very tight again, even though she was following him along the path. He stopped when they came to a place where they could sit down and again, as he had the previous evening, he took off his jacket and carefully laid it down for her to sit upon, a gesture which seemed to Ottilie to be infinitely touching and at the same time heartbreaking as she tried not to think about Philip going away and perhaps never coming back, ending up in some foreign field which might then be for ever England, but would eventually come to mean precious little to those who loved and missed him.

Ottilie stared out to sea. She knew that Philip was thinking of her the way young men always did think of 'their girls' before they went back to their regiments. He was thinking that she was the girl he would be coming back to, that as soon as he was out of the Army he would marry her and they would go to live at Tredegar.

'I am all right, Philip, really.' She turned to him. 'There's nothing to worry about. I can work, really I can.'

'I shall worry about you more than I shall worry about getting it right in Cyprus.'

254

'You mustn't worry about me, really. I shall find a job quite easily. With my experience of running the Grand, can you imagine? People will fall over themselves to employ me,' she joked.

'Let me give you some money—'

'No, absolutely not. It's not about money, all of this, it's about doing it on your own. Making your own way. Besides, I know you don't have any more than I do, not after your mess bills!'

'I only really drink soft drinks except on leave. "Orange juice Jim" they call me in the mess, but it's more expensive than champagne, would you believe? You can go and stay with Constantia at Tredegar, she would love it.'

'Sweet of you, but it would be quite unfair to Constantia to go to live at Tredegar. Can you imagine? I would be under her feet all weekend when she would be wanting her friends there, and then because she would be away in London during the week I would be sure to try and reorganize everything my way – which comes I'm afraid from growing up in a hotel – and then Constantia would come back and find everything not to her liking, and it would be awful.'

Philip smiled, recognizing, at once, thank God, the truth of what Ottilie was saying.

'No, I shall be fine, really. I will write to you, wherever I am.'

'And I will come back to you from wherever I am.'

'Will it be long?'

'A matter of a moment.'

'Maybe, but it will seem like a lifetime to me, and perhaps when we meet again we shall both be old and changed, and nothing will be the same again. I always have that feeling when I'm happy, that nothing will ever be the same again, and of course it won't.'

Just at that moment it seemed to Ottilie that Philip had never looked more handsome, his fair hair brushed back, somehow every inch the hero. But now the hero must return to his house and change into his uniform, and Ottilie must wait in the car for him, knowing without being told that it would be more tactful not to go in with him, to allow him to say his goodbyes to Constantia and his friends without her, and instead of accompanying him she lay back in the car and listened to the sound of the trees outside, barely moving and yet utterly alive.

Because she had been standing on the platform for too long Ottilie realized that she hated not only the Station Café at St Elcombe, but also the station. Not that it was not pretty in an idyllic English way, with flowers set about in tubs and a station master with a cap and a collection of smart flags, no, it was all the other people standing around, as they were – waiting with too much of an air of pretending that they were not waiting – who were so hateful. All those other people staring at her, other people seeing Philip holding her hand. Other people knowing who he was, or who she was, nothing any longer private, and Philip going off and pretending to be so brave but both of them knowing all the time that everything they were trying to say was just pretend and everything they were not saying was actually real.

What they were not saying was that they might never see each other again, and that if they never did see each other again in this world, this was it. Nothing more nor less.

This would be the last time they held hands, walked side by side, tried to find something to talk about to take their minds off the time on the station clock whose hands now seemed to be bending over double to hurry forward to summon the train and spell out the final moment of goodbye.

Ottilie knew from the old general who had given Philip his soldiers all those years ago that young men were not brave before battle. He had described to her young Guards officers in tears on the eve of battles, crying their eyes out like little boys on Victoria Station before they went back to their boarding schools, not at all like in war films where everyone was bright-eyed and ready to do battle.

As they waited for the train it was the general's sad descriptions that kept coming into Ottilie's mind, and though she turned away from them as much as she could they would keep coming back as Philip kept talking about anything and everything – his posting, the party the night before, the amount of champagne they had all drunk, how Ottilie had missed the best scrambled eggs ever by leaving before breakfast had been served.

At last the train arrived and it was almost a relief to put an end to the waiting and the pretending.

'I shan't say goodbye.'

'No, don't,' Philip agreed in a low voice, removing his Army cap and kissing her long and hard, neither of them caring at all who saw or who told.

'I want you to keep this in your uniform.' Ottilie handed him the small black and white photograph of himself as a boy with Ludlow. 'They say hares are lucky, you know.'

'You will be good until I get back, won't you, Ottilie?' Philip asked, holding her tightly to him.

'You know I will.'

It was such a very Philip way of saying something intimate to her that Ottilie could not help smiling, although it was actually the last thing she felt like doing at that moment.

After that of course it was very difficult, just a question of clinging to each other briefly because the station master was looking pointedly at them as he slammed door after door behind them, and then as the train pulled out of the station Ottilie found herself running as fast as she could down the platform until it came to an end, when she stopped to wave and wave until the train was so far away that, quiet as it was at St Elcombe on a Sunday evening, Ottilie found that she couldn't even hear it any longer.

Thirteen

It had been easy enough at first for Ottilie to be brave, to walk out of the Grand and find herself lodgings in St Elcombe. Just as at first it was very easy not to miss the daily grind of bed-making, and seeing to everyone and everything, and usually all at the same time. Not to miss standing in for a waitress or a maid, not to miss Chef's grumbling, the chaos and the heat in the kitchen, and most of all not to miss the endless hostility she had known over the last eighteen months at the hotel. But now, after five weeks without a job and with her money running out, her early courage started to desert her.

She dared not risk driving to another town in search of work because every penny had to be counted, and if she wanted to be sure that she would be able to eat and pay her rent for the next few weeks she simply could not risk throwing away pounds on petrol. She knew that she could always sell her car, but a question mark lay over that too, because although the Cartarets had given it to her, Ottilie had no actual proof that they had done so. They had bought her the second-hand Citroën, but a suspicion lay in Ottilie's mind that should she put poor Oscar up for sale, St Elcombe being such a small place, her parents might find out and claim back the money on the grounds that they had only bought her the car for her use while she worked at their hotel. The memory of the police station and Ma's howls of despair as she protested her innocence still haunted Ottilie, and kept her from wanting to invite any kind of disgrace upon herself.

On her own now, night after night, watching endless feet walking past her on the pavement by the railings which reached down to her basement window, she knew for the first time what it felt like to be really desperate and not to know which way to turn. She was far too proud to write for help to Lorcan or Mrs Le Martine, and besides, having not heard back from either of them for many months, she felt that if she described her new circumstances too fully to them it might appear as if she was asking them for money anyway, so she did not write at all.

But if Ottilie was too proud to beg, she was also too poor not to realize how it came about that girls of her age took to the streets. They did so because they were desperate. But in her letter to Philip, waiting to be posted, she naturally made a joke of it all.

I am lodging in downtown St Elcombe where the nightly entertainment is taking bets on how many steps the local drunks can make when they come out of the Pirate's Cabin, and how soon they fall into the road.

Sometimes she could hardly bring herself to get out of bed she felt so hungry in the mornings, and so dismal at the idea of setting out on yet another search for a job. She had signed on at the Labour Exchange but it would be some weeks yet before she could draw any money, and anyway it would not be enough to cover the rent and her food. Desperate, Ottilie took to praying again, and even to going to church. It didn't seem at all right after all these years of not praying, of not going to church after Ma had died so suddenly, to start beseeching the Almighty, but at least it was warm in church, and the brightly painted statues seemed to exude a Mediterranean cheerfulness with their bright blue or red garments and their silver orbs and bare feet.

'Catholic churches are so ugly,' Melanie used to say as if that excused her ever attending one, and she certainly never bothered to take Ottilie.

But as she grew up Ottilie had realized that Melanie was right. The Catholic church in St Elcombe was little more than a tin hut, but the people she met there were not unfriendly and suspicious like so many downtown. Ottilie found that when she went to church people who did not know her smiled at her, and it wasn't like the Grand – they never stopped you going in because you had poor clothes or were not wearing a tie.

It was after early morning church one day (Ottilie had gone less because she wanted to pray than because St Antony's was a great deal warmer than her basement room) that she clearly heard a voice behind her calling her old childhood name.

'Ottie! Ottie Cartaret!'

She was so caught up in her thoughts, so full of the usual mixture of elation and despair that going to church seemed to bring on, that when she turned she fully expected to see some sort of statue come to life, calling her back to prayer once more, calling her back to kneel among the other sinners and ask God's forgiveness for offending her parents. Instead, she saw a face she only barely recognized, the face of a priest.

It was also the face of her eldest brother Lorcan.

'Lorcan!'

'Well now, let me look at you.' He held her away from him, and shook his head in a kind of avuncular wonder. 'Ottie. You're a young lady. Will you let me look at you, will you look at that?'

When Lorcan had last communicated with her – and it must have been two years ago – it was from Ireland, from the priests' college where he was still studying. He had wanted her to come to his Ordination Mass but Ottilie had been needed at the hotel, so she had sent him a present of a silver crucifix and although he had written hastily to thank her she had not heard from him since, for – as Edith had often gently reminded her – 'Brothers are not like that, I don't think, Miss Ottilie, they just think of you as

261

being there, and not really needing them, not really. They don't think like girls.'

'Lorcan.'

As she said his name, and to her horror, Ottilie felt a devastating embarrassment sweeping over her. She might be a young lady but Lorcan was a priest. He was a person set apart, someone to whom she could confess her sins, someone who would come to her if she was dying and say the Last Rites over her, someone who was empowered to hold up the Host at daily Mass. Lorcan, who had always seemed to be either building something or painting something. Lorcan, who had appeared at her birthday party when she was ten, was now a person whom she could ask for a blessing like the nuns and the priest at her first school.

Could she treat him like Lorcan and tease him, or would it be more fitting if she respected the barrier that she sensed was already between them?

'You have changed so much,' Lorcan told her, as if he had not, and he stood back to openly admire her still smart coat and shoes, a residue of her former life, her long hair brushed back, her treasured leather gloves and shoulder bag. 'You are really beautiful now, Ottilie.' Ottilie must have looked embarrassed for him, because he went on quickly, 'Oh, no, don't look shocked, Ottie. It is perfectly all right for me to say so. In fact Father Peter encourages us to admire women and their beauty. They are all part of God's Creation.'

'I should think so too!' Ottilie said, laughing suddenly, and her embarrassment started to dissipate as she realized that although he was mostly not the same at all, a part of Lorcan was still very much the same.

Of course they were not like brother or sister any more, that feeling could never come back, they had grown too far apart. Yet when he smiled so endearingly down at her, Ottilie could see that he was still the same tall, handsome eldest brother who used to swing her onto his shoulders and jogtrot her up to the cottage door.

'Are you at the eight o'clock every morning? Being the youngest I take the six o'clock, for my sins!'

'Practically every morning,' Ottilie replied.

She did not dare to tell Lorcan that she was attending Mass regularly not just to pray but to warm up after a long damp night in her lonely basement.

'It's good your faith still means so much to you, Ottie.'

Seeing the sincerity in his eyes and hearing the warmth in his voice, Ottilie did not make a joke of her recent regular churchgoing as she might have done to Philip, for the sweetness and solemnity of Lorcan's look prevented her.

'Look, Ottie. Wait until I change, will you? Father Peter will allow me half an hour with you, I'm sure, great man that he is.'

Ottilie put out her hand to delay Lorcan, but he was already walking quickly off towards the priest's house, his gown billowing behind him. Time enough perhaps to tell him of her newly reduced circumstances.

But as she waited for him to change to a dark suit Ottilie herself changed her mind, deciding not to take Lorcan back to her lodgings which were a good twenty minutes' walk from the church anyway. Instead she would take him to a local café for a cappuccino coffee, using the excuse that she did not want to upset Melanie by bringing Lorcan back to the hotel as her guest in the middle of the season.

They had hardly sat down when Lorcan, with his suddenly familiar slow, kind smile which reached up to his eyes and took Ottilie back to the dear days of Number Four, said, 'So tell me, Ottie, what did you do that was wrong enough for Mrs Cartaret to throw you out of the Grand?'

Ottilie looked up from sprinkling sugar on the top of her coffee. To gain time she helped herself to another spoonful which she scattered thickly all over the white froth before finally saying to Lorcan, 'How did you know?'

'St Elcombe's a small place, and I had hardly arrived back in the parish last week when I rang the hotel and was told, "Miss Cartaret no longer lives or works here." And then of course I asked Mr Hulton and he told me of the scandal at the Grand and how you had been thrown out in disgrace, or so they said.'

Lorcan succeeded in looking both sage and grave at the same time while Ottilie only managed to look rueful.

'You know me, Lorcan. I could always get into trouble when I really wanted to, couldn't I, no matter what? Always out in the corridor in some kind of disgrace, always in trouble. Ma used to laugh and think it funny, but the nuns didn't think I was very good at all, I'm afraid.'

'Ma. She thought the sun shone every time your eyes opened.'

Lorcan shook his head, remembering, and smiled, but his eyes never left Ottilie's face and from his quiet but determined manner Ottilie quickly realized that she was talking to a trained priest, not just to an elder brother whom she now hardly knew. 'Priests,' Ma used to say with a laugh, 'have minds like athletes, pet.'

'It will shock you, what happened will shock you.'

'Very little, you'll find, shocks even a young priest. The Bible is shocking.'

'Well, if you really want to know . . .' Ottilie took a deep breath and began, only to stop a moment later as she remembered how Philip had laughed and teased her on the day she had been kicked out. 'If you really want to know, I was given a drawing of a nude when I was in Paris,' she went on, finally unable to stand the silence. 'It's really rather beautiful, actually, even though I say it myself, and it is of me, though it was drawn from the artist's imagination, how he remembered me.'

Lorcan nodded, and Ottilie noticed that not even his eyes blinked, so reassuringly unshocked was he. 'Go on.'

'I never posed for it, Lorcan. I mean I don't actually

think it matters a damn if I did, for heaven's sakes, God made our bodies, didn't He? But as it happens I didn't.'

'You once fainted clean out in a shop when Ma removed your pullover, even though, as Ma said, you were wearing a blouse, a skirt, a petticoat, a vest, long tights and little lace-up boots,' was all Lorcan thought to say with a fond smile.

This encouraged Ottilie to go on, which it was obviously meant to do.

'What happened was that this much older man, "Monsieur" I called him, I can't even remember his name now, but he was a friend of a friend and he owned the apartment where I was staying. Anyway, he saw me coming out of the bathroom wearing only a towel. I mean it was quite by mistake, and he went away and drew me from memory, but without the towel, if you can imagine?'

Lorcan obviously did not seem to find this as difficult to believe as Alfred and Melanie, because he merely nodded for her to go on.

'And to be honest, when he gave it to me I was thrilled. I love it. It reminds me of Paris. But even so I didn't frame it or hang it, in case the staff saw it and jumped to the wrong conclusion, you know how staff can? Not because I was ashamed of it or anything. What I did instead was, I bought a special sort of folder to put it in, and I really didn't think anything much more about it, except that it was beautiful. Then Philip Granville came home on leave. You remember Philip, Lorcan? He used to come to the hotel and play tennis sometimes when you were still working there? Anyway, he was home on leave for forty-eight hours and he came to the hotel and he asked me to this party and I went, but without telling the parents, because I knew they would try and stop me. That *was* wrong, I do admit, and, well, when I got back – you can imagine, the heavens and the earth split open.'

'They would have done . . .'

'Yes. They had spent most of the night going through

all my things to see if I had a diary and had written about where I was going or something. Anyway, of course they ended up finding the drawing, and of course—'

'They didn't believe you hadn't posed for it.'

'No. They didn't believe me, and perhaps worse – they didn't want to believe me, which was strange, because even if I don't believe someone I find I always want to believe them, because it helps when it comes to forgiving them, don't you think?'

'Certainly.'

Lorcan had watched Ottilie slowly drinking her cappuccino with small appreciative sips, having made a meal of the froth and the sugar off a teaspoon first, which was why he now said in his usual down-to-earth way, 'And now, you're starving.'

'No, I'm fine, really, Lorcan.'

'You're starving,' Lorcan corrected her. 'I know.'

'How do you know?'

'Because I fast, Ottie. I know the signs. Look at you, you're as thin as a pencil, there's nothing of you. I would hardly have recognized you at Mass but for those large eyes of yours staring out from under your black veil. You must eat to live, you know.'

'I just can't get a job, Lorcan,' Ottilie confessed, knowing the game was up. 'You see I haven't a reference, despite all my experience at the hotel.'

'So, what are you going up for, Miss Cartaret?'

'Waitressing, cleaning, anything—'

'Dressed like you and speaking as you do, you haven't a hope,' Lorcan told her, at his most practical. 'Folks don't want cleaners who speak like ladies, Ottie, you should know that. You've employed enough people at the Grand. People want cleaners who speak like cleaners; and they don't want beautiful girls waiting on their tables either. It distracts the customers from the main business of the day, spending their money on food, eating it and clearing off as quick as time will allow. Waitresses who are too pretty make the customers linger over their food or their drinks, but they do not necessarily spend any more. A full table is not necessarily a paying table. However, no matter. I think I can get you a job, as it happens, a very good job, as a matter of fact, and one which will not only suit you perfectly, but for which you are perfectly suitable. When I heard of your disgrace I thought you might need me!'

He grinned, suddenly very much the elder brother.

'Come back with me to the presbytery and we'll ring up Mrs Blaize.'

Although Lorcan looked smart and handsome in his dark suit and clerical collar, Ottilie started to feel distinctly uneasy as she was walking down the street with him towards the Angel.

Ottilie paused on the threshold of the ancient coaching inn.

'It's no good, Lorcan, I can't go in there. They're sure to know who I am. Staff from here used to come dressed up as customers and spy on our menus.'

'It's all changed now, Ottie, I promise you.'

'Yes, for the worse, I heard.'

'Exactly, that's why they're looking for a new manageress. Someone young with a light touch but experienced in the old ways, someone who will attract back their old customers and bring them new ones.'

'I know, the usual camel that a committee has in mind.'

Lorcan laughed. 'You've become some kind of a right hard young businesswoman then, now haven't you, Ottie?'

Ottilie smiled at his constant use of her childhood nickname. Just hearing 'Ottie' said with an Irish accent was like pressing a button which brought back golden memories of warmth, and in a second she could once more feel herself a small child, her hand clutching at Ma's index finger as they ambled away from Number Four and towards the shops, and hear Ma's voice saying, 'Come on, pet, and maybe we will even be able to have ourselves a sweet when we get to see Mr North at MacDonagh's?'

So along they'd go, and first there would be the railings across which Ottie would be allowed to run a stick as she passed, making a satisfying clatter as they walked round the corner into the High Street, and all the time Ottilie's grip on Ma's index finger would become tighter and she would glance up anxiously every few seconds just to make sure that not only was Ma's finger there, but Ma was too.

And sure enough Ma would be there, her great thick plait of hair tossed back, her lips parted in a smile as at every turn they seemed to pass someone they knew, or who knew them. But once they had trailed on past them, Ma, still preceding Ottilie with her stately amble, would glance down at her and mutter, 'Heaven only knows who that was, pet, and who cares for heaven's sakes? Just so long as they don't come round wanting supper we should be all right.'

But all that was over, and now it was Lorcan saying, 'Here we are, Ottie.'

The new priestly Lorcan had a quietly confident air about him, so unlike the young man Ottilie remembered walking towards her birthday table, painfully shy, seemingly all too aware of his thick clothing and heavy boots, his Irish accent most particularly because he must have felt himself to be such an awkward contrast to the Cartarets in their fine tailoring and with their refined accents and gentrified ways.

Ottilie glanced at the clock. It was after half past nine and yet there was no staff about, giving the Angel Inn a neglected air. Mentally Ottilie compared it to the Grand at the same time of the morning, when all the flowers would have been changed, and the carpets cleaned, when the receptionist would be ready and smiling, and even Blackie striding about as if the Grand was a station and he the station master.

'Ah now, good morning to you, Father O'Flaherty, we

were expecting you.' A dumpy little grey-haired woman in a much worn tweed skirt appeared to have arrived from what looked like a broom cupboard under the stairs. She spoke with an Irish accent and looked worn and harassed. Not a welcoming sight, least of all if you happened to be an arriving guest.

'This is my sister, Ottilie O'Flaherty.' Lorcan turned and his eyes warned Ottilie, 'You're O'Flaherty here, OK?'

As she picked up the warning look Ottilie warmed at the familial closeness which Lorcan and she were able to resume so quickly, as if no time at all had elapsed since they were both living under the same roof, and she suddenly remembered the old days when Lorcan would give her just such a look if Ma had one of her 'bad' days, and they needed to help her upstairs and he didn't want Ottie opening her trap and saying something that might set Ma off.

'This is Mrs Blaize. She is leaving very suddenly and having to look for someone to replace herself, Ottilie. A bit of a novel situation, isn't it, Mrs Blaize?'

Mrs Blaize nodded, all the time trying to smooth down her skirt while indicating for them to follow her and sit down in the small, overcrowded office to which she had conducted them.

'There's been no time to tidy up since I arrived, I'm afraid, Father O'Flaherty,' she told Lorcan apologetically as she removed telephone directories and full ashtrays from various worn seating arrangements around the room. 'It's terrible to have to ask you in here, but there's been no time to turn my hand to anything, and because I have to return immediately to Liverpool to nurse my poor husband there's no time to advertise either. And then too, as you may imagine, since the Clover Group have taken over we're all at sixes and sevens. Now tell me, Miss O'Flaherty—'

She stared at Ottilie for the first time. 'Oh dear, you

269

look really rather young for this position, if you don't mind my saying, Miss O'Flaherty. What might your previous experience in the hotel trade be, may I ask?'

'She has been helping to run the Grand for the couple who adopted her, a Mr and Mrs Cartaret, but there has been a misunderstanding and so she is looking for a new position,' Lorcan put in quickly, speaking for Ottilie.

Ottilie saw suspicion flash into Mrs Blaize's eyes at Lorcan's words, but perhaps it was the dog collar or Lorcan's confident manner because she seemed to pause only for a fraction of a second, long enough to allow suspicion to enter her mind and be rejected, and then she said, 'I see. In that case perhaps you would like to tell me what you were in the habit of doing – your normal day and hours, as it were, at the Grand?'

Ottilie told her, exactly. There was a short silence during which Lorcan smiled his slow, warm smile, and Mrs Blaize also smiled, only with relief, but then she made an impatient little sound and said, 'Such a nuisance about your references, though as I understand it from Father O'Flaherty there will be some difficulty in obtaining any at all. With such experience you are obviously perfect! And what's more, which is more important, willing. As we both know, even in a small hotel, that is almost more important than anything. Still,' she sighed, 'I have to be able to recommend you with utter confidence.' She turned to Lorcan. 'Father O'Flaherty, much as I appreciate your recommending your sister, and clearly as I can see she would be perfect for the position, the Clover House Group will not accept my recommendation, however warm, unless backed by a reference of some sort. It is just not possible.'

There was a long disappointed silence which both Lorcan and Ottilie were wise enough not to try to fill with explanation. After all, if there was no way out, there was no way out.

'Mrs Tomber, the housekeeper, might give me a

reference, but she knew me as Miss Cartaret – my adopted name,' Ottilie volunteered, suddenly desperate at the idea of returning jobless to her wretched basement once more. 'I'm sure she would give me a telephone reference if you rang her, in fact I know she would. But you would have to ring her at her sister's house. I think she would be frightened to say anything nice about me otherwise.'

'Well now, this is more hopeful.' Mrs Blaize paused and nodded at Lorcan as Ottilie wrote down Mrs Tomber's sister's number from her own small address book, and handed it to her.

'Mrs Tomber always goes there on Saturday night.'

'I will ring her on Saturday night then.' Mrs Blaize nodded, quickly interrupting. 'It will be a great relief to me if I can get this matter settled as soon as possible, as you will appreciate. Thank you for coming, Father, and what a miracle it was that you heard about our plight. Something for your favourite cause, Father.'

Lorcan looked embarrassed as Mrs Blaize slipped him an envelope, but he took it none the less, saying, 'I take this in a spirit of humility and I thank you, Mrs Blaize.'

Outside, as they walked along, Ottilie could hardly believe what she knew might be about to happen. She might actually be about to be able to leave the basement with its constant dreary sight of feet walking or shuffling or stopping by her windows, the lavatory that took seventeen pulls to work, the basin that only ran hot water for five minutes and the gas ring that was forever consuming shillings and running out just as she tried to boil a kettle.

'But how did you hear about this?' she said, stopping and frowning, although she knew that Lorcan most probably would not tell her anyway because he always did have a way of working things without letting on to anyone. 'How did you hear they were looking for someone, Lorcan?'

Lorcan carried on walking as he answered, 'Put it this

way, Ottie. The good Lord brought the position to my attention, and when I heard from you of your plight it seemed to me that restoring the Angel Inn could be just the job for you.'

'I hope so,' Ottilie said fervently and she closed her eyes for a second and prayed, for if there was anything that might drive her to the edge of despair it would be the idea that she would have to spend another month in that basement in downtown St Elcombe.

'There's a call for you, dear, at least I think it's for you. Ottilie something, that's you, i'n'tit?' Ottilie's landlady always called down the stairs, never came down herself, as if she was afraid of entering the appalling reality of her own basement flat. 'A Mrs Blaize on the telephone for you, dear.'

Why she called Ottilie 'dear' Ottilie could not imagine, but it didn't matter what she called her just so long as Mrs Tomber had given her a good reference. Ottilie jumped up the stairs to the narrow hallway of the main part of the house with its shiny linoed floor and its public telephone box ('for incoming calls only, dear') that made walking down the corridor anything but sideways so difficult.

'Don't be long, dear.'

Ottilie could hardly hear Mrs Blaize, her soft Irish voice being almost drowned by the landlady's harsher English accent.

'Yes, this is Mrs Blaize from the Angel Inn.'

'Hello, Mrs Blaize.' Ottilie could suddenly hear just how much she wanted the job from the tension in her own voice.

Mrs Blaize sounded equally tense, but, as it turned out, for other reasons. 'It's very embarrassing, Miss O'Flaherty, particularly in view of your brother's position, but I'm afraid – well, I'm afraid that Mrs Tomber does not recommend you for the situation.'

'What?'

There was a long pause.

'Mrs Tomber says she does not think you are at all suitable for the position for which you applied,' Mrs Blaize repeated. 'She says, moreover, that she herself would never employ you.'

Ottilie could hear her heart pounding in her ears as she tried to take in what Mrs Blaize had just said, and make sense of it.

'Are you sure it was Mrs Tomber you spoke to?'

'Positive. I spoke first to her sister and then to her.' A pause and then, 'I think you should come back and see me, Miss O'Flaherty. I think there is definitely a great deal more to this than meets the eye. I am suspicious, let us say. That's why I think we should talk it over at once.'

'I will be with you as soon as I can.'

Ottilie ran down the familiar winding streets of St Elcombe that seemed, on bad days such as this, to be mean and more than ever full of ugly people with narrow minds and hard feelings. She pounded up the short hill towards the Angel, where she stopped suddenly to regain her breath. She was angry with Mrs Tomber, but whatever her feelings it made no sense to arrive in a state of breathless indignation. It would only look as if she was over-reacting like a guilty person. She should arrive calm, collected, and above all not defensive.

At least Mrs Blaize had given her a second chance to speak for herself, she had that for which to be grateful.

'Good girl, you came back as soon as may be.' Mrs Blaize gave Ottilie an approving glance as she walked her from the hotel foyer back to her small, overcrowded office. 'Sit down now while I order us both some tea and we talk this thing through. I need to know more from you about this Mrs Tomber and why she might be so intent on preventing you taking up this position?'

'I really don't know. I actually thought she was my best

friend, my only friend I mean after Edith – the other housekeeper at the hotel – died. Edith looked after me, you see, when I was little, and she and Mrs Tomber were the best of friends. I thought I was too, but obviously not.' Ottilie's voice dropped as she realized the full implications of Mrs Tomber's betrayal. 'It was an odd situation, you see,' she continued after a few seconds' thought. 'Mrs Tomber was the official housekeeper, but Edith and I were too, in a way. Mr Cartaret was a bit disorganized like that. I mean no-one quite knew where the dividing lines lay. We all had to step in for each other, so finally, in the shake-up, we were all doing a bit of everything, if you know how that can be?'

'Certainly. I used to be a nurse when I was young, Miss O'Flaherty,' Mrs Blaize said briskly. 'We had sisters on the wards like that. Chaos usually resulted, but if it did not it was no thanks to the sister. Now.' Mrs Blaize paused, having spent the previous minute staring at the top of her fountain pen. She looked directly at Ottilie. 'I don't know how much I can tell you, or how much I should tell you, but since I made that call on Saturday night to Mrs Tomber . . . oh, I really don't know – Father O'Flaherty would say I am causing scandal – but I suppose I must tell you if we are to come to any satisfactory conclusion. The thing is, Miss O'Flaherty, I made a few enquiries for myself before calling you this morning. St Elcombe is a small town – I myself come from a small town in Ireland, and in my experience everything comes to light sooner rather than later in small towns. It is very difficult – impossible – for people to keep things to themselves, or indeed for people not to talk about each other. Gossip let us say is a recreation, for there is very little else to do in small towns, is there?'

Ottilie stared at Mrs Blaize, realizing that she obviously knew a great deal more than Ottilie herself. She wanted to say, 'Come on, come on' but she couldn't, so she sat very still instead, her large eyes never leaving Mrs Blaize's face until Mrs Blaize's own eyes seemed to be wandering round the room looking at everything except Ottilie.

'So. After I telephoned Mrs Tomber, I telephoned Father O'Flaherty and we set to putting our thinking caps on. It occurred to us that there would have to be some other reason why this woman should let you down in this way. I mean I could see that you gave her name with complete confidence. Frankly, I have a wide experience of people in this work, Miss O'Flaherty, and why in the name of all that is holy should you have given me this woman's name if you had any reason to believe she would not recommend you? No, there had to be a reason for her "spinning" you, as they say in Ireland, and I felt I had to uncover her motive, if only to satisfy my own curiosity, and of course for my own selfish sake too, because as you know I want to leave here and be with my poor husband as soon as I possibly can. It is so terrible to be here when I should be with him, caring for him.'

More and more Ottilie wanted to urge Mrs Blaize to come on, and the front of her knees hurt in her effort to keep still and not show the impatience she felt.

'This is how it is, then.' Mrs Blaize paused, considering her words. 'First of all Father O'Flaherty and I, we thought it must be that she did not want to lose her situation. She has only a year or two to go before she is due to retire, and she would not want to do anything to risk her pension, which is understandable all right. But then I said to Father O'Flaherty, that's not quite right either. The woman was most vehement. She was most insistent on, let us say, running you down, and that does not make much sense. If she just did not want to be discovered recommending you, even verbally, she would merely have said so and replaced the telephone receiver and that would have been that. She would not have gone to the lengths she did to run you down to me. She was, to put it mildly, most unkind. Poisonous, actually.'

'I really can't believe it,' Ottilie said, unable to keep

275

quiet any longer. 'She has always been such a friend to me. These last months, she was the only person I felt I could really trust. She cried when I left, for heaven's sake.'

'Things change very quickly in any establishment, Miss O'Flaherty. Most of all in a hotel, as you might have observed.'

Ottilie stared at Mrs Blaize.

'To put it delicately, I believe that Mrs Tomber is more than influential in your parents' establishment nowadays.'

Ottilie heard herself asking, 'Mrs Tomber?'

Mrs Blaize nodded. 'Housekeepers have a habit of taking over hotel proprietors. It's often seen as a natural progression, especially if a wife dies. One person goes, and another takes their place. In this case, though, it was not the wife dying, but the daughter going. You, after all, as I understand it from Father O'Flaherty, more or less ran the Grand in place of your mother, didn't you?'

'Of course. It makes such sense,' Ottilie said to herself, but out loud. 'The last thing she wants is me setting up in opposition to them, so she gave me a bad reference.'

'Indeed it does make sense, Miss O'Flaherty. When you left, Mr Cartaret would have suddenly found himself having to rely upon someone new and strange. Proximity is the first step towards temptation.'

Mrs Blaize looked at Ottilie, and Ottilie knew at once from the solemn nature of the words she was using that she was probably quoting Lorcan. 'So you see, it seems to me, given that this is so, and we have it on good authority that it is, we know now that this woman's testimony as to your character not only cannot be relied upon, it must not be relied upon. I shall recommend you for the post of manageress. Head Office will be told you are the subject of a calumny. It happens a great deal, I assure you!'

Mrs Blaize put out her hand in a strange little gesture of formality, but her eyes were full of warmth. As for Ottilie, she could hardly believe it.

Indeed, so great was Ottilie's happiness that as she

walked out into the winter sunshine she was quite sure that she could hear Edith's voice reading to her from their favourite book – '*The sunshine struck hot on his fur, soft breezes caressed his heated brow, and after the seclusion of the cellarage he had lived in so long the carol of happy birds fell on his dulled hearing like a shout.*'

That was just how Ottilie felt now, as if the song of the birds was more like a shout, as if the cold wind blowing so strongly from the sea was just a soft breeze. She started to run back to her lodgings, but she was hard put to it not to stop each person she passed and tell them, 'I've got a job! I've got a job!' It didn't seem possible that after all this time someone wanted to employ her at last.

Mrs Blaize was explaining to Ottilie that the Angel had not always been a hotel. It had once been an old coaching inn, so now, Ottilie found, standing in the centre of its cobblestone courtyard, it was not at all difficult to imagine the scenes at the end of the eighteenth century when the inn was at the height of its popularity and sometimes horses would be changed at such speed it was breathtaking, and at other times coach and horses rested overnight while men and boy passengers climbing stiffly from the outside of the coaches and the ladies and older folk from the inside would all retire thankfully to stand by glowing fires and eat warm food, to be served by cheerful staff and sleep in comfortable feather beds.

'You know of course that it was actually the fine quality of its coaching inns that made England famous, now, don't you?' Mrs Blaize told Ottilie as they walked round the old place on Ottilie's first day, for Mrs Blaize appeared briskly expectant that Ottilie would take over from her within hours of her arrival. 'The fact is, and it was a fact, I'm afraid, that until the improvement in the services at the old coaching inns foreigners dreaded to come to England, and worse than that even English people could not travel about freely without taking their lives in their hands, such was the low quality at the inns at which the staging coaches halted. People were regularly robbed of their possessions. There were nothing but brigands and ex-convicts to change the horses, and nothing but slatterns and prostitutes staffing the inns. But then someone or other realized that things had to get better because it was affecting the coaching trade and only the aristocracy could travel safely, and so they took out the convicts and put in proper grooms, which led to faster changes for the horses and better stabling, and from the end of the eighteenth century until the coming of the railways the English coaching inn was the most admired hostelry in Europe. And still could be if someone new could see sense!'

As Ottilie was listening to Mrs Blaize's potted history lecture she was pushing open the doors of the old stables, her eyes narrowing in the darkness of each interior, trying to find old-fashioned light switches, and staring at the great tangling muddles inside the old unkept storage spaces, some full of nothing better than old lawnmowers and petrol cans and garden shears and other ageing or rusting implements. There was even a set of heavy old harness from a team of horses, now long gone, their names carefully engraved on a copper plate down the side.

'What's the Chairman of the Clover House Group like, exactly, Mrs Blaize?'

Mrs Blaize abandoned her history lecture and thought for a minute before answering, 'Sir Harold Ropner? All right, possibly.'

'So if say someone wrote to him with an idea, he might listen?'

'Oh no, Miss O'Flaherty, Sir Harold might be nice, but he's not that nice. Someone like you couldn't write to him and expect a reply, really you couldn't. Chairmen of groups do not have anything to do with area managers or manageresses of individual establishments, nothing at all.'

'In that case, Mrs Blaize, perhaps it is high time they did?'

Seeing the determined look on Ottilie's face, Mrs Blaize smiled. As they turned to retrace their steps back to the main part of the hotel, she gave a satisfied nod. 'I knew you'd be the right person.'

Two days later she was gone.

Fourteen

Ottilie flung open her grey curtains to see the winter sky which exactly matched them. The curtains were most definitely going to be dyed a vibrant shocking blue in the hotel washing machine, and the walls of her dingy housekeeper's room painted a pure snow white. There was a secondhand shop in St Elcombe, selling antiques and old clothes for charity, and nowadays Ottilie never passed it without going in. She had seen an old white Victorian cotton cover in the window. They were actually using it to display ornaments, but if Ottilie had her way in exchange for a couple of pounds and the added purchase of a packet of soap powder by this evening it would be on her bed.

But before this evening something rather more important was about to happen. Sir Harold Ropner was visiting Cornwall, and more particularly the Angel Inn. Ottilie paused on the stairs leading down to the main hall. Since getting up that morning she had tried not to think about what the outcome of Sir Harold's visit might be, or indeed how she had managed to persuade him to come to this small out of the way hotel in St Elcombe. Luck of course had played its part. He had been due to visit his old friends the Staffords at Christopher House, near St Elcombe, but that was not all, it seemed, because the secretary had added on Sir Harold's behalf, 'Sir Harold is very interested in much of what you had to say in your letter to him.'

Ottilie's carefully penned letter had taken her hours. She had handwritten it most meticulously, calculating that it would have far more effect if she wrote it herself in what Edith used to call 'a rather fine hand' rather than have Miss Little, the hotel secretary, type it for her. People like Sir Harold were only ever presented with typewritten letters.

As she put the finishing touches to her self-designed uniform of navy dress and jacket and fastened her long brown hair into a big black velvet bow at the nape of her neck, Ottilie felt so nervous she set herself to breathe in and out very slowly and deeply several times. She knew she had to win Sir Harold over, and she knew that if she showed she was in the slightest degree nervous she would alienate him and make herself seem to be what Philip always called 'a cracking amateur'.

The night before, in an effort to quell her nerves, she had sat on the edge of her bed lecturing herself.

If you show you're nervous it will make him nervous, and if you make him nervous he will feel nervous about what you have to say, and if he's nervous about what you have to say he won't feel like investing in you, so grit your teeth and just pretend as hard as you can, as hard as when you used to be beaten and you had to pretend you didn't care, that's how hard you have to pretend.

Downstairs in the hall, Nantwick the hotel boots, barman, and man-of-all-work was up, already waiting for her orders for the day. At the Grand it had always been Ottilie who tried to make it a point to be up and about long before anyone else, thereby fixing her imprint on the running of the place. She had to hand it to Nantwick. So far he had beaten her to it for every one of the twenty-eight days since she had taken over the management of the Angel.

This morning, however, she was actually grateful for the sight of him padding about, busying himself with the hall fire. Deciding on how best to present her case to Sir Harold had been agonizing. She knew that if she dressed the place up too much for his coming he would not see the need to give them any money. On the other hand, if it was presented in such a way that it looked too dingy, he wouldn't think it promising enough to warrant any more money's being spent on it.

Finally she compromised, and Ottilie, Miss Little, Nantwick and Jean the maid-of-all-work, as she jokingly referred to herself, had repainted and rearranged just one of the main rooms, making it look as nearly as possible how Ottilie would ultimately like the whole inn to look, and then left the rest exactly as it was. This too was a risk.

The risk was that Sir Harold might love the current post-war Station Hotel dingy look that the Angel affected. Or he might be one of those men who simply did not notice anything except the quality of the beer, or the precision with which Nantwick could mix a dry martini.

Drink, however, was not the real problem. The list of Sir Harold's favourite foods discreetly acquired by Miss Little was a much greater one, not least because his preferences seemed to Ottilie to embrace so many foods that she disliked. Oysters, jellied consommés, lobsters, very small game birds, cream sauces on all the vegetables, and a large choice of nursery puddings including 'Queen of Puddings'.

The problem was not that she and Cook – they did not run to 'chefs' at the Angel Inn – were unable to produce these dishes, nor that they did not enjoy the challenge of producing them from the very finest ingredients and the best-written of the classic cookbooks. No, the problem was that Sir Harold was not the only person who would be required to eat them. Ottilie would be too.

Afterwards, long afterwards, Ottilie would wonder at the audacity she showed that morning and tremble for her younger self, but now as the famous flying lady on Sir Harold's pre-war Rolls-Royce pushed her nose past the kitchens and came to a halt where once the coaches would pull up with cries of 'Ostler!' there was only Ottilie, trim and tidy in her navy blue skirt and jacket and dark stockings, her long dark hair tied back in a black velvet bow.

When she had sat down to write to him with her request for him to visit them at the Angel Ottilie had not stopped to consider the character of the man to whom she was writing, or why he had earned for himself such a fearsome reputation. All she could see was what she wanted to do to the inn, and how much money she needed to do it. Nothing else seemed to matter, until she saw him.

As soon as she clapped eyes on him it came to her why his name had seemed to have such a familiar ring to it. She had supposed it was because he was chairman of the Clover House Group and she must have read about him in the business section of *The Times* or the *Telegraph*, or because she had seen his photograph in one of the magazines escorting some beautiful divorcee to a ball, but as soon as she saw him now walking towards her, and she said, 'Good morning, Sir Harold,' it came to Ottilie why it was that she knew the man.

Sir Harold had once been a regular at the Grand at St Elcombe in the days when it was fashionable. He had been handsome in a florid sort of way, dark finger-waved hair, a fresh complexion, and an affable presence, but now he was grey-haired, fat, and red-faced with broken veins running from his nose, a large handkerchief flopping too far out of his expensive suit and his handshake as 'wet as a rector's'.

'What shall I say, Miss O'Flaherty?' he asked with a sigh, looking round at the dirty cream walls of the reception hall, his plump square-fingered hand indicating the door. 'Probably *nothing* would be best.'

Ottilie's returning smile was far too wide but there was nothing she could do about it. It was the relief. He obviously had not recognized her. She surrendered a short prayer of thanks for Lorcan, since it was he who had advised her to change her name back from Cartaret to O'Flaherty so that there could be no possible confusion with herself and 'the folks back at the Grand'.

Having walked ahead of her into the lounge and seen the dreariness of the interior, the grease on the walls, the dingy furniture, he now turned round and asked, 'Miss O'Flaherty, where can we sit and have a drink where we will not be in some kind of danger to our health?'

'Practically nowhere,' Ottilie told him ingenuously.

There was a short pause and then Sir Harold looked at Ottilie and started to shake with the kind of laughter that in such a large man made Ottilie nervous he might do himself damage. 'My dear Miss O'Flaherty,' he said finally, 'in all my tours of these wretched old inns, that is one of the few honest things anyone has ever said to me.' He spread the handkerchief with which he had mopped his face over the seat of an armchair and sat down quite suddenly.

It was then that he looked up at Ottilie, waiting, expecting the next move, and Ottilie knew at once that her professional trial had begun.

'Sir Harold, might we offer you something to drink?'

'You might indeed, Miss O'Flaherty.'

For a second Sir Harold's eyes, so full of anxiety and unease, narrowed as he tilted back his head, lit a cigarette and waited as Ottilie again prayed, silently and passionately, that Sir Harold's secretary, whom Miss Little had telephoned to know of his preferences, would not have betrayed them by giving them the wrong information.

'I can offer you an anise, a Pernod, or a pink gin made with Bombay gin?'

At the mention of those three drinks, Sir Harold let out a sigh of relief, a sigh which seemed to run down his large, closely tailored and amply upholstered body in ripples, as if the sigh was a brook and his body some sort of embankment through which the brook was sinuously threading its way.

'Miss O'Flaherty, I can see that despite the greasy spoon decor and the much used seating I am going to be in safe hands.'

'I hope so, Sir Harold.'

'Bombay gin. Imagine. Normally only Laurie at the Ritz offers me Bombay.'

Ottilie did not like to tell him that she had sent to Fortnum and Mason's in London for it and that the gin and all the other specialities that she had laid on for him had cost her as much as Nantwick was likely to take in a whole two weeks at their bar. If the expenditure did not pay off Ottilie was not at all sure whether she would be able to balance the books ever again.

The luncheon table was set in the one freshly decorated room, and on Ottilie's orders in the French manner, white linen cloth, heavy white napkins – all bought secondhand for the occasion from the thrift shop by Ottilie – not to mention the flowers which she had fled to the early morning markets to purchase so that the scent of the white hyacinths was discernible as they walked into the splendidly inviting room decorated with many bunches of daffodils upon whose pale trumpets little drops of dew were still visible.

'Ah, oysters.' Sir Harold breathed in appreciatively as if he could smell their freshness before he sat down, and he stubbed out his cigarette in one of Miss Little's ashtrays that she had brought from home for the occasion.

'Ugh, oysters,' is what Ottilie would have liked to have said, but instead she sat composedly looking down the length of the table at her illustrious guest, unpicked her starched napkin with assumed verve and smiled with equally assumed cheerfulness before facing the agony of squeezing the lemon on each one and then tipping them down her throat, all the time being watched approvingly and then matched, oyster for oyster, by Sir Harold himself.

He evidently approved heartily of a young woman who could eat as many oysters as himself and even lifted his head slightly, his mouth falling open just a little as he watched Ottilie tilting her own head back to swallow them, one after wretched one, only to feel the awful slither as she gave the large gulp necessary to down the wretched thing.

Ottilie would never forget the horror of that first course, the awful feeling of something which was technically alive slipping down her throat, and then the worse feeling that they were actually alive inside her. After the oysters came a confection of lobster and crevettes served with a mayonnaise and thin brown bread.

Possibly because she was only barely holding on to the first course the second did not appeal to her either, and this despite the fact that she had made the mayonnaise herself, drip by little drip. Normally she was happy to eat shrimps and lobsters but at that particular moment they appealed to Ottilie as a wondrous part of God's creation, living and beautiful, not dead and edible, and the matchless pink of the lobster seemed heartbreaking in its purity, not deserving to disappear for ever down Sir Harold and herself. Yet she ate on, asking questions and making conversational replies which carefully concealed anything about herself and showed only interest in Sir Harold and his career.

Next came the *médaillons* of beef on softly fried rounds of toast and accompanied by a béarnaise sauce which again Ottilie had taken care to make herself. They were served with tiny early carrots and small French fries and were, she had to admit, pretty perfect. After that came a salad, a very good olive oil found abandoned in a cellar, vinegar from the Loire, and finally cheese presented in the French manner to finish up the red wine. With the pudding she served a really very delicate white dessert wine.

'My dear.' Sir Harold pushed his chair back from the table and lit a cigar so big that for one awful moment Ottilie was sure that it was going to be too big for him to manage. 'My dear, what a perfect luncheon. You are to be congratulated, Miss O'Flaherty. I haven't had such a delicious lunch since last week at the Savoy, and even then

I am not sure that the freshness of the ingredients quite matched up to yours, by any means.'

Sir Harold smiled and then slowly pulled on his cigar.

'Now tell me, why on earth should I give you money for your enterprise here?'

'Because,' Ottilie said slowly, 'if you look round this place it needs it, and if I can impress you with a good luncheon then you know I can do it for others. I know I can make this place really successful.'

'But Miss O'Flaherty, don't you realize you have done quite the wrong thing?' Sir Harold's eyes seemed to be full of mocking pity. 'I mean how can you possibly lay on a lunch like this for me and then expect me to give you money?'

Ottilie felt her blood running cold. She had done something terribly wrong and she knew it before she had even begun to reply. She knew it from the expression in his eyes, and yet for the life of her she could not imagine what it could be. The food had been as near to perfection as was surely possible, and the wines had not lagged far behind, although admittedly she had been rather restricted by cost in that area. Even so, she thought, her mind racing, where had she gone wrong? Why was she about to be refused what she so desperately needed to make a success of the Angel?

'Tell me, is this the sort of lunch you are hoping to give your guests, Miss O'Flaherty? Is this the sort of menu you think might be suitable for these parts?'

'Good heavens no.'

Quick as a flash Ottilie had seen what was coming.

'No? Are these not your standards then, Miss O'Flaherty?'

'No, not at all.' Ottilie gave him a measured look. 'These are your standards, as I understand them. In a place like this I would never be able to afford to produce a menu like that for anyone but Sir Harold Ropner. No, our menus here at the Angel are quite different, just as our ambience will be quite different. Luncheon a choice of hot or cold home-made soup and rolls, all made on the premises. Also a large selection of every sort of salad – rice, potato, tomato – with a choice of home-made pork pies and sausages, and of course a large home-cooked ham. Puddings will be perfect but homely, treacle tart, lemon meringue, proper trifle made with home-made cake and Cornish cream, a choice of cheeses to follow, and coffee, also properly made, of course.'

There was a long pause as Sir Harold's eyes narrowed again, but this time because of his own cigar smoke.

'You must include your Queen of Puddings. That was one of the best I have ever tasted.'

'Certainly,' Ottilie said, and she smiled although she still felt as sick as a dog. Not purely on account of the oysters, but because she surmised that she had just been within seconds of losing everything.

'What is it you are going to try to achieve here?'

Ottilie folded her napkin and stood up. Sir Harold remained seated. Ottilie waited, pointedly. Sir Harold at length rose from his chair and replaced his own napkin on the tablecloth.

'Is it time for the Loyal Toast?' he asked ironically.

'No, it's time for the historic tour,' Ottilie told him. 'You asked the twenty-thousand-dollar question, Sir Harold, and I am now going to try to answer it for you. If you will follow me?'

'With some difficulty after that luncheon, Miss O'Flaherty,' came the suddenly good-natured reply.

Equally suddenly Ottilie took a step or two towards him and held out her arm which, after a second, Sir Harold took.

'I will take the shortest route.'

'Short cuts are some of the longest ways round, didn't Mrs O'Flaherty tell you?'

'Oh, Ma, yes, she told me that. And—' Ottilie stopped as Sir Harold's hand seemed to be growing heavier and heavier on her arm.

'And?'

'And to be thankful for the day and never look further.'

Sir Harold snorted. 'Not a philosophy that will take you very far, Miss O'Flaherty. What a good thing you learned to make mayonnaise and *sauce béarnaise* and arrange flowers.'

They were out in the stableyard once more, and Sir Harold seemed to be benefiting from the cold fresh spring air. The hand on her arm grew lighter as he became caught up in Ottilie's imaginings of how the stableyard could be converted, of just how the style and feeling of the place could be preserved, of how she wanted to make all the colours, quite against the current fashion for bright oranges and dark browns, soft, pale and old-fashioned in feeling. She told him of the fountain that she wanted to put at the top of the courtyard, of the fresh-cut flowers that she wanted to grow in a greenhouse and of the new cypher she planned, the 'A' of the Angel Inn woven around a cherub-like angel.

She had been talking non-stop when of a sudden she fell silent, realizing that Sir Harold was no longer taking in what she was saying and was staring not at the old courtyard but at Ottilie herself.

'Well, well, well, what a positive person you are, Miss O'Flaherty. Do you know, your enthusiasm and excitement about your subject even convert me.' He stopped, throwing away his cigar butt into a flower bed. 'But do you know something? With all your ideas, all your energy, it seems to me that you are not in the least suited to this place. No, my dear, with your breadth of vision, in my view you would be far better suited managing that run-down old palace, the Grand.'

At which remark Ottilie tried to smile, but failed.

Days passed and turned into a fortnight, and still Ottilie had heard nothing from Sir Harold, just a formal note from his secretary thanking her for luncheon and saying that he would be writing to her personally in the near future. It wasn't long before Ottilie came to realize that it was quite possible she would never hear anything again from her distinguished guest. To guard against the hurt that his rejection would bring she started making up her mind to accept defeat long before her letter of dismissal arrived. It was better, she told Miss Little, to accept that she had not only failed personally to impress Sir Harold, but undoubtedly failed to impress on him why what she had wanted in terms of warmth and style would suit an establishment such as the Angel.

'I mean you always think you can get other people to see things your way, but you can't, can you?'

Miss Little, who was thirty, slim and dark, pale, anxious and conscientious to a fault, smiled nervously as she looked up from changing the ribbon on her old-fashioned sit-up-and-beg typewriter.

'I wish I wasn't so pig-headed,' Ottilie went on, trying to find a new ribbon for her in the old office desk that was being propped up by a telephone book of about the same vintage as the typewriter. 'But you see I am so convinced that this is the way for these sorts of places to go. Stop them being down and dirty pubs and transform them instead into the old-fashioned, medium-priced, warmly welcoming old-style inn, just like in Dickens' time when the fires would be roaring and the pies home-made and everyone jumping about to make you welcome. Here in the land that invented Myne Hoste we would be fulfilling a need, wouldn't we? God, do you realize this telephone still says "St Elcombe 234"!'

Ottilie raised her eyes to heaven and handed Miss Little a new black ribbon for the typewriter.

'You won't want to stay here much longer, will you?' she asked her secretary suddenly. 'I don't blame you, it's terrible.'

'I like a challenge, really I do,' Veronica Little told her just a little too quickly.

'I'll go for the post before I start to get any more tiresome than I am already,' Ottilie said, sighing and leaving poor Veronica to blackened fingers and a still unworkable 'h' on the typewriter.

It was a relief to walk out of the office and into the courtyard where the post was still left in an old box in the archway, enabling the horsemen of yesterday to throw it in without dismounting. Ottilie turned her head away from the post, grabbing it and not looking at it, which had become a sort of superstition with her, not to look at the letters until she was back in the office – rather like getting down the last bit of stairs before the loo finished flushing – and stared at the courtyard. She longed so much to pull it all down and rebuild it sometimes it was all she could do not to start, at once, with her own hands.

'Please, God!' she prayed to the leaden sky above, but she knew that God had something rather more important on His mind so she quickly went inside and put the post on Veronica's desk, saying as she did every morning, 'You look, I can't.'

Veronica paused in her typewriter-servicing duties, shook her head, and went to wash her hands before returning and saying, 'Very well, fingers crossed, Miss O'Flaherty, fingers crossed!'

She sat down at her desk, very much the secretary now, and started to leaf through the letters in complete silence. She stopped one before the last and looked up at Ottilie.

'Oh Lord, it's come,' she breathed, at which they both stared first at each other and then at the square, thick white envelope with its small, shiny red crest engraved on the back and the neatly written 'Miss Ottilie O'Flaherty' on the front and then at each other again.

'A letter from Sir Harold himself, handwritten.'

Veronica who had stood up at once, as if he had come into the room, reverently handed the small white envelope over her desk to Ottilie, who took it and stared at it.

'No, it's no use, I can't read it.' Ottilie handed it back.

'It's in his own handwriting.'

'I know. That's why I can't read it. You read it to me.'

Veronica put on her glasses, very modern and up-to-date with black frames.

'"*Dear Miss O'Flaherty*."' She stopped for a second.

'What's the matter?' Ottilie stared at her. 'There must be more, surely?'

'Yes, of course there's more, it's just that I can hardly bear to read it. In case you're disappointed.'

'I see. Well, never mind.'

'"*Dear Miss O'Flaherty, I have given much thought to your idea, and regret to say—*" Dear, his handwriting is really rather appalling, Miss O'Flaherty, really it is. It seems to be pulling in both directions, a sign of a rather weak personality I'm afraid. But to continue. Where was I? Yes. "*I have given much thought to your idea and regret to say—*"'

'Oh damn, damn, damn.'

Ottilie fell into the old office sofa and buried her head in a cushion. Damn, damn, double, double damn, she screamed silently into the worn old brocade cover.

'There is more,' she dimly heard Veronica telling her. 'Yes. Now where was I? Ah yes. I "*regret to say that your – idea*" yes "*your idea is remarkably*" what's this word? Oh yes, I see "*apt.*" I think that's it. "*I say I regret it, Miss O, because it means considerable company expenditure, but as you said at our luncheon there is a definite need for this kind of hostelry and there is nothing in England at the moment between the very grand and the spit and sawdust. I will therefore have no hesitation in granting you the monies that will be needed for your improvements at the Angel Inn, and provided you keep to the budget and make the mayonnaise yourself I would think you will soon be sitting in my chair at Head Office.*

'"*Thank you again for a most enjoyable luncheon. Yours sincerely, Harold Ropner.*"'

Ottilie took her head out of the cushion and straightened up as Veronica removed her glasses. They stared at each other.

'Oh, Miss Little – Veronica.'

'Yes, Miss O'Flaherty?'

'Would you mind terribly reading that letter again to me? Word by little word?'

'Of course not.' This time Veronica read it far faster.

'And again, Veronica. And again. And again. Once more with feeling! You're getting better at it every time!'

Obediently Veronica put back her spectacles and word by little word repeated her by now really rather polished performance, after which Ottilie jumped all over the sofa and Veronica looked as if she was about to burst into tears.

'Do you know I really think this is the happiest day of my life, Miss O'Flaherty?'

'Do you know, Veronica, I think this might be mine?'

Fifteen

It had never been open to Ottilie to change anything at all at the Grand. The Grand had been like a great old ocean liner. There was only one way it operated and that was the way it had always done, and even when the staff shrank and it became an almost insuperable problem to keep the huge floral arrangements on every floor fresh, with the water in the vast vases changed daily and each flower stem checked for peak perfection, even when just the polishing of the twelve pieces of silver set at every place for every meal took until midnight, that was how it had always been done, and that was how it seemed it would always be done at the Grand, St Elcombe.

Even in her own suite Ottilie was never allowed to change anything. Once she had decided to privately adopt the seven-year-old Ottilie O'Flaherty, Melanie had sent for a designer from Truro to come and draw up a design for the ideal little girl's bedroom and sitting room, and he had done so with an eye to detail which was quite perfect and his design was one which Mr Hulton and his team were more than happy to implement.

Hence the curtains were of a pale salmon printed with small girls wearing Kate Greenaway dresses and hats, the dressing table was draped with organza underlined with a pale salmon silk, and the carpet was of palest French blue with a flowered design arranged in Madame de Pompadour fashion – small knotted bunches of pale pink roses set at discreet intervals.

The books too were all arranged in alphabetical order on

mahogany shelving of the most delicate kind – Queen Anne copies – and the books themselves were all old, beautifully printed children's books of the kind that still have tissue paper over the illustrations and dates never later than 1939. Dresses were hung in wardrobes with mahogany shelving, drawers lined with scented flowered paper and lavender bags placed everywhere 'against the flies, Miss Ottilie' Edith would always say.

Ottilie's private bathroom was a designer's dream of what a little girl's bathroom should be. The bath itself was built into an edifice that was shaped and painted to resemble a swan. The 'la-la' as Edith called it was a little throne with salmon-pink carpeted steps up and a salmon-pink satin embroidered cover over the lid with 'O.C.' sewn on it in raised blue silk.

Wherever possible everything else in the bathroom and bedroom had also been salmon-pink satin and embroidered. Ottilie's sponge bag, her nightdress case, her dressing gowns – always ordered from the same shop, year in year out – her slippers, her ribbons for night-time, her counterpane, even her lawn nightdresses were trimmed with the same salmon-pink satin ribbons.

Of course, after living at the cottage and sharing her bed with Ma, her suite at the Grand had seemed to be a sort of paradise of space and luxury to the young Ottilie, with toys and books that Lorcan and the boys, and up until then Ottilie herself, would not have even glimpsed in a shop window, so exclusive were they to the rich.

But then, inevitably, she had matured and her feeling for colour developed, and long before she went to Paris Ottilie had started to feel absurd bathing in the painted swan, however pretty. But there was no question of change. She had been adopted into salmon-pink satin and in salmon-pink satin she would remain.

All this was why being granted the money she wanted to redesign the Angel was such a heady moment for Ottilie. More and more it seemed to her that the Courtyard Suites, as they were destined to be known, were going to be the best suites in the place, principally because when starting afresh it was easy to design rooms more spacious and bathrooms more luxurious than the bedrooms and bathrooms in the inn itself. Using a local architect, she commissioned a series of ground-floor double bedrooms with windows overlooking the courtyard and picture windows overlooking the gardens, but first she and Veronica went in search of that most elusive event, the genuine country house sale.

Ottilie and Veronica arrived early at the old house clutching their catalogues and convinced that they were about to find Old Masters for a few pounds and Knole sofas for only a little more than that. Instead, faced with someone else's treasured possessions all marked and catalogued, not only unwanted but so unloved by anyone in her family that they sought only to sell them, they both became quite low with the sadness of it all, and Ottilie could not help thinking of Philip and how he loved not just Tredegar, but everything in it. Supposing everything there had to be put up for sale as it was in this house?

Suddenly the last time she had seen him seemed even more likely to be the last time she would *ever* see him.

She remembered how tall and handsome he had looked in his uniform, and how courageous he had been, perhaps knowing all the time that he might not come back, and trying to pretend not to care. She delayed going into the main rooms and from there to the marquee where the sale was being held, fascinated and appalled by a brass plaque with the roll call of the dead from two world wars upon which was inscribed not just the names of the sons of the house but the names of the gardeners and grooms who had once worked on the estate. There was even a Granville.

'Let's go for a coffee.'

'I usually only feel sort of sad like this when autumn

comes and I hear my mother or my aunt singing "The Last Rose of Summer",' Veronica tried to joke to Ottilie when they found the impromptu refreshment area set out in the stables. 'It's all those little things – the boot jacks and the old hunting boots, the silver christening mugs. You'd think someone in her family would have wanted to treasure them, wouldn't you? Or even just some of the framed photographs of their relatives who died in the war. You'd think they'd be of interest.'

Ottilie nodded, but Veronica could see that she could hardly concentrate on what she was saying and was polite enough to fall silent and study her catalogue, for all Ottilie could see was Philip dead like those young boys whose pictures lay marked up and priced for sale in the very reception rooms in which they would have once played as children, or danced with their girlfriends to the wind-up gramophone, or as one of their aunts or sisters played the old Steinway.

It was a relief when, minutes later, the auction started.

To begin with it was a little boring waiting for the items they had marked to come up, but when they did Ottilie became quite tense with the excitement of waving her catalogue at the right moment. Perhaps because the weather was bad there were not as many people as anticipated, and in what finally seemed like seconds two lovely old Persian rugs became the property of the Angel Inn. After that it was Veronica's turn and she bid for and won a Chippendale-style chest of drawers, a very well made Victorian copy, and what guest would complain that it wasn't genuine Chippendale?

Sets of three dozen plates, old cake dishes, fish knives and forks – old linen tablecloths, a mahogany barometer. Ottilie and Veronica, while keeping a keen eye on their budget, started to grow in confidence as the day wore on, nodding and flapping their catalogues until they gradually acquired the kind of furnishings that would grace the old inn and make it look as if they had always been there.

Staying right until the last pitchfork and garden bench had been bid for, they finally walked out into the dark of the early spring evening with the largest fountain sold privately in Cornwall in recent years, or so the auctioneer had said. It was vast, far too large for most people's gardens, but perfect for the courtyard of the Angel Inn. Three stone horses prancing, the water destined to come from a fountain at their centre.

Driving home in Oscar and practically whooping with joy at their success, Ottilie confided to Veronica that there was only one thing that had puzzled her. 'I don't understand why there were not more people there?'

There was a sudden silence from the secretary in the passenger seat beside her. Veronica stared ahead into the darkness, seemingly concentrating on the narrow road ahead lit dimly by Oscar's lights, on the high hedges either side, on the rain that was falling to be lightly swished away somewhat haphazardly by the Citroën's windscreen wipers.

But Ottilie would not let it go. 'Veronica. You know something I don't know. Please tell me?'

'Well,' Veronica began, stopped, and then glanced at Ottilie's profile as she drove. 'You must promise not to tell, but the auction was a bit of a sort of a fix, I'm afraid, according to Mr Pennington.'

Ottilie frowned. She took her eyes from the narrow country road with its high hedges momentarily and stared at Veronica, who she had only just begun to realize really had hidden depths. 'You've got your still-waters-run-deep look. What is it? You know something I don't. Mr Pennington knows something I don't. You both know something I don't. I want to know something I don't, so please, please, tell me.'

Veronica bit her lip and paused, but then she spoke.

'I'll tell you, Miss O'Flaherty, but you must understand that neither Mr Pennington nor myself had anything to do with it. We just knew about it, if you understand me, we didn't organize it?'

Ottilie nodded briefly, still frowning to see through the evening rain and unable to risk turning to look at her secretary again. 'Very well. Go on.'

'The reason there were only just locals at the sale, if you noticed, and a few people from Truro and Plymouth after the books, no real London dealers, is very simple. You see, local people really liked the owner of the house, old Miss Princeton Blount, and when she died her relatives had no interest in taking on anything of hers – just interested in the money and that was it – so they determined to buy as many of her lovely possessions as possible not just because they were rather old and rather nice but because they knew the old lady would have wanted her things to go to people she knew and liked – that way they would stay in Cornwall, which old Miss Princeton Blount loved. But of course at London prices the locals knew they wouldn't possibly be able to afford them, would they?'

'Well, no. So what did they do?'

Without turning her head Ottilie knew that Veronica was smiling despite her serious tone.

'Well – you mustn't tell anyone, but they turned many of the country signposts to the auction round so that the dealers from London arrived either too late or not at all.' Ottilie started to laugh as Veronica finished, 'Not for nothing do they say never cross a Cornishman!'

And so back to dinner at the Angel and that odd feeling of real achievement that the purchase of bargains brings. As the work on the conversion of the stables progressed that too brought new excitement. Ottilie found that for the first time since her month in Paris she was springing out of bed earlier and earlier, sometimes arriving in the office or on the site before even the builders arrived, and as each rotten timber was thrown out and new wood arrived, as she decided on keeping the rough stonework in the small halls and entrances, as she searched out shops that would give her discounts on new beds and designed four-posters that looked like four-posters but were really just curtains, as she chose Spanish lamps decorated in the old manner but gave them large white silk shades sewn by Veronica's mum, and white bathroom suites with pale carpets and small oil seascapes that she was able to buy from local galleries, without realizing it she started to bloom with health.

'You're looking much better, Miss O'Flaherty.'

Ottilie looked up from her account books, surprised by Veronica's sudden statement. The state of her looks, never one of her own preoccupations, was not something she thought anyone else noticed.

'You – well, you won't mind me saying this, will you?' Veronica went on, hesitant at first, but obviously encouraged by the glass of whisky Ottilie had fetched her from the bar. 'But when you first arrived here, frankly I thought Mrs Blaize had made a grave mistake. You seemed far too young for the position, only then I could see from your very first day that you knew what it was all about, that although you were young you were quite tough, which you certainly have to be in this business. But you were always so pale and tense. And, as a matter of fact, I started to feel sorry for you having to shoulder so much in a greasy spoon place such as this was. It didn't seem right, so instead of leaving, which frankly I was about to do, I stayed on, and I'm very glad I did.'

'I'm glad you did too.'

They smiled at each other, which prompted Ottilie to say, 'I was wondering if you'd like to call me by my first name?'

'Thank you, but no.' Veronica smiled, shook her head and went back to typing out the rewritten brochure. 'Frankly the last manager before Mrs Blaize had everyone calling him Geoff and it didn't stop the place going to rack and ruin.'

'I don't suppose it was because of what they called him.

301

More to do with what he drank, from what I hear.'

But Veronica would not be moved, frowning and shaking her head and saying again, 'Thank you, but no.'

Veronica, like Ottilie, took making a success of the Angel very seriously, and yet Ottilie could not prevent herself feeling lighthearted when she walked round the Courtyard Suites once the carpets had been laid, and saw just how smart and welcoming everything looked. And then it was somehow magical to wander out again into the courtyard and stand and admire the horse fountain that had been such a bargain, and from there to step back into the inn and see the fires, warm and welcoming, and watch more and more new customers arriving.

As she had promised Sir Harold the bar menu was a welcoming choice of soup and salads all for one price and dinner a simple classically based menu. In fact everything had turned out how she had hoped. The reception rooms painted in old-fashioned pale colours, the flagstone floors laid with faded rugs, candlesticks commissioned from a local potter arranged on the dining tables with the new cypher Ottilie had designed set in the middle of their bases; and what with the old cream holland blinds that she had found in the attics cleaned up, and parchment lampshades over pink light bulbs softening the look of everything, it was probably not surprising, so speedy is 'word of mouth', that the Angel rarely had a table free.

Thanks to Lorcan, in a matter of months Ottilie had gone from a sort of hopeless boredom to that state of being happily busy from early dawn to late at night without a moment to think of anything beyond the welfare of her staff and guests. All the more shocking therefore when one night she heard a scream coming from the dining room.

A childhood spent in a hotel meant that even as Ottilie started to hurry towards the dining room she already knew that it would only be a matter of a moment before she was confronted by a white-faced waitress. At the Grand it had always been known as 'the spider in the salad scream' and whenever it had happened Alfred or Mrs Tomber had always sighed and shrugged their shoulders.

As she waited in the service area for Jean to emerge from the dining room clutching a plate of roast pork and potatoes, half eaten, the knife and fork still on the plate, Ottilie reminded herself that this was always the first symbol of success in the hotel trade.

'I just can't believe it. I served the lady myself, Miss O'Flaherty, really I did. I know I would have noticed a piece of glass that size. 'Sides, no-one's broken anything for days.'

Quickly calling Veronica to deal with the customer who had screamed, Ottilie herself rushed off to examine the piece. Having satisfied herself as to its exact shape and design she beckoned to Jean to follow her into the main part of the kitchen.

'Crowd round, I want witnesses. Good. Now, Jean, you have not touched this piece of glass since the lady in question found it?'

'No, Miss O'Flaherty.'

'Mrs East,' Ottilie turned to Cook, 'please remove the piece with one of your serving spoons, and Martin – come here, please, bringing with you each of our glasses. Now you are all witnesses to this, and thank heavens we opted for the same design for all the glasses so there are definitely no variations in the rims. Now, see, the rim of the plant – because believe me this is what this is – if you look you can see it is quite different from our own, having a rolled edge to the top, whereas you can see our own glasses have no cheap rolled edge, they are quite plain.'

There was a ripple of relief and then admiration from everyone around Ottilie. Barely able to contain her indignation, she said, 'If you will please all follow me, bringing with you the plate, and the piece of glass on a napkin, we will see this one down and very publicly too.'

Yet another murmur and the staff, looking amazed, followed Ottilie back through the service doors into the restaurant. Ottilie clapped her hands for attention as she remembered seeing her father do many times.

'Ladies and gentlemen, I want your attention please.' She looked sharply round the room as she began to make her speech and saw at once to her immense disappointment that the woman who had screamed, and her companion, were no longer present. 'As you no doubt just heard the lady who was only recently sitting at that table found a piece of glass in her food. A piece of glass that had no business in her food. A piece of glass, ladies and gentlemen, that had no business not just in her food but anywhere in this hotel since, ladies and gentlemen, and I have seven witnesses here to this effect, not one of our glasses have this design to their top. Hold it up please, Jean. Here is one of our glasses and here is the piece of glass just found. Take them round to each of the tables, please.'

The strange little ceremony that followed started uncertainly but as each set of guests could see the point of what the management was trying to prove it gained in popularity. Ottilie once more clapped her hands for attention.

'I think we are all agreed therefore, ladies and gentlemen, that this piece of glass did not come into this dining room via the kitchens?'

'I've read about this sort of thing happening in restaurants, but never actually seen it for myself, d'you know? Fascinating, absolutely fascinating,' one guest announced to everyone. 'People like that should be shot.'

'Yes they should be,' Ottilie agreed, overhearing her. 'Only trouble is that some minutes ago "they" disappeared before we could have the satisfaction of shooting them!'

At which there was general laughter and eventually a return to the sort of heightened normality that always accompanies averted crises.

'What a good thing you dealt with the situation as fast as you did,' Veronica congratulated Ottilie. 'Like something in a murder story, wouldn't you say?'

'I knew from my previous life at the Grand just what to look for. My father warned me, years ago, that they often make a fundamental mistake – with glass especially. They plant just any old piece, not one that matches the kind used at the hotel.'

Veronica nodded but looked pensive suddenly. 'Hope they don't try again,' she said, voicing Ottilie's own fears.

She had suddenly realized just what the real reason for Mrs Blaize's sudden departure must have been, nothing to do with a sick husband and everything to do with sabotage. That must also be the reason for the Angel going downhill under previous managements, the usual dirty tricks. They'd already had false bookings but she had paid little attention to them.

Poor old Geoff and Mrs Blaize, perhaps they had refused to pay protection, perhaps that was indeed why they had been in and out of the place so quickly?

Ottilie breathed in deeply.

'Do you know who it might be?' Veronica persisted, her face anxious, her darkly lined eyes frowning, glasses on top of her head, her expression more earnest than ever.

Ottilie couldn't say 'Yes, I have a horrible suspicion I do' so instead, she said, 'No.'

When all was said and done Veronica was far too nice to be told whom it was that Ottilie really did suspect.

Sixteen

There it was. Ottilie stared at it hard, convinced just for a moment that it would go away. But no, it stayed. Quite black, confidently black, in fact the figures appeared to be so black that they almost seemed to be sitting up on the page on which they had been typed. But sitting up or lying down there they were and they were insistently exciting, because they meant there was money in her newly opened bank account, and in her name, and she had earned it all for herself, by herself.

She put the envelope with her bank statement into the top drawer of the old white-painted chest of drawers and sitting down at her dressing table she stared at her image in the mirror in front of her. Things would not continue so well unless she found out, and soon, just who was behind paying that couple to put glass in their food the previous week. It would only take a few more such incidents and trade could be ruined in months.

After all not every piece of glass could be proved not to be the property of the hotel, or as Veronica said, succinctly, 'It's going to be more difficult to prove that, say, a corn plaster in the soup is not the property of the Angel Inn, isn't it?'

She was right, and because she was right, Ottilie made. light of it. 'Yes, that will be difficult,' she agreed. 'Still, all is not doom and gloom. I see the share price for the Clover House Group has rocketed.' She gave a little whistle. 'It seems Sir Harold's enthusiasm for the individual is beginning to pay off.' Ottilie placed the business section of the *Daily Telegraph* across Veronica's typewriter.

From the time she was quite small Ottilie had grown into the habit of consulting share prices, because she had so often been put to read them aloud to the old ladies and gentlemen staying at the Grand. The habit of reading the business news first had become strangely ingrained.

'Oh dear, have you seen this?'

This time it was Veronica who laid the newspaper across Ottilie's own desk. Ottilie picked it up. Amid all the words in front of her, small items of late foreign news, she saw only three – British officer killed.

Right up until his posting, all through the winter, Philip had occasionally written to Ottilie, letters full of humorous observations and funny little cartoons of himself and fellow officers in the mess, himself with hangover, and all the usual sort of jokes doing the round of his regiment. Ottilie had read and re-read his few letters so often that they had become quite faded with the intensity of her devotion, and since he had been posted abroad she had tried to tell herself that crossing the road in St Elcombe, or driving too fast to London, was probably just as dangerous as being in the Army. Unfortunately, she was unable to convince herself.

She knew just from the way he talked that being in the Army *was* all about being killed and no matter what Philip said or wrote to her about 'keeping the peace' in reality his life was all about being shot at. So that try as she might again and again, in the middle of the night, or when there was a slight lull in the day, she would find herself turning away from the image of Philip's flag-draped coffin arriving back at St Elcombe station.

Sometimes Ottilie had longed to ring Constantia, knowing that she was most probably more up to date with news about the conflict and surmising that she would doubtless have the kind of news that would never reach a newspaper. Most of the Granvilles' friends were in the Army. Constantia would know wives with husbands in the same

308

regiment as Philip, be friends with other sisters whose brothers were his fellow officers.

Yet much as Ottilie longed to ring Constantia she knew that to do so would be to risk a rebuff. Philip's disappearing to the island with Ottilie the night of the dinner dance would have been too public a display of ardour for Constantia. She was Philip's only sister, his only real relative – his falling in love with Ottilie would not have been something she could welcome. Which was obviously the reason that Ottilie had not heard from anyone at Tredegar since the night of the party, which made it all the more surprising when minutes after seeing under 'Late News – British officer killed in Cyprus' Veronica, having answered the telephone, called quietly across the office, 'A Miss Granville on the line for you, do you want to speak to her?'

Ottilie nodded and took the receiver from Veronica, but as she did so she was so sure that Constantia was telephoning to tell her that Philip had been killed that she found she could not find her voice enough to say 'hello'.

Constantia spoke first, not bothering with 'hello'. 'No longer a Cartaret, eh?' she said in her strangely boyish voice. 'Well, never mind. Whatever you are now come to lunch tomorrow, will you?'

Without saying any more she replaced the receiver, and Ottilie handed Veronica back the telephone. It was not until a few seconds had elapsed that she realized with relief that Constantia had never even mentioned Philip.

She must have looked shaken because Veronica asked, 'Are you all right?'

Ottilie nodded, but Veronica could not have believed her because seconds later she sprang up and going to their refreshment cupboard quickly poured her a glass of water.

Twenty-four hours later Ottilie found herself looking round the Angel's restaurant and imagining what Constantia might be doing at that moment. Preparatory to their luncheon she would probably have been woken at around eight thirty by her maid bringing her the news-papers and a Lord Roberts Workshop tray laid with fresh orange juice, fresh coffee and some healthy toasted home-made bread.

After that she would most likely have gone for a ride around the estate on her part-thoroughbred, jumping logs, cantering across meadows, her hair streaming out behind her, before returning to throw the reins at the groom and walk slowly up to the house for a long soak in a bath. Next she would dress slowly and carefully, probably choosing a plain silk shirt and immaculately cut trousers, which, after she had carefully knotted an Hermès scarf around her neck, would make her look just as everyone, everywhere, wanted their daughters to look. Correct, conservative, beautifully dressed, obviously and becomingly well bred and immensely suited to country life, and most particu-larly the front picture of the magazine of that name.

By contrast, in order to take the necessary time out to go to lunch with Constantia at Tredegar Ottilie had had to set her alarm an hour earlier – at five o'clock instead of six. She went to market to buy all the fresh flowers preparatory to arranging them, and then checked with Mrs East as to the state of breakfast, especially for those guests who were having it in their rooms. The quality of the bread rolls and brioches must always be tested daily. (Two of Ottilie's many hatreds were over-baked breakfast rolls or a brioche that was in any way greasy.)

Next would be the luncheon dishes – which cold or hot soup they would be making, and which salads; and it never went amiss to check on the quality of the vegetables and taste the stock. Again, Mrs East, if not watched like a hawk, had the shocking habit of using cooked bones for stock which gave the soup a greasy edge.

After this Ottilie had hopped upstairs to the dining rooms and checked on the table settings, the state of the cloakrooms and the bookings for the day, and popped in to see Veronica – this morning she had been in fine fettle, the inn having received a strong commendation in *Saxone Addington's Guide to England*. Although not a Michelin star, they both agreed it was at least something.

After all this Ottilie had just enough time to run up to her newly painted white room and throw herself into a cotton dress, at the same time pulling on her new navy shoes – which had to double both for good occasions and work – and equally hurriedly brush her hair, freshen her lipstick, jump into Oscar and drive herself to Tredegar, and so it was only as she was heading out through the high hedges, her mind still back at the hotel, that Ottilie realized with a sudden rush of feeling that she was, after all this time, actually on her way to Philip's old home, and that even if he himself was not there, something of him would be.

More than that perhaps something of both of them would still be there? Perhaps their auras had been left on the island dancing to his small portable gramophone. As Oscar chugged noisily through the winding lanes, Ottilie once again lived through waiting in Philip's car at Tredegar while he said goodbye to family and friends. She remembered the way they held hands even when he changed gear on the way to the station, and how the sounds of the train doors closing seemed so final as they clung to each other. And then the sight of his fair hair out of the window and his hand still waving, until the railway track turned and sloped away and the train disappeared from sight.

Ottilie felt sure that all that part of her life would still be there waiting for her at Tredegar, and suddenly she felt so excited it was almost as if she was driving to meet Philip himself. Being at Tredegar again would be like holding hands with Philip. It would be magical.

There was a mile-long drive at Tredegar but no way that visitors could arrive outside the Elizabethan front door except on foot, feet that took them over an old, worn, and slightly sloping stone path flanked on either side by immaculate lawn, a walk which was so quietly executed in the quiet of the English countryside that Ottilie imagined that not even the dogs could have heard her, yet somehow Constantia had – managing to throw open the old oak door the moment Ottilie stretched out her hand to reach the door knocker, able to stand framed in the old entrance with her family's coat of arms over the front door and greet Ottilie as if she had known to a second when she would arrive.

'Ot-ti-lie. How good of you to come. And at such short notice.'

Ottilie had forgotten Constantia's habit of breaking up her name into three syllables making it sound strangely foreign and Frenchified. As a child Ottilie had found it vaguely irritating, as she did now, but they bumped cheeks adroitly in greeting, neither of them wishing to leave lipstick on the other's face.

'Come in, come in.' Constantia beckoned to Ottilie, even though she was already stepping over the threshold into the cool air of the still familiar large hall with its rush matting, its suits of armour, but no dogs. 'Both the dogs died, I'm afraid,' Constantia said, as Ottilie's eyes looked and did not find. 'Danes don't live that long, and what with Philip being away I didn't know what new beasts to order, really.'

She was speaking of the magnificent Great Danes with their dark grey-black coats and their yellow eyes as if they had been part of the inanimate fire ornaments, iron 'dogs' or toasting forks or pokers, not the beautiful creatures that Philip loved so and upon whose heads he and Ottilie had used to lean and stare into the fire while they toasted muffins or roasted chestnuts.

'Tredegar doesn't seem Tredegar somehow without Great Danes,' Ottilie told Constantia who immediately looked irritated, her eagle's eyes becoming cold and dismissive, and once again Ottilie realized just how quickly things changed within only a few months.

'Let's go upstairs to my private sitting room. We're lunching in the breakfast room, or if it stays fine we'll eat out under the mulberry tree in the Courtyard Garden, if you like.'

But seconds later the heavens appeared to have opened, so that when they approached the landing and turned to go down the main corridor off which Constantia had made herself a sitting room, Ottilie could see the rain bouncing erratically off the old diamond-shaped window panes, and lightning zedding across from the sea that lay beyond the trees. Lunching outside did not seem to be going to be an option.

Constantia's sitting room was immensely private and completely Constantia, so much so that it appeared to Ottilie to resemble nothing more or less than a designer showroom, or some specialist shop licensed to trade in small household items for the county, but housed in a much larger building, as if Tredegar was the main store and her sitting room an in-house boutique.

Here there was not only no touch of Philip anywhere, there was no sight of anything that would have been allowed by him anywhere else in the house, where nothing could be found that had not been there for at least fifty years.

To begin with everything, without exception, was new. The china ornaments, the porcelain dogs, the bookends, the flower vases from the General Trading Company, the yellow carpet with the small design of keys on it, everything was new and recently designed, and very pretty, but not at all Tredegar. The sofa which, like the ruffled blind at the window, was Colefax and Fowler chintz, was very feminine, and Ottilie knew after just one glance at it how Philip would hate it.

'Iced sherry?'

Constantia moved easily and elegantly across her closely carpeted sitting room talking about her chic 'other' life, as she called it, in London, while Ottilie sat down in one of the chintz-covered chairs, a rather small chair more suited to a bedroom, and gazed around her in some interest. She never opened a conversation, force of habit from working in the hotel.

'I hear,' Constantia went on, eventually, handing Ottilie a very small iced sherry in a Stuart crystal glass, 'I hear from everyone that you are executing miracles at the Angel. Very brave of you to take it on, Ot-ti-lie, really, really brave.'

Ottilie smiled. She smiled because it was amusing to think that everyone Constantia knew was talking about Ottilie's so-called achievement and yet no-one had deigned to come and visit her, and because she knew that by not mentioning it Constantia was also indicating to Ottilie that she knew all about her having been thrown out of the Grand by the Cartarets, and doubtless too about her impoverished sojourn in the unheated basement.

'My dear, why didn't you simply sell your car? Really, you could have sold the car, surely, and not lived in such a terrible place?'

'I could have,' Ottilie agreed, 'but I didn't fancy being thrown into Truro gaol.' And then to Constantia's questioning look she answered, 'The car was registered in my father's name. He could easily have come after me.'

'He could have done, but he would not have. Your father is much too much the gentleman.' Constantia lit a cigarette and smiled through the smoke at Ottilie. 'Much too much the gentleman,' she repeated.

'Have you heard from Philip?' Ottilie asked her, impatient to hear news.

'Not since his posting; you know boys. He's wildly in love with you, you know that? Terribly sweet.'

There was something awful about Constantia's describing the innocent treasured romance of those last two days and the loneliness that followed as 'terribly sweet'. A dress was 'terribly sweet', an invitation to a dinner party could

314

possibly be 'terribly sweet', a Shetland pony or even a pet canary, but not someone madly in love. It was so dismissive. Made all the endless pain seem really rather ridiculous, pathetic even.

I am out of place here, Ottilie thought. *I am completely out of place here. It's a wonder she hasn't commented on how rough my hands are and the fact that there is mud on the edge of my skirt. I should be talking about Courrèges boots and miniskirts and whether or not I like geometric haircuts. I am so provincial, such a country bumpkin, my hair is not cut at Vidal Sassoon, I'm still wearing shirtwaister dresses and flat shoes, and I've never even been to a Beatles concert, let alone to an all-white première with Michael Caine and Peter Sellers. Not only that but one of my eyes won't stop flickering because I have not had more than five hours' sleep in weeks.*

Constantia must have seen or felt something of Ottilie's impatience at being locked into what seemed now to her to be an unnecessary waste of time, time when she would normally be working, because she returned to the subject of Philip.

'I expect you saw an officer had been killed in Cyprus?' she stated, not pausing to have this confirmed. 'Well I heard this morning from a friend of a friend that the officer killed is – or rather was, poor chap – a great friend of Philip's and they had been together only the evening before. A sniper, you know? But anyway, this friend, she thinks he's all right, that Philip is all right, so we can only hope that he will be home soon and then we can all stop worrying.'

At that moment Ottilie really envied Constantia her cigarettes. They must be such a relief at times like these.

'Shall we lunch?'

Ottilie did not really feel like lunch after such grim news, but since Constantia was indicating for her to follow her to the small informal dining room at the back of the kitchens she did so, passing on the way memories of

Philip, of them all playing in the corridors on rainy days like today. Or waiting impatiently at the windows to go outside to go fishing. Now perhaps he really was in danger, not just the pretend danger that they had loved to imagine as children, and there would be no more running around the lake. Indeed so much had Tredegar changed since he left it, by the time Ottilie sat down for lunch she felt that Philip might already be dead, so little of him seemed to have remained in the house.

It was not just that the house now seemed to be filled with the kind of Constance Spry flower arrangements that he always professed to loathe, not just that *Sporting Life* no longer lay thrown carelessly crumpled across some armchair, or that the house seemed immeasurably hotter with fires still lit even though it was summer, or that his .22 rifle was not sticking out of the landing window on red alert for shooting at marauding magpies intent on stealing the swallows' eggs. Not just that Ottilie could see from the breakfast room window that there were last year's leaves on top of the swimming pool cover because only Philip liked to swim at all temperatures and all the year round, or that there were bright orange marigolds in the kitchen garden which he would hate, or that smoked salmon was being served for lunch – Philip always called smoked salmon 'the bane of the upper class kitchen' – but the whole of his presence was gone from Tredegar, as if it had never been.

The truth was that until now Ottilie had never realized just how much her enjoyment of Tredegar depended on him. She thought all this over as she ate politely and listened to Constantia talking about 'the Snowdons' at 'KP' and endless London personalities who all seemed to be from another planet to Ottilie whose whole life centred round her work leaving no time for anything else.

The lunch coming to a close, at last, Ottilie was just rising thankfully to her feet, looking forward to going back to work which now seemed most especially welcoming, most particularly warming, when Constantia said, quite casually, 'I thought you'd like to know that I'd heard from a friend that Vision Hotels are looking to take over the Clover House Group in the next few weeks. I thought I ought to tell you, because if this is so I would think that putting in too much effort at that funny little place where you're working, well, it would be really rather a waste of time, wouldn't it?'

Of course Ottilie herself knew nothing of the sort but what she did suddenly know was that this was the sole reason that Constantia had asked her across to lunch, nothing to do with Philip or his friend who had been killed.

Like the fatal PS in a letter where the sender so often unveiled the real motive for writing to the recipient, Constantia had finally revealed the true reason for asking Ottilie to lunch, and it was to tell her that her days at what she referred to as that 'funny little place where you're working' were numbered.

Back at work, but feeling stunned by the news, Ottilie nevertheless went about her usual duties, smiling at guests, helping in the kitchens, supervising the dining room, yet all the time all she could see was the 'V' for Vision sign on everything. For God's sake it must have been only yesterday that she had been entertaining Sir Harold Ropner and praying for a budget to do the place up, and now it seemed it was only seconds later and everything that she had accomplished would be swept aside and replaced by corner-cutting, profit motives and worst of all, the pride and joy of the Vision group, *portion control*. She resolved to go to bed purposefully late having tried to overtire herself.

But she knew the moment she climbed into bed she would lie awake for the rest of the night unable to switch off Constantia's voice as she left.

'It's one of those things, Ottilie dear, it's happening

everywhere – takeovers, you know. You will have to find somewhere else to devote yourself to, you poor thing, and after all your hard work. Tut, tut. Never mind.'

But Ottilie did mind, she minded terribly, far more than she would have thought possible.

Seventeen

Ottilie stared down at the news items on the damp floor in front of her. When the newspaper was laid on her breakfast tray in the morning she never found anything to interest her outside of the headlines, but once put on the dampened floor by Jean last thing at night certain items appeared to take on a fascination and a vitality that they had never had when Ottilie was first flicking through them.

Who wanted to know whether or not miniskirts would be allowed into the Royal Enclosure for Ascot? Now that they might all be going to be chucked out just as everything had started to come good it all seemed so trivial. Ottilie sighed suddenly and straightened up, but finding that she was afraid to go to bed in case she could not sleep she sat down suddenly instead in Mrs East's rocking chair – ''tes mine and no-one's else's, Miss Flar-tee', she always told Ottilie, patting it as if it was a dog.

The whole hotel, above Ottilie, and across the courtyard was completely quiet. It was that nearing-midnight kind of quiet that made her think of the old days at the Grand when she was little and she would have nightmares and wake up to find herself completely alone, because her parents slept on another floor and Edith on another corridor.

Sometimes she would feel so frightened that she would go right to the bottom of her bed, right to the end, and shut her eyes tight and just hope and pray that morning would come soon. Her eyes would close, as she could feel they were doing now, and she would fall asleep as she seemed to be doing now. She knew she shouldn't sleep, that she should go upstairs to her room, but somehow what with the tiredness and the warmth of the kitchen range, and Mrs East's rocking chair slowly tipping her backwards and forwards, sleep was irresistible.

How much later she wouldn't at first know, but she was suddenly bright awake hours or possibly minutes later, with that feeling that someone or something was watching her. She stood up and looked around her. The kitchen was still warm, but she felt cold, and even colder when she heard what had woken her. Someone or something was scratching at the window. After a few seconds she knew that such an insistent sound must belong to a human being, and that the human being could not be someone who knew her or they would surely be calling to her instead of watching her.

Fear always had the same effect on Ottilie. It made her go forwards rather than backwards. Edith would always say 'Grasp the nettle, dear, and then it stings less' so now Ottilie straightened her shoulders and forced herself forward to the old-fashioned kitchen windows which ran in one long small-paned length down the whole of one side. The kitchen was halfway between the courtyard and the cellar so that it was quite easy for people outside to look down into them. Determinedly she climbed on a chair and pressed her face to one of the square pieces of old glass in front of her. Seconds later a face appeared, suddenly and instantly pressed against the same pane, but pressed far too hard so that the features were squashed beyond recognition. Ottilie jumped backwards from the window and as she did so heard a man laughing, but before she could run to the door and up the stairs into the main body of the hotel to fetch Nantwick, she heard her name being called. 'Ottie! Ottie!'

She didn't know why but half asleep as she was she immediately went and unlocked the door and flung it open to see a tall man in a polo-necked jumper and dark trousers, dark hair, grey eyes. Her hands flew to her face, and she said faintly, 'My God, Joseph, what are you doing here?'

'Now, Ottie, why on earth would you say Joseph like that, and after all this time? That is really quite, quite extraordinary.'

Lorcan stepped out of the darkness as Ottie stepped back, only realizing when Lorcan stood in front of her that, half asleep as she was, she had mistaken him for his middle brother, which was ridiculous because Lorcan had always been taller than Joseph, and although they shared the same colouring their manner was quite different. Well, practically everything about them was different except their grey eyes which were precisely the same, as if Mother Nature having given the eldest boy beautiful clear grey eyes with brown flecks had decided that they were so arresting she would press the button again with the second O'Flaherty boy.

'I had to abandon the old dog collar because I've been down on the quays, hence the un-priest-like appearance.' Lorcan indicated his polo-necked jumper. 'You know how it is, Ottie. So many of my parishioners have the less than virtuous habit of spending their money on beer I have to try and meet them informally and remind them of their duties to their poor families before they get so insanely inebriated after returning from sea there is nothing left for shoes and food for their childer. Can't go down to the quays dressed as a member of the clergy – I'd end up being thrown to the sharks. A dog collar is a red rag to a bull down there.'

Ottilie didn't like to tell Lorcan that he had actually given her the fright of her life. Instead she went to one of the cupboards and brought out a bottle of whisky and two small glasses. She held up the bottle questioningly to Lorcan.

'Well now thank you, Ottie, just a very small dram will

not go amiss. Staying sober while everyone else is intent on getting footless is an enormously taxing occupation, believe me. It's trying to get through to the poor fellows before the hop completely fogs their brain and they even forget where they live that exhausts you – did you know that's why they paint their doors such different colours, so that they can remember where they live?'

Lorcan sighed and laughed, and shook his head as he watched Ottilie pouring them both small glasses of Scotch. Ottilie raised her glass to him, noting as she did that he, as she herself must be, was pale from tiredness.

'Imagine your mistaking me for Joseph of all people, Ottie,' he exclaimed, shaking his head and returning to their first conversation. 'It's almost like telepathy, so strange, really strange, that you should suddenly mention his name that way.' The first taste of the Scotch had obviously had a reviving effect.

'I was fast asleep—'

'I know. But would you believe it, I have just, today, had a letter from him?'

Ottilie would not have believed it for one second had she not already read about 'Joseph Maximus' in the American magazine in Paris all that time before. She had not felt that she could tell Lorcan, fearing that after all their anxieties, after all they had been through thinking that Joseph might be dead, Lorcan might be unimaginably hurt.

'You've had a letter from Joseph?' she repeated.

'Yes, Ottie, our brother Joseph is alive and well and coming to England. Imagine! All this time he has been in America, alive and well.'

Lorcan stared at Ottilie. She stared back, completely silenced, but not as Lorcan must imagine because she was in shock from the realization that their brother was alive, but from having to cope anew with the realization that it was she, Ottilie, not Joseph, who had been really to blame, the cause of all Lorcan's suffering over his brother. The immensity of this suffering, which up until that moment she had only ever been able to imagine, she could now see and hear for herself because it was reflected in the sheer relief in Lorcan's eyes, and in the wonder in his voice as he caught at her hands, his own so warm and strong. 'After all this time, Ottie, we have heard from Joseph at last. He is alive, he is well and he is coming to see us, here, in St Elcombe. Imagine, our Joseph is coming back to us. Our prayers have at last been answered, Ottie.'

Lorcan knocked on the table at which they were both seated in a steady, unceasing manner as he repeated, 'Joseph is alive and coming back to us. Joseph is alive and coming back to us. God is good, Ottie. God is so good.'

Ottilie took a much larger sip of her Scotch and smiled but she still could not find words that were suitable for the moment. Of course Lorcan must be right, God was good, and of course it was wonderful that Joseph was coming back to them, alive and well, but then Ottilie herself had known that he was alive and well for three years now.

What she was not sure of was how much God Himself had to do with Joseph's return to St Elcombe. But seeing the shining look in Lorcan's eyes, his utter sincerity and belief in the goodness of the Almighty, she had to attempt to suppress her feelings, push aside the guilty knowledge that by throwing those wretched earrings at Joseph that night, some people might say it was she who had been responsible for his disappearance.

'May God forgive me if I am wrong, Ottilie, but at last everything seems to be coming right for us all, everyone settled the way Ma would have wanted us to be, everyone with some good purpose, some place to which they can really direct their efforts.'

Forget about God forgiving you, Lorcan, Ottilie thought. *May God forgive me.*

But aloud she said, 'Let's have another little Scotch, shall we, Lorcan?'

Lorcan shook his head and stood up.

'Many thanks, Ottie, but I must be on my way, for I am surely late as it is. Father Peter likes me to take him a hot cup of cocoa when I get in. The poor old priest has terrible trouble sleeping. I keep teasing him that if only he would give up the cocoa he would probably sleep like a baby. God bless you, Ottie.'

Lorcan smiled and waved to her from the door, and Ottilie began to shut it, feeling nothing but relief at the idea that her eldest brother was going, but before she could put the chain across again Lorcan turned back. 'Oh, and one more thing, Ottie. I forgot to tell you in the excitement of my news. You'll never guess what?'

Ottilie could not guess so she remained silent but she smiled nevertheless and waited for what her overwhelmingly kind eldest brother would have to say.

'Our Joseph's not no-one any more. Do you know he is a very important young man now? Not yet thirty and managing director of Vision Hotels, Europe. How about that? Our Joseph? All those days hanging around doing odd jobs at the Grand, they obviously really paid off.'

Ottilie felt that it had to be a miracle of sorts that she was able to make any kind of reply to this news, but as Lorcan was clearly so happy she was able to get by with a murmur. She waved him goodbye for so long after he had actually gone that had anyone come into the kitchen she imagined they would have thought her both mad and drunk. Eventually, unable to control her feelings, she found herself turning back to the bottle of whisky, unscrewing the top, and pouring herself a second glass of Scotch which she sat and drank all by herself.

Veronica was giving Ottilie one of her shrewd looks.

'You've been up all these nights worrying,' she said flatly.

'How do you know?'

'Probably from the lines under your eyes, the fact that you have not eaten any lunch in a week, let alone I suspect any dinner, and you are sounding tired and depressed. Otherwise you're fine.'

Veronica carefully removed her with-it glasses and pulling at her polo-neck jumper cleared her throat. 'I think you're making a mountain out of a molehill. One single piece of glass planted in a salad—'

'Roast pork, actually—'

'Is not something with which we cannot cope, and will not cope again, and again, and again, if need be.'

'No, true.' Ottilie put her cup of coffee down with unusual care. When Veronica wasn't looking or was answering the telephone, she determined that she would quickly rummage in the bottom drawer of her desk and swallow some aspirin to relieve her throbbing head. 'But what I think you will agree we cannot cope with, Veronica, is Vision Hotels taking us over.'

'You are joking.'

'No, I am not.'

'No you are not. Oh, sh— ugar, just as everything was going right,' said Veronica morosely.

'I couldn't agree more.'

'Perhaps one of us could seduce the managing director?'

Ottilie sighed. 'Well, maybe you, but certainly not me.' And then in answer to Veronica's questioning look, 'He's my brother. Besides, I don't think you'd want to, not really.'

But one look at Joseph and Ottilie could see that Veronica did not believe her. One look at Joseph and Veronica fell for him, hook, line and sinker, and Ottilie could not really blame her. He walked into their office the following week looking every inch the successful businessman, dark suit, white shirt, dark tie, gold cuff links, except Joseph had the looks of a movie star. More than that, he had the tanned even-featured looks of a young god. In all the months that Ottilie had known Veronica she had never once known her to take any real notice of a man of any age, but one look at

'Joseph Maximus' and she fell for him. And that was before he had even opened his mouth and started to charm not just Veronica but the whole of St Elcombe. Certainly from the moment he gave notice of his arrival he could do no wrong for Lorcan. Arriving back in grand style – Mercedes, chauffeur driven – he invited Ottilie and Lorcan to join him at the Grand where he had taken the top suite – Blue Lady's suite.

Lorcan was in such a state when Ottilie went to pick him up for their reunion dinner that she thought he would most likely burst out of his dog collar within seconds of seating himself beside her in the car.

'Imagine Joseph, in the top suite,' Lorcan kept saying, over and over. 'Can you imagine, Ottie? Our Joseph in the top suite at the Grand, as rich as a rajah and even now ordering caviar and champagne most like, and in the very place where we both once painted the railings and put up wallpaper? It's hard put to understand it all I am. Wait until we hear about his adventures, Ottie, that is indeed going to be something. How did he do it? My, but how proud Ma would be on this day, wouldn't you say? An O'Flaherty in the top suite at the Grand, and a managing director at that.'

Ottilie was finding Lorcan's enthusiasm understandable but embarrassing. To her the Grand was just the Grand, a place that was either successful or not successful. Besides, Lorcan's overt enthusiasm reminded her of the bad old days when she was the little princess in the castle and her brothers were the workmen. She herself was dreading her return, walking up the steps of the Grand again, dreading the looks that she would get from those staff that had not yet incurred Mrs Tomber's displeasure and been dismissed – although she reasoned that the likelihood of still seeing anyone she knew there was very small.

Nowadays probably only Blackie would be a face that she would recognize. And after their last encounter he certainly would not want to even pass the time of day with her. Alfred she knew would not bother to mind or not mind where she was. After finding the nude drawing of Ottilie it seemed he had put his adopted daughter out of his mind for ever. And Melanie, it being past midday, would be on to at least her second large gin and tonic and not caring who was in the hotel unless room service was not responding to her calls.

'Do I look all right, now, Ottie?'

Ottilie turned round to Lorcan. Standing there looking so nervous outside the heavy old mahogany doors of the Great Suite he was no longer a priest but her beloved brother who had arrived so hopefully at the hotel that day of her tenth birthday. As she patted his jacket and smiled reassuringly at him Ottilie remembered how even as a child she had noticed how cheap Lorcan's suit had looked, and how heavy his shoes must have seemed as he walked bravely down that whole flight of stairs and into the dining room of the Grand.

'You look grand,' she said, squeezing his hand the way she remembered Ma would always do when Lorcan went off for school of a morning from Number Four. 'Really grand.'

Lorcan nodded, and Ottilie noticed that he looked slightly flushed with excitement. Seeing what a wonderful moment it was for him her own sense of dread about what Joseph's revelations might be, about the diamond earrings, about everything, quite vanished and there and then she determined to take the attitude that with Lorcan so happy and Joseph so successful everything had surely all turned out for the best?

'Lorcan. Ottie.'

Joseph turned from the balcony and came quickly back into the large sitting room, his arms outstretched in welcome. Lorcan had always been taller than Joseph, but no longer. Now Joseph seemed to tower over his older brother, and even if he had not, dressed as he was, and with his aura of success, and power, and money, he

327

swamped poor Lorcan in his cheap priest's suit – until, that is, Lorcan held his younger brother at arm's length and said in his warm fatherly way, 'Well now, will you let me look at you, will you let me look at you, my little brother?' at which point all Joseph's confidence seemed to visibly melt away and for a second he appeared to be waiting for Lorcan's verdict on him. Would he 'do' as the O'Flahertys would say? Would Lorcan be proud of him? Perhaps, most of all, had Lorcan forgiven him for disappearing?

'You look grand, just grand, Joseph,' Lorcan said quietly. 'God bless you.'

'Ottie.'

It was like some religious ceremony, for seconds later it was Joseph who was holding Ottilie away from him.

'How *about* this girl?' he asked Lorcan. 'I mean, how about this girl? Isn't she grown beautiful? Isn't she grown smart? You are one hell of a smart and beautiful girl, Ottilie. Turn round. My God, you must knock them all out around here. You look, well, so – New York, Paris, Tokyo, London, nothing to do with St Elcombe.'

Ottilie had her hair knotted as Monsieur had taught her and was wearing a navy blue silk shirt dress, just above the knee, very new, terribly expensive from a dress shop in Plymouth, but she had felt that no less was required for the return of a prodigal brother.

As Joseph poured some champagne Lorcan started to wander around the suite and they began reminiscing about the old days when they had both worked on the rebuilding of the hotel, and all the eccentric characters they had known. Mention was even made of 'Blue Lady' and how she used to scare the pants off everyone with her strange clothes, always talking to someone who wasn't there.

As he sipped at his champagne Lorcan kept shaking his head and saying, 'Ah God, yes, imagine you remembering that, Joseph'. But as she stood laughing and talking with them, that awful moment when Ottilie had agreed to put

Melanie's earrings in her pocket seemed to have happened only the day before, and she could smell Joseph's cigarettes and see the pot of tea on the dirty table as she handed them to him and said that she thought they were worth a thousand pounds.

'I told the waiter to go away,' Joseph said as he handed the champagne round. 'I wanted us all to be quite, quite alone, to be able to talk, to be able to tell each other things that no-one else should hear. Like how much we love each other, like how much we loved Ma, all those things. Things that we must say to each other, no holds barred, don't you think?' Joseph raised his glass. 'Come, let us drink to Ma, to Number Four, to us all.'

Joseph was so much the young managing director of a business, had adopted such a Churchillian manner, that Ottilie was hard put to it not to smile. Nevertheless, she raised her glass. 'To Ma.'

There was a short awkward silence while they sipped their champagne and conjured Ma back from their childhood memories, and it seemed to Ottilie that they could all hear her rich laugh and see her throwing back her thick plait of auburn hair and hear her say 'Well now, isn't this fine?' and Ottilie thought of how her eyes would have really sparkled as only Ma's eyes could at seeing Lorcan an ordained priest, at seeing Joseph in his fine suit, and how she would have wondered at the miracle of his success, and how she would have loved to have seen her two sons standing in the Great Suite at the Grand.

'I still miss her, you know,' Joseph said, sighing. 'I still hold on to those wonderful years when she was all right, when we were all so happy at Number Four.' He turned to Lorcan. 'How proud she would have been of you. Her eldest son a man of God, a priest.' Joseph shook his head.

'And you,' Lorcan said warmly. 'You, Joseph, how proud she would have been of you. All we are missing today is little Sean and he will surely make his mark. Did you know he had gone into Australian television? Oh yes, he is making his way all right. He will get on, will our Sean.' Ottilie's heart went out to Lorcan as she watched him speaking, he was so much the proud eldest brother, and she could see that there was so much that he wanted to say, and yet it was almost as if the words would hardly come out so great was his love for and pride in his brothers. And then, realizing that she had not rated a mention, she felt a little sad, as he finished by saying, 'This is a wonderful day, a great day for the O'Flaherty brothers.'

And it *was* a wonderful day and it was a great evening, and when at last they left, Lorcan smiling from ear to ear, and Joseph waving goodbye from his front balcony way above them, Ottilie could not bear to lower Lorcan's mood by questioning him about his own impressions. But the next morning as soon as Veronica came into their office Ottilie pounced on her, saying, 'I don't know what has happened to the Grand. I wouldn't have known it, filthy food, thick with dust, no flowers—' but finally she ended up, quite despite herself, looking rather pleased.

'You're making such a success of this place soon they'll be on their knees begging you to go back.'

As she spoke Veronica handed Ottilie a letter stamped PRIVATE. The envelope had no familiar look to it, no Clover House crest on the back, so she was not it seemed being given her marching orders, and yet it had a London postmark. As she always did when she did not know what the contents of a letter from London might be, Ottilie set it aside, giving herself the necessary time to think about where the letter might have come from, what it might have in it, to prepare herself in some way mentally in case it should be something that she would not like. It was a seemingly incurable habit of hers stemming from the days when Melanie would leave letters in the downstairs hall for her, letters of bitter crossness, full of indignation at the way the hotel was being run – usually written at half past one in the morning when the wine was flowing if not the ink. They were sometimes completely incomprehensible, sometimes all too comprehensible.

Still feeling in some superstitious way that the letter might contain something she would not want to hear she passed it back to her secretary saying, 'Tell me the worst. It's probably a demand for money from the charming couple who put the piece of glass in their food.'

'It might be good news.'

'Oh my God it's a lawyer's letter. Don't tell me, I'm right, they're suing us.'

Veronica cleared her throat before beginning. '"*Dear Miss O'Flaherty, We understand from our investigations that you might be the former Miss Ottilie Cartaret who lived for many years at the Grand Hotel, St Elcombe, but that you have now changed your name back to O'Flaherty and are residing at the above address.*"'

Veronica looked up, briefly lowering her glasses and looking at Ottilie over the top of them. 'So far, so good. To continue. Yes. "*If this is so might we ask you to get in touch with our Mr Nicholas Lyall Phelps, and arrange a convenient time for you to meet him? Or if this is difficult he could come to see you in Cornwall? The matter concerns a bequest made to you by the late Miss Edith Emilia Stanton. We regret having taken so long to be in touch with you about this matter but all letters addressed to Miss Ottilie Cartaret at the Grand Hotel, St Elcombe, were returned 'address unknown'. Yours sincerely, George Gray Phelps.*"' Veronica smiled across at Ottilie. 'It seems that chance might be a fine thing after all.'

'How kind of Edith to leave me something.' Ottilie sighed.

'Who *was* this Edith that you're always talking about? Was she your nurse or your teacher?'

'No, no, she was one of the housekeepers at the Grand, but she turned into a sort of nurse. She took me everywhere with her really, because my adopted mother, Mrs Cartaret, didn't believe in schools, only in reading books, learning French – oh, and dancing.'

'What do you think it is that she could possibly have left you?'

'I know what I would like . . .' Ottilie said after a second or two's thought as Veronica looked questioningly in her direction, momentarily distracted from the rest of the post. 'It may sound really rather dreadful but I would simply love it if she had left me her cameo brooch.'

Nicholas Lyall Phelps was what Edith herself would have described as 'quite a dish'. Tall, even-featured, but with a good big head of hair. Immaculately suited, beautifully shod, his shirt crisply white, his tie dark but not too dark. Only the colour of his socks – like his lapis lazuli cuff links a quite bright blue – showed just the right amount of dash.

'Miss O'Flaherty, I am Nicholas Lyall Phelps. How do you do?'

'Very well, thank you,' Ottilie replied, and she looked up at him mischievously, realizing at once that although his fashionably thick gold wedding ring might declare him to be married, he was certainly not dead. 'Do sit down, and would you like some coffee?'

'I would love some coffee, Miss O'Flaherty, thank you.'

Ottilie picked up the telephone, ordered coffee and sat down opposite him. It was a sunny morning, as yet there was no bad news of Philip, and she had every reason to feel as sunny as the morning, particularly since Edith might, just might, have left her the little cameo brooch which Ottilie loved and thought of as so much 'Edith'.

'I hope you are staying somewhere comfortable, Mr Phelps.'

'No,' he said quickly and then looked embarrassed before he went on. 'I regret to say that I am staying at the Grand. My grandmother used to stay there every summer and always enjoyed it but I fear she wouldn't know it today. I ordered coffee for breakfast and a poached egg and was served tea and a boiled egg and that was only the

332

last straw. Before that my room was not ready when I arrived at four thirty, the tea tray not removed when I went to bed, and they forgot to wake me up at eight o'clock. Frankly it's hell at a horrible price.'

'It's a wonder you're still alive.'

Nicholas Phelps coloured slightly, but not for the reason she might have thought. 'I'm sorry, I forgot you used to live there. You must find this rather rude.'

'No, I entirely agree. For my sins I was there a few days ago and I found the service shocking and the food inedible. It was heartbreaking.'

'There is some ghastly woman in charge who seemed quite drunk,' he continued. 'A Mrs – Mrs Coffin or something.'

'Mrs Tomber?'

'That's her. Slurring her words, hardly able to stand up. It seems to have become a home for derelicts. When I went down for a nightcap I found even the hall porter was drunk.'

'The poor old Grand. In its heyday it was so lovely.'

'Still could be if the right person was in charge.'

After which Jean came in bearing an immaculately laid coffee tray with fresh white tray cloth, coffee pot gleaming, cups and saucers shining, home-made biscuits on an old Masons Ironstone plate. As Ottilie poured them both coffee and offered the lawyer a biscuit, she tried not to think nostalgically of Edith's cameo as the lawyer first sipped his coffee and then broached the matter of their meeting.

'Now, I have to ask you once, very boring, but necessary. Are you the former Miss Cartaret who resided at the Grand Hotel, St Elcombe? This is just for our records, you understand?'

'Yes, I am the former Miss Cartaret, Mr Phelps.'

'Good.' The fact that Ottilie was indeed the former Miss Cartaret seemed to please Mr Phelps no end, for he was now smiling broadly. Then he frowned and cleared his throat. 'I have been told – this is always rather a difficult moment for lawyers, Miss O'Flaherty. One never quite knows how to break this sort of very serious news.'

Ottilie stared at him, made uneasy by his sober look. Edith was dead. Surely there could be no more news that could be difficult to break?

'I have been sent here today by my firm to tell you that you have been left a bequest by Miss Edith Emilia Stanton, a somewhat sizeable bequest. No – a more than sizeable bequest.' Nicholas Phelps paused and shuffled the papers he had taken out of his elegant briefcase as if what he was about to say would embarrass them both. 'This is what I mean by its being difficult for lawyers to break things to people,' he continued more gently, lowering his voice. 'Any news that one has to tell someone that will change their entire life is very, very difficult indeed, as I am sure you will appreciate. Some people of course completely refuse to let this kind of news change their lives. Some people just wish to carry on as they are despite whatever is coming to them. They may be what we would call "contented", or they may be people who have lived their lives in so fixed a fashion that to change at some late date is quite impossible. I imagine that is what happened to Miss Stanton, because she herself was left this bequest late in life.'

He paused and then sighed.

'In fact as I understand it, from everything my senior partner told me, it was, alas, the news of this bequest that caused Miss Stanton to have the first of her heart attacks. But you are considerably younger. I dare say we will not have such problems. I dare hope not, Miss O'Flaherty? I certainly hope not.'

'Please go on,' Ottilie said, with assumed calm, because she was having to suppress the surge of relief that she felt on hearing the reason why Edith had suffered her heart attack.

'To continue. As we understand it from her letters, by

334

the time my senior partner was writing to her of her mother's bequest to her Miss Stanton was already suffering from a weak heart, and was not able or was completely unwilling to change her life in any degree at all. She continued as she was, undisturbed, and determined to leave everything to you to enjoy.'

'What do you mean by "everything",' Ottilie asked, clearing her throat and suddenly feeling as if the world had stopped turning on its axis and Mr Phelps was actually an elegant apparition who would shortly disappear.

'What I mean by everything is – literally – everything. You see Miss Stanton was a very rich woman, Miss O'Flaherty, although I am sure you would never have thought it. She lived all her life as a spinster, as you know, worked at the Grand, and looked after her mother who was one of those miserly reclusive women whom you have no doubt read about in the newspapers from time to time? Not to put too fine a point on it, Miss Edith's mother literally lived in dread of anyone finding out that she was rich and consequently became quite mad as a result. Her own father was a Conroy, Miss Edith's maternal grandfather that is. They made the tops that fit into Biro pens, do you know what I mean by them?'

Ottilie nodded, finding herself speechless and at the same time overcome with a deep desire to laugh. 'Biro pens' sounded so terribly funny. Why didn't he say 'Biros' like everyone else?

'To continue. Edith Stanton knew nothing of her mother being an heiress and her mother determined that she should know nothing of it either. The daughter lived and worked, as you know, all her life in St Elcombe, looking after her mother until she died. The house was quite bare when we went there to value it for probate, nothing but bare boards, no curtains at the windows – and yet all the time Miss Stanton's mother had a fortune on tap, but no desire to spend it, just lived with the terror that somebody might find out she was rich. She would only eat at the weekends and took nothing but toast and tea during the week, and she saved paper bags so obsessively that what with the state of the electricity quite frankly it was a miracle that the place did not catch fire and herself with it.

'She finally departed this life leaving poor Miss Edith to cope with the running of this huge fortune, which of course she could not do. Nothing in her life had prepared Miss Edith for such an eventuality as being rich and the very idea of it was impossible for her to grasp. She had lived all her life in service and that is how she wanted to continue, which is why when she died she left it all to you. As of today, Miss O'Flaherty, you are a very rich young lady indeed.'

Ottilie stared at Nicholas Phelps and then rolled her eyes towards the door and gave him a panic-struck frown. Years of living in close proximity to resident staff had made her permanently afraid of eavesdroppers. As a result she found herself frequently dropping her voice, or, as at this moment, whispering in case someone overheard what she was saying. Now she murmured to the lawyer as quietly as it was possible for her to murmur and him still to hear, 'Quickly, say "Only joking!" in case someone's listening.'

'Only joking, of course!'

'I knew you were. You lawyers. Imagine if I had believed you.' Ottilie laughed a little loudly and long while at the same time springing to her feet and encouraging Nicholas Phelps to do the same. 'I expect you'd like some sea air? Let's go for a walk, if you wouldn't mind.'

This time the young lawyer was on to what she was telling him with her eyes, his own eyes fixed on hers, which were sliding towards the door, so he said, 'Of course, sea air. Just what I need after London.'

He followed her out of the door, and into the courtyard outside. It was not a particularly cold day but Ottilie found she was shivering, from the shock she supposed, and her teeth were chattering.

'Let's go into the town,' she murmured, 'there's a café down near the quays, it will be so noisy no-one can overhear us. Staff can be such a problem in hotels, always listening in – it's a sort of hobby with them, like fretwork or knitting.'

They walked along to the café at a brisk pace. Once seated either side of the formica table Ottilie said, 'Look, just to begin with, I think you'd better just write down the amount I've been left. That way there's less chance that I will make a fool of myself and faint or something.'

'Very well.'

'And then I'll swallow the piece of paper and we can both forget about it,' she joked and insisted on ordering two coffees before looking at the note that Nicholas Phelps had pushed towards her. Ottilie took a good sip of coffee when it arrived and then opened the piece of writing paper which was headed, inevitably, PHELPS, PHELPS and PHELPS. 'And now for the awful truth,' she continued as she stared blindly at the figures written down for her benefit by the lawyer. Having tried to take them in she finally looked across at him. 'Nothing about a cameo brooch, by the way?'

'Nothing about a cameo brooch, I'm afraid.' Nicholas Phelps smiled. 'Still I expect you can afford one yourself now, if not a dozen,' he added, holding her look a little too long.

Ottilie nodded. It would not be the same at all just to go out to buy one, and she dropped her eyes.

'I also imagine that you would like us to put you in touch with the people who manage all your new investments.'

'Oh, I'll leave all that to you. But. I mean. This changes so much. I mean. What will I do about my job? Will I have to leave it? How strange it all is.'

Ottilie frowned, trying hard and failing to imagine how it would feel not to have to work. It seemed to her that all at once she knew a little of the awful panic poor Edith

337

herself must have felt on being told of her inheritance, as if she had been used to swimming backwards and forwards in a swimming pool, touching one end one minute and the other the next, only to find of a sudden that there was an ocean in front and behind her and no edges that needed touching.

'Tell me, does everyone feel when they're suddenly told they're going to be very, very rich as if – well, as if there's not much point to anything any more, as if they perhaps don't know who they are or what they should be doing?'

'Of course. That's why their first reaction is so often "nothing's going to change". Dreaming of wealth is one thing, reality rather different.'

There didn't seem very much to say after that.

Certainly Ottilie felt there was very little she could say. She listened to the lawyer talking about how the financial people were investing for her, and having only too recently prided herself on taking such an interest in how shares were doing Ottilie now found that she had no actual interest in them at all.

She could only think of Edith and her calming smile and how she had used to take her part so often against Melanie, but in such a way that Mrs Cartaret never knew, smuggling her up biscuits and little petits fours from the dining room once Madame was safely downstairs. 'Just put it out of your mind, Miss Ottilie,' she would say after Ottilie had been punished for some new offence. 'Just put it out of your mind.'

At that moment that seemed just about the best piece of advice Ottilie could give herself.

Later, returning to the office, Ottilie found she was not to be alone with Veronica. To her irritation Joseph had somehow found his way down from the Grand to the inn and was sitting on the side of her desk charming her, one leg swinging to and fro, and Veronica who had always seemed so sensible was blushing and giggling in a way that made Ottilie want to shake her. Had she forgotten that Joseph was after all Vision Hotels – the enemy?

But instead of standing around being made to feel foolish listening to Joseph charming her secretary, Ottilie left them and went to the kitchens to see how the luncheon buffet was going. Once there a voice in her mind kept murmuring, 'What does it matter? What does it matter now that you are so rich?'

Try as hard as she could it didn't seem to matter any more whether or not Mrs East had overdone the rolls or the butter pats were looking warm, or whether they should take another ham out of the fridge. Two hours earlier, before Nicholas Phelps had arrived, it had seemed not only important but vital. Now, do what she would, in the light of what the lawyer had just told Ottilie, and always providing that he was not some sort of sick confidence trickster, it seemed faintly absurd to worry about such things as butter pats and hot rolls.

'Mrs East, this cheese has had it, and these tomatoes – I thought we agreed yesterday that they were tasteless and we would not put them on the buffet any more?' Without realizing it and probably to compensate for how she was feeling Ottilie's tone had become hectoring, and she saw the kitchen staff turning round and staring at her in surprise. 'Sorry, I'm expecting a food inspector,' she lied on seeing their stares, and then disappeared up to her room before they could ask her any more.

Lying on her bed she tried to think of Philip, but even he seemed confused and far away, not real, and although she continued to try to imagine what he would say to her, how he would make her laugh and tease her the way he had when her parents threw her out of the Grand, she somehow could not hear his voice any more, or even see his face in her mind's eye. Later she went back to her office.

'I can't wait to know. Did you get left the cee ay em ee oh?' Any outbreak of spelling was always a sign that

Veronica had just seen Jean approaching through the half glass of the office door.

'Sorry, what was that?'

Ottilie turned and frowned at Veronica who once again started to spell out the words 'cameo brooch' silently, using her finger to indicate the letters that she was slowly and carefully writing in the air. Watching her, Ottilie felt almost guilty. Cameo brooch! If she knew.

Over the next few days Nicholas Phelps and Ottilie met frequently. At these meetings they both struggled to reach some agreement as to what to do with the money – now code-named It. In her heart of hearts, try as she might (because she could see that he wanted so much to interest her in her new inheritance), Ottilie found that just the sight of the young lawyer undoing his briefcase started to fill her with unreasoning panic.

'I can see business is tedious to you,' he said sorrowfully one afternoon, actually catching Ottilie smothering a yawn after only ten minutes.

'No, it's not that. It's just that I have really no interest in simply making money. My fascination is in making something from something I have done, not just being given it. I suppose what I'm saying is – I can't see the point of money just being there for you, without working for it.'

'You are only just twenty.'

'Of course,' Ottilie agreed. 'Far too young to have so much money and much, much too young just to live off investments like old ladies do. I could give it away, of course, but Edith wouldn't like that. I could travel, but I would be alone, and travelling alone for no purpose doesn't sound much fun, does it?' There was a long silence while Nicholas Phelps waited for Ottilie to voice her conclusions. 'As a matter of fact, something did occur to me last night, in the middle of the night. I mean I have been thinking of what I really, really would like to do, a wonderful, crazy,

340

hilarious thing that I could do with all the money, and what's more I think Edith would approve.'

She paused.

Nicholas Phelps leaned forward and waited.

Ottilie cleared her throat and wondered how she should phrase what she was about to say. She found herself staring at his serious expression and, due to the tension of the moment and the protracted length of the meeting, suddenly started to laugh helplessly because it seemed impossibly, ridiculously funny to think that she was actually about to say what she was about to say, to think that she, Ottilie O'Flaherty, who had grown up with Ma at Number Four in London's Notting Hill, could be even thinking of what she was thinking and that it might even be possible.

'I'm so sorry, really I am,' she said eventually, wiping the tears from her eyes. 'I'll start again.' This time Nicholas Phelps leaned forward even more eagerly and the solemnity of his expression was even greater. Ottilie started to laugh once again but even less controllably, the tears actually running down her face until, shoulders still shaking, she eventually managed to straighten up, wiping her eyes and apologizing, 'I'm so terribly sorry, so rude, oh dear, it's just your face – so serious. Oh, I am sorry.' Taking the laywer's handkerchief for her eyes. 'Thank you. Oh dear. Goodness, how rude. No, I'm fine. Really. No. Very well. Start again. What. I would. Like. Is – no, it's no good, I'm going to go again. I'll just have to write it down.'

She sprang up and going to a writing desk took a pen and some paper and wrote down what she wanted to do with her inheritance. The lawyer took the piece of paper from her, read it, folded it, and then put it among his papers as if it was a legal document.

'You must be mad,' he said, quite factually.

Eighteen

It was Joseph's last night and he was in a party mood. He rang Ottilie to say so.

'You must come and celebrate with me.'

'I don't think I can, Joseph. Really, I have some sort of bug. I'm full of antibiotics, feeling terrible.'

'You're going to feel worse when I tell you that the news has just come through – we are about to buy you out, Miss O'Flaherty. The Clover House shareholders are about to be made an offer that will make them all as happy as clams. From now on you will be employed by your brother, how about that?'

His tone was so gloating, so cock-a-hoop, that Ottilie could hardly bear to listen to any more. Instead she put her hand to her throbbing head and said, 'Are you sure about all this?'

'Sure I'm sure. Clover House have had it – it's official, Ottie. The new group will be called Clover Vision. Don't worry, it won't affect you. They can't afford to lose people like you, it's the slack undergrowth they'll cut away—'

'I have actually been in a Vision hotel, I do know what they're like, Joseph. Slack undergrowth means no more night porters, no more real fires, one waitress to six tables, watered down drinks, bland food, and no atmosphere at all, just as we had all set our hearts on bringing back the old-style small hostelry. Vision is so characterless, Joseph.'

'It is nothing of the sort. You forget yourself if you criticize Vision to me, Ottie. Vision is my whole life. I believe in Vision. It is my faith.' She could hear him pounding the telephone table with his fist. 'I eat, drink and live Vision. You must never criticize it to me.'

There was no point in continuing so, head throbbing, pulse racing, Ottilie curtailed the conversation. Seconds after she had replaced the telephone receiver she found herself wondering why in heaven she had not successfully pleaded illness? Who cared if it was Joseph's last night in St Elcombe? If Vision were taking over he would soon be back among them, if only to supervise the ruination of the Angel and whatever other hostelries they had bought. She sat down suddenly.

What on earth would she say to her little staff? Once a place was taken over by one of the big groups that was it, no-one stayed. It was said to be a sign of weakness to dismiss staff once an acquisition had been made, but that was not something that would trouble the organization that Joseph worked for. Everything they had all done together was about to disappear.

Depressed beyond measure, Ottilie managed to drag herself upstairs. After swallowing one of her antibiotic pills she changed once more into her blue silk shirt dress, and set out once again for the Grand. She felt ghastly, but at least there was a time limit to the party since Joseph had already announced that he was leaving for London later that evening. Handsome and charming he might be but in Ottilie's eyes Joseph already stood for all that was grey and mediocre. He had become yet another zombie executive. He stood for people who cared not a jot for adding to the beauty of the world, but only to paper profit.

This evening he opened the door of his suite to her, drink in hand, every inch the immaculately suited businessman, charm back in place, exactly the right amount of shirt cuff showing beneath the tailored sleeve of his suit.

'My but you sounded mad at me on the telephone. You're not mad at me, are you?'

'No, no, of course I'm not mad at you, Joseph, I'm just not feeling too good.'

'I'm sorry about that, Ottie, but I really needed someone to get loaded with tonight. Lorcan's out on a call and only coming along later,' he went on, pouring her a whisky and topping up his own.

Without thinking, distracted by both her fever and the worry of the Angel collapsing and taking the staff down with it, Ottilie took the whisky while all the time knowing that she absolutely did not want it. It was as if she was sleep-walking, what with the tiredness and the fever.

'I can't stay long, Joseph, I'm afraid. I really don't feel at all well, and I'm just so worried about my staff. You know how it is, you hire these people, you build up something together and then suddenly the rug is pulled out from under them and they're on the scrap heap again.'

'At Vision we never put anyone worthwhile on the scrap heap, Ottie—' Joseph interrupted.

'It's as if I've been building a house, and then after only a few months the bulldozers are being sent in to raze it to the ground—'

'Oh come on, Ottie, you always exaggerate so.'

'It's people's lives, Joe,' Ottilie insisted suddenly with passion. 'It breaks your heart when you see how people respond to being treated with respect, paid properly, what a real spring it gives to their step.'

'Trade is about survival of the fittest, and to stay fit companies must stay lean and trim,' Joseph said, walking up and down the room, but she could see from his eyes what he was all too anxious to keep out of his voice, that he was really enjoying this moment, that he was – as she had suspected when he telephoned her earlier – gloating.

'If you're giving bad service, if the end product is poor and unjoyous, what's the point of being anything?'

'For a beautiful girl you talk too much. People who are good always survive.'

'Not always. People matter. They must do, or else there's nothing left.'

'They'll all find other work. Vision might employ them, who knows? I tell you, I can't wait to get out of this place. What a dump.' Joseph looked round the suite taking in the faded furnishings, the drooping flowers – the vase of the inevitable long-stemmed too-tall red roses with their too-small heads leaning down towards the floor as if even they were ashamed of their surroundings. 'Do you know, ten years ago I would have given my right arm just to paint this place with emulsion and brush, now I would give my right arm to get out of it.' Joseph obviously could not stop indulging himself in his sense of victory. 'Ten years ago I couldn't hold down a job painting the railings down there, and now look at me! By the way, your lawyer's popping in tonight for a celebration drink with us. Nice guy. Good choice.'

Ottilie hoped against hope that her face did not register any surprise at Joseph's words, that it did not state publicly, wordlessly but all too clearly, 'My lawyer? But how do you know Nicholas Phelps is my lawyer?'

'It's all right, Ottie, I *know*.'

Ottilie looked at him dazedly. 'What do you know now, Joseph?'

How she loathed him suddenly. His gleeful face, his gloating, his careless attitude to other people with lesser lives than his, less money than his.

'I know that old Edith left you money. I saw the letter in his room. It's a trick of mine, leaning over desks and reading letters. Go on, admit it, you've been left money by that old maid who looked after you.'

'Edith wasn't an old maid, Joseph, she was much more than that.'

'You know what I mean. What did you she leave you – a couple of hundred quid and a parrot?'

'Edith left me what she had,' was the only way that Ottilie could think of putting it truthfully. Quickly she

346

turned the conversation back to him. 'You are the all-American success story now, aren't you, Joseph?'

'I certainly am,' Joseph agreed. 'And I tell you what, Ottie, I intend to stay that way. I have worked for what I have got. Even changed my name to give myself the will to succeed on my own account. I have not had to accept leg-ups on the "Murphy Circuit". No, I started on a street corner selling newspapers, like Bob Hope, like Nelson Rockefeller, like all good Americans I worked my way up the hard way, saving dimes, putting aside a dollar a week—'

'Tell me what happened after I left you that night, Joseph, I've always wondered?'

'I started by selling newspapers,' Joseph continued inexorably, seemingly unstoppable on the subject of himself, 'and then went into hotels, starting at the bottom as a bellboy and working my way up to the top, where I am now. And I have done it all myself, and all by myself without any help from anyone, except the United States of America, God be praised. Ah now, this would be Lorcan' – Joseph flung open the door in answer to a discreet knock – 'no, it would not, it would be Mr Nicholas Phelps himself, come to join the Joseph Maximus farewell party. I think you two know each other?'

Nicholas Phelps had arrived obviously intent on striking an informal note for he was without his tie and the top button of his shirt was undone. He looked just like any other vaguely patrician young man intent on enjoying a drink with an American he had befriended on a rather dull trip to Cornwall. 'You don't look too good,' he told Ottilie, looking at her slightly shocked.

'No, I'm not feeling at all well, I shouldn't have come. I'll have to go home. Lorcan will take me—'

'I was just teasing Ottilie about her inheritance,' Joseph said, rocking back on his heels and laughing. 'Imagine that old maid Edith leaving her a couple of hundred quid and a parrot!'

'She's left her a great deal more than that,' Nicholas Phelps told Joseph. Before Ottilie could stop him, he had added, obviously dying to cut the all too gleeful Joseph down to size, 'Miss O'Flaherty will soon be buying you out, chum, if you don't watch it. Miss O'Flaherty has inherited a very, very large fortune indeed.'

Ottilie's eyes flew first to Joseph's face and then, too late, to the lawyer's. She was so horrified by his indiscretion she forgot to put out her hand to cover her glass as Joseph stopped yet again in front of her to top it up.

'He'll know soon enough, when you buy this place, won't he?' Phelps asked her, half apologetically and half factually.

'You're kidding me?' Joseph looked down at Ottilie and because he was standing too near her she could see that the pulse in his neck had increased its speed and hear the intake of his breath. 'Tell me you're kidding me, Ottie? Edith never left you a fortune, did she?'

He looked from her to the lawyer and back again.

'It's all right, Miss O'Flaherty,' Phelps continued smoothly. 'If you want it kept a secret, I'm sure your brother won't tell anyone.'

'You stupid bloody idiot, of course I wanted it kept a secret! You know I wanted it kept a secret!'

Ottilie turned on the lawyer, and then back to Joseph who had backed off from her down the room, shaking his head in disbelief, whisky glass in hand.

'And to think that minutes ago I was about to offer you a job, and feeling sorry for you, and you were busy lecturing me on the profit motive!'

'We were talking about principles—'

'Principles, don't give me principles, Ottie! You and principles, what did you ever know about principles? You never did have any, not even when you were a child. Why, you were a thief even then, you started off life stealing your own mother's earrings—'

'You know that's not true, Joseph.'

'Of course I know it's true – and aren't I glad you were, Ottie?'

Staring into Joseph's furious mocking face Ottilie heard the word thief and it brought everything back, Ma, the police, waiting for Lorcan to come. It was like that now – she was still waiting for Lorcan to come, if only he would come . . .

Phelps took Joseph's arm, and she heard him say in a lowered voice, 'I say, old chap, I think you've had just a little too much to drink.' And then turning back to her he said, 'Miss O'Flaherty, why not take some air? You really do look very unwell.'

'No, I'm fine, really I am,' Ottilie heard herself trying to reassure him.

'Look, Ottie, I'm sorry, really I am.'

'Never mind, Joseph. I know the truth of what you said, and that's all that matters.' Ottilie felt terrible suddenly, sick and faint. She tried to walk towards the balcony but knew that she was swaying more than walking, and she could hear Joseph laughing and saying in a teasing voice, 'Silly girl, you're as pissed as I am!'

He strode across the room and took her in his arms.

'Come on, let's kiss and make up, Ottie! Let's dance. We're both rich, that's all that matters, we're rich!'

'I'm not drunk, am I, Joseph?'

Valiantly Ottilie tried opening her eyes a little wider, but it was too late, darkness was crowding in, and before she could protest she had started to dance with him and she knew she was smiling stupidly and she could hear that awful lawyer suddenly joining in Joseph's laughter, and herself saying woozily, 'Lorcan's coming soon, isn't it?'

'It? You mean he! Course he is, big brother to the rescue, Ottie!'

She knew at once when she woke up what must have happened. She did not have to look, she did not have to stare down at herself, and indeed she felt so terrible, so ill, so sick, all she could think of was that she had to somehow get herself to the bathroom. It seemed to take for ever, she didn't know why, but at last she felt the coldness of the chrome taps to which she found herself clinging just as a passenger on a liner might hold the edge of the boat. Next came the blessed cool of the basin.

She had never thought being violently sick could be a blessing but it was now, for despite her dizziness, despite that tell-tale feeling of total revulsion, it meant that she might sometime be rid of the nightmare that she had allowed to happen to her body.

Dimly in the bathroom mirror she could see that her beautiful dress might be ripped, but that was nothing. Calmly after what must have been many minutes she thought, *Right, I know what to do now* and she looked round the bathroom for a razor. There was no razor. There was nothing except a piece of used soap, some towels, towels she pulled towards and started to put about her, pulling her dress into place as she did so, frantically pulling up her clothing around her, under the towel as she had used to do when changing on the beach with Ma fondly watching her.

Propriety restored she put on her shoes. Because she was still drunk that too seemed to take an age, and she wobbled helplessly at one point because she had on one, and could not seem to find the other without difficulty, and then she edged slowly towards the door. Thank God she knew the hotel so well. She knew where the fire escape was, she knew how, even in the darkness, she could escape.

She crept slowly towards the door. There was no sign of any of the men anywhere, not in the bedroom, not in the sitting room, nowhere, no suitcases, nothing. Whoever had done this to her had gone. Now all she had to do was to get out, and down, and back into her car, so quietly that she knew that no-one could follow her.

Just the smell of the interior of her car was somehow reassuring, and finding her keys in her handbag beside her make-up compact was so good, sort of like a balm, and putting the key into the ignition and hearing Oscar starting up was dream-like, and the fact that she could pull the steering wheel and the lights went on, and the car went where she wanted it to go – and the road in front of her, that too was out of this world. Its dull, pale colour might have been the yellow brick road itself.

And at last it was there, the smell of her own kitchen, the smell of the wood they still used in the kitchen range, and the old-fashioned buttermilk cream that she had recently had it repainted, that was there too, and the herbs that Mrs East dried by the range, they were there, and the smell of the cloves that Mrs East used to cook the hams once a week, that was hanging in the air, and despite hardly being able to see for the pain in her head Ottilie could see her chair, Mrs East's chair, and she sat down in it and began to rock it, to and fro, to and fro, to and fro, and as the rocking eased her pained body something burst out of her, a sound, a sound that she could hear from far away, the sound of some poor woman sobbing. Poor woman, she thought, listening to her, poor, poor woman. Imagine crying like that, imagine making that sound, poor creature.

And then there was another sound and it was the same poor woman screaming and there was a face pressed up against the window and she saw this woman – she was quite young and she looked oddly like someone Ottilie knew – she saw her grabbing a knife from the rack near the sink as the back door swung open, and she heard her screaming, 'Don't come near me, Joseph, don't come near me or I swear I'll kill you.'

But it wasn't Joseph. It was someone who looked just like him and he was saying to her in a gentle voice, 'Ottie, give me the knife. No, don't turn it on yourself. Please. I don't know what's happened, but whatever's happened to you, don't do that.'

351

Ottilie stared at the man. It was Lorcan. Her brother. And of course he didn't know what had happened to her, why she needed to put the knife in herself.

'Give me the knife.'

Ottilie shook her head. No.

Nineteen

Ottilie had forgotten the words of confession. She stared at Lorcan.

'*Oh, for Christ's sake,*' she wanted to shout at him. '*I mean, really, for Christ's sake, tell me, I mean, really, really tell me, for His sake what on earth anything has to do with anything, particularly confession?*'

'It's no good, Lorcan,' she told him out loud, thankful only that he could not read her thoughts. 'I've forgotten the words, what the hell are the words? It's my head, I suppose,' she went on, 'my head throbs so, and what with the 'flu and the antibiotics I feel just as if I have been hit on the head. I knew I shouldn't have drunk anything, I shouldn't even have gone out.'

Lorcan's eyes were steady, his hands cool, and he was seated opposite her on the other side of the big pine kitchen table. It was so quiet, the night around them was an ocean of darkness, the kitchen a liner spilling out light, and themselves in the middle of it, passengers. For no reason Ottilie turned her face towards the large windows to the side of them and stared out at the black. It was still so tempting to end it all. She looked at the knives on the rack now, and then cursed the fact that the kitchen had no gas, and there was no garage nearby. She had always heard that garages were good for going into, closing doors and turning on engines and ending it all in blissful, welcoming unconsciousness.

'Lorcan.'

'Yes.'

'Why do they call the devil the Prince of Darkness when darkness is so lovely?' she asked, mystified.

'If I say the words, Ottie—'

'Don't call me that,' she screamed, suddenly crashing her fist down on the table. 'Don't call me that, don't ever call me that again, please.' Lorcan stared at her. 'That's what he kept calling me.'

Lorcan's eyes. They were his eyes too, yet they were not his eyes, they were Lorcan's eyes because they were so full of concern.

'He kept calling you that?'

'Yes, he kept calling me that in an American voice. I know he did. I can hear it, even now.'

Ottilie stared at Lorcan through aching eyes.

'It must have been Joseph, Lorcan. Who else would call me that? Only you and he and Sean ever call me Ottie. My brother molested me. So what use is that in confession, Lorcan? Words can't take that away.'

'Well, for a start, he's not your brother any more than I am, and whoever molested you of the two men present – believe you me, he was no relative, thank God. You will not have that burden, thank heavens. That's why I'm trying to get us both into a confessional state, don't you understand, to try to bring us both round to the truth of what has happened? I want you to confess to me and in the sanctity of the confessional – we can do it here, it's perfectly allowable, we have no need of the confession box itself – you can tell me what you remember and know, absolutely, that I will not divulge it to anyone, not a single person, not a living soul. You will be quite safe with me.'

'I hate confession,' Ottilie heard herself sobbing. 'I hate it, and – and I just told you, I can't even remember the words.'

'I will remember them, and you can repeat them after me.'

Lorcan took out something, Ottilie could hardly see what it was, nor did she care for the pain in her head was so intense she thought she might faint. Why was Lorcan getting her to confess, and to what?

'It's as well that I came by,' he said as he kissed the thin piece of stiffened purple silk he was putting round his neck. Purple was for death, and for sin forgiven, and for mourning and for all sorts of things that were nothing to do with what had happened to Ottilie but everything to do with Lorcan, which was probably why he was talking so much, talk, talk, talk, what difference did it ever make? 'I feel that it was my fault that this party became an occasion of sin, but I was delayed from reaching the Grand – delayed by my poor parishioners on the moors. In the event it transpired that Mr Dibble had passed on before I arrived, but I anointed him, and was able to bring comfort to his wife,' he added, half to himself. Then to Ottilie, 'Now I will say the words and you may continue to think on what has happened to you – the truth, the all-important truth of what has happened – and ask God's forgiveness for those moments where you yourself may indeed have been at fault, Ottie, do – ask God's forgiveness if you can. We are all at fault somewhere. We find, really we do, when we examine our consciences, that we have usually, despite our best efforts, occasioned sin in others.'

Lorcan started to mutter words and prayers, or so it seemed to Ottilie, but they made no sense to her. If they brought him comfort well and good, but they did nothing for her, they only made her want to scream, 'I am in hell. Words are no good to someone in the hell that I am occupying.'

'Very well, now tell me. In your own words, in whatever way you wish, what happened.'

'What. Happened.'

Ottilie wiped her eyes with her hands. Somehow handkerchiefs always eluded her.

'Very well. What happened was this,' she said slowly and her words sounded thick and slurred, as if it was someone else speaking. 'As I remember it, I was given away, by you, to this couple who ran a hotel, and that is where I grew up, not as Ottilie O'Flaherty but as Ottilie Cartaret, and Mrs Cartaret, my mother, used to beat me. Not often, mostly she was kind in her own way, but when she was drunk or had a hangover, she beat me. And I didn't like it. And so after that I told her lies, all sorts of lies, but I went on doing what she told me because I didn't want to be beaten and one day she told me to run out of the hotel and throw away these diamond earrings she had, but I couldn't, I don't know why. Each time I came to a drain I looked up and Edith would be looking at me, and when I went back to the hotel I was too frightened to even throw them down the basin because the police were—' Ottilie stopped and despite every effort she started to cry again. Eventually she continued. 'I think it was because the police were there, and ever since Ma was arrested I have such a fear of them, of the police, and so I jumped out of the window and I ran to find you, but you weren't there, there was just Joseph and he took the earrings because he thought they were just worth a few pounds, but when he realized they were worth at least a thousand pounds and that Mrs Cartaret was doing away with them so she could get the insurance, he ran off with them, and never came back.'

Lorcan's eyes said, 'Ah, I see now, so that's how Joseph could afford to go to America,' but his mouth said, 'Go on, I'm listening.'

'After that, well, you know about after that.' Ottilie stopped, raising her swollen eyes to Lorcan's face. 'I grew up and went to Paris and – well, you also know about the drawing being found and all that, and how I came to be here and how happy I have been here, because of you. But now this.' She stopped again and stared down at her dress. 'I think this happened because of something else. I mean I think he did this to me because – because Edith – oh God, Lorcan – I didn't want anyone to know but Edith only

356

went and left me a fortune, and I mean a real fortune, and you see her lawyer was staying in the next-door suite to Joseph and when Joseph heard just how rich I was he became contorted with jealousy—'

Lorcan put his hand over Ottilie's as she broke down once more, her shoulders shaking, the tears seeming to be scorching, but Lorcan's hand was the hand of a priest, cool and consoling.

'Was there any way that you could have led him on, my child? Was there any way that you could honestly say that without realizing it you encouraged him to go too far in a way that may have made him go out of control? Think seriously. I mean – your dress is very attractive, although it has long sleeves and its hem reaches to the knee; and it is quite low cut. That could be, wouldn't you think, deemed quite provocative to the men present, both of whom obviously already had drink taken?'

'For Christ's sake!' Ottilie jumped to her feet, the tears gone, anger exploding inside her. 'For Christ's sake, Lorcan, this is a bloody designer dress. Look at me. It's in perfect taste and you know it. Don't try that kind of "Oh but you must have led him on would he not have been better if you had have been wearing a twinset and pearls" rubbish with me. I'm not one of your dumbo parishioners to be brought to their knees sobbing with guilt over someone else's crime. Face it, Lorcan, I'm not like this because of my dress, or the colour of my hair, or my shoes, or my twenty-two-inch waist, or the mole on my cheek, I'm like this because of your brother, my brother. How can you drivel on about dresses when I have been raped! Have some bloody compassion—'

'Sit down, my child, sit down, and try to stay calm.'

'I don't want to be calm, I want to kill myself.'

Lorcan stood up and taking Ottilie's shaking hands he led her to Mrs East's chair.

'Sit there while I make you some hot milk.'

'I don't want hot milk.'

'Just sit—'

'You won't know where anything is.'

'I'll soon find everything, you'd be surprised. After the number of parishes I've been in I can find my way round most kitchens nowadays.'

He took off his vestment, kissed it and put it away and then moving quietly and methodically while Ottilie swung to and fro in Mrs East's chair he found milk, and sugar, and brandy, and put them on to boil.

'Now,' he said, turning from the stove back to Ottilie. 'First, you know very well I am not your brother, and nor is the man you think molested you tonight. He is not your brother. He is Joseph O'Flaherty, but he is not your brother. We were brought up as your brothers, and we think of you as a sister, but we are not related by blood. Ma must have told you all about how you were born, but I'll tell you again. Wait, I'll just get the milk into the mug and then I'll tell you again for you have undoubtedly become confused with the shock of it all, you have been shredded into confusion.'

Ottilie took the mug and sipped at the milk and brandy as Lorcan drew up a chair near her and started to talk to her as if she was a small child again, as if he was in charge of reading to her to put her to sleep.

'You were born at Number Four Porchester Terrace,' he said in a low, measured voice, 'but not in our flat, you were born in the flat above us. I remember your mother, she lived in two rooms above us, a slip of a girl, not unlike yourself with long hair and a pretty little face, coming in and out of the main doors of the block, but of course being that I was only a gossoon I never took much notice. Eventually it seems, nine months after she came to Porchester Terrace, you were born, but your poor mother died, alone, giving birth, for want of someone attending her, afraid to tell anyone of her state, I think. Anyway, the local midwife was a friend of Ma's – well, everyone was a friend of Ma's, weren't they? And she came and gave Ma the baby, just to look after at first, you understand, but Ma fell in love with you – Da was well gone by then, and she longed I think for more children, and along came you. And of course you were a girl after all us boys, you were a longed-for girl. So – well, I don't know how they managed it because I doubt there was anything official happened, but you came to stay and be our longed-for little sister, and of course Ma always told me and the boys that if anyone asked we were merely to tell them that you were brought and left at the door by the Little People. Remember that? You were brought by the Little People – we always joked with you about that, didn't we? I always thought Ma had told you, I swear to God all the time you were growing – I always thought Ma told you. She did, didn't she?'

'Ma never said anything, Lorcan, you know Ma. I always thought that my having been brought by the Little People was just a joke, because of Da being away, and everything . . .' Ottilie said, but her own voice seemed so terribly far away, it was as if she was being spoken for, and all the time trying to understand everything Lorcan had just told her through the throbbing of her head. 'I thought it was just a joke when everyone said that. I always thought you were my family, and the Cartarets were in place of you, because of Ma dying.'

'Dear God, Ottie, I thought – we all thought – that you *knew*. It never occurred to me to think otherwise. You poor creature, and now – to have to find out now, at this late date. I never thought for a second that Ma hadn't told you.'

'Why didn't you tell me when you gave me away? It would have made it much easier. All that time I thought you were my real brother and you weren't. I could have made more sense of it all if I'd known then. It makes so much sense, if we're not related. It would have – stopped some of the pain, for Christ's sakes, the awfulness of thinking that none of you wanted anything to do with your sister any more!'

Lorcan was silent for a minute, then he said, 'Do you not think that I would not have given anything, anything at all, to have kept you with us? That was the worst of Ma's going like that, more than anything else, even the suddenness of her death, it was having suddenly to find a home for you because out of all of us you were the one who couldn't be left. If you could have seen yourself, you looked so pathetic, going off with your little cardboard box filled with your rag books and your teddies and wearing Ma's old black Mass veil, and you were so brave.' Lorcan shook his head. 'I remember it as if it was yesterday. Ah, but you had such a way with you when you were little, Ottilie. Always standing on chairs making speeches, or saying to Ma "Let me dance for you" or "Wait there till I make you laugh." One day, I'll never forget it, one day I got back from the building site and there you were in your best dress, what a thing, and dancing away for her, and of course Ma – it was one of her bad days, you know? She was passed out on the floor, *flutered* poor thing, but you'd just gone on dancing away to some old seventy-eight record, waiting for her to wake up and laugh with you. That's why Joseph was always so jealous, d'you see? It's not this money you speak of, that wouldn't have affected him so much, no, it's because it's you who was the apple of Ma's eye, her golden girl. That's why she joked so often that the Little People had sent you to her. She just thought of you as her little miracle sent by them. Maybe in her confusion she even came to believe it, who knows? Perhaps that's why she delayed telling you that you weren't really hers?'

He stopped, sighing, a deep down sigh at the memories, suddenly not a priest at all but just a boy, a son.

'But to get back to the story. Who your real mother was we'll never know, you know? All we do know is that we came here, to Cornwall, because the poor girl had these pictures of Cornwall stuck on the walls of her poor auld room. And when the midwife gave them to Ma, well, Ma, she thought it looked like Kerry a bit, where she came from in Ireland. So down we all came, after Da sent her the pay-off money. And that's all we know. Except of course the bracelet, which I gave you, on your tenth birthday, I think it was.'

Ottilie thought, *What does it matter if it was my eleventh, twelfth or twentieth, Lorcan, when you know very well what you're really telling me is that we have spent all this time caring for each other quite needlessly. Even my guilt over you being sent away by Melanie from that wretched party, that was all needless.*

'God, I remember what a complete gombeen I felt in my thorn-proof coming to that party with all those smart people there. But you would have it that I must come. Anyway, the bracelet that I brought you that day, that was said to have belonged to your own poor mother. Ma always said it had belonged to the poor girl. But that's all we do know of her, that she lived at Number Four and that it was hers – the bracelet. So d'you see now what I meant when I said the man you think molested you was not your brother, it was mine?'

'What is done, is done,' Ottilie said on a tired sigh, her eyes still closed because the hot milk with the brandy seemed to be getting through to her, soothing her and making her feel suddenly spent, without any fight or interest left in her, what with the rocking of the chair and Lorcan talking and talking. 'But brother or no brother, when he did what he did *I* thought he was still my brother and maybe even *he* was thinking it too, and that's as bad, isn't it?' She opened her eyes and stared at Lorcan as her voice rose on a suddenly sarcastic note. 'After all, Lorcan, you're a priest, isn't intention meant to be everything?'

'I still can't believe that either of those two men – least of all Joseph.'

Lorcan started to walk around the kitchen clasping and unclasping his hands as Ottilie closed her eyes again.

'Can't you, Lorcan?' she heard herself saying in a tired

voice as the rocking chair went backwards and forwards. 'I think you can. Joseph was always the bad one, Ma said. She used to say to me, "Out of the three I wouldn't mind throwing out the middle one, too like his father for my liking." She was always saying that on our walks together. She wasn't that doting a mother, you know, and because I was so young, and a girl, she talked to me all the time about you, about all of you.'

'Did she, Ottie? Did she really?'

Ottilie opened her eyes again and standing up she carefully put the empty mug on the kitchen table. She was now barely able to think, yet somehow she must get herself to bed and in the morning the staff would come, life would start up again, and she could begin to not care too much about what had happened. Just get on with life, not care.

'Oh yes,' she told Lorcan slowly, because he was obviously hungering after what Ma had said. 'She talked about you all the time. It was always Lorcan this and Joseph that, and little Sean the other. She never stopped talking about you all on our walks, and of her dreams for you. She wanted so much for you all, for us all. The French say women divide into two – wife/mother or wife/mistress. Ma was all mother.'

'In that case, can you tell me, could you tell me what did she say about me?'

'About you?' she said, and her tone softened as she saw the anxiety in Lorcan's eyes. 'She said you were a saint, Lorcan. She said that after Da left she could never have got through a minute of her life without you.'

At which Lorcan stopped pacing and put his head in his hands and started to cry like a child, and Ottilie walked slowly over to him and stroked his head.

'Poor Lorcan,' she said. 'So much to bear, poor Lorcan.'

Twenty

Ottilie stared in the mirror. Although she was pale, she was up at last, and when she drew her navy blue curtains winter sunshine was transforming the courtyard outside, and she could see departing guests moving about, carefully crossing the old cobblestone in overcoats and hats, waiting for each other to leave, their luggage piled high by the doors of their suites. Mrs East suddenly appeared by the back door of the kitchen, shook out one of the old fashioned mops to which she was so devoted, and then disappeared again to be followed, shortly, by Nantwick who picked up some of the waiting suitcases, piled them expertly under his arm, and set off down the courtyard to the front to help put them into waiting cars. Ottilie watched all this seeming mundanity at first dutifully, finally with interest. Life was still going on down there, and from now on she must make herself part of it.

She turned from the window and going to her cupboard she picked out her most cheerful winter dress. A red dress with a high collar, close fitted and with a circular skirt, the many folds of which showed off her slim figure, making a feature of her sudden loss of weight.

'Sea air. You must get out in the air,' Veronica had kept murmuring, arriving in her room every day with papers to sign, and in the evenings a glass of champagne, which she encouraged Ottilie to drink, always saying, 'There's nothing like champagne to restore the human spirit. Believe me, I know.'

At first, dreary day after dreary day Ottilie hated seeing

even Veronica and for some reason she especially hated the champagne, but to please her secretary and because she could see how worried she looked, she sipped at it, and after a while, some few weeks, she found she had started to look forward to its evening arrival, and to seeing Veronica and hearing about what was happening downstairs where life still went on, and things still mattered.

Veronica was too mature not to realize that something terrible had happened to Ottilie, but also, thankfully, too sensitive to say more than 'drink your champagne' or 'sign here, Miss O'Flaherty'.

One day – Ottilie could not and did not care to remember which day it was – she said to her suddenly, 'Don't call me that any more. I know you don't like first-naming, but if you don't mind, from now on please call me "Miss Cartaret".'

Veronica had merely nodded, not seeming to take much notice, but after that Ottilie did indeed become 'Miss Cartaret' again, not just to Veronica, but to the rest of the staff who telephoned to her room. The change made a difference to her somehow. As if the other person, Ottilie O'Flaherty, had died the night of Joseph's farewell party.

Once she had satisfied herself that her dress was up to the neck, and the hem of it fashionably long and sufficiently demure – nearly to her ankle – Ottilie brushed back her thick dark hair and pulled it tightly into a large black velvet bow at her neck. She stared at herself in the dressing mirror behind the door. She was far too thin – keeping weight on always being a problem for her – she was still pale, and there were shadows under her eyes, but she was up at last, and she was about, and she was alive, and more than that, incredibly, and in time for her recovery, Philip was about to arrive home.

Constantia had telephoned the great news. Her patrician tones seemed suddenly healing to Ottilie, and, like Veronica, her tactful ability to not say too much a balm. After that night with Lorcan she was sure that she absolutely did not want anyone saying anything emotional to her ever again. She had spent weeks feeling bereft of everything that had once seemed to matter. Her family, her brothers, who were not her brothers, everything appeared to have been taken from her in a matter of a few hours. For weeks her belief in life had hovered between the blackest despair and inability to see any point in living, and a gradual awareness that there was still something to live for, the boy she had known and loved since she was ten.

It was staring at Philip's photograph, remembering him as he had been their last day in St Elcombe, that had pulled her through. After all, he had laughed at the story of the nude drawing, teased her about her effortless ability to get herself into hot water. Of all people Philip would understand she was sure, and although his words kept coming back to her, *You will be good until I get back, won't you, Ottilie?* and she remembered how she had worried that they would both change, for ever, that nothing ever stayed the same (and so it had proved), nevertheless even if she had been changed, perhaps – and in this she saw her salvation – perhaps he would not and so on seeing him she would change back again, and everything could be as it had been before, and he would still be the boy with the hare.

'Of course I would love to come and see Philip the moment he gets back, but only after you have had your own welcoming party,' Ottilie told Constantia. 'Really. I would love to see him, but you must come first, you and everyone at Tredegar.'

Constantia had sounded surprised at Ottilie's words, and unwillingly grateful, as if she would have liked to have said 'I never expected you of all people to be like this, Ottilie, so accommodating', but instead she made a funny little 'oh' sound, like breaking glass, and put the phone down after continuing in her clipped way, 'Oh, very well. I'll tell him. I know he'll want to take you out to dinner.

No, I tell you what – come here, for dinner, on Saturday. I'll lay everything on. I won't be coming down, I've been promised a day out with the Beaufort and a stay-over at Badminton. Philip should be quite better by Saturday night. They need to unwind after these tours of duty. Particularly when there's been fighting.'

Philip's endearingly cryptic letters festooned with little caricatures had ceased as soon as the regiment had left for Cyprus, and she had heard nothing more from him, not even when she had written to say how sorry she was that his best friend had been killed. Perhaps because of this she had been only too willing to believe Constantia when she said that 'boys will be boys and when they're abroad they sort of go into limbo', but nevertheless, she was not prepared for what she saw crossing the hall towards her at Tredegar. Philip had always used to walk with such a quick step and he was always making a noise, whistling, or singing, or calling for the dogs.

She always remembered him, from a boy, coming towards her with a smile on his face, whereas the man approaching her now walked with a slow deliberate step, had no sign of gaiety in his face, and was not whistling. There were no dogs to be called. In seconds Ottilie realized that young Philip, like young Ottilie, had gone, that the young man who had waved so gaily and for so long as the train had pulled out of St Elcombe station that mellow Cornish evening had disappeared as if he had never been.

Of course this Philip, the present Philip, was still tall and handsome, his fair hair still wavy and thick, and his figure slim and upright, but his tanned skin was taut now, the lines around his mouth tight. Worst of all was the changed look in his eyes. His eyes were no longer Philip's eyes, perpetually filled with the sudden joyous gaiety of life, the certain knowledge that something wonderful was just about to happen, a fish was about to jump, or Ludlow belt across the grass towards him, or the sun was up and climbing the sky and they were about to go swimming and picnicking and Berenger was promising to show them how to call down an owl by whistling in a special way. Even the possibility of such joys was gone, and Ottilie realized that the expression in Philip's eyes was now watchful. He, like Constantia, now had the look of eagles.

'Ottilie, my darling.' He swung her round with a sort of dutiful false gaiety, and he kissed her on the lips, but his eyes said nothing at all, while his lips said, 'Let me look at you, after all this time. You look marvellous.'

Ottilie smiled.

'You look really marvellous,' Philip continued mechanically. 'Come upstairs where it's warm. Constantia's loaned us the use of her sitting room, it'll be cosy there. After Cyprus, you can imagine, Tredegar feels like the Arctic.'

It was all terrible, just awful little words and neither of them saying anything that was real, Ottilie saying in bright tones, 'Oh, I love Constantia's sitting room,' which she didn't at all, thinking it was just like a shop. And 'Ooh, good, champagne, I love champagne,' just as if Veronica hadn't been in the habit of bringing her a glass every evening for strictly medicinal reasons. So that now it seemed it would always taste like medicine to her.

'So.' Philip sat down opposite her. 'What's been happening here while I've been away? Plenty, I'm sure.'

Before, when they talked, Philip had always sat stroking dogs, but now there were no dogs to stroke he kept fiddling with his gold cigarette lighter, putting it up one way and then down another and turning it back, over and over again, and it was terribly irritating because he kept watching the lighter and his eyes deliberately avoided hers as they talked about all the things that had happened since they had parted at the station that evening and none of the things that had really happened to make their young selves go away for ever.

He said nothing about his sorrow at losing his friend,

and Ottilie said nothing about what had happened to her. She said nothing about why she was so thin, why she was so subdued, even her voice sounding tired and thin, as if she was suffering from a sore throat.

Finally, unable to bear the falsity of the situation, and unable to eat or drink very much of the cold meats and salads left out for them either, Ottilie put down her wine glass and said quietly, 'Philip don't let's pretend any more. We've known each other for so long.'

'How do you mean?' Philip stared at the base of his wine glass.

'I mean that we've gone, haven't we? The bits of us that were here before you went to Cyprus and before I got chucked out of the Grand, the young bits that thought something pretty wonderful was just around the corner, they have quite gone, and we're just pretending to have dinner and conversation as if we had only known each other socially, instead of saying what we really feel, aren't we?'

As soon as she had said it, Ottilie realized she had made a terrible mistake, because Philip immediately looked exactly as Constantia would if confronted by real, stated, feelings. He looked as if Ottilie had been sick in front of him, as if she had deeply offended his sense of propriety. His look put her behind a glass partition, mouthing soundlessly at him, worst of all it put her firmly on the other side of the tracks.

'I simply do not know what you mean, Ottilie,' he said.

Ottilie suddenly saw from that look that he had not only changed because of seeing friends die, he had changed because of being for so long in the company of other officers, men of his own kind, men who had not taken joy in keeping tame hares called Ludlow, but shot hares, or raced them and let hounds tear them to pieces while they gambled on the outcome. Men who drank at regimental dinners until they could no longer stand. Men who took girls when they could, but married their own kind. Men who did not understand emotions and certainly did not talk about them.

Ottilie put her napkin down. Too much had happened to her for her ever to want again to conceal or deny her feelings. She would not sob, or cry, or look for sympathy, but would just state them so that it would be as if she was holding them in her hands, as if they were different-coloured pieces of ribbon, or semi-precious stones, that she could hold up to the light and say, 'Ah yes, this is jealousy, and this – this is confusion, and here, here is love.' Or not.

'Philip. I know you won't like this, and I know you won't want to see me again, but I also know that it is quite fatal for people not to talk about how they are, how everything is.'

She stood up and walked towards the fireplace with its two Herend greyhounds facing each other and its General Trading Company china clock with its gold hands, and its small cut-glass vase of flowers, and its pale pine mantel and its awful log-effect fire – Constantia had such strange taste – and stared down into the flickering falsity of the logs that were not really logs, and the fire that was only electric, and then she looked across at Philip, hoping that somehow all the new stiffness would suddenly go and they could both laugh and talk as they had always used to do.

'I know you've had a horrid time, losing your friend and having to bury him, because Constantia told me, but all the time you've been away I have done nothing but think of you and pray for you and read your letters, and at night your photograph was the last image in front of my eyes before I fell asleep. But that's not enough, is it? I mean, I promised you that I would keep myself for you when you came back, and I really did, except something terrible happened to me too, Philip.'

He was unmoving, still sitting in front of his stupid salad, and his eyes were so different from how she remembered them, and perhaps because he had not once touched her hand or made any attempt to do so, Ottilie suddenly knew that he already knew all about what had happened to her; and that he had known all the time, right from the moment when she had arrived at the old oak door with his family coat of arms above it, and it was that knowledge, about Ottilie, nothing to do with being in the Army, that had lain between them from the moment he had kissed her and swung her round.

'I must admit I did hear something had happened to you. You know St Elcombe, they start to gossip before they even open their eyes in the morning.'

Ottilie did not know from where she now received her strength, but although her heart felt as if it had iced over as he spoke, she straightened her back and looked across at him, not wanting sympathy, but certainly still seeking some kind of understanding.

'Yes,' she said. 'I do know St Elcombe. But I must tell you everything, in my own words.' She began again. 'Something terrible happened to me, Philip, one of the worst things that can happen to a woman, and it was not my fault. There is nothing I can do about it, because to do anything would mean bringing scandal and hurt, and Lorcan – you know, Lorcan, my sort of brother – well, he says it is best forgotten, put behind me, and I think he's right. But anyway I'm all right. I'm better now.'

At last, remembering his manners, Philip too stood up, but he didn't walk towards her.

'I'm glad,' he said slowly. 'I'm glad for your sake that you're better. But – this is a bit awkward to say – but the trouble is, we have to face it, you're damaged goods now, aren't you, Ottilie?'

He said it quite casually, as if she was a parcel arrived from Harrods which, most regrettably, he would have to send back.

'Well, I – well yes, I suppose, put like that, I suppose, yes, I am.' Ottilie stared at Philip, not really believing what he had just said.

'I gather it was the usual girl's party story, of course, and don't get me wrong, I don't blame you for sticking to it – your drink was spiked. But I'm not the only one who knows, I'm afraid, the whole of St Elcombe knows. Apparently the housekeeper or someone saw you leaving the hotel the night of the party, or whatever it was, in a bit of a state. Rather embarrassing for you in such a small place, but I expect they'll all get over it. But it does, well, it does make things a bit awkward, doesn't it?'

'What do you mean by "awkward", and "things", Philip?'

'By "things" I mean' – he took out a cigarette from a slim gold case and slowly lit it, using his lighter. He did not bother to offer her one but drew on his own with such open satisfaction that Ottilie felt she could almost see the smoke going down to his lungs and then returning, slowly, slowly, at last to be expelled through his nose. 'I suppose I mean "us" really, not "things". I mean – yes, we must be frank, I suppose you're right to say we must be frank. Before I went away I thought I was in love with you. When I wrote to you before the regiment was sent to Cyprus, I was crazy about you, but now – well, it's just one of those things that happen, you know, lovely memories and all that, but it is over, really.'

'I see.'

Emboldened perhaps by Ottilie's cool reaction, Philip continued. 'Constantia did try to warn me, after our party, that any girl who was sporting a Parisian model dress was not likely to be a plaster saint, but I didn't believe her. Besides, you looked so cracking in it, I don't suppose I cared how you got the dress either. But now it is quite different. I am back here for good. I will be out of the Army in another few months, and you know how it is, Ottilie. St Elcombe is such a small place. I must be careful to retain respect for my family. Father's family having been here for so many hundreds of years we are expected to behave ourselves, anyway publicly. You see, traditionally, we usually end up as Lord Lieutenants of the county, greeting the monarch and members of the royal family and so on, and with this kind of story about you being such common gossip, in such a small place it makes it – well, quite frankly, it makes it a bit awkward to even go on taking you out. Constantia tells me that you have quite a good job now, that you've made quite a success of the Angel, and that you are all right, not in a bad way at all. So.' He must have seen the astonishment in Ottilie's eyes, for he turned to walk down the far side of the sitting room and stare up at a rather poorly painted portrait of his father in regimental uniform. 'So, well, that's how it is,' he finished.

There was a long silence as Ottilie stared at his back. So this was it. This was the end of all those months of worrying and thinking and, yes, praying.

'Fine,' she said aloud. 'Now let me just see, Philip,' she said, continuing despite the fact that his back was still turned to her. 'What you're saying is that it would be bad for you and your position in the county to go on taking me out or being friends, because you believe what happened to me was my fault, and that I am the sort of person who would sleep with someone for the sake of a couture gown?'

'In short, yes.' He turned back from his father's portrait, obviously relieved that Ottilie had stayed outwardly calm, had not screamed or protested her innocence or anything embarrassing. 'It won't matter to some other man, Ottilie, that you're that sort of girl. It's just for someone like me, with my position here at Tredegar, and all our connections in the town – well, it makes things very different for me, you understand? Some other man won't mind. In fact from what I gather from others in the regiment, a great many girls are damaged goods now.'

'If they have the bad luck to fall in love with men like you, yes, Philip, I would think they would be, very damaged.'

'I mean, if you really want to know, if we put our cards

on the table,' he continued, ignoring her, 'I didn't mind about the nude drawing of you, I thought that was quite funny when you told me and I thought your parents were being a bit stuffy because taking your clothes off for some old Frenchman, well, who cares? But this is rather different. It's actually caused a bit of scandal among the kind of people who come to work here, whose families have always worked here, and country people are very conservative. But don't mind too much. I mean you're still young and beautiful. You'll find someone else, I'm sure, if not this year, next year.'

Ottilie picked up her handbag. Her heart was beating so fast it actually sounded like a drum in her ears, so hard was it thumping. She moved towards the door, but only once he had moved away from it, because the idea that he might even touch her hand was abhorrent to her. At the door she turned her head and directed her large eyes at what she saw now was a most arrogant face.

'I shan't protest my innocence, Philip. I've already done that quite enough in my life. Besides, I don't see why I should. I know what happened, and I shall have to live with it. But I'll tell you something now. What happened to me I admit was quite definitely my fault. I was foolish, I went to a party and drank too much when I should not have done, but I promise you, here and now, I shall prove to you how wrong you were about me, how wrong you were about my character and about the sort of person I am. I am not as you so sweetly call me "damaged goods" and I am a person not a chattel, and so long as I keep away from people like you I expect I have a good chance of becoming mended.'

She closed the door behind her and ran down the many stairs, past his long-faced wigged and velvet-coated ancestors, under his coat of arms and out into the cold night air. As she ran towards her car she could hear the sea beyond the gardens, and feel its breeze on her face, and it lifted her to a sudden dizzying sense of freedom. She could not lie. In her heart of hearts as she had said goodbye to the person that Philip now was, she had felt not sadness, but only a profound sense of relief.

After all, in a few weeks, or months, or however long it took, and in defiance of good sense, of Phelps her lawyer, of everything logical, she would be the new owner of the Grand, St Elcombe. This time it would be she, Ottilie, who would be doing the adopting. Damaged goods or not, she would survive, and win.

Twenty-One

The probate on Edith's estate had been through for many months, and Ottilie was now so rich that when she awoke in the morning she determined that the only way to go on living sensibly was to put the realization to one side, thinking that to dwell in any way upon the possibilities of her new wealth would make her less determined.

Following the takeover by Vision, she and Veronica and the rest of the small staff started the long task of packing up the Angel, and preparing to move themselves out and up the road to what Jean kept referring to as 'the sea-side' in deference to the Grand's famous view, which was not shared by any other building.

'Only a few more weeks in this old place,' Ottilie said, sitting back on her heels, and bored with wrapping glasses in newspaper she sighed suddenly and looked round. 'I'm afraid I may be going to miss it. It seems so awful to have to leave it just as we made it comfortable. And now bloody old Vision is going to flatten it all into a place that could be anywhere in the world. Are you sure you and Jean and Nantwick want to come to the derelict old Grand? I mean you have seen it, haven't you?'

'It's a bit late for that sort of talk, Miss Cartaret,' Veronica told her crisply. 'Besides, we are all looking forward to the new challenge. Nantwick calls it "Operation Grand", like the war, you know? Very appropriate. What about your parents, though?'

'My parents are going on a long cruise to enjoy spending some of their new wealth, and then they're going to live in a hotel in Devon – not run one, which will be a change for the better for them, I would think.'

'If you don't mind my saying so, I think that is a great deal more than they deserve after what they did to you, turning a blind eye to what that housekeeper was up to when she got that couple to plant that piece of glass in their food. What a dreadful thing to do.'

Ottilie's jaw dropped. In fact as she turned towards her secretary she was quite sure it was actually on the office carpet, and as she continued to stare at her, Veronica smiled.

'Sacked chef told Nantwick. You know St Elcombe, it all gets out, one way or another.'

Two months after that particular conversation, almost to the day, Ottilie and Veronica, followed by Jean and Nantwick with most of their possessions piled into a hired van driven by Nantwick, drew up outside the Grand. Ottilie alighted from Oscar and stood on the green sward running up to the old mahogany swing doors and breathed in. No matter what happened she was determined that she would not regret having bought the old place, but when she looked up and took in what was now actually hers, her courage nearly failed her entirely.

Ottilie knew that the ideal is always far from the reality, and although all during the long and protracted negotiations conducted by Phelps she was sure she had known exactly the sort of state into which the old hotel had fallen, now that she actually stood in front of the old place it was only too clear that seen from its proud buyer's point of view the Grand was not so much a subject for restoration as in need of complete resuscitation.

The stucco was crumbling visibly, the white paint, always the pride and joy of dear old Mr Hulton, stained and worn from neglect and the weather. Those of the dark green balcony shades that were still being used were frayed and some had torn at the sides from their iron fixings so that as they all approached the front steps carrying a few of their boxes and cases they could hear them flapping gently in the breeze. There was no sign of any bulbs or flowers in any of the boxes placed outside the windows or by the front doors, and the green sward in front of the entrance was poorly kept, with tufts sprouting at the sides of the paths from being mown by a machine set on a too-high blade.

'There are no guests nowadays, surely, Miss Cartaret?' Nantwick asked, as he and Jean looked up at the large crumbling exterior in complete amazement and they all avoided mentioning the fact that even the gold 'R' and 'D' were missing from GRAND.

Ottilie looked at Nantwick and then at Veronica and after that up at the Gothic façade of the hotel, a façade she had always thought so like a children's drawing, or a sandcastle on the beach, all castellations and a flagpole, but without a flag. She breathed in deeply. 'No, no-one stays any more, Nantwick, I'm afraid, not unless they're mad.'

They all walked with slow sad tread up the weed-strewn steps and pushed at the old mahogany swing doors which edged their way only with difficulty in the same old circle, finally allowing the four of them to squeeze out of them into the foyer. Here there was still no sign of life, and as Ottilie gazed round while they waited for someone to emerge from the office behind the desk it seemed to her that she could almost smell the dust in the air.

'It's maybe a hundred times worse even than when I last had the misfortune to be here,' Ottilie said, hoping that she had not just seen a rat appearing at the door of what had once been Blackie's cubby hole.

'It doesn't take much, Miss Cartaret,' Jean said sagely. 'Just a few months with no heating on and no staff and the damp and the rot creep up, 'specially at the seaside. I dread to think what we're going to find in the kitchens.'

Ottilie smiled and she chewed the inside of her cheek, discovering that now she was once more in the hotel she

377

had to fight hard to hold on to her courage.

Veronica seemed to feel this because she said to Nantwick, 'Why don't you go and take a look at the kitchens for Miss Cartaret? There's nothing in them, I believe, all the effects were sold off, but it'll give you an idea of what we're up against, and then you can take your picnic lunch into the garden and we'll be down to help you plan what's best to tackle first.'

A girl, a Danish student, perhaps an au pair Mrs Cartaret had engaged, appeared at the top of the stairs and called down to them, 'Mr and Mrs Cartaret are expecting you. Please use the lift if you might.'

'I'm not going in that. I'm the sole support of my mother,' Veronica said firmly.

'I abstain for more or less the same reasons,' Ottilie agreed, and she and Veronica proceeded to walk up the many flights that led to the Cartarets' apartments with the determined air of hitchhikers who are not expecting a lift, but would not say no if they were offered one.

'Ottilie.'

Ottilie had had no idea what she would feel like confronting her parents now that she actually owned the place from which they had so summarily ejected her. She had hoped she would feel a sort of justifiable anger, that she would be able to make an eloquent speech about how she hoped they would understand that she was not doing to them what they had done to her, but when she saw them again they looked somehow so forlorn and so helpless, she just wanted to gather them up and make them young and happy again. And so the speech fled and Ottilie reached forward and kissed them both. They did not offer their cheeks, but on the other hand they did not seem to mind Ottilie kissing them in a deferential sort of way, the way a child, she imagined, might kiss grand-parents that she hardly knows.

'See you're wearing your hair down, suits you,' Alfred stated and then he turned and stared at the view.

'This is Veronica. She is my business assistant.'

Veronica smiled at them both, and Ottilie could see that she felt the same, she would have liked to have said something cold and clever, but instead she smiled and accepted a glass of sherry from Alfred's small silver tray.

'Well, well.' Melanie's hand trembled slightly as she raised her sherry glass to her lips. 'Isn't this exciting, a Cartaret once more buying the Grand, St Elcombe?'

'Indeed, indeed.' Alfred sat down opposite Ottilie and Veronica who were now seated on a worn chintz sofa, old velvet cushions supporting their backs, the continuous sound of the sea sweeping up to the balconied windows outside. 'Well, now,' he said, shaking his head in wonder, 'who would have thought that our dear Edith would turn out to be a vastly rich woman? No-one could possibly have guessed such a thing. What a dark horse she was to be sure.'

'Certainly none of us knew anything about our Edith having money,' said Melanie and she too shook her head in wonder. 'It's too extraordinary to think that Edith had money, after all the years she spent here in service, really too extraordinary. Of course, when you made us your offer we in fact had already had another offer, as you probably know, from that awful Vision Clover group? But it was too little, of course. Insulting, really. Particularly given that the place has such a good reputation.'

Ottilie started to say something and then seeing Veronica looking at her she stopped. There was no point. She owned the place now, that was all that mattered, and as she had realized only too well, and for some time, buying the Grand with Edith's money was in reality her revenge on her parents.

Of course in her mind she had made many speeches to Alfred and Melanie remonstrating with them for throwing her out so summarily, for not caring what happened to her, but seeing them now, having to pack up and leave the place they had been a part of for so long, she suddenly

379

could only remember the good times and the style they had brought to running the hotel in the old days, just as when someone died she found she could only remember their virtues.

'Miss Edith was, I gather, a very good woman?'

Ottilie smiled thankfully at Veronica, who seemed most wonderfully adept at filling in awkward pauses.

'The absolute prop of the establishment,' Melanie agreed, lighting a cigarette. Her eyes filled with tears. 'When she went our hearts rather went out of the business, I really think that. And now, well you can imagine, with the retirement of Blackie, our long-time hall porter, and our builder Mr Hulton dead, and all the other regulars – we simply cannot manage any longer.'

'Of course you heard about poor Mrs Tomber, did you, Ottilie? Did I tell you? She too went, you know,' Alfred put in, at which Melanie cleared her throat over-loudly as her husband continued, 'yes, she went too.' Melanie was looking pointedly at her empty glass and continuing to clear her throat. 'You did know about Mrs Tomber, did you?' he asked Ottilie again after he had finally refilled his wife's glass.

Of course Ottilie and Veronica knew all about Mrs Tomber, but at the mention of her name they merely murmured sympathetically and stared resolutely ahead, unable to look at each other at all.

They had every reason to know all about the wretched Mrs Tomber, for the housekeeper had not only embarked on an affair with Alfred the moment Ottilie had left, but, judging from the appalling state of the hotel books, she had also set about altering accounts in her favour, writing herself cheques to the tune of thousands of pounds. Following the acceptance of her offer on the hotel, Ottilie had quickly and promptly set about dealing with Mrs Tomber before the wretched woman could set about effecting any more 'shrinkage', as it was known in the trade.

It was probably regrettable, Ottilie thought, but as her father still continued to drone on about Mrs Tomber's many and wonderful qualities of loyalty and sweetness she could not help recalling the enjoyment she herself had felt when, the papers having come through, she had driven round one early morning with Veronica to the staff entrance of the Grand, and they had personally thrown Mrs Tomber's possessions into suitcases and escorted her out of the hotel to a waiting taxi, while all the time Alfred and Melanie pottered about upstairs, unaware that their old housekeeper had written her letter of resignation to their daughter's clear instructions.

'Well now, there we are,' Veronica said, standing up suddenly in accordance with their preconceived plan to cut down on any pain that the Cartarets might feel on leaving the old place. 'Hire car is waiting, time to pack the suitcases.'

'Everything's labelled, isn't it, Melanie?'

'It's going to be exciting, isn't it?' Ottilie heard Melanie ask Alfred with a sudden catch in her voice that made Ottilie's heart reach out to her.

'Very, darling, very exciting indeed, a new beginning, just imagine, so much to look forward to,' Alfred could be heard reassuring her.

On hearing this Ottilie's eyes filled with tears. 'Lucky things,' she said with heartfelt intensity as she waved them off on their pre-paid cruise from the crumbling front steps of the hotel. 'I wish I was going with them.'

Veronica turned and stared at Ottilie. 'I don't understand you. How could you be so nice to them?'

Ottilie continued to stare ahead for a few seconds, and then she finally turned to Veronica and said, 'I knew you were thinking that, all the time we were having our sherries, I knew you were wondering when I was going to tell them what I thought of them. And I was going to, really I was, but then suddenly I couldn't. You see, I kept thinking of how they must have been in the old days when they were so smart and everyone who was anyone came here, and before their little girl was drowned and they adopted me and my mother took to the bottle and pills because I could never really replace her own little girl. She was a nice person before their tragedy, everyone said so. I really think she was nice, they both were, but people change, Veronica, so quickly. Even you must have seen that, I certainly have. And besides – they're gone, and I'm here.'

Veronica began to say something and then stopped as she heard someone running out to the front of the hotel where they were still standing.

'Oh, Miss Cartaret, I don't know how to tell you,' Ottilie heard Jean saying from behind her, and turned to find the maid was standing looking as if someone had just thrown a bag of flour at her.

'Yes, Jean?'

'I don't know how to say this, but some of the kitchen ceiling seems to have fallen down.'

Ottilie blinked, once, twice, and then said, 'Ah, yes. Well, as a matter of fact, Jean, I don't think you could have put it better if you tried. No, in fact you have put it very well indeed, I would say. The kitchen ceiling, if not where it should be on the – er, ceiling, must be said to have fallen down. Shall I come and inspect?'

Jean nodded. 'If you wouldn't mind, Miss Cartaret. I think it might help.' She looked down at herself. 'It's ruined our uniforms, mine and Mr Nantwick's, as you can see.'

'Yes,' Ottilie agreed, looking at poor Jean and wondering if she had become that pale because of the fright or the falling plaster. 'Yes, I can see, very well. Yes, it has fallen down and over you.'

'And that's not all, as you will see, Miss Cartaret,' Jean said, lowering her voice and letting her eyes drift towards the green sward in front of the hotel. 'I think you'll be seeing more than the kitchen ceiling falling down soon.'

'Mmm?'

Ottilie turned at the sound of a large car drawing up beyond the green sward and the swaying palm trees.

'Yes, Miss Cartaret, I think you'll be seeing a guest who has been booked in and no-one has let them know that we're closed for repairs until further notice.'

Ottilie's eyes followed the line that Jean's were taking and seeing what Jean was seeing she quickly closed them again.

'Tell me I am not seeing what I am seeing, Jean, please.'

'I can't, Miss Cartaret, I wish I could but I can't. And judging from the amount of suitcases the chauffeur's unloading it's not just a week she's booked in for, but a year.'

Ottilie clapped her hands in front of her mouth and started to laugh helplessly when she saw who was now climbing stiffly, but disembarking with great determination none the less, from the parked limousine. She simply could not help herself. The lettering had been plundered from the front of the place, but whether or not it read G*AN* HOTEL, whether or not the kitchen ceiling was lying all over Jean, Nantwick and the old red-tiled floor, whether or not the roof was leaking in places, and there was no chef, and someone had pinched most of the hotel plates and the glasses, not to mention a yard or two of linen and most of the wine cellar, it was that time of year.

It was the time of year when Blue Lady arrived, come hell or high water, and here she was, standing in her strange 1948 New Look clothes and staring about her as if everything was just as it had always been and she was on her honeymoon and any minute now her husband would be coming round to lead her up the hotel steps to their bridal suite.

'Oh well, at least it's not the outbreak of war,' Ottilie consoled herself out aloud.

'No,' Jean agreed, looking more like a ghost than even

Blue Lady. 'Although once you've visited the kitchens, Miss Cartaret, I think you might change your mind.'

'Look, you cope with her, and I'll fly up there to make everything right.' Ottilie turned to Jean, throwing herself on her mercy. 'Say anything to delay her downstairs until I can get it all sorted out with Nantwick.'

'If she's from the old school she'll have brought her own sheets with her, don't forget, Miss Cartaret,' Jean warned in a low voice as they both watched Blue Lady advancing on them in her calf-length clothes. 'And she'll like the blinds half down in the bedroom, and a nice tray with fruit and biscuits in a box, even though she won't touch them, and the place must be dusted so there's not a speck in sight. Oh, and a nice smell of fresh flowers,' she went on inexorably.

'Don't I know it, Jean,' Ottilie called. 'Just delay her somehow. Get back into the car with her and take a toddle with that dear old chauffeur of hers. Take her on the scenic ride, while you explain everything that's happened, and by that time I will have the place looking as it always has for her.'

She turned for a second before flinging herself through the swing doors and as she did so she saw Jean offering Mrs Ballantyne her arm, and the two of them turning back to the car, Jean still talking.

Minutes later Ottilie stood outside the top suite. She had always known, ever since the sale of the Grand went through, that it would take a superhuman effort for her to go in without reviving such terrible memories that she would want to throw herself from the balcony, but it had to be done, it just had to. She closed her eyes, willing herself to put her hand on the door handle, but the message stayed in her head and her hand by her side. She opened her eyes and then clenching her hand she thought again. Finally it came to her.

If I treat this experience as one that will help me understand better when I hear of it happening to other people, then it will not be wasted. What I must actually do is to remember, not forget, that is what I must do. I must remember every detail of what a fool I was and then I will become more human, not less.

And so as Uls the fresh-faced Danish girl arrived to help her make up the bed and do the thousand things that needed to be done, including hijacking flowers from all over the rest of the hotel, flinging a rug over a piece of carpet that a previous guest had burnt with the inevitable iron, and rearranging the awful old chintz curtains so that they did at least look charming rather than decrepit, Ottilie knew that she was helping to lay her ghosts, as much as she knew that Mrs Ballantyne was arriving to revive hers.

Later Jean told Ottilie that Mrs Ballantyne's face had literally lit up the moment she walked into the suite of rooms that nowadays she undoubtedly considered her own and that she had walked straight through to the bedroom and placed her handbag on the bed as if there had been no unseemly delay and the fire had always been kept burning and the lamps lit.

By the time Ottilie had reappeared with a perfectly laid tea tray the atmosphere in the room was quite as it had always been. As always on the far horizon there was a ship, or perhaps it was a tanker, being pulled along as if by a hidden string. Seagulls flew overhead, dipping towards the distant curve of the cliffs, preparing to land with their slow measured flight, but happily too far away for their ugly looks and curved beaks to spoil the distant impression of beauty their snow-whiteness created against the grey backdrop. Mrs Ballantyne was standing, obviously content, still in her veiled hat, watching the scene in front of her.

'Oh, darling, this is everything that we had hoped, is it not?'

Ottilie heard the words as she came into the room, and froze, turning as she did so to look at Blue Lady. She saw

385

that not only was her voice the voice of a lover, but even her face had changed. All of a sudden Mrs Ballantyne was twenty again, and it was her honeymoon.

But if Ottilie felt she had frozen it was nothing to the effect she herself seemed to have had on Mrs Ballantyne.

'Kitty,' she exclaimed, 'what are you doing here!'

Twenty-Two

'My dear little Miss Ottilie, how are you?'

The newly installed telephone had rung on her newly acquired partner's desk, the sound seeming to echo round the still barely furnished room making it sound louder and more demanding. Ottilie had stared at it and allowed it to ring several times before she finally picked it up and heard Mrs Le Martine's voice. She had not heard from her old friend for so long it was almost shocking to hear her again. Too much had happened to her 'dear little Miss Ottilie' for her to be able to explain very much, and yet she had to explain something or else why was she answering the telephone? What was she doing back at the Grand?

But Mrs Le Martine seemed to know more about her than she realized because she said, 'I heard on the jungle drums that you were back at the Grand, running it once more, and your sainted parents had departed. What a miracle! Have you married a millionaire without telling me, my dear Ottilie?'

Ottilie felt far too shy to tell her exactly what her new position at the Grand was, so she obfuscated by merely saying, 'No, I haven't married a millionaire.'

'What a pity, but you will, *n'est-ce pas*?'

Ottilie felt like saying 'Actually I don't need to, Mrs Le Martine' but instead she said, 'I know you're just the person who can help me.'

'I love that phrase.'

'We are pulling the old place apart and need someone to help us with drawings and suggested alterations, plans for the builders to work from, and also someone who will know what is needed for new designs for the Grand, someone who will help me furnish it comfortably, but with good taste and a feeling for the past.'

'My dear little Ottilie, but of course! I know everyone. And that is why I have telephoned to you, because I knew you must be in need of me! I think I know exactly who you must want.'

Ottilie smiled and replaced the receiver. It was quite clear from her immediate resumption of their relationship that Mrs Le Martine must have forgiven Ottilie for whatever she had imagined 'Monsieur' in Paris might have told the sixteen-year-old about her starting life as the Countess's maid, which was good, but it was also clear that Mrs Le Martine was as incorrigible as ever, still doubtless wearing 'Shah-nelle' clothes, still gossiping too much, and devouring Charbonnel and Walker chocolates which she kept hidden, for some reason best known to herself, in her lingerie.

Ottilie looked into Veronica's office. She was busy typing at her usual breakneck speed of seventy words a minute, despite the hotel typewriter's being as old as Ottilie herself.

'I think we may have an architect coming to our rescue, and quite soon,' she told her secretary.

'The sooner the better,' Veronica told her, stopping briefly to hurl a large book across the room at what she obviously imagined was a mouse. 'But first a cat. *Then* an architect.'

'And some dogs.'

Veronica straightened up, having crossed the room to pick up the book only to ascertain with some disappointment that it had missed the mouse yet again.

'Dogs indeed. What kind of dogs?'

'Black labradors. Very welcoming in the hall, like a real house—'

'As long as they are good at catching mice.'

388

Ottilie smiled. She sensed that spring was on its way, and with it that blessed sense of renewal and purpose that makes even the dullest day seem filled with promise. Upstairs Blue Lady would be busy chatting to the ghostly presence of her husband, downstairs Jean and Nantwick were preparing for the arrival of new linen and glass, not to mention new casseroles, new *marmites*, new *batterie de cuisine*, for everything that had been there had been so badly kept that in Jean's opinion 'It's a terrible risk to everyone's health, even the kitchen mice. There's even verdigris on their traps, Miss Cartaret, and really – that must be a first, wouldn't you say?'

Things were beginning to happen, the past was being walled up behind the present. Already she had engaged some builders to come from Plymouth to give estimates and start as soon as possible on the more straightforward tasks around the place. Even the missing gold letters on the façade had been ordered. Now all she had to do was to sit back and wait for the architect-designer that Mrs Le Martine was so keen to recommend.

It was only when she found herself frowning through the upper half of the old glass into the lounge bar the following week that Ottilie realized that relying on her old friend's choice might not have been so very sensible. Not only did the man whom she could hear saying, 'Coffee would be fine' sound resoundingly American, he looked far too young. Ottilie had hoped for a conservative, older man, someone with greying hair and highly polished laced shoes and dark socks, not a dark-haired restless young man in a suede jacket and polo-necked sweater.

'Mr Justin?'

He turned and Ottilie stopped frowning.

'Mr Pierre Justin?'

'That's right,' he agreed, a little absently, still looking round at the lounge in which he stood as if he could not quite believe what he saw. 'I'm waiting for Miss Cartaret, and someone is already fetching me coffee, thank you.'

'I am Miss Cartaret,' Ottilie told him, lifting her head, and looking at him slightly sideways which was a new habit she had adopted in the hope of making herself seem older and more remote in manner. If she looked too young to own and run an hotel, Pierre Justin could hardly have been more than twenty-five or six.

'*You* are – Miss Cartaret?'

'As a matter of fact, yes, I am, that's one thing I am quite sure about.'

'I see.'

She felt he looked let down, disappointed, and that the 'I see' meant 'If you are Miss Cartaret you are far too young to own this place', so she said crisply, 'You don't, Mr Justin, but you will.'

Ottilie sat down determined to be all proprietor while he too sat down, pushing at his small, gold-rimmed spectacles and frowning as if he was still sure that she must be the wrong person. Seconds later he sprang up again as Jean came in with coffee on a tray, and in an effort to clear the coffee table he managed to throw a pile of *Country Life* magazines under her feet, and all this before he lit a cigarette which threw sparks all down his sweater, not to mention all over the old Persian rug which was about the only one Ottilie actually wanted to keep in the whole hotel.

'I expect you're regretting that Mrs Le Martine recommended me already, Miss Cartaret,' he joked, stamping on one of the larger sparks and at the same time pushing his spectacles up his nose again. 'Don't worry – places do recover from me, eventually.'

He looked across at her, suddenly helpless, frowning past Ottilie's shoulder as if he had seen something of great interest, and then cleared his throat as if preparing to say something which he then quite forgot and so quickly frowned again.

'Mr Justin, let's start again. I am Ottilie Cartaret. Hello.'

'Good idea. Hello.'

They leaned towards each other and shook hands this time. As they touched he suddenly smiled at her, a wonderful smile full of modesty and kindness. It was a smile that was reflected from eyes that had never felt anything but warmth towards the world and its inhabitants, the smile of a boy who had always been loved. A smile quite at odds with his nervous behaviour.

Ottilie frowned momentarily. Something about that smile reminded her of someone she had once known, but for the life of her she could not remember who it was, except that she was quite certain that the smile had belonged to someone she had really liked.

'Are you engaging that funny American man for the refurbishments?' Veronica asked Ottilie.

'I *am* engaging him for the refurbishments, Veronica, and what's more today we are going to try and find some furniture for this barn of a place. Pierre says the only good thing about it is that it's big and the bigger the pieces of furniture the cheaper, because nowadays people only want small pieces for their refurbishments.'

Veronica started to laugh as Ottilie said 'refurbishments' yet again. It was ridiculous but for some reason at that moment they were both going through a phase when they found the word 'refurbishments' terribly funny.

Actually Ottilie was quite relieved to be able at last to laugh directly at something, because she had spent the previous half-hour consciously trying not to look happy in front of Veronica and she felt that Veronica knew it and was eyeing her beadily. She turned from the office mirror, pulling yet another of her high-necked dresses right up to her chin and tightly re-tying the black velvet bow that held her long brown hair in check, and faced her secretary.

'Pierre Justin's so frightfully good-looking, I have a feeling that he must be one of those,' Veronica said in a warning voice. 'Do you think he is?'

Ottilie frowned. She had not thought of Pierre Justin as

being anything but now she did she said, 'I don't know — hadn't thought.'

'Interior decorators usually are, aren't they?'

'As long as he has an eye for colour I don't really care if he's a eunuch,' Ottilie called back to her, quickly closing the office door.

Pierre was waiting for her at the front of the hotel and although she was already twenty minutes late for him, he only smiled and pushed his spectacles up his nose, opening the door of his Mini Cooper.

'Morning, boss,' he said, taking the picnic basket she was carrying from her, and then as he closed the door with a nod towards the sunshine and the sparkling sea, 'and what a morning, *n'est-ce pas?*'

Ottilie pulled up the polo-neck collar of her cashmere dress. Cashmere was one of the reasons that she was enjoying being rich, and expensive perfume, and being able to take the day off whenever she wished. There were a few compensations for all the responsibilities that Edith's money had brought her.

If Ottilie had had time to really talk to Veronica about Pierre, she would have told her that, despite his tall, dark good looks, from their very first meeting Pierre Justin had appealed to Ottilie as being perhaps quite the shyest and least confident man that she had met.

In fact setting fire to his clothes with his cigarette turned out not to be an occasional incident but a regular routine. When he went into a room, any room, hitherto innocent furniture that had never misbehaved itself before seemed to throw itself in front of him as he walked across a room. The handles of coffee cups fractured as he picked them up and rugs equipped with discreet weights became instantly lethal, before fires decided to throw logs out onto valuable carpets in sudden rebellious fury.

Pierre Justin behaved in such a way that it seemed he felt that any moment he was about to be an embarrassment both to himself and to everyone else, until he started to work. Miraculously, the moment he started to talk about his ideas, about his subject, he became elegant where he had seconds before been clumsy, articulate where he had been hesitant, and supremely confident where he had hardly a minute previously looked as if he wished the earth would open up and swallow him.

Happily it was evident to Ottilie from the start of their meetings and discussions at the hotel that despite his frequent mishaps – colliding with marble busts which had never before given anyone any trouble, drenching himself with a shower whose water had been turned off, falling over Veronica who had never been known to be under anyone's feet – he quite definitely had the 'eye'.

'If there is anything more exciting than a picnic in the trunk of a car, and the idea that you have a whole day ahead in which to search for unknown treasure, I do not know it,' he told her as he started up the car, and drove swiftly off in the wrong direction.

'Never mind, we can take the scenic route,' Ottilie reassured him once he realized his mistake. 'It's much more beautiful.'

Ottilie stared ahead at the day, thrilled at the sudden feeling of freedom from everyone and everything. 'What is the perfect day, do you think?' she asked him after a long silence in which he took the scenic route past sparkling sea views and deserted white coves.

'Probably going to be today, I think,' he said, suddenly smiling.

The moment they had parked in Truro, Ottilie realized that her life was about to become considerably more lively than it had previously been, for once he had confidence it seemed that Pierre could no more stop trying to entertain than he could breathe.

'Right, now what we do here,' Pierre instructed outside their first antique shop, 'what we do here is to stand outside and decide how much everything should cost, and then we go inside and ask the price and whoever laughs when they shouldn't buys both of us coffee.'

Ottilie had always found it calamitous to be told not to laugh so she took a pin from behind the jacket of her lapel and stuck it into her thumb. She had to prove to Pierre that she had complete self-control.

'Well howdee, sir, I'm from Texas and I would very much apprecia-ate to know the price of this 'ere beautiful chest.'

'The price, sir?'

For a fleeting second Ottilie wondered why it was that shop assistants always managed to look quite so amazed if asked the cost of something. Surely it was something they must grow to expect at least sometimes?

Pierre looked unblinkingly at the assistant and repeated his question, but at an even slower pace. 'Yes, sir, if you don't mind, I would sure apprecia-ate to know the price of this 'ere beautiful chest, if you would be so good?'

One glance at the serious face of the supposedly gullible Texan in front of him and the shop assistant in his tight black suit and his large mauve silk tie cleared his throat and said without even a blush, 'Five hundred pounds, sir.'

'Really, sir? May I repeat that? You want five hundred pounds for this—'

Pierre touched the chest.

'It is a very rare Charles II walnut coffer, sir, remark-able of its kind as I am sure you will appreciate?'

'It must be very remarkable of its kind,' Pierre said in his normal voice, lifting the lid of the piece and closing it again while talking at twice his normal rate, 'since this is not walnut but oak, and it is no more Charles II than I am. This is a Victorian piece – please look at those hinges and that lock – and undoubtedly Welsh, and you, sir, are equally undoubtedly a charlatan.'

Ottilie had done very well with her pin stuck into her thumb up until the moment that she saw the expression on the assistant's face at the word 'charlatan'. It was as if he had been slapped. He seemed to reel backwards at the word and Ottilie turned and walked quickly from the shop to the street outside where Pierre found her doubled up with laughter a few seconds later.

'Not very good, Miss Cartaret,' Pierre said, taking her arm and crossing the road. 'I saw you were gone rotten within a second of my opening my mouth, so guess whose going to be buying coffee?'

They found a café of sorts and sat quietly working out from a street guide where to go next as the waitress put down a tray in front of them and poured out some black liquid into stoneware cups. She topped them up with milk and then sauntered off, flicking at dirty tables with a tea cloth as she retreated behind a door marked 'Private'.

'That's something I miss so much, decent coffee,' Pierre said, sighing and staring at the over-hot slightly bitter brew which had been carelessly topped up by milk from a pot with little pieces of skin floating in it. 'The British drink coffee which tastes stewed and then they put boiled milk in it – ah God this is really disgusting.'

Embarrassed by the awfulness of the brew Ottilie quickly told him, 'I am ordering proper coffee pots, individual coffee pots, for the hotel from a shop in France – it is ridiculous in this day and age not to get decent coffee. I mean the war's been over twenty years and you still get that awful stuff with chicory added if you're not careful, or that bottled coffee, all left over from rationing. But I'm preaching to the converted beause you are half French anyway. Mrs Le Martine—'

'Oh, she told you the awful news, did she?'

'Not awful, no, she just said you were educated in the States, and your mother was American – and then of course she went off on one of her tangents, you know how she is, something to do with Nancy Gordon having a terrific crush on you, and about your brilliance. She was very anxious to sell you to me.'

'Well she would be, she's an old friend. Do you know

you have the most beautiful-coloured eyes?'

Ottilie stared into her now empty coffee cup. 'Yes,' she said, mischievously.

'And absolutely no modesty.'

'None!'

They both laughed and despite winning the bet Pierre paid for the perfectly awful coffee which said something about him to Ottilie, although precisely what it was she didn't exactly know.

'Come on, there's still more fun to be had at the expense of the antique trade.'

As they walked along Ottilie found herself hoping that Pierre wouldn't continue to pretend to be a Texan in every shop. Perhaps he sensed how she felt or perhaps he knew enough not to go on, but he dropped the game, obviously now satisfied that he had proved he could make her laugh whenever he wanted, and so began the serious business of buying.

'After our meeting yesterday at least I know exactly what you hate now,' Pierre told her as they hurried along the streets, stopping, staring and then moving quickly on the moment they discovered there was nothing of particular interest. 'To recap, as I remember it, you hate overly patterned wallpapers, you hate fringes on sofas and curtains. You hate large ornate vases and lampshades with yet more fringes. As a matter of fact, why is it that I have the feeling that you hate all fringes? You hate still life paintings with dead geese, dead ducks, dead hares – in fact anything dead in a painting, although maybe a dead leaf suggesting decadence might possibly pass. You do not like fuss or clutter – unusual in your sex I have to tell you – oh, and you don't like patterned carpets either. You know what, Miss Cartaret? I get the feeling that what you really are is – yes, you are – you're really a Quaker at heart, aren't you? As a matter of fact, Miss Cartaret ma'am, what is it that you do like, because that is something of which I am beginning to think I am not exactly sure?'

Ottilie thought hard as she followed him into a small, dark shop. What she did like wasn't something she had ever really summed up for anyone else.

'I suppose, just recently, I've only thought about what I dislike.'

She began slowly but then gathered confidence when she realized that she had rather more definite ideas than she had at first thought.

'Since you ask, I like wooden floors with old rugs, I like soft colours which look old and old colours which look soft. I don't like change for the sake of it, but if it means more comfort I want change immediately. I don't like anything ornate, nor do I like collections of things – you know, china in glass cabinets and collections of vases on shelves. Too museum-like for me. I loathe mock Chinese or Japanese, in fact anything mock Oriental, however old or beautiful. As a matter of fact I don't like anything Oriental except in the Orient, or in a restaurant. I hate orange, including marigolds. I prefer a garden to have old trees and look really rather unkempt rather than stiff and – well, stiff. I like white roses in gardens but not inside where I always think they look too white. I like black cherries in or on practically everything; and velvet. I like straw hats but only if they are made of panama straw. I like tea to be at teatime, but at no other. I like fourposter beds, but not if they have lamps sticking through the drapes. I like plain carpet if it makes a room cosier, but not if it's covering a beautiful wood floor. I like large lamps with large shades but not if they look angular and stiff. I like a mixture of everything. I mean . . .' she hesitated, thinking. 'I mean I really hate to walk into a place and see it all done correctly with everything in the same style – like some sort of a room set in a museum—'

Ottilie stopped suddenly pulling a little face at Pierre because she realized she had been really talking out loud to herself rather than to Pierre whom she had been following round the little dark crowded antique shop as she spelt out

397

her likes and dislikes. He turned as she finally finished, and looked down at her. 'I do believe we are going to get on infamously, Miss Cartaret, do you know that?' he said delightedly. 'As a matter of fact, after that, there is only one more thing I need to ask and that is – will you marry me?'

Ottilie laughed, realizing that he was joking as he turned back to his task of sorting through a medley of old books, picking up vases, bending down and examining small dark uncleaned paintings close to, and pulling an old dress out of a trunk. It was long, velvet, gold-embroidered, with slightly large sleeves, tight at the wrists, low across the bust.

'Very Tudoresque, probably made for some grand lady performing at some Edwardian house party,' Pierre said, holding it up against Ottilie. 'Suits you. That dark green is great with your hair. As a matter of fact I am determined that I will buy it for you, Miss Cartaret, as my gift, on this sunny day.'

Ottilie stared at it for a brief moment, and then turned abruptly on her heel.

'Thank you but no,' she said curtly and after clambering back over and through the many objects in the old place she found her way thankfully back to the sunshine outside.

Pierre did not follow her out of the shop for some quarter of an hour and so she was left to hang around outside wondering what he was doing, only to see from his expression of triumph as he finally emerged that it was all too obvious what he was doing. He was what he called 'truffling' and seeing his delighted expression Ottilie forgot her disquiet and found that all she could do was to smile at his delight.

'I think you are going to love me when you see what your very own truffle hound has bought you,' he said, as he walked briskly towards his car, and carefully placed a large cardboard box covered in old newspaper in the boot.

'I think what we may have here are two very fine small eighteenth-century paintings which when cleaned up will grace the walls of your hotel with an ease hitherto unknown to them. No frames, which is a pity, but we can fake those. Oh and you must not be too angry, but I couldn't resist one other thing—'

Ottilie looked at him. It was Pierre's turn to pull a face.

'And now these you are going to hate me for, but they will be great in the dining room. A pair of Ming vases, would you believe?'

'Oh no.'

'Oh yes.'

'You have them.'

Pierre looked suddenly so hurt at her reaction Ottilie started to laugh.

'Look, I'm sorry, but didn't I just tell you I don't like anything Chinoise—'

'Not even Ming?'

'Not even double or triple Ming.'

'What about our picnic then?'

'Oh I like picnics all right.'

They found a beautiful white beach, a tiny cove embraced by rocks. Ottilie put down a rug, and Pierre assiduously found stones to hold down each corner of its tartan wool as Ottilie began the joyous task of unpacking Mrs East's picnic. Thank heavens the old cook's idea of a picnic was not some miserable pile of sandwiches wrapped in greaseproof paper and a hard boiled egg with no salt. Mrs East's picnics were made up of pies with meltingly soft pastry whose inner mixes were a surprise of tender chicken in lightly flavoured sauces made from their own stock, or tiny vegetables parboiled and chopped before being wrapped in pastry made with cream cheese. Home-made sausages, home-made sausage rolls, home-cooked ham baked in honey and cloves and served with peaches and potato salad made with just the right amount of home-made mayonnaise. Everything that could be home-cooked was home-cooked by Mrs East, but it seemed to Ottilie that never had Mrs East's cooking tasted quite so delicious, so light, so meltingly perfect as it did that lunchtime on the beach as she sat staring out to sea with Pierre.

Later, as the wind became sharper and they walked along the sand barefoot, Ottilie slipped on a piece of seaweed. Catching her hand quickly Pierre steadied her and she clung to him laughing, but he held on only for a second, letting her go immediately so that she could go on paddling, allowing the cold frills of water to lap her feet, relishing the change in temperature.

'You have very elegant feet for a man, most unusual,' she told him as they went on paddling and staring at the water as if they were looking for something, momentarily calmed, as people so often are at the edge of the sea.

'You sound as if you've made some sort of study of feet.'

'For heaven's sake, I was brought up at the Grand! I was always seeing men's feet, when I took them breakfast, when they passed me on their way out for their inevitable "dip before breakfast", when I had to take them fresh towels if they were sunbathing on the beach. They almost became an obsession with me. And do you know why? Because I hardly ever met a member of either sex who had pretty or elegant feet, except perhaps Blue Lady, and now you.'

'Who was Blue Lady?'

'Not was – is. Blue Lady is still a regular guest. She is in the top suite. Doesn't mind the alterations, doesn't mind who comes or goes, she must always be in her suite at this time. She commemorates her honeymoon every year, and as far as we know she always will. Her husband, who was much older, died you see, just at the end of their glorious six-week honeymoon, and it seems that she never got over it. She loved him that much.'

'What a strange story . . .'

'Mmm, she talks to him, out loud. It's quite spooky if

you go in there because you have to lay tea for two and she makes you put the teacup just so where he would have had it, and she goes through the kind of day they have had – you know, "Wasn't it bright out today, darling?" that sort of conversation, and for years I couldn't understand it because there she was stitching away and going on about how beautiful the day had been when anyone could see it had been raining stair rods and then I clued in suddenly when I saw her consulting her diary one morning, and I realized that she must re-enact each day up there in that suite just the way it was twenty or more years before, each day just the same, all over again.'

'Is she beautiful?'

'Very beautiful, but she even dresses from that era you know, the New Look from Dior kind of clothes that you see in old movies? I was scared stiff of her when I was younger but now – well, particularly now – she seems almost like a touchstone from the past, something precious that I want to preserve just as she is preserving her few weeks of happiness – you know, how it is before life happens and everything goes wrong?'

Ottilie could see Pierre wanted to ask, 'But what has gone wrong?' Yet he didn't because he could see from the way she turned her eyes away and looked ahead down the beach that she wasn't prepared to say any more.

'Perhaps we should call the top suite after her?' Ottilie wondered as they continued to walk to the end of the beach, where they turned. The wind had got up and the waves were pounding and growing white tops that curled over and rushed up the tiny cove, so they quickly packed up and went back to the car.

'Bit difficult for men to book a suite with "Lady" in the title. But the Blue Suite might be quite chic. I'd love to meet her,' Pierre said, as they drove on in search of more treasure. 'What a story. I keep trying to imagine her and yet I know I'm nowhere near what she's really like.'

But if Pierre wanted to meet Blue Lady he had no

interest in hearing any more about Alfred or Melanie.

'From what I have heard of them, they sound a bit – er, Victorian for my taste,' he explained to Ottilie as they drove back, but Ottilie, realizing that he must know about the incident when Mrs Le Martine left the hotel, felt the need to justify her upbringing.

'I didn't mind that they were strict, really I didn't, because I never was any good at being young. I mean even now I don't like doing the twist, I prefer waltzing, and I hate the Beatles I'm afraid. If you want to make a nightclub in the hotel basement, fine, but don't ask me down there. I can't stand nightclubs unless they're in Paris and really a jazz club like the Blue Note. I'm afraid I'm a flop as a young person and I always have been. Too much time spent with old ladies at the hotel.'

Pierre laughed and she knew at once that he completely understood.

'You sound just my sort of person. When I was a little boy I always hated other little boys because they were always coming round and ripping up your train sets and smashing your Lego and then telling you they were bored and going outside and blaming you if they fell off your slide. Couldn't *wait* for them to leave.'

'I don't know anything about you,' Ottilie teased Pierre as they had dinner in the hotel restaurant that night. 'Except, of course, that you like to make the lives of antique dealers miserable.'

'I *do* love to be the bane of their lives, that's true. I hate what they do to beautiful things – tearing apart wonderful books to frame the prints, cannabalizing furniture, pretending age, overcharging, it's anathema to me,' Pierre agreed, and lifting his glass he toasted, 'To the destruction of cheats, everywhere.'

Ottilie raised her glass to his toast, and a little later she said, 'You must tell me a little about yourself, please? You know, like where you were born and how your middle finger came to be that shape, shockingly intimate things.'

Pierre shook his head and for a second Ottilie remembered the sudden sharp sense of disappointment she had experienced when he had released her so quickly on the beach.

'I never talk about myself to clients.' He looked at her. 'In what is after all a professional relationship, nothing matters except how I do the job for you, wouldn't you say?'

As he finished speaking Ottilie remembered Veronica's feeling that Pierre 'must be one of those' because so many interior decorators were, and although she had not cared in the least then, now, suddenly, for some reason she found she did mind, which was pathetic, because as Pierre had just said after all their relationship was professional.

'No, of course not, no, I mean, yes, just professional.' Ottilie dropped her eyes. 'No. It was just that I really enjoyed today, and now, of course, it's over.' She fell silent thinking of Philip on the station at St Elcombe and of how he had said he would be back in a matter of a moment and how she had pleaded with him to reassure her that nothing would change, and yet everything had changed between them. In the end it could not have become more changed, and he had come back with no trace of the boy he had once been in his eyes or his voice, anywhere. She had thought that he would be like one of Peter Pan's Lost Boys and would come back the same, but he had come back just a conventional Army sort of person.

Thinking of this in the silence that had fallen Ottilie realized that she was just about to make the same mistake with Pierre. She was just about to try to pretend that each second of each minute did not change everything.

She stood up suddenly, pushing her chair back and replacing her napkin.

'This has been a coloured glass of a day, and I shall always remember it, thank you very much.'

'But you haven't finished your coffee.' Pierre looked up

at her in utter dismay, still seated. 'Mrs East has made very good coffee!'

'No, I know.' Ottilie turned to look at Pierre. 'I suddenly don't feel like coffee, so if you'll excuse me?'

She had always taken such comfort from walking down to the beach, particularly at night when it was empty, and when she was younger she had imagined that she had a dog, or even two dogs, and that they would be running ahead of her and then running back, and that she could throw them sticks and they would run into the waves barking and back again as she collected shells and stones that looked so wonderful on the beach but always faded indoors, as if pining for the sea and the rain outside where they really belonged.

Tonight, outside, the wind had got up and was making the trees sway so she did not hear someone following her out and down the green sward in front of the hotel, and when she did and saw it was Pierre she no longer wanted to walk but to run off towards the sea, to be quite alone.

'Why did you get up and leave like that?' he asked as, catching up with her, he finally managed to force her to a halt. 'I didn't say anything to hurt you, did I?'

Ottilie shook her head and lied, 'Of course not. I just wanted some air, that's all, I get claustrophobic sometimes, you know—'

'No, I don't. I mean one minute we were fine, really enjoying ourselves, and the next minute you just – disappeared.'

'I told you I wanted some air,' Ottilie insisted, not looking at him.

'That's not it at all, is it? That is not it at all!'

'It is, really.'

'No, it's not. It's because I said our relationship was "professional", that's why you became upset, and you know it. The "you" bit of you suddenly disappeared, by that I mean the Ottilie I've been with all day suddenly disappeared. Please bring her back again.'

Ottilie tried to turn from him, shaking her head, determined to keep her pride intact but Pierre pulled her back and put his hand under her chin, murmuring, 'I've been longing to kiss that pretty mouth of yours ever since I first arrived and tried to set fire to your rug,' and bending his head he kissed her so beautifully that Ottilie realized that the kissing she had done with Philip had been just kissing and that this kissing was nothing less than the wondrous confirmation of what she had been feeling all day, utter happiness. He stepped back a little, but still held on to her.

'I'm sorry. That wasn't very – er, professional, Miss Cartaret.'

Ottilie was silent for a moment, and then, looking up at him, 'Oh, I don't know,' she said and started to laugh. 'I should think most girls would give you ten out of ten!' And after that they kissed again, and again, until Ottilie, feeling a little faint, murmured, 'or perhaps even eleven out of ten.'

She touched Pierre's cheek and without saying anything they walked back up to the hotel hand in hand. They passed Jean who tried not to stare, and Nantwick who did not bother to pretend not to see them, but only smiled in almost paternal approval. Ottilie did not care a jot. If life had taught her only one thing it was that when that beautiful-coloured piece of pink glass known as happiness was put into your hand you held it up to the light and looked through it, and never mind if next day someone stole it from you, or you dropped it, it was yours for that moment.

As it turned out the delightful oasis of a day that she had spent with Pierre was the high point of Ottilie's week. There was so much office work to be done she had to leave Pierre to get on with the plans upon which they had agreed while she and Veronica sorted through files of old papers, staring at the small print of previous agreements which governed the day-to-day running of the hotel, and up-dating valuations which were so long out of date they were laughable. All important, but endlessly dull after the laughter and the fun that she had enjoyed with Pierre searching for antiques and bric-a-brac to bring the old hotel back to life.

She found herself shifting in her seat and yawning when she should be attending to something, or staring out of the window and dreaming of more days spent hunting antiques and more picnics on white sandy beaches with only the sound of the waves and the wailing cries of the seagulls to break or add to the happy harmony that being with Pierre seemed to bring.

And so it was, faced with so many dull papers through which she had to sift, that on hearing the telephone on her private line ringing, instead of feeling irritated at having her concentration broken on such a rainy, cloudy after-noon, Ottilie felt only a glorious sense of relief. Hoping, indeed thinking, that it would be Pierre telephoning from his London office to which he had returned for a few days, she quickly picked up the receiver after only two rings, despite knowing that Veronica was watching her, she knowing only too well that Ottilie was praying it would be Pierre, no matter how much she pretended.

'Hello.'

Disappointingly it was not Pierre. Worse it was Nicholas Phelps, the lawyer.

'Oh, good morning.'

Ottilie could feel herself tensing up. It was not just the embarrassment, knowing that he must remember just how drunk she had been that night, it was everything. The fact that Joseph had accused her of being a thief in front of him, the fact that she had so demeaned herself, swaying about the room, arguing with Joseph and then finally passing out. Phelps was so proper, always so meticulous about everything, almost an old woman in his ways, not someone who would ever be so stupid as to drink on top of antibiotics and make a display of himself.

'Long time no see you.'

Ottilie murmured agreement even though she hated the phrase, always wondering what people expected in return when they said it.

'How is everything?'

'Everything's fine.'

She wished that he would get to the point so that she could ring off and then Pierre could telephone, every second delayed the moment. Nowadays Ottilie thought she knew what it meant to be 'sent' by a voice. Pierre's voice literally 'sent' her. Briefly she wondered if she was at last becoming 'young' and thought she could hear Pierre laughing at the idea.

'I have a friend who would like to try to interest you in a new cold drinks machine for the hotel. Would it be all right if I give him your office number?' Phelps asked.

'I don't know that we really want a cold drinks machine, except perhaps if we build a games annexe, might be all right there.' She was talking out loud to herself and not him. 'OK, give him my number, fine.'

'I will warn you however, he's a bit like your brother Joseph.'

Ottilie suddenly knew that Phelps was dragging Joseph's name into the conversation in some effort to embarrass her, that he actually wanted to remind her of that awful night.

'He's not my brother. Joseph is not my brother.'

'But he was so proud of "Ottie".'

'No, he's not my brother. He's no relation. His mother adopted me for a few years, until I was six, and then I was re-adopted, and that's how I came here. And by the way, no-one calls me "Ottie" any more.'

Ottilie suddenly felt strong because she could talk about Joseph, say his name and not *mind*.

'But that night we had drinks he stated categorically that he was your brother. *Although I must admit, Miss*

407

Cartaret, he is so – well, so American, my dear, I admit I did have a problem with that.' Nick Phelps' voice on the other end of the telephone had changed into a remarkably good imitation of Jack Kennedy, slight lisp and all.

Ottilie was silent for a second, and then she said quietly, 'That's a very good American accent that you do.'

'*I am afraid, Miss Cartaret, I have a horrible ability to mimic.*'

'Obviously.'

'At Cambridge I used to be known as the second Peter Sellers. Want my Peter Lorre?'

'No time for that I'm afraid.'

'*OK, Miss Cartaret.*' He did his Peter Lorre anyway. 'Good, don't you think? But not as good as my Kennedy. *Mrs Kennedy is responsible for the White House decor.*'

The American voice continued but Ottilie quietly replaced the telephone receiver and when she looked down at the hand that had done so she saw that it was shaking and she sat watching it as if it belonged to someone else.

Veronica must have noticed that she had not said goodbye because she looked up from her work and frowned.

'Don't tell me, not a dirty phone call?'

Ottilie nodded. 'In a way, mm, 'fraid so.' After a minute she sprang up from her chair and bolted towards the door, snatching at her coat. 'Going to see Father O'Flaherty,' she called back to Veronica.

Ottilie had not seen Lorcan since that awful night when he had tried to force her to confess that it had been in some way her fault that she had been molested. Of course, in a way, he had been right, and Ottilie knew it now. It had been her fault, but *not* because of the way she dressed – if that was the case then a nurse in a uniform, or a nanny pushing a pram, could be considered *provocative*. No, she had been stupid to *drink* and because of that a man had taken advantage of her, and that *had* been her fault, nothing to do with her blue silk dress.

Because she had considered Lorcan to have been totally wrong to even suggest such a thing Ottilie had not been able to face him. Also, knowing that he knew such a thing about her, that all St Elcombe seemed somehow to know, that too had meant that she could not face him and appear normal.

She left her office in such a hurry that Veronica called after her to take her umbrella because it was raining, but Ottilie could not wait for that, she had to run through the rain because yet again in her life she had to reach Lorcan. But this time she was not running towards Ma, she was not a child running back to find the only real mother she had known, she was a grown-up woman running through the downpour of a wet afternoon and the cold and the wet of the rain was a blessing and a relief because it was real and not something from the past.

The presbytery door was never locked, but Ottilie was afraid to go there in case she bumped into Father Peter and he would detain her. With his gentle kindness he would probably lead her to a fire and ask after her and the hotel, and worse he would feel sorry for her, and so she would start to feel sorry for herself, and it would make her cry, and this was not a moment for that. So she made her way through a different door and rang the bell for confession, praying that it would be Lorcan's day to be hearing them.

'Lorcan, I had to see you.'

'Ottie!'

Lorcan always seemed taller in his priestly clothes, but he was pale too and the lines around his eyes were marked as they had used to be all the time when Ma was alive and he was having to carry the burden of them all.

'You want me to hear your confession?' he asked in a lowered tone because they were in church.

'Oh no, Lorcan, no,' Ottilie whispered. 'At least yes, but not the way you mean. I hate confession, Lorcan! I

409

think we all feel so guilty about everything most of the time it should be changed to "Feel Better" and people should go in and try and find a few good things to say about themselves instead of feeling it's their fault about everything like the bomb and starving babies—'

'Shsh, Ottie, calm yourself.'

At that Ottilie stopped whispering so fast. Drawing breath for a second, she demanded in a normal voice, 'Lorcan. In all the time that you have known me when have I ever been calm?'

They both laughed, and Lorcan said, 'You're such a rebel, Ottie. Come into the presbytery and we can talk better, not disturb those at prayer.' As they walked down the corridor to the end room he said, 'It's extraordinary, you know, Ottie, you always did have a sort of intuitive thing with you, didn't you? Because as it happens I was just about to come and see you. Now.' He went to an old dusty cupboard and taking out two strangely unmatched glasses he said, 'Let's warm ourselves with some of Father Peter's lethal sherry.'

'I could do with something lethal.'

He lifted out a dusty bottle. 'Some parishioner gave it him last Christmas but he thinks sherry's for nuns!'

Ottilie laughed but watching Lorcan polishing the bottle with his handkerchief she thought how cold the presbytery was after the hotel, and how bleak Lorcan's life was in comparison to hers, but then it seemed to her that if your life was so bleak, perhaps it made the real things stand out better, the things that mattered?

'Now. Let us drink to the future, Ottie.'

They raised their glasses and Ottilie drank the rather too sweet sherry gratefully, because it was at least warming, whereas Lorcan pulled a face and said, 'I think Father Peter's right, this is strictly for nuns!'

A second of silence and then Ottilie started.

'The thing is, Lorcan, I had to come to tell you at once. Because you know that awful thing that happened to me?'

410

Lorcan nodded, his gaze unswerving, suddenly very much the priest and Ottilie was grateful for that, for his detachment, because it made it easier for her, and for him. 'I told you that it was Joseph, because it was an American voice. But I don't think it was at all, I don't think Joseph would do such a thing, I think it was someone else. And you were right, and I was wrong. Not that it matters, now, because it doesn't. It's like Jackie Kennedy said – what does it matter who killed her husband, he's *dead*. What happened to me is over, for ever. I was ill for a long time afterwards but now I am quite better. I should never have accused Joseph to you. I think I did because – well, because of the awfulness of his running away and our thinking he was dead all that time. I think I wanted to prove to myself that he was really more wicked than he is.'

All the time she was talking Ottilie did not once drop her eyes.

'I shall not even go into who I think did what he did, but I know that sometimes when men do these awful things they don't get – well, they don't get the thrill out of it that they are searching for unless they let you know that it was them. And I think. I say I *think* I know who the person is, because I think he just phoned me, and that is precisely what he was doing. Letting me know that it was him. Apparently it is sort of compulsive with men like that.'

Lorcan nodded and quickly poured them both another tot of the perfectly revolting sherry.

'You had no need to come here, Ottie, but I am glad that you did. I knew that Joseph was not capable of what you had thought, but it was up to time, and circumstances, perhaps even God's will, which let us face it we shall never understand, to find the truth for you. Your truth, perhaps the real truth, who knows? Let me tell you, now, if you can spare a minute, about what happened when I left you that night. Remember? I obtained Father Peter's permission for leave of absence and I drove after

Joseph. I knew that he had been due to catch the afternoon plane next day and that he was stopping over at another of Vision's hotels near Exeter and then on to one near Salisbury, which is where I caught up with him, and God forgive me – I gave him such a belting.'

'My God, how awful, and all the time he was innocent!'

'Joseph wasn't innocent, Ottie! He was guilty. I belted him not for you, but for us. All those years, not knowing, thinking he was dead. But I said nothing to him about what had happened to you because he might be an egomaniac and many things but I knew, absolutely, that Joseph was not capable of what you thought, not even remotely and if he knew what had happened to you after he left that night I dare say, knowing his temper, he would have murdered the man by now, so it was as well I said nothing I think. Anyway, thank God you yourself have come here and the matter is now put to rest before I leave. God be praised for that.'

Ottilie stared at Lorcan. 'You're not leaving?'

'I am, Ottie, I am going to Africa, which is such an honour for me, to be chosen to go. It's something for which I have prayed.'

'Oh, Lorcan.'

'I know, I know, our little family, we're all flung far and wide now, but it won't stop us thinking of each other, will it? Thank heavens I'm leaving knowing that you are quite healed, that is such a relief to me, Ottie. More than I can tell you.'

'You will be awfully good with all those black babies, Lorcan. You're so good with children. And just think, they'll be a cinch after looking after all of us, wouldn't you say?'

Lorcan smiled, and Ottilie could see he was grateful that she was trying to make it easier for both of them.

As for Ottilie, it seemed to her that even as he stood in front of her Lorcan was fading away, and she was fading from him too, and that lying between them was the uneasy past and their devotion to Ma, and out of all of them that had driven down in Sullivan's hearse and Mrs Burgess's car that day, only she was left in Cornwall.

The next day Pierre was back. Springing through the hotel doors at breakneck speed, followed by his assistant, Alanna, a young girl about whom he was inclined to joke but who, it was immediately apparent to Ottilie, was utterly devoted not just to Justin and Gordon, the company recently started by Nancy Gordon and Pierre, but to Mr Pierre Justin himself. Pierre referred to her as 'Orange Crush' because she had a crush not just on him but on orange with which it seemed she wanted to decorate the world.

The arrangements for the decorators to move into the top suite having been finally confirmed for the time when, by long tradition now, Mrs Ballantyne left it and retired to Devon for two weeks, Ottilie and Pierre were able to leave Alanna in charge of it, and move down to concentrate on Ottilie's own rooms.

She preceded Pierre up to them, jumping up the stairs and pushing open the door to the large, spacious rooms. He followed her as quickly, and then stood quite still, looking round at the childish decor, before pushing his gold-rimmed spectacles up his nose a little and saying, 'Well, yes. This is all rather charming but a little juvenile for *toi*, I should have thought, Miss C.'

To begin with Pierre paced up and down a little, as he always seemed to do when he was thinking, and then he picked up his drawing pad and pencils and started to make notes, and then to sketch, during which time Ottilie fell to silence, for she was filled with reverence for anyone who could draw. While he paced and sketched she pushed her way out on to the balcony to see the sea, and to be out of his way.

'I'm sorry, it's no good.' Twenty minutes later he pushed the balcony doors open and looked moodily at

413

Ottilie and then out to the sea and the horizon. 'I can't.'

'How do you mean?'

'Well.' He frowned down at her. 'Well. Let's face it. If these are to be your personal rooms, Miss C, what do I know about you? *Rien*. We have only ever discussed the public rooms. These are "Ottilie's rooms", or will be.' He looked at her with sudden sadness. 'For you and you alone, *n'est-ce pas*?'

'Well, yes, I suppose so.'

'Exactly, so whom am I designing for? I mean am I designing for a single professional lady? Or – what?'

Ottilie frowned and shook her head, but finally said, 'Well, I suppose, yes, the owner of the Grand, yes, that is whom you are designing for, yes.'

'Exactly, and I don't know anything about her, except that she is divinely funny, loves to play games and have picnics, has the most beautiful eyes and hair and kisses like no-one I've ever kissed. That's all I know, and that, quite frankly, is not enough.'

Ottilie groaned. 'I can't tell you about myself, Pierre, really I can't. Believe me I would have before if I could have but I couldn't so I haven't, that's why you see—'

She stopped as she started to break up and as she looked across at Pierre she realized that he had too and they caught each other up laughing.

'Oh, Ottilie, that was so funny, what was that you said – "I would have if I could have but I couldn't so I haven't"?'

Ottilie looked up at Pierre, silent for once, which she never really was with him, and then she reached up, took off his glasses, and this time she kissed him, and it was wonderful, and once again she realized that he had a taste just like his sweet nature and she put both her hands up round his face and kissed him a second time, much longer this time, and he kissed her right back and it was wonderful what there was in a kiss, and Ottilie realized that love could be even more intoxicating and ecstatic than she had imagined. Passion, commitment, love of life, it was all there in a single kiss.

'I'm afraid I love you, Pierre.'

'I love you too, but you know that, you've known that all along.'

'I realized that I loved you two days ago, when you were in London.'

'You can't be serious? I fell in love with you much earlier than that. What kept you?'

'OK, I'll start again. When I went to say goodbye to Lorcan the other day – he's one of my sort of brothers, except he's not – well, it was very sad and so I started to run home to stop the sadness and as I ran home I realized two things. First that this was my home, and I mean my real home, and the second was that I was running faster and faster so that I could get back home to you ringing. To Pierre. And although I had started off feeling so sad I began to feel happier and happier and when I arrived outside the front here I realized why I had felt better and better as I ran towards this place was because all I could see was your face.' There was a small pause. 'Well look surprised, at least look a little surprised,' she begged.

'Yes, ma'am, I will look surprised for you, in my own time though.' Pierre put his hand under her chin. 'Two can play at being difficult.'

'I'm not difficult, I'm impossible, that's different.'

'So what from here?'

'I don't know, I wouldn't know.'

'In that case how about Pierre Justin asks Miss Ottilie Cartaret to dinner at the completed top suite on a date to be arranged with the painters, the curtain makers, the upholsterers and not to mention Miss Cartaret's secretary, Veronica of the same name?'

'As long as there's not twisting to that awful Chubby Checker—'

'No twisting, just dancing to Johnny Matthis?'

'I'm not sure.'

'Now, Ottilie—'

'I was only really going to say that I'm not sure who Johnny Matthis is,' Ottilie confessed.

'Not sure – not sure – not sure who Johnny Matthis is?'

Pierre did a pretend stagger back clutching his head and shaking it, and then eventually he raised it once more and with a mock brave expression he said, 'Well, it's about time you were sure, mademoiselle from St Elcombe. Dear heavens, where have you been all your life? No, don't tell me, as you said with your upbringing here I suppose all you ever heard was a quickstep or a waltz drifting upstairs from the dining room. If you haven't danced cheek to cheek to Johnny Matthis you have never lived or loved. And by the way, while I'm in a masterful mood I am going to choose our celebration dinner in the completed Blue Suite. I want none of your vapid steamed English Dover Sole, thank you. I want strong tastes to go with my passionate Yankee nature.'

At which they would have started to kiss again had Pierre's secretary Alanna not burst in with what she called 'the best news ever'. The curtains for the top suite had arrived.

'Exaggeration is Alanna's middle name,' Pierre said affectionately, watching his secretary's retreating dirndl skirt with one of his mildly puzzled looks. 'I hardly think that "the curtains for the top suite have arrived" would rouse most people to excitement, but for Alanna this is "big news", so who are we to argue?'

Ottilie stared at her face in the mirror. She actually could not wait for Pierre to tear all her rooms apart. She didn't know why but it seemed to her to be going to be the most exciting moment of all the transformation of the hotel. She wasn't in the least sentimental about her old furnishings. She could not wait to say goodbye to the swan-shaped bath, to the endless pink, even to the curtains with their Kate Greenaway figures. She thought of all this as she turned and turned in front of the mirror with its childish decorations of deer, looking anxiously at herself. She wondered what Pierre would think of her in her new dress? He had hardly ever seen her out of navy blue. She had to admit that deep down she feared that when he saw her dressed up he might laugh at her as Monsieur had done that evening in Paris.

This fear had not been helped by Veronica who when she saw the dress being lifted from its box had murmured, 'Very seductive, Miss C.'

'A Gina Fratini silk jersey dress is bound to be a *little* revealing.'

'After you with it, I've got my eye on the newly arrived *sous chef* one Bruno by name. So handsome, so charming, I have already started learning real live Italian – so much better than from a book.' Veronica rolled her eyes, and they both laughed. 'You're going to look fantastic in that.'

But was Veronica going to be proved right? Ottilie sat down and pulled on her evening shoes, or rather stepped into them, for they were very high heeled. There was little point in wondering what Pierre would think of her. If the recent past had taught Ottilie one thing it was that anxiety and above all guilt were a destructive waste, just so many dead leaves that had to be burnt.

Ottilie stood back in front of the mirror. Jean, who had come in to help her put her hair up, hovered anxiously behind her. Now the shoes were on they could both really assess the dress, and Ottilie saw at once that Veronica was quite right, the dress was very clinging indeed. It showed every contour of her body.

'Not many girls could wear a dress like that, Miss Cartaret, and you are one of the few,' Jean murmured and she gave a satisfied sigh as if she had just finished a glass of champagne. 'Colour's wonderful on you, with your dark hair, couldn't be better.'

Jean was right about the colour, it was a beautiful shining deep brown and what with the dress having such a high collar with its long sleeves, and its skirt cut to fall in graceful folds, the waistline emphasized by a thick gold chain belt, it couldn't have been a better choice. Even so, Ottilie turned away saying, 'I don't know, maybe I can't carry it off.'

Seeing how nervous she was, and probably knowing why, Jean clucked maternally. 'Course you can. Sit down while Jean does your hair for you. You've got yourself in a right tizz, haven't you? Course you can wear it. Not many could, but you can. Now you let me see.'

Swiftly she pinned up Ottilie's still damp hair, and with the hair dryer on high she started to dry it. The drying process had necessarily to be done fast and furiously, leaving neither of them time to talk, because Ottilie hated her hair to frizz. Jean ended by pinning up the thick fall on top of her mistress's head, while allowing a few small strands to wisp at the back.

'You look what my dad would call "peachy", you really do, Miss Cartaret, and don't forget your bracelet.'

She handed Ottilie the bracelet that Lorcan had brought to her tenth birthday party. Realizing the time Ottilie snatched at it and started to hurry towards the door, but then abruptly she turned back.

'Thank you, but I think I will just stay here – just a moment. On my own. I think perhaps I need a little quiet, if you don't mind?'

Jean gave her a worried little look but she left her saying, 'You look like a film star, really you do, Miss Cartaret, a real star.'

Once Jean had left Ottilie started to pace about her room. She knew that Jean was right, she did look like a film star, her mirror told her that, but inside her, right inside her, Ottilie still felt that she was in Philip's phrase 'damaged goods' and consequently in her own eyes she was ugly. Ottilie had told herself, and she had meant it, that what was over was over, but now that she was wearing this beautiful dress, her hair put up, her make-up immaculate, in contrast to her appearance those awful feelings of self-disgust were returning and no matter how she tried to stem them they were coming back, threatening to be a tidal wave which would prevent her going out of the door, dressed as a beautiful woman, looking to be loved.

She turned in desperation, near to despair, looking round her room for reassurance, something to which she could cling, something that would send those feelings away. Finally, she found herself going to her old toy chest, filled as it was with all her childhood souvenirs which she never really looked at, but which were too infinitely precious to throw away. In among the treasures, where she always kept it, a little hidden, lay the beautiful hand-marbled folder in which she kept Monsieur's drawing that she so loved.

There it was, or rather there she was, herself before the awful event of Joseph's party. There she was without a stitch on but glowing with health, happy and innocent. She pressed the drawing to her, willing it to send away the revulsion, the feelings of disgust, the ugliness that she felt was still inside her.

As she held it to her she remembered the happiness she had enjoyed in Paris, she remembered that evening as she came out of the bathroom, the turban of towelling on her head, the larger towel caught up around her, and how they had both spontaneously delighted in the moment, and all the subsequent wonder of those days and weeks, and she shed everything that had happened since, so that by the time she replaced the drawing, opened her door and started to climb the stairs towards the top suite, where she knew Pierre was waiting, it seemed to her that although it was evening the sun was shining, and she could hear the laughter and the slight pause in conversation as she had made her way through the crowded restaurant.

'*Courage, Ottilie!*' Monsieur would have said. '*Courage!*'

Outside the newly renamed Blue Suite Ottilie stopped and caught her breath. She must not rush in and talk too much. She must not become flushed with excitement. She put up her hands to her face and happily they were ice cold from nerves and they cooled not just her face but the whole of her, as if the cold was reaching down to her very centre. Next she breathed in and out a few times, but still she could not bring herself to put her hand on the door knob. *Come on*, she urged herself, *it's just an evening for heaven's sakes!* She breathed in once more and then, head held high, turned the handle of the suite.

As promised there was a tape stretched across the door and Pierre was in the middle of the room waiting for her, himself in immaculate evening dress, but carrying a large pair of kitchen scissors. He turned as he saw the door opening and as soon as he saw her he walked towards her with one hand stretched out and Ottilie knew straight away that everything was going to be all right because there was that wonderful smile of his lighting up his eyes.

'Stay there, stay there, you have to make a speech and cut the tape.'

'No glasses?' she asked as she took the scissors, the tape dividing them, their eyes uniting them.

'I sat on them, would you believe? Just as we all had everything in place, I stepped back and sat down in that lovely armoire over there. At least for once I knew exactly where my spectacles were.'

The newly hired hotel waiters standing behind him in the candle-filled room all laughed and clapped after Ottilie announced in clear royal tones 'I declare this suite open' and cut the tape.

Pierre bowed deeply from the waist. 'Welcome to the Blue Suite, Miss Cartaret, ma'am.'

Ottilie stepped into the room, into this place that she knew so well, and yet was unrecognizable, so changed had it become. What Pierre's artistry had wrought was not a transformation so much as a miracle.

The place embraced you as you came in, and without being in the least bit nautical its whole ambience directed your senses towards the sea beyond the French windows, for the room was indeed blue, as Pierre had promised, but like the waves seemed to be reflecting the colour of the sky for although it was blue to the eye it was in actuality a French grey which is a grey with much blue in it yet subtly suggests blue not grey. And the white, like the cliffs on either side of the bay, a bone white, but there were many gradations of both, so that each when present in either curtains or upholstery, like the presentation of one colour in a painting presented not one colour but many. Pierre took her round explaining the provenance of each piece of furniture, and how he had brought back, from one of his many treasure hunts, a set of 1930 reproduction eighteenth-century furniture.

'Very well made and can be adapted without a tremor,' he had joked when he had first shown them to her, but now they too had been repainted a French grey and they looked charming, not pretending to be antiques in any way at all, but graceful none the less, and as Pierre said, very well made.

Outside the long windows there was a beautiful sunset such as sometimes happens in Cornwall even after the rainiest day. As Ottilie took a glass of champagne and moved around the room it seemed to her that the glow that was lighting up the skyline reflected itself in every corner of the room.

'There's always been something about this suite that I just can't explain, as if I knew that one day it would mean a great deal to me,' she confessed to Pierre but couldn't say any more because the waiters were hovering and there was more champagne to be drunk and finally dinner to be eaten.

After the waiters left, wheeling the old mahogany trolleys towards the newly mended lifts, Pierre closed the doors and holding out his arms and smiling he said, 'All alone at last,' and Ottilie ran into them and they started to dance to the record he had just put on but only for a minute or so, for what with the moon outside standing still and small dark clouds starting to run across it and the rain starting to fall once again, and above all the sound of the sea outside the windows, kissing and making love became a matter of what was both best and beautiful.

The following morning so early that not even Nantwick was up and about they crept down to Ottilie's suite wearing only the newly arrived white towelling hotel dressing gowns. Pierre was unshaven and Ottilie's hair was around her shoulders. They held hands, creeping like children, both of them longing for the coffee that Ottilie kept in her suite, made in a secondhand cafetière brought back from a shop on the Left Bank. Coffee made, they drank it and watched the sun rising over the sea from the safe warmth of her sitting room. There was much to talk about between coffee and kissing. Their future plans and present problems, and how Ottilie came to be left enough money to buy the Grand, and how the Cartarets had thrown her out, but not why.

'I know I am the only child of indulgent parents, but I simply can't understand what you could have done for the Cartarets to have treated you that way. I mean we are in the so-called Swinging Sixties.'

Pierre shook his head, but Ottilie only said, 'We won't speak about the past any more.' She looked up at Pierre. 'Last night you made me a whole person again, this morning I know that even if you leave tomorrow I will still be a whole person. And how can I ever thank you enough for that?'

'I'm not leaving tomorrow unless you intend to fire me.'

'Yes but one of these days you will be leaving, and I have to understand that, the hotel will be finished, the ball we are planning will be over – literally – and you won't want to be here any more. St Elcombe is a small place and you are too cosmopolitan to want to stay.'

'Where do you get your ideas from?' Pierre asked, shaking his head in mock wonder.

'Living here all this time, seeing things that I have seen, I know only too well what happens to people. Life is transient, made up of a few memorable moments. To cling to even one second of what has been perfect would be to destroy it.'

'So how come my parents were happily married for years and until the day he died last year my father lived only to see my mother again? Even when she was gone he still spoke to her every day, spoke to her photographs, to the paintings he had done of her. He died still living for her. These are not transient emotions. Of course not, they live on for ever, in my heart, in all hearts that knew them, as everyone who has truly loved always will, you must understand that, you little pagan.'

After a small pause Ottilie said, 'Pantheist actually, not pagan. I worship nature. As a child just imagining the life beneath the sea used to fill me with a sort of religious wonder.'

'You fill me with wonder, but you do know that you are going to have to fire me to get rid of me? Now that really will be a transient moment.'

Ottilie frowned and stared out at the sea. She didn't really know how to say what she knew she had to say as she saw Pierre sinking dramatically to his knees in front of her, his chin still unshaven, but she knew, no matter what, that nevertheless it had to be said, for both their sakes. Making love was one thing but by no means everything.

'Will you marry me, Miss Cartaret?'

Ottilie stared down at him on his knees. 'You look like a pirate, I don't want to marry a pirate,' she said, running a finger round his chin.

'Ottilie, if you don't say yes you know what will happen to you, don't you?'

'Yes.' Ottilie was laughing and moving away from him

423

when Pierre caught her hand and started to pull her towards the bedroom. 'Yes, yes, I do know, thank goodness.'

Later she laughed a great deal more as she watched Pierre bathing in her swan-shaped bath. A more incongruous sight she thought she had never seen than six foot of Pierre sitting with still unshaven chin in a child's bath.

'How will you do these rooms for – us?'

'How will I "do" them? I will "do" them as you call it in a way that will make it habitable for both sexes, in other words I will give the place a classical calm. I have great ideas for the bed. I was thinking about it, I shall design it myself. A fourposter, but a modern fourposter, extra large, because once all the clutter is removed this is actually a very large set of rooms. We will twist cloth around the newel posts, round and round, plain linen – and the top of the canopy will be a great roll of cloth descending towards the front, but caught up finally, before it drops, by two great leather buckles.'

'Sounds – interesting.'

Pierre looked at her over the top of the swan. 'You are being cheeky, aren't you?'

'No, no, it does, it sounds very – interesting.'

'Just an idea,' he said shooting her a look from under his surprisingly long black eyelashes.

'What about the floors?' Ottilie wanted to know as Pierre stood up and climbed out of the bath, grabbing a towel and drying himself with great speed and vigour.

'Follow me,' he commanded, and without a stitch on but with the towel hung around his neck as if it was a scarf he strode through to the main room and started to indicate how he thought he could draw the whole suite together using natural linens and basket weaves, again so that the eye would inevitably be drawn, as in the top suite, back out to the scene beyond the windows but this time to the sand and the rocks.

'And what about paintings and things?' Ottilie wanted to know.

'I hadn't really thought. Beach scenes perhaps, nudes – but only if they are modern, none of those slab-like figures, although a Picasso might be nice,' he joked.

But Pierre wasn't really listening, he was concentrating on what he might do and what he might not do, and so Ottilie went to her old toy chest, and once more opened the precious marbled folder and took out the drawing that Monsieur had done of her.

'I have something that might do, something that I love so much. But if I show it to you, you mustn't get ideas because I did not pose for this, although my parents did not believe me when I said as much. The artist did it from his imagination and then he gave it to me as a present, my last night in Paris.'

Pierre was standing over by the window, murmuring, 'The light bright sand of the coves around here, that is what we will have in here. Linen blinds, everything uncluttered. And what is this?'

'I was just telling you.' Ottilie pushed the marbled folder towards him. 'It's one of my treasures. A drawing of me, but I did not pose for it, the artist did it from his imagination.'

Pierre stared at it, completely silenced, and after a moment he said, 'But it's beautiful. And it's just like you. May I ask you something, none of my business, but did you love this man?'

Ottilie stared at him in astonishment and then started to laugh.

'I do not find this a laughing matter, I do assure you,' Pierre said coldly. 'Not at all. Please tell the truth. Did you love this man?'

'Love him? Good heavens, I hardly knew him! It was just that Mrs Le Martine knew him – "Monsieur" is what we nicknamed him and she somehow talked him into letting me stay in his Paris flat for a month. And well, I think he thought I was a bit lonely, and so on my last night in Paris he took me out to dinner and gave me this drawing as he left to go back to Lyon. I mean I think it's brilliant because he really did do it from his imagination, from just meeting me once. He was obviously very clever.'

'Very clever,' Pierre agreed. 'Very clever indeed. In fact I should say from looking at this that he was a man after my own heart, which was just as well, since he was my father.'

'Le Bonnier is my father's name,' Pierre continued, much later for as always with lovers the interval between the discovery of something new and astonishing and continuation with their conversation had been delightfully filled.

'Justin was my mother's maiden name. But you know how it is in France, you take both the names of your parents. Mine are Le Bonnier Justin, which is too much of a mouthful for anyone, so when my mother died so suddenly I took her name shortened, in her memory, for professional use. When I joined Nancy, my partner, we called the company Justin and Gordon. My full names are Jean-Pierre Le Bonnier Justin, but I sidetrack.'

'No, no, please, I like detours.'

'At the end of last year when my father died I returned to France from America not just for the funeral, but to pack up everything, and to sort through his personal effects with a view to giving as much as was possible to his so-devoted friends and staff, and of course his servants on his estate. It was while I was going through his things that I found the same drawing as you have, except in mine – or rather in his – you are actually wearing a towel, exactly, I suppose, as you were that evening when you and he first met. He must have done two drawings, because the one that he gave you, you know how he loved to tease – it seems he has removed the towel!'

They were walking down the beach hand in hand. Back at the hotel breakfast would be being served but Ottilie did not care if the croissants were too brown and the toast stiffening, all she could think about was her evening with Pierre's father and how when she had met his son she had indeed had the strangest feeling that they had somehow met before.

'As soon as I saw that drawing, in grief as I was, I knew that I had to meet this girl that my father had drawn with such obvious delight. But I did not know who the girl was, can you imagine anything so irritating? I knew from his friends and servants that there had been no young mistress in his life, so who was the model for this so joyous drawing? Who had so captured his imagination that he had been able to go away and draw her with such tenderness, whom had he known, whom had he seen, that had such an innocent look to her? And then Mrs Le Martine came to the funeral and we talked, and she came back to our family home and I showed her the drawing and she laughed so much – she knew you straight away, and that is why when she heard that you were looking for a designer she sent me hotfoot down here on her recommendation, because she knew I longed to meet you.'

'That's why you were so nervous that morning. You must have been in dread of my being a disappointment, and let's face it – I was.'

'No, you were no disappointment, but you were a shock. I could see that something terrible had happened to you. You were so thin, and you had the haunted look of someone who appeared to have been very ill and was only now getting better.'

'I had been ill. And now I am better.'

'So now we know everything that there is to know about each other, will you marry me? Preferably by special licence, tomorrow?'

Ottilie shook her head. 'I can't marry you, Pierre, at least not yet, not until I've found out who I really am. Coming back here to the Grand, seeing everything again, but through such different eyes, I know now that I have to know who I am before I go any further, or make any more changes in my life.'

'But I thought – you just said earlier that the past didn't matter!'

'No, not my past,' Ottilie agreed. 'But their past. The people who made me. I must know where I came from, why I'm here at all.'

Pierre looked down at her and carefully brushing back the hair that was blowing across her face he sighed and warned her, 'Be very careful of the past, Ottilie, anyone's past. It can sometimes prove to be more hurting than your own.'

But Ottilie had hardly heard his last words before springing back and putting her hand across her mouth as she remembered. 'Oh my God, oh my God, Blue Lady is due tonight, I must have everything ready for her. It's so important that she likes the way you've done the suite, everything must be perfect for her.'

She turned. 'Jean is in dread because Mrs Ballantyne's so set in her ways and since she came back – before you, as it were, sent the troops in to pull the suite all apart – Blue Lady's been going dottier than ever. We warned her the suite would be changed, when she came back, but you never know how much she takes in.'

Ottilie started to run back towards the hotel, Pierre following her and calling, 'But I thought she'd left?'

'She has, for her time in Devon. It's difficult to – too difficult to explain now.'

Pierre shook his head, but he refused to follow Ottilie any further, and realizing that their time together was temporarily at an end he turned back to the beach to continue their walk alone, although calling back with an attempt at humour, 'I could learn to hate this woman, Blue Lady, and really quite quickly too. And Ottilie, don't forget we're invited to the mighty Granvilles for lunch today. Or as they said in Jane Austen's day, to Tredegar we are invited, Miss Cartaret.'

Who could forget it, Ottilie thought, as she jumped back up the steps of the hotel, realizing that because of all the love-making and the wonder of last night and this morning she had nevertheless nearly forgotten Mrs Ballantyne's all-important return.

Yet she doubted very much that she could possibly have forgotten that they were invited to Tredegar since it was after all Ottilie who had found Philip and Constantia wandering round the hotel. Happily the knowledge that she owned the place in which they stood meant that when she bumped into them she felt quite able to stand tall and look both of them in the face, and it was they who looked away, dropping their eyes as dogs do, knowing that they might well be, indeed were, not just caught in the act of snooping round the hotel, but highly unwanted by its new owner.

'We just had to come and look, we heard so-o much about what you were up to, Ot-ti-lie dear,' Constantia drawled, puffing a little too hard on her cigarette.

Ottilie could see Veronica hovering protectively some yards away. She would know immediately that the Granvilles were snooping and would be waiting to see if Ottilie wanted them shown the door.

Constantia smiled at Ottilie, mouth only, eyes as hard as ever, her thoughts reflected in the hardened expression and it wasn't difficult to read at least one of them. 'Who would have thought *you* would have done so well for yourself, Ottilie Cartaret?'

'Thank you, Veronica,' Ottilie said smoothly, turning and pulling a gargoyle's face at her behind the Granvilles' backs.

As Veronica bit her lip and hurried off Ottilie turned back to the Granvilles.

'Now how can I help you?' she drawled in a fair imitation of Constantia herself.

Philip, realizing what she was doing, reddened, but Ottilie stared at him stonefaced. She was determined to show him that she had changed completely. The damaged goods were now whole again. And yet, proud of her professionalism as she was, Ottilie would not deny them access to her hotel, for to do so would be to give them far too much importance. Constantia and Philip might be the Granvilles of Tredegar, but they were only human beings, and as such she had found them wanting in both kindness and tolerance, believing in rumours, rather than the person they had once known so well and, in Philip's case, even loved.

The hotel, because its structure was so sound, because all the doors were good thick polished Edwardian mahogany made from wonderful, aged wood, must now seem like a palace to the Granvilles compared to how it had been recently during its bad sad days. Pierre had hardly even begun but the little he had accomplished nevertheless was already reflecting his determination to bring about an atmosphere of, as he called it, 'being aboard a luxurious liner before the war'. And, although working to a self-imposed tight budget, he had actually wrought miracles with the paintings and furniture that he had already bought on Ottilie's behalf, not to mention the ubiquitous Ming vases.

Nevertheless, proud as she was of Pierre's achievements in such a short time, all the while Ottilie was proudly showing the now rather effectively silenced Granvilles the just completed new dining room, she kept praying that Pierre would not bump into them.

It wasn't that Ottilie was ashamed of having once imagined that she was in love with her old childhood friend, or that she was not proud of Pierre, it was just that she had every idea that Pierre would loathe the Granvilles and their haughty ways, and wonder how she ever came to be friends with them in the first place, and nowadays that was something which Ottilie herself found difficult to explain. Thankfully by the time the tour ended Pierre had yet to be seen and Ottilie had every hope of sending the Granvilles on their way.

Until Constantia – and she *would* – doubled back to the dining room saying, 'I just must see that marvellous Fowler pink that your designer has used. Just the same colour as Roberts Animal Ointment, I always think.'

And suddenly there was Pierre in the middle of the dining room talking to Alanna and staring at some china that had newly arrived and as always on seeing him Ottilie immediately felt immensely glad despite not wanting him to meet the Granvilles. She couldn't help being glad because every time she set eyes on Pierre anew, it seemed like both a wonderful surprise and a reaffirmation, and yet at that particular moment she wished him a million miles away.

Pierre himself had seemed benignly oblivious of the Granvilles' patronizing attitudes, waving a swatch of silk and saying, 'Look, Ottilie, that stupid old Knightsbridge fruit has come good at last.'

'This is your designer, is it? We must be allowed to meet him, surely?' Constantia immediately insisted as she saw Pierre, his spectacles on his nose, Alanna hovering with her clipboard, as always her hair scraped back, face scrubbed and generally shining with devotion.

Of course as soon as Philip saw Pierre walking towards Ottilie with his face lit up he knew. And as soon as Pierre saw Ottilie with Philip he knew that Ottilie had once thought herself in love with Philip, and that being so as they shook hands Pierre removed his glasses and put them on top of his head, as if he did not want to appear disadvantaged by them. And Philip having engaged Pierre in conversation kept referring to his occupation in thinly veiled sarcastic terms, using the words 'interior design' and 'interior designer' with a lightly sarcastic emphasis that was nevertheless unmistakable in its meaning. So much so that had Pierre not frowned a warning at her Ottilie would have felt tempted to say something, but that was before Constantia knocked one of the Ming vases 'by mistake' to the floor and it broke into several pieces.

'Oh I *am* sorry!'

She leaned down to pick up some of the pieces while essaying to look remorseful.

There was a small silence as Ottilie stared at the pieces, and then at Constantia, knowing that what she had just done had been far from a mistake. Philip at least had the grace to look embarrassed for the first time, before Pierre said, stooping down to help Ottilie pick up the pieces, 'Don't be sorry, Miss Granville. Ottilie certainly won't be. She hates these vases, as soon as I bought them I could see they set her teeth on edge. Besides, they're actually worthless, one of them having a crack in it. Not only that but they're fakes – all so-called Ming is fake as you know. As it happened these were rather good fakes, but fakes none the less. As I am sure you will appreciate one would never dream of putting out the real thing in a hotel.'

There was nothing but good humour in Pierre's eyes as he said all that, whereas Ottilie had the feeling that there was a look of something near to defeat in Constantia's, and she suddenly remembered seeing Constantia, when they were much younger, scratching a mark with a red Biro down the back of a friend's new cream winter coat simply because it was new and pretty and did not belong to Constantia.

At long last, feeling embarrassed by his sister's obvious lack of grace, Philip had quickly diverted the conversation and asked Ottilie and Pierre to lunch the following Sunday. 'We must at least try to make it up to you both,' he said with a gracious smile, as if Pierre and Ottilie were badly in need of a hot meal.

'Don't let's go,' Ottilie had begged, but not nearly hard enough she realized as Pierre drove them both towards Tredegar, and anyway it was useless, because Pierre was avid to see such a famous old house, particularly since it was still in private hands.

Soon they were standing outside the old oak doors that

were so familiar to Ottilie and he was saying, 'This is a pretty perfect example of Elizabethan domestic architecture.'

'Hi.' Constantia opened the door herself, although there was a maid hovering in the background.

She smiled, which for Constantia was quite something, except that it had to be faced that Constantia's smile was a little like that of an alligator, one third on the top, two thirds concealed. Right from the start she addressed herself solely to the man, ignoring Ottilie, which Ottilie had noticed some women have the habit of doing, and which she, at the hotel, was most careful not to do. Not that Constantia's lapse of manners was important. After all they were not going to be staying at Tredegar, just having to suffer a meal there.

Compared to Pierre's work on the Grand, Tredegar with its too-crowded walls and dark wood, while undoubtedly beautiful, appealed to Ottilie as being gloomy and claustrophobic, so she was glad to follow Pierre and Constantia quietly round, all the while feeling doubly glad that she did not live there.

'I expect Ottilie told you that we invited you especially early knowing that you would probably enjoy a quiet ride with Philip before luncheon while Ottilie and I catch up with our gossip?'

Constantia turned as they returned once more to the Great Hall, and before Ottilie could say 'You never mentioned riding when you phoned to confirm, Constantia' she beckoned Pierre to follow her upstairs.

'No riding clothes,' Pierre told his hostess, as Ottilie reflected that there was nothing she cared for less than what Constantia called a 'quiet gossip'.

'Borrow some of Philip's riding clothes, no problem. Ottilie doesn't ride, I know, but Philip has plenty that will fit you, and we have a whole family of riding boots,' she went on, glancing at Pierre's elegant feet. 'But perhaps you don't, ride I mean, perhaps you can't?'

433

'Of course I can. Sure I ride. I spent much of the American half of my childhood riding on a horse farm.'

Ottilie knew that this would appeal to Constantia as being boastful, and she could imagine only too well Constantia, after they had left, mimicking Pierre to Philip using words like 'horse farm' and 'sure' in a mocking way.

'Oh I don't think Pierre wants to ride,' Ottilie put in quickly, because she knew very well from way back that one of Constantia's more savage houseparty jokes was to put inexperienced riders up on unrideable hacks, usually hirelings brought in for the weekend, and then watch in glee while they fell off them. This practice had ended rather abruptly when one of the many unfortunates had broken a collar bone.

Pierre frowned a warning at Ottilie, a frown meant only for her, before turning back to Constantia. His voice immediately changed to a higher register, and he flapped his hand at his hostess as he said, 'It's ages since I had a ride, darling, do please let me, please!'

In her turn Ottilie pleaded with him with her eyes 'Please don't!' because he just didn't know the kind of horse that the Granvilles would lend people, he had no idea what he was letting himself in for. But Pierre turned away from her appearing not to notice either her grimace or the pleading look in her eyes.

No sooner had Pierre changed into a pair of Philip's jodhpurs and some boots than Constantia glanced out of the window and sighed. 'Oh dear, look, it's started to rain, would you believe? And not just rain, hail too. That will be no fun to ride in for either of you.' Ottilie heaved an inward sigh of relief. 'No, no fun at all,' Constantia said, smiling up at Pierre. 'Tell you what, how about some jumping in the indoor school? In view of the weather, eh? You jump, don't you?'

'Jump?' Pierre said. 'No, I don't jump, Miss Granville, I soar.'

'Oh, I shouldn't—'

But Pierre removed Ottilie's hand from his sleeve, giving it a warning squeeze.

'I just love jumping, really.'

With that they all set off with umbrellas in the pouring rain across the fields at the back in the direction of a large barn, Pierre, outwardly anyway, as cheerful as ever, and Constantia looking like a cat who has just caught a large mouse and is going to have great fun playing with it before killing it.

The horse that the girl groom led towards them as they entered the barn was a large bay, but it had short ears and plenty of white to its eye. Ottilie knew nothing about horses but it seemed to her the moment she saw Pierre's mount that it looked mean and bad-tempered. She wanted to dive at the wretched creature and lead it back out of the great barn that acted as a covered school for the Granvilles and their employees.

Pierre on the other hand seemed blissfully impervious to the obvious imperfections of his proffered mount, merely removing his glasses and giving them to Ottilie while smiling and chatting with Constantia. The groom lowered the leathers and pulled down the stirrups for Pierre to mount, but he turned to her as she led the horse up and said, 'Oh no, thank you. No saddle, thank you. I always ride bareback.'

The groom looked more than astonished and for once even Constantia seemed silenced, not even making her little 'oh' sound, like breaking glass.

'No saddle?' she asked, an eye on the distant figure of Philip on a thoroughbred making perfect transitions from trot to canter and back again, while hardly disturbing the sawdust as he rode in perfect unison.

'Oh you know us Americans,' Pierre joked. 'We actually prefer frontier conditions. Plenty of sawdust here,' he went on, indicating the heaped sawdust on the floor of the barn, 'all we need now is the saloon and a barman and two fingers of redeye.'

'You're going to ride bareback?' Constantia persisted in asking him.

'Not ride bareback,' Pierre called gaily as the groom gave him a leg up and he promptly swung forward clasping his arms around his mount's neck thereby setting it off at a fast trot, 'heck no, nothing like that. Jump bareback, much more fun. If you'll excuse me, ma'am.' At which he appeared to nearly fall from the horse, leaning and swaying and exclaiming, 'Oh my, oh my, it's years since I did this, oh my, oh my. Maybe if I call to it it will stop,' he shouted, bolting off in the direction of the jumps as Ottilie closed her eyes.

He was going to be killed. Ottilie was quite sure that he was going to be killed and her life would be at an end.

Twenty-Three

'Never ever do that again!'

They were on their way home and Ottilie was pretending to be furious with Pierre, because following his pretence of not being able to ride he had proceeded to trot and canter bareback round and round Philip's wretched school, riding sometimes clinging to the front of the horse, sometimes appearing to disappear underneath it, all the time whooping and hollering, finally ending by jumping over a set of jumps so fast that when he finally pulled to a stop Ottilie was quite sure so had her heart.

'Oh come on, admit it, it was funny! Seeing their faces was so funny, you must admit. Did you like the screams of terror, by the way? I modelled those on Peter Patent, you know the man I was telling you about the other day, the one in the London office? Only he does them when he thinks he has seen a flaw in a roll of cloth.'

Pierre repeated the high-pitched screams fortunately not as loudly as he had reproduced them while riding.

'No. Yes. No. Yes. Really. They were hilarious.'

'I think we taught Mr Granville a lesson, didn't we, Ottilie?' Pierre was unable to stop himself from laughing even though Ottilie was still sitting poker-faced. 'He thought, I mean come on, from the moment he met me, because he's in the Army – and the Army is such a man's world, my dear – he thought, "Well here's a right fruit that Ottilie Cartaret has in tow, so I'll put him up on a bad-tempered old cob and have fun watching him fall off." That's what he hoped, didn't he?'

'Well yes, that was exactly what he did think, and what he wanted. I was terrified, no – I was petrified.'

'Don't worry. I was on to him at once. That's why I kept frowning at you. You see what he didn't know was that at that horse farm I used to attend as a child back in the States there was an old film stunt man, name of Walter – naturally – what else should old film hands be called? Anyway, the moment my mother left me at that place to learn to ride like a little gentleman, Walter forgot all about teaching me the gentlemanly bit and set to and taught me all the things that I wanted to learn and not what my mother had in mind at all. He taught me everything he knew from film stunting, falling off, jumping on, standing up, sitting down, yes sirree so much so that by the age of twelve I could have made myself a mint in them there movies, ma'am!'

'Oh dear.' Ottilie's reserve finally broke and she started to laugh for the first time, because now that they were speeding away from Tredegar in retrospect the whole episode did seem hilarious. Just the memory of Constantia's face and the sound of her voice saying 'Oh – does he always do this sort of thing when he sees a horse?' as Pierre careered round the school doing acrobatics was too funny for words.

Still laughing at the memory Pierre and Ottilie parked the car and walked up the green sward in front of the hotel. Ottilie looked up at it, thankful that the façade was once more being returned to its old dignity, with the lettering mended, the painting completed and the new blinds about to arrive.

But as she was about to walk on Pierre pulled her back, frowning at the building ahead.

'You know what we need here,' he said and 'we' suddenly seemed to sound quite natural to both of them, 'we need some separate villas, in keeping of course, but designed with a much simpler architecture than the main house, less Gothic, more Pompeiian, colonnades, square.

You know at the back of the property there's plenty of room to build, don't you? It could be enchanting, very Continental in feel, which is all right here in Cornwall which after all prides itself on not being part of Britain anyway. I'll draw what I have in mind. I can just see it. Classical façades, pale paint.'

Ottilie looked up at him. How strange that what he had just described to her seemed suddenly familiar, a place where she had been before, but it was getting dark, and she thought she could already see Jean waiting, and so she hurried on up to her without pausing to try to recall where it was that she had seen or heard what Pierre had just finished describing to her.

As it was, she was hardly within a yard of the hotel when Jean sprang out at her, as always looking fraught, and Ottilie had not even reached the swing doors before she had already begun to tell her the bad news.

'It's that poor Mrs Ballantyne, she's had a terrible accident, at that place in Devon she would insist on going to.' Jean started to cry. 'Oh the poor dear, I'm afraid she's only gone and died, the daft woman. Her chauffeur rang through to reception, Miss Veronica being off, today being Sunday. Poor Mr Butterworth, he's that upset, it seems he's been with her ever such a long time, too. They pulled Mrs Ballantyne out of the river. Oh, Miss Cartaret, I knew all along that she shouldn't have gone away on her own. I did say. I don't know her like what you do, but I had a feeling that nothing good would come of it. She was acting so very strange. Miss Veronica has the police with her, and they are at a loss I must say. There's no answer to her home, of course, Mrs Butterworth having gone to her mother in Ealing it seems, and only the chauffeur at the Devon place, and he's distraught as you can imagine, because he found her, poor fellow. It's not suicide they don't think. Just must have fallen in and that's that. Or gone for a swim and got overpowered.'

Ottilie put her hand on Jean's arm.

'You go and have a nice cup of tea in the kitchen, Jean,' she told her, 'I'll deal with all this.' And she sighed. Five minutes before she and Pierre had been laughing so much Pierre had nearly had to stop driving the car, and now Mrs Ballantyne was dead.

There was no good reason to feel so unreasonably cast down by the death of a guest. Ottilie knew this. She knew this, she told herself this, and she accepted that this was sensible, but there was no reasoning with the unreasonable, and for some unaccountable reason Mrs Ballantyne's death, helping to pack up her things and deal with all the little details over the next few days, threw her into an unaccountable depression that was difficult to shake off.

The chauffeur was visibly upset when he returned from Devon and came to see Ottilie. Mrs Ballantyne had no family, he told her. 'I know she made a will, but it was many years ago now. She laughed when she told me. "Left everything to Battersea Dogs Home, Butterworth," she said, "I think dogs are a great deal more kind than humans, as you know." Not that she ever kept a dog. More's the pity, poor woman,' Mr Butterworth told Ottilie. 'Her bank acts as her solicitors, and they should take care of everything here,' he added with a discreet cough.

'That's the least of our worries,' Ottilie reassured him, knowing he was worrying about paying the bill. 'Will you come upstairs, Mr Butterworth?'

Ottilie and the chauffeur stood in the Blue Suite, and looking round its new fine furnishings she said in a desolated voice, 'I so wanted her to see all this, after all these years she's been coming, I really thought she would enjoy everything that Justin and Gordon have done here. I even thought it might change things for her, drive away the ghosts.'

'And it might well have done, Miss Cartaret, might well,' Mr Butterworth reassured her, stroking his magnificent

440

white moustache. 'This really is a changed place, hardly known it I wouldn't have, Miss Cartaret. Just Mrs Ballantyne's sort of taste too, Miss Cartaret, just her taste, a bit Noel Coward, sophisticated, but nice.' He looked round appreciatively, himself momentarily cheered, and although Ottilie knew that there was a strong chance that the rooms' new decor would not have been to his mistress's taste she saw for a second that he was enjoying imagining her delight.

'Well, now. We've packed up all her remaining . . .' Ottilie paused, she hated the word 'effects'. 'We've packed up all her things, and put them back in these suitcases. If you would like to check them through for me, and sign for them? And of course there was this—'

'Oh yes, her precious papers.' The chauffeur looked at the shabby little vanity case that had traditionally always followed his mistress up the stairs of the Grand to the suite. 'I always understood that's all her life in there, Miss Cartaret, not that there was much to it, not after her honeymoon, as you may have gathered.'

'What did happen, Mr Butterworth? I know I shouldn't ask, but what do you think really did happen to Mrs Ballantyne?'

'I know no more than you, Miss Cartaret, and I worked for her, six days a week for the last ten years. It all happened long before my time, you know. She was all right, day to day, she wasn't certifiable or anything, the doctor reassured my wife and me about that when we first came to work for her, definitely not dangerous, nothing like that. But this last time, as Jean probably told you herself, I don't know why but I noticed as soon as I was driving her up to Devon that she was definitely not herself, so much more distracted, just not herself at all. She seemed to be suffering from some kind of a delusion.'

'Yes, I realized that when she thought *I* was someone else, but I hardly saw her this visit, what with dealing with all the alterations, and so on. But Jean did say she was acting really quite strangely. Every time she opened the door Mrs Ballantyne would look round as if she was frightened that a ghost was coming in, and Jean said she would stare at her in such a funny way.'

'It was the loss of her husband, truly. It was just that, quite simply it turned her mind. She loved him that much. And the Devon thing, that was where they had gone you see, at the end of their honeymoon to this old hunting lodge, just the two of them, very cosy and romantic, so that was why – that was why she went back there, every year, part of re-enacting the whole honeymoon. Course if she'd had children, or anyone else in her life, not just people like me, it might have made a difference, but she didn't, and no interests neither. In London she just spent her whole day either walking round the shops or going to museums, up and down and round and about, and then back to the flat. Very eerie I thought, quite honestly, but if that was how she wanted to spend her life, who was I to say anything? My wife kept the place, her flat, like a new pin, and I drove her round to the shops every day and waited, but though she saw us day in and day out she hardly talked. Not what I would call talk. Didn't seem to notice what year it was, never had the radio on, never watched the television, never cared to talk about politics, nothing. But she never had a bad word to say about anyone either, I'll say that for her.'

He turned away suddenly, perhaps overcome by the realization that he would never now take his mistress round the shops or back to the flat again, never drive her down to St Elcombe on her annual visit. Ottilie put a sympathetic hand on his arm.

'Go down and have something to eat and drink with the others. They're all lunching early. It will do you good after all this, to have lunch.'

Butterworth nodded, giving Ottilie back the pen with which he had signed for the luggage and turning his cap in his hand.

'I'll have the cases taken down to the car meanwhile, and don't you worry about a thing. My secretary's in touch with her bank and they have everything in hand. I'm afraid your wife and you may have to do all the arrangements for her but if the bank are her executors, they will be sure to tell you most precisely.'

The chauffeur seemed only too grateful to get out of the suite, striding off quickly in the direction of the lifts as Ottilie rang down to reception to send up Nantwick to fetch Mrs Ballantyne's elegant suitcases, and an hour or so later Ottilie and Veronica saw Mr Butterworth and the car off.

'I should shoot off early today,' Ottilie told Veronica who looked suddenly grateful although murmuring, 'Are you sure?'

Ottilie watched her secretary's car drive off. Downstairs in the kitchen and the staff rooms they would still be talking about Mrs Ballantyne and her watery fate, but there were none of the old guard left, no-one who had really known her all down the years, as Ottilie had. Recently Jean had taken her meals up to her every day and become really rather devoted but it wasn't the same as having known her, as Ottilie had known her, since childhood, looking forward to her arrivals and witnessing her departures, both soon becoming as much part of the changing year as the sunshine or the gales.

As she wandered about the hotel distractedly checking the flowers Ottilie kept hearing Mrs Ballantyne's voice, so pretty and light, saying 'Put the tea down there' or 'You may remove the tea tray now, thank you' and seeing her turn towards the chair that was unoccupied except to her, with the inevitable 'Do go on, darling'.

At the time it had all seemed so wrong to be living in the past the way Blue Lady had, but now she was gone it seemed to Ottilie that it was intensely, passionately romantic and that the fierce way that she had clung to the memory of her dead love was impressive in the way a great piece of music or a painting is impressive, in the way that the sea outside her suite was impressive.

Feeling at such a loose end and not wanted by anyone in particular downstairs, lonely for Pierre's company, longing for him to ring and talk endlessly as he did every evening now, Ottilie's sadness intensified. It was raining and she longed to hear Pierre's deep warm baritone, longed to look up at just the sound of his quick light step, see him arriving in her office, drawing board in hand, Alanna in hot pursuit, her suede sandals making flopping sounds on the hotel floors as she tried to keep up not just with him, but with all his exuberant ideas.

Alone in the hotel, and perhaps because it was raining, Ottilie did what she had always done on such days, if she could, she wandered up to the top suite to be alone, only this time it was to remember. To look out of the windows of the Blue Suite and remember dancing and making love with Pierre up there, that would lift the sense of darkness descending.

She pushed open the familiar double doors, half expecting to see Blue Lady still, and fully expecting to see the old decor, the old brown furniture, the rug, the chintz, all the old familiar objects and Mrs Ballantyne by the window with the empty chair opposite her, sewing and talking to a ghost that no-one but her could see.

But there was no Mrs Ballantyne and the new French grey of the curtains and the gradations of the same colour reflected in the upholstery, everything in the room was once more a revelation which momentarily lifted Ottilie's spirits. Beyond the windows seas were running, their white tops seeming to chase each other endlessly, fruitlessly, backwards and forwards, but the sound of the wind moaning and crying around the Blue Suite was eerie, and all of a sudden Ottilie didn't want to be up there on her own any more. She turned quickly to go because her blood was changing, because she was sure, she was quite sure, she had the quite definite sensation, that Blue Lady had been standing behind her all the time that she had been at the windows looking out. She thought she could smell her scent, 'A La Fuite Des Heures' – fleeting time. Edith had always said that when the spirits of those recently departed returned that was how you knew they were beside you, because of the smell of their perfume.

She's dead! She can't come back! It's just her scent lingering on the air! Ottilie told herself neverthless moving towards the door as rapidly as she could, but as she turned to pull the old double doors to behind her, she noticed a small piece of hand luggage over by the new desk. It didn't seem possible, but after all that packing up and labelling Nantwick had only gone and left Mrs Ballantyne's old vanity case behind.

Seeing it Ottilie went back into the room. He couldn't really be blamed because Nantwick, like all hall porters and hotel staff, was such a suitcase snob, he would never have thought that such a small, cheap piece of luggage could possibly belong to the late chic, rich, imperious Mrs Ballantyne.

Ottilie picked the shabby little item up and then promptly put it down again, bored at the idea of taking it all the way down to the hall where she would have to leave it in her office which was already full to bursting. Much more sensible to leave it for Nantwick to take down tomorrow. She glanced down at it briefly. Really, Nantwick could not be blamed for leaving it behind, it was such a dreadful-looking thing, and what Mrs Ballantyne was doing, poor old bat, taking a few old papers around in it she could not imagine. Ottilie picked it up again. She had changed her mind, she thought tiredly, she would put it outside in the corridor in case Jean or someone brought visitors up to the suite. Honeymooners were always arriving unexpectedly and demanding to see round the best rooms.

As she picked it up a second time, she glanced down at the label because in what had once been a bold hand was written not MRS BALLANTYNE as might be expected, but MISS K. SHELBORNE.

Ottilie straightened up after reading the label and picked up the vanity case once more. Miss K. Shelborne must be Mrs Ballantyne's maiden name before she married the unlucky Mr Ballantyne who died so tragically on their honeymoon. She started to walk towards the door with her tatty burden but after a second or two paused. There was no-one about, no-one in the hotel, it was raining, it was wrong, but she suddenly felt irresistibly drawn to opening the case and finding out just a little more about poor Mrs Ballantyne. Knowing her as she had for so many years, it was too tempting not to have a look at what her personal papers might say about her. And after all, she was gone, and she had no dependants. The bank, or Mr and Mrs Butterworth – they would just throw the papers away. In reality they would be of no interest to anyone but Ottilie.

She put the small suitcase on the floor, and greatly daring because she still had the feeling that there was someone else in the room with her, she tried the locks. But they were locked, and there was no key attached. Mr Butterworth would have charge of all the keys now. Ottilie stared at it and then shook the case. It rattled with what sounded like a few papers, not much more, just a few old papers. Finally becoming exasperated she tried to hit the cheap locks open with a nearby paperweight. That failing, but definitely committed to her crime now, she took a steel paperknife and started to prise the cheap locks apart. Cheap the vanity case might be, but it was stubborn too. It simply would not open. Desperate now, and knowing that she had already gone far too far, she continued until at last the case opened, spilling out its few papers on to the floor and looking up at her in a pathetic fashion. It was as if the papers were a too-small fish that Ottilie had been playing for hours and had at last landed, only to feel embarrassed by its size and insignificance.

Yet having gone so far a little further was inevitable, and as she picked up the papers the first thing she noticed was that all the letters inside, and the diaries, were addressed to the same person as the label, Miss K. Shelborne. The second thing she noticed was that there were a great many exercise books and that when she picked them up the handwriting inside was more or less the same as that on the luggage label.

Having piled up the cheap exercise books, none of which were dated, Ottilie started to read. But not without guilt, for it was obvious from the start that these were private diaries and none of her business.

Part Five

Love, all alike, no season knows, or clime
Nor hours, days, months, which are
   the rags of time!

John Donne

Twenty-Four

An hour and a half after she had begun delving into Miss K. Shelborne's private diaries, Ottilie stopped. They were so predictably dull, just endless jottings, day after dreary day, and for all her pains, Ottilie was now stiff with cramp, still sitting in the same position on the floor and wondering why on earth Mrs Ballantyne had seen fit not only to keep but to treasure such boring diaries belonging to this Miss Shelborne, who was some kind of a governess or a nurse to her. It wasn't as if Blue Lady herself hadn't kept her own diaries. Ottilie had often seen her consulting her honeymoon diary in order to hold those strange conversations about weather that was not happening, and all the other things that weren't happening but which annually Mrs Ballantyne came back to the Grand to make happen.

'You meet the strangest people and hear the strangest stories in a hotel, Miss Ottilie,' Edith used to say sagely. 'That's one of its attractions, it's like it has a great river of stories flowing in and out of it every day, always full of surprises. Mark my words, and I can predict it knowing you as I do, this place will always have a hold on you, because you're a nosy little imp at the best of times.'

And knowing her as well as she had Edith must also have known that if she left Ottilie all her money she would end up buying the place, Ottilie thought, standing up and stretching her legs.

She must have known that all along, but being Edith she would leave that part of the story for Ottilie to find out for herself. Just as she never did say anything about Mrs Cartaret to her, only left Ottilie to find out what she felt about her for herself. Edith didn't believe in influencing things one way or another, and she often said so. It was because she must have had too much of that herself, being told what to do by her mother, too crushed herself to ever want to crush anyone else.

Ottilie stooped down and picking up all the exercise books in one guilty armful she started to throw them into a laundry bag retrieved from the bathroom. Perhaps if they had belonged to Mrs Ballantyne they might at least have thrown some light on her character, but as it was they were merely the jottings of a girl whose life had not added up to much, and who, it was obvious, was good but really rather dull. Nothing of real interest seemed to have happened to poor Miss K. Shelborne. Dull school with a dull home, just an orange and a bag of sweets at Christmas, and then thinking all the time that she was so lucky to be sent to look after Mrs Ballantyne who was obviously the 'Miss L' that she kept referring to in her later entries. Miss Shelborne had lived for the young Mrs Ballantyne, so admiring was she of her, obviously loving all the excitement her young mistress had brought to her life.

Once all the cheap little exercise books were in the laundry bag Ottilie pulled the string tight and made for the fireplace on the landing outside.

Having set fire to everything with the aid of some firelighters and some old newspaper, and feeling strangely relieved, she returned to the Blue Suite and set about tidying it. As she did so she stooped to find yet another of the wretched Miss Shelborne's – or was it Sherborne's? – exercise books. Ottilie started to throw it into the wastepaper basket this time, when her eyes were caught by the first of the entries.

It was actually interesting to her, if only because of the tragedy that she knew had followed this particular event, and yet again she felt as if her blood had changed and she could smell the scent of 'A La Fuite Des Heures' upon the air, as she started to read the diarist's entries. Knowing as she did what had happened to poor Mrs Ballantyne on her honeymoon the entries regarding her engagement became suddenly enthralling and Ottilie herself, reading of it, wanted to step back all those years to 1947 or 1948 or whenever it was and stop it all.

The sea outside the window was pounding and disintegrating against the rocks as Ottilie sat down, this time at the repainted boudoir desk, and started to read. The wind too was howling as if in prepared grief for the tragedy that Ottilie knew had to be about to unfold. And now too it seemed to Ottilie more than ever that Blue Lady was standing behind her, and she was crying.

Monday 15 November

Engagement announced. Both very relieved. This will make old Mr Waldo keep in his place and stop pestering. Fiancé a picture I keep telling Miss L, everything a man should be, tall, handsome. Much older of course, but then, as we keep saying, much richer too! No bad thing as I keep saying, no bad thing at all. Newspapers all very interested because of Mr Waldo himself being so recently married to Miss L's mother. Meanwhile Miss L miserable but sees sense. Because it is sense, nothing she can do now except marry. Nothing else will keep Mr Waldo's hands off of her. She pretty miserable and lonely too. But there. There may still be a happy ending I keep telling her. Fiancé very much the gentleman.

Wednesday 29 November

Engagement continues still. D.V. Mr Ballantyne took Miss L to choose trousseau and they came back and I

453

did Miss Lavinia's hair. Mr Ballantyne is a very nise (sic) gentleman, very nise indeed. He interviewed me about the future. Full of kindness he was, and Miss L said behaves like a gentleman all the time they was shoppin'. No hanky panky. Which is good. Good things can come out of bad, then, I say. They are to be married in New Year, but not in a church, just ordinary with only myself and Mr B's valet as witness. No fuss. He is very old fashioned and shy Miss L said. Just as well, I say. Honeymoon to be spend (sic) in Paris and Rome, and then back to good old Blighty which I personally think will be the best bit. But then. None of my business.

30 December

Soon be New Year and get on with it I say. Miss L delighted with her trousseau what Mr Ballantyne ordered. Her mamma disgusted. She don't agree with it, the New Look, skirts practically down to the ankles and clothing coupons and rationing still on, she don't agree with it at all. But she can be stuffy poor lady. New Look she kept saying to me, whatever next? But she is old and Miss L and I think she looks perfect, and does she. Course she does. She looks good in anything I say. Only two weeks and we will be leaving good old England for France and the frogs, but Parker, the valet, he says there is food in Paris and fuel and we will like it much better than London, which is good I say. You wouldn't have thought it was us that won the war my mother keeps writing to me, would you? What with all the money going to Germany and all the food to France? What was it all for? Never mind, I say to Miss L, we'll soon be free of Hitler which is what we have nicknamed Mr Waldo. He was sniffing round yesterday, sniff, sniff, sniff he goes outside her door, and us

454

on the inside, locked it, thank God, both thinking back
sniff, sniff, sniff you can bugger off Mr Waldo.

Tomorrow is the great day what we have all been
looking forward to so much. When I say we; I mean
Miss L and I. Everything's packed and we're as excited
as snakes, wondering what the 'Trifle Tower' as Miss L
calls it will look like but most of all thinking 'no more
Mr Waldo, no more Mr Waldo'. It's a shame that Miss
L had to marry so young and to such an old man really
but on the other hand he's a nise man really he is. And
he still has his hair, and old as he is and old in his ways
I'd rather him than most of the younger men. Specially
when he's in evening clothes. You can see he was very
handsome in the old days then.

PARIS!

Miss L sick as a dog on its last legs all the way over on
the boat. We were warned by her mother I must say
about how it would be in January, but Miss L didn't
care she just wanted to be out of that place and away
from Mr Waldo – Sniff Sniff we called him. Sniff Sniff
Waldo. I held her head and Mr Ballantyne most kind
and nise. He is nise. Really really nise. We are to stay
here in the hotel until she is better and then see the
sights. The valet is also nise, Mr Parker, but he does
like his drop. Still, he is older and as long as Mr
Ballantyne stays sober we should be all right. Miss L
still being sick and not up too much. Not very romantic
really but there it is. He's an old man. What can you
expect I say.

Mr Parker his valet and I went for a walk to allow them
to get to know each other better. Mr Ballantyne had
lunch sent up to their rooms and we went for a walk.
The French children are very gay and nise, with pretty
clothes, but they don't look bonny like English children
and yet there is food everywhere in the cafés and people
are looking more cheerful than they are back home.
Saw a woman who'd had her head shaved but it is
growing again. Mr Parker said this means that she lived
with the Gestapo rather than eat rats. I don't think we
should judge starving people myself. Who knows what
we wouldn't all have done in the same place? Back
home to Miss L in a right old state. Being sick again.
Mr Ballantyne calls the French doctor, but Miss L
won't have it, not at all. She's too fussy by half about
her body she says to let a French doctor give her things
that she don't know what they are. Myself I think she's
nervous. The honeymoon has been delayed so long now
and Mr Ballantyne must be wondering? He's a man
after all. Last night she locked herself in and her hands
were that cold when she clung to me I felt that sorry for
the poor girl. We're the same age but she's been
brought up different from what I have. Not tough. The
things I've seen you couldn't write down.

Miss L still sick. Doctor came again. Suppositories!
That's all the French think of. They've got them on the
brain I say. Miss L throws them down the la-la and then
pulls the flush hard. But the doctor has told Mr
Ballantyne he can find nothing wrong so I think tonight
will be the night and I feel that sorry for her. She don't
no (sic) nothing and it's not up to me to tell her. And

saying about thinking of England's not going to help her or anyone else. Sometimes I'm glad I'm working class after all you know what's what from the year dot and no mistaking, and nothing more to say on the subject. I can't tell her what her mother should ought to have done any more than I can fly to the moon.

PARIS

Well the deed is done and nothing more to be said. It's all over and she's most grateful to me. Although why she should be I wouldn't want to know. Her husband is the handsomest kindest man and she's the luckiest young girl you ever did hear about. To marry to get away from Sniff Sniff which let's face it is what she did and then to end up with such a wonderful lover is more than most women could dream of. She asked me and I came right out with it I must say. I told her. Beautiful. Just beautiful and she looked most surprised and then pleased so maybe she'll relax now who knows. I don't care. It was beautiful.

PARIS

Still the same. Miss L still the same. I keep telling her but she won't have it. I'm terrified now that old Parker will discover because he's a shrewd old man. But as to Mr B he is as happy as I've ever seen him. Sings all day and keeps buying his bride everything in sight. I tell Miss L to ask to go to England. There's a crossing soon. Once she's back in old Blighty she'll probably relax. So off we are going and I can't say that I am that sad to leave the frogs because there might be food here and there might be wine here but England's England and I start to pine for the old white cliffs. Miss L wants to go

457

to Cornwall where she went as a child. Very nise too. There'll be butter and cream there all right, not like London. And besides we all like the seaside don't we?

Arriving here. Straight away we all said what a good idea this is. Hotel is just what it should be. Mr B says it takes him back to before the war. Miss L still low in her spirits though. Myself I don't know what will bring her round. I tell her if the seaside don't do the trick what will. Mr B wants to take her to see some place he once used to stay as a boy. Dear old chap he loves to walk along the front with her. Hand in her arm. I could feel jealous but I don't. Love should be spread around and shared like jam I say!

That was the last entry. Ottilie put the incomplete exercise book down and stared around the room as someone might who is looking for someone to talk to and only realizes on seeing an empty room that there is no-one else besides themselves in it.

She stood up suddenly, infuriated with herself. Why had she thrown all the other exercise books out? What an idiot she was. Pierre was always teasing her about her habit of throwing things away, and Veronica too. For some reason no-one had been able to explain to her, the moment Ottilie thought that there was no reason to keep something any more, she threw it away, and now she had set fire to a whole set of diaries one of which, like this one, might have proved riveting.

Ottilie stared out to sea frowning. She had to find out what had happened to Mrs Ballantyne's maid. She had never seemed to enter the story before. If they had been so close why had Mrs Ballantyne not kept her on even when her husband had died? What had happened to Miss K. Shelborne that was so beautiful?

Something to do with Mr Ballantyne obviously, but why had she disappeared? She turned back to the room asking its ghosts, not caring at all if Blue Lady was with her now, not minding one bit, she just wanted to know what had happened. What had caused the maid to write 'Well the deed is done'? What *deed* was it? She went back to the desk and once more flicked through the diary.

No more entries, nothing except an address written in pencil at the back. It had often struck Ottilie that the sight of addresses and telephone numbers written in haste on anything from notepads to the front of telephone books could seem strangely emotive, but never before had it struck her quite so forcibly as it did now as she stared at the hastily scrawled writing. It was generous if childish writing, not all the letters joined up, and it sloped forward. It was not the writing of the diarist either, but it was writing that Ottilie recognized from bills and cheques over the years.

Impulsively she went to the telephone and picking it up she dialled Pierre's office in London. He sounded busy, surprised but nevertheless delighted to hear her even though it was normally he who telephoned her every evening.

'I'm coming to London,' she told him abruptly.

'You never come to London. Swinging London is just not your city, Ottilie, darling.'

'According to the fiction that is on my birth certificate, I was born at Number Four Porchester Terrace, to a Mrs O'Flaherty, and now I think it is high time I returned there.'

'Darling, do be sensible,' Pierre begged her. 'Remember lifting stones is not always a good idea, creepy crawlies so often result.'

'I have just discovered something that I think will stop even you in your tracks. I mean I think even you would be tempted to lift this particular stone.'

'Don't tell me? Blue Lady has left you all her money provided you become a nun? What could possibly stop me in my tracks besides you, Ottilie Cartaret?'

'Well. I found these boring old diaries in an old vanity case—' Ottilie could hear Pierre suddenly being distracted by Alanna, probably showing him something, but she continued even so. 'And I know I shouldn't have, but I read them, and they were so dull, Pierre, until I came to the end, at least I didn't come to the end – they were so boring I set fire to them. But then, just as I was tidying up I found another one, and I won't go into it too much, because you're obviously busy, but this one's all about Blue Lady's honeymoon, you know the famous honeymoon when her husband died?'

'Yes, yes, yes.' Ottilie could tell that Pierre's attention was now very much back on her, and so she continued.

'So it's all about – this diary is all about the honeymoon and her being sick and what not – oh, by the way, it's the maid's diary, not Mrs Ballantyne's diary, and it's actually quite riveting but I won't go into that—'

'Too late!'

'OK, you can laugh, Pierre, but at the end of this one, and I've got it in front of me, the writing stops after Paris, and Mrs Ballantyne being ill all the time, and so on, and then it ends most strangely, because obviously something happened in Paris, but that's just one thing. The other thing, the thing I want to tell you about, the thing I found, why I just had to tell you, why I have to come to London, was that when I flicked through the book to see if there was any more, guess what I found?'

'Can't, darling!' Once more Pierre's voice rang out gaily.

'I found an address scribbled in pencil. And, Pierre, it's the address where I was born.'

Chapter Twenty-Five

Pierre had wanted to meet Ottilie at the station but at the last minute he could not make it so she went to his office instead. Justin and Gordon was in Pimlico, a chic premises with discreet paint, discreet bells, and a discreet reception. Only Pierre seemed out of place, flinging open the door of his office, his glasses on top of his head, his arms stretched out, but because Alanna was hovering and he had a client in another room he could not linger longer than to kiss Ottilie and beg her once more not to go round to Number Four Porchester Terrace.

'Please, do us both a favour, please, don't go – please?' he begged, as they walked along the road, arms around each other, towards the taxi rank. 'It's always fatal to go back anywhere, I know, I've done it. Even the horse farm I used to go to as a child, looked such a dump – and so small. It'll look such a dump and so small you'll destroy all your golden memories in one fell swoop.'

'I must go, Pierre, really, I must. I mean if it was you, if you knew as little, or as much, as I know of your own story, wouldn't you go back?'

'I tell you I never yet heard of a story where "going back" ended up with anything but a slap in the face.'

He blew her a kiss nevertheless, and called through the cab window, 'I'll meet you on the station – good old Riviera Express where would we be without it?'

'Four Porchester Terrace, Notting Hill Gate,' Ottilie told the cab driver before Pierre could say any more although he sighed when he heard her, and then shrugged his shoulders in a resigned sort of way.

'You're not going to like what you find, Ottilie, no-one ever does,' he called but he waved even so.

Despite her bravura Ottilie was very glad that Pierre was not going with her. Lorcan had said that the girl who was Ottilie's mother was 'a pretty little thing with long dark hair' but he had also said that she 'died'. But supposing she had not died? Supposing she had simply given the baby away to Ma to adopt and pretended that she had died because her husband had died and she didn't want to bring the baby up? Could Lorcan's description of this slender young girl, could it possibly have been a description of Mrs Ballantyne who had long dark hair? Or was it a description of someone else, say the maid?

Ottilie kept asking herself all these questions on the taxi ride, until at last the cab stopped right outside what the taxi driver assured her must be Number Four since it was situated between numbers two and six, but no longer had a discernible number of its own.

The way Ottilie remembered it Porchester Terrace had always been filled with sunshine, and the cars and the buses that had pulled slowly past it had been few, and the people that Ma and she passed, or stopped and talked with, had always been stopping and smiling despite there still being rationing and life not being easy. But now, looking around her as the taxi driver put his 'For Hire' sign back up and drove off, it was all too clear to her that not even sunshine could cheer Porchester Terrace. It was also perfectly clear that having, many years ago, fallen on bad times, it had not yet picked itself up from them again. With its blackened Victorian exterior and the traffic edging moodily past its door, Porchester Terrace was probably as dreary as it had always been.

Ottilie looked slowly up and down the street. Opposite her a tramp was staring into a dustbin lodged by a pile of builder's rubble. On her side of the street people were passing her, their faces marked with despairs of different and desperate kinds. People who had despaired of the world, of finding a job, of finding love, of being able to change themselves, people who hated themselves or other people, people who were indifferent to life, they all seemed to be passing Ottilie at that moment, and it was beginning to rain.

She walked to the entrance of the block of flats and pushed open the handleless, lockless door. The inevitable smell of cooking cabbage hung in the air as she stared up at the names on the old-fashioned Victorian board in the hall. It looked strangely decorous in its surroundings although proclaiming every occupant of the flats to a person to be 'out', even a Mrs Burgess.

An old woman stepped slowly and noisily into the dingy hall. She was half-stooped and sighing loudly, her clear plastic hat covered in rain, her flowered umbrella also drenched. She straightened up as she shook out the umbrella and sighed noisily. Following this she removed the pixie hat that had covered her hair. Ottilie stared at the apparition that had finally emerged from under the hat. She was old, her hair was brightly dyed, her eyelids were lined with bright blue and her lips as brightly coloured as her hair.

'Do you want something? Are you looking for someone, dear?' she asked Ottilie.

'I'm not sure . . .'

'Oh very well then.' The old woman turned towards what was obviously her front door, her latch key already out, and slowly, very slowly, she turned it in the lock, the sound reverberating in the dulled silence of the dingy hallway.

'As a matter of fact,' Ottilie heard herself say, 'as a matter of fact you might be able to help me, after all, as a matter of fact. I am – looking for a Mrs Burgess.'

'Mrs Burgess has moved.'

'You wouldn't possibly know to where?'

'Mrs Burgess moved to East Sheen—'

'East Cheam?'

'No, East Sheen, the Avenue, number twenty-four. It's a long way out, dear, you'll have to tip the taxi driver, they do so hate to cross Putney Bridge. I know because I went to see her at Christmas.'

As she had predicted it took some little while for Ottilie to find a cab that would take her out to East Sheen and when at last she did she realized that she was already pushed for time if she was going to make it back to Paddington in time to catch the Riviera.

At last the taxi drew to a halt outside a small Thirties immaculately maintained cottage. Ottilie could hardly remember what Mrs Burgess looked like until a plump woman in her fifties opened the door and suddenly, all at once, she knew exactly what she looked like. She looked just like Mrs Burgess had always looked only grey-haired now, but she was just as smooth-faced and smiling as she had always been, and still smoking.

'Mrs Burgess?'

'Yes.'

It was obvious that she did not recognize Ottilie at all.

'It's Ottilie, do you remember – Number Four? Ottilie and her brothers? You took us down to Cornwall?'

Mrs Burgess's heavily ringed hand flew to her mouth as it always had and she started to laugh.

'Little Ottilie? I wouldn't have known you from the Queen, dear! I can hardly believe it, and after all these years.' Mrs Burgess's obvious excitement was touching. 'Come in, come in. It simply does not seem possible, after all these years.'

Ottilie stepped into an immaculately kept hall, oak-floored, grandfather clock, everything just so, and as she did so Mrs Burgess leaned forward and hugged her impulsively.

'I can't tell you what this means to me. I always wondered how you all were, but I never was a letter writer. Course Lorcan wrote to me of your poor mother's sad demise, and after that I just never did get back to Cornwall to see you all. Then I moved here a year ago, and sometimes some of my old friends come out to see me from Porchester Terrace, but not many. Let alone such a person from the past as you. Well, well, darling, sit down while Mrs B gets you a cup of tea and some fruit cake.'

She bustled off to prepare something leaving Ottilie in a sitting room whose shelves, she realized, were completely dominated by dolls of all kinds.

'What a wonderful collection,' Ottilie said when Mrs Burgess returned with tea on a tray and biscuits and cake on a plate.

'Imagine you saying that. Do you know,' she sat back in her chair and having poured the tea for both of them she lit a cigarette, 'do you know your own mother helped me to sew some of those very dolls, darling? Cake?'

Not really wanting it Ottilie nevertheless took it. She was surprised that Ma had helped to sew dolls, she had never seen her sew anything.

'Not Mrs O'Flaherty, dear. I mean, not that mother, your real mother.' As Ottilie said nothing to this, she went on. 'Course you know the story now, don't you? But probably not the whole story. I mean I expect that's why you've come to see old Mrs Burgess, isn't it?' She laughed as Ottilie still said nothing. 'Don't worry, dear, I would want to know, if it was me. In your shoes I'd have come. So. Yes, poor child, your mother. She arrived from the country like so many of them did in those days, you know, knowing nothing really, not really, and I had to help her in every way I could, because she was that innocent, really she was – but of course as soon as I realized she could sew I roped her in because good out-workers are not easy to find, dear, not at all, and you can imagine in those days trying to get materials for my business – murder, dear, sheer murder. But we managed, but only if the girls were handy, we couldn't afford a shred of waste.'

Between puffs on her cigarette Mrs Burgess was

unstoppable. It was as if she was telling a story she had told so many times to other people that she knew it off by heart, and Ottilie suddenly had the impression that Mrs Burgess must have told this story many times, to other people, perhaps people in some local pub that she frequented.

'Yes, so your mother and I we got to know each other really well when I started up my little crinoline doll business and she was as good a seamstress as you'd find anywhere. I have letters from America, from Japan, you'd be surprised where my dolls get to, really surprised. But that's how come I got to know your mother so well, you see, dear, through the dolls. Seeing that she had been brought up in service, and that, she was not just a dab hand with a needle, but as neat as a pin when it came to arranging their hair and I know not what. And of course, because of being in service, she knew what good taste was. She used to help me choose the kind of faces and the hair and that, and then back they would come and we'd make every stitch of their clothes, by hand, all the embroidery, everything, covered buttons on the shoes. Oh I missed her something terrible when she went like that, poor child, something terrible. She was ever such a sweet little thing. You don't look like her, I mean I wouldn't have known you as her daughter until I saw your hair, that rich dark brown hair, that would give me a clue, and your nose, perhaps—'

Mrs Burgess had her head on one side and was inspecting Ottilie for all the world as if she was one of her dolls, underneath a glass dome.

'No, I wouldn't have known you. You probably take more after your father. Course he was such an old man by the time he was married to Mrs Ballantyne.'

'Did you know him then, I mean did you really know my father?'

'Your father, no. Bless you, my dear, I only knew your mother. Mrs O'Flaherty, and people like myself, we never

466

would associate with people like the Ballantynes, remember this was 1948, dear, not the Sixties. No, I never knew your father, never would have done in the way of things then, but I knew the whole story. Although none of us knew your mother was having you, and I don't think she knew in a way, I mean I think she denied it to herself. It transpired afterwards that she'd had this thing they call a dry pregnancy, at least that's what the midwife thought. There's no water round the baby – not that I've ever had a baby myself, dear, but no water means nothing shows. And not only does the mother not show, but she can lose weight instead of putting it on. Course I noticed her getting thinner, and I was that worried about her looks and her weight after a while, but I never could say anything because she wasn't a relative of mine. I just thought she might be pining, for the country, for Cornwall or wherever it was that she had come from.

'She must have known, I suppose, I realized that afterwards, poor little thing, but I don't think she could bring herself to admit it, that's all I can think, dear. It does happen. Girls can't face up to the fact of their pregnancy and then they get theirselves in all sorts of trouble. Mrs Mac, your Ma, she and I we kicked ourselves afterwards, when we realized, but Mrs Mac hardly knew her, only to see her. But she was funny that way, Mrs Mac, very funny. I mean she liked babies and children the way some people like dogs, if you know what I mean? She liked them better than people, if you get my meaning? And there was another thing.'

Mrs Burgess put down her teacup and wiped her mouth very carefully on the back of her hand.

'She did not approve of my dolls, Mrs Mac didn't. She hated dolls herself, called them "tart's toys" if you please!' Mrs Burgess laughed hugely and suddenly, obviously remembering her friend's disapproval, and shook her head. 'Tart's toys if you please! Oh she was a one all right was Mrs Mac, she really was. Well, I will agree some of the ladies of the night from around here did buy my dolls and they did come here to buy them from me, but what harm did that do? The way Mrs Mac was on about my line of work you'd have thought it was the dolls the men were calling on! Still, we were friends, one of the best she was. Shame she died.'

All the time she had been talking Ottilie had been trying to imagine where she herself came into it, but Mrs Burgess was unstoppable. It seemed rude to interrupt her but it had to be done.

'Mrs Burgess, can I ask you, did my mother know my father?'

'Did your father know your mother?' Mrs Burgess put down her teacup. 'You mean you really don't know any of the story? Well bless your socks, and me going on all this time, and there you are wondering how you came to be on this planet.'

Having sat back in her chintz armchair Mrs Burgess began.

'Listen dear, your father was a gentleman, even if he was old, and I do know that for certain. And your mother, this Kitty Shelborne, she really loved him, even though what she did was wrong, as I understand it, she really loved your father, if only because he was a gentleman. And I mean I do know, she did tell me that this Mrs Ballantyne pushed her into it, that what happened was not of her choosing, it wasn't voluntary.'

'Yes, but what? I mean what was not of her choosing?'

Mrs Burgess stood up abruptly, obviously wondering how to put the next bit of the story, and to cover her embarrassment she started to clear away the tea things. Ottilie immediately set to and helped her for she had a feeling that if she was not very careful Mrs Burgess would stop talking and she never would know how she came to be put upon this earth. Carefully and methodically they stacked the tea things in the plastic washing-up bowl and returned to the sitting room, during which time

Ottilie found it hard not to take hold of the woman and scream her question at her, 'What happened? Tell me what happened?'

'Where was I now? Ah yes. Well, as I understand it,' said Mrs Burgess, and she crossed thick lisle-stockinged legs comfortably in front of her knowing all too well perhaps that for the next few minutes it was she who held the stage. 'As I understand it, as it was told to me by this Kitty Shelborne, this Mrs Ballantyne-to-be, she was only a young thing still when her mother remarried suddenly. Well that might have been all right, but she was always being pestered by the stepfather, her mother's new husband, he was always outside her bedroom waiting for her, or trying to grab her when she passed him in the hall, and so nothing must be, but she and the maid, this Kitty that I knew, they decided that there was only one way out, and that was that she would have to get married if only to get away from this Waldo, this stepfather.'

Mrs Burgess stopped and sighed, her eyes fixed on the middle of the window that overlooked the dreary street outside before turning her attention back to Ottilie.

'It wouldn't happen now, of course. But in those days there was no way a girl could get away from home until she was twenty-one, and it soon became clear that this young girl had to get away from him, and fast, you know? Well, at all events, apparently, it so happened that just at that moment this old Mr Ballantyne he'd just returned from abroad, a tea planter or some such I think he was, and he saw this young girl out riding in Richmond Park and fell for her, lock, stock and barrel. Course he was far too old, nearly seventy I think he must have been, but nevertheless he determined on marrying her, and she, to get away from this stepfather, she decided to accept his offer, and you couldn't blame her, because he was very, very rich, even if he was old. Tons of money for anything she wanted, and of course being young that had great appeal. New Look clothes from Dior, anything and everything she wanted he bought her, he was that besotted about her. Anyway, they married, and your mother, Mrs Ballantyne's maid, she went with them, on their honeymoon. And of course that's when all the trouble started.'

Mrs Burgess nodded and sighed once more, first to herself and then to Ottilie.

'Yes, that was when the trouble started, all right, as it was bound to do. See, girls weren't like what they are now, they weren't full of theirselves and knowing everything, and as I understand it this poor young girl, this Mrs Ballantyne, his wife, she was terrified. Night after night went by and she just couldn't get herself to go through with it, she just was sick, night after night, sick as a dog—'

'Yes, that was in the diary, the maid's diary.'

Mrs Burgess shot Ottilie a sharp look at that but continued after a small pause during which Ottilie understood from the look that if she wanted to hear the whole story there must be no more interruptions.

'As I was saying, the young girl was as sick as a dog, and on and on it went, all the time they were in Paris on honeymoon, until I suppose the husband, old as he was, became suspicious and after a while I suppose he must have insisted, you know, on his rights—' Mrs Burgess coloured a little at this. 'Yes, he must have insisted, and really, as I say, things was very different in 1948, girls didn't know what happened, they was nearly always terrified for most of their honeymoon, they was really. Some of them never got used to it. I know I never did. But then Mr Burgess was quite the gentleman even though he was in the City.'

Mrs Burgess nodded towards her husband's photograph in its silver frame and refrained from continuing for a few seconds, perhaps in reverence to his memory.

'Well, anyway, this Kitty, she told me about it one night when we was having a bit of a jolly together, and by that time I do think she knew that she was expecting you, although I certainly didn't, and perhaps she wanted me to

470

know? Perhaps she even knew that she might not be going to live, who knows? No-one knows the human heart, do they?

'See, what happened was that they both, both the young girl and the maid – your mother – they both had this long brown hair and they were both slim and young, the same age practically – to tell you the truth I think that's why I noticed your hair directly you come into the house, because of knowing this story. Anyway the night came when she couldn't put the old gent off any more – and well, you can imagine. She was petrified this young girl, this Mrs Ballantyne, so apparently she flew into a right fury and she threatened your mother with dismissal and cried and shouted and became hysterical, and your mother realizing that nothing was going to get her young mistress into bed with the old chap and if she didn't go through with it they'd both be on the streets – well, she hid behind the screen in the bedroom and slipped into the old gent's bed, in her mistress's place.'

Ottilie stared at Mrs Burgess, imagining the scene, two girls brushing out each other's hair, one covering the other with the scent. Mrs Ballantyne perhaps pushing the maid towards the bedroom door. What must it have been like?

'Kitty told me herself that they put all the lights out, and covered her in the girl's perfume, this Mrs Ballantyne's perfume—'

'"A La Fuite Des Heures."'

'Really? I wouldn't know. Well, anyway apparently she covered herself in it, and that was that, she slipped between the sheets with him, and the deed was done, and the old gent was satisfied and everything would have been fine, if it had been left at that. Except something always does go wrong, don't it? In this case it was that the maid, this Kitty Shelborne, I mean she only went and fell in love with the old gent. And I mean really in love – whenever she talked about him I could see she was besotted of him, and the young wife, this Mrs Ballantyne, after that she

471

couldn't stop young Kitty from slipping off to see her husband. Finally, she had to sack her to stop her! She cooked up some story to her husband about wanting to be alone with the old gent and she took him away, somewhere in Devon, I think, and sacked the maid. Course she paid her off, quite handsomely, but really, how long does that last? But that's how she came to be here and took up sewing with me.

'But then of course, and you probably know this, this Mr Ballantyne, the poor old gent, Kitty Shelborne found out from the valet, he only went and died on his honeymoon just as the girl herself, seeing the maid had been so dotty on him, had begun to realize what a treasure he was, very handsome and nice, apparently, never mind his age. So you can imagine, what with your mother dying on us upstairs and none of us knowing she'd been up the spout anyway and the poor old man dying on his honeymoon, while he was away in Devon, or wherever they were, it was a right old muddle, if you like. But you probably knew all this?'

'No. I have this bracelet. Lorcan gave it to me one birthday thinking it had belonged to my mother.'

'And so it did, Lorcan was right. This Mrs Ballantyne she gave it to Kitty, in all honesty she did, it was on one of her impulses, after the honeymoon night, that she gave it to Kitty. I mean, she never took it, Kitty didn't, and yet when she asked for all her diaries to be sent on the girl only went and accused her of taking it and slammed down the phone. Poor Kitty, she regretted those diaries, I know, all her life was in those diaries, she told me, she'd kept them since she was knee high. I know she rang the old man's valet and asked him to send them on here, but she never did hear from any of them again. Well she wouldn't, would she? She knew too much, Kitty did. And of course that was it, she was poor and they was rich, and we all know how equal the world is when it comes to that.'

'But – Kitty really did love Mr Ballantyne, didn't she? I mean she did at least have that.'

'I wouldn't know, dear, really,' she said, 'I only know that when the doctor and the midwife turned up with you on the doorstep, that your ma, Mrs Mac, she thought it was a miracle. She loved you so much, you know. She was your real mother, dear, not poor little Kitty Shelborne.'

Finally, with one eye on the clock and the time of her departing train, Ottilie was able to extract herself from the flat, and from Mrs Burgess, but not without having been given a doll.

And so she found herself eventually, alone once more on Paddington station, a crinoline doll under one arm and thinking not of the poor girl who had made it, but remembering instead Ma with her thick red plait of hair and her rich laugh, and it came to her that Pierre had been wrong. It had mattered a great deal to Ottilie to find out where she came from, or to go back to where she came from, but now she realized that he had been right too, for it did not matter in the least who had actually made her.

She felt so exhilarated by this thought, and by the realization that she had been truly loved as a child, and remembering the boys and all the laughter they had shared, the hustle and bustle and warmth of a family life where there was not much to go round except plenty of Ma's love, she hurried back out into the rain to telephone Pierre's office.

'He's gone to France, Miss Cartaret, for the linen for the Maize Suite. He said it was quicker, the manufacturer has been driving him mad. But he left a message – it says "Gone for linen, Ottilie darling, *and* a rather beautiful wedding dress. Made from the best Lyon silk, and designed for my grandmother. I can picture you in it. Make it a day in May, kid!"'

Ottilie put the phone down and wandered once more back into the station. Despite her disappointment she had to admire a man who went to France at a moment's notice to fetch linen and a wedding dress. It was worse than romantic. It was cataclysmically romantic, and it had made Alanna sigh with envy as she put down the phone.

The train was not in so Ottilie wandered restlessly around the station, eventually settling on a bench where a young family joined her minutes later.

Ottilie looked across at the mother. She was a poor woman, but like Ma she was proud, for everything about her and her children was neat and clean, polished shoes, mended gloves. Ottilie turned suddenly to the mother.

'Don't think I'm mad, but I was wondering – I was wondering if your daughter would like this doll? It sounds funny, but I don't really like dolls.'

The woman stared at Ottilie in astonishment.

'It belonged to my mother, but I actually don't want it any more.'

The woman looked down at the obviously expensive doll in its crinoline and cloak that Ottilie was holding, probably feeling suspicious.

'I've grown out of it, you might say.'

The woman still looked doubtful but seeing the expression on her daughter's face as Ottilie held out the beautifully dressed doll to her she must have changed her mind, because she said, after a moment, 'Are you sure?'

'Of course I'm sure.' Ottilie stood up. 'She'll love her more than I possibly could. I know that, you see, because I was given away.'

At which she walked off towards her train, and home.

It was very late when Ottilie eventually arrived back at the Grand, but as the taxi drew away from the green sward outside her home, she looked up at its lights spilling out over the grass, just reaching the edge, and gave a great sigh of contentment. There was her home, and she knew every room backwards, and now she even knew how she came to be there, and why the top suite had always held a fascination for her. Mrs Ballantyne was gone, never to return, and the top suite would, even now, be playing its romantic part and bringing joy to some more fortunate honeymoon couple. The old colonels and the lavender-scented ladies and their moustached husbands from long ago were gone, but they had been replaced, and would always be replaced by other couples and other old colonels. In a few years Ottilie knew she would walk through the old swing doors into the dining room and hear Constantia longing for the good old days and deploring the ways of the young, which heaven only knew, thanks to the human heart, were exactly the same as the old.

She walked up the steps, slowly, savouring her home-coming as if she was a guest and not the owner of the great white house in front of her. The first person to greet her was Nantwick, despite the hour. His face lit up as soon as he saw her.

'They've arrived, Miss Cartaret, and they're beautiful.'

Ottilie stared at him. She was worn to a thread paper, as Edith would say, but Nantwick's enthusiasm was so infectious she too smiled.

'Oh good, Nantwick, that is good,' she said, not having the faintest idea what he was talking about.

'And very nice too, Miss Cartaret, if I may say so.'

'Oh good, Nantwick,' Ottilie said, still smiling, hoping for a clue. 'They' might be new guests, or new plants for the greenhouse, or even the new machines for the laundry. Such was Nantwick's enthusiasm for the place, and such his devotion, the slightest innovation or arrival was always greeted like Christmas.

'Yes, yes, they're here,' Nantwick agreed and his shrewd eyes twinkled.

'Oh good,' Ottilie agreed. 'That is good.'

'Shall I bring them up, Miss Cartaret?'

If he was going to bring them up, Ottilie somehow doubted that they could be new machines, and nor could they, she supposed, be guests, for she would have thought by this hour even the most celebratory of guests would be more than reluctant to meet the proprietor.

'Oh yes, bring them up, Nantwick, do.' Ottilie gave him an encouraging nod. 'Meanwhile I am going to the bar where I am going to have a soothing nightcap after my journey.'

She poured herself a small brandy and sank down into one of the new large sofas, avoiding the memory of how and where and with whom she had chosen them, concentrating instead on the more immediate question of what or who Nantwick was going to bring in to show her. Not remembering she had ordered anything, too tired to try.

'Here they are then,' Nantwick said, proudly bursting through the door.

Ottilie looked down at 'here' and 'they' and saw before her two resplendent black labrador puppies in matching blue harnesses and leads.

'Course they only came the moment you left, Miss Cartaret, just as you left for the station. We ran after the station taxi, but of course you'd gone by then. Nothing to be done. Still, now you're here, all's well. Nothing like it, is there, Miss Cartaret, coming home?'

Veronica never forgot to read the births and deaths columns in the *Daily Telegraph*. Ottilie often wondered why it was such a duty with her, since she did not seem to have a wide enough circle of friends to warrant spending such a meticulous amount of time on them, but read them she did, and most religiously.

'All right,' Ottilie said to her the following morning, seeing her involved in her usual daily occupation, 'today, you can read me some names out loud from the births column.'

'Anyone we know expecting?'

'Us. We have had two boys.'

Veronica stared at her for a second and Ottilie could see

476

her thinking that not even Ottilie could have given birth to twins during the time she was in London.

'Yes, now – did this happen last night in the hotel?'

'Black labradors. I need to name them, hence my request for you to read from the columns of that noble newspaper to which you are even now referring.'

'Black labradors. How very jolly.'

'I chose black labradors because I thought they would look welcoming. In the winter they can sit in front of a roaring fire in the hall, and in summer they can look noble on the top steps. Nantwick is thrilled with them already, and I think you will find that they are training themselves beautifully to the new Persian rugs.'

'We surely can't force names on the poor things without at the same time having a look at them and seeing if they will suit?'

As soon as the puppies had been brought in Veronica started to read. '"AINSLY, to Richard and Elizabeth, a son, James Richard." "BARRACLOUGH, to Paul and Emily, a son, Ian Barry."' By the time Veronica was filleting through the Gs and Hs each birth seemed to be getting duller and more unsuitable than the last.

'So many Johns and Jameses,' Ottilie complained as she stared at the puppies and repeated the names to them, while they in their turn busied themselves tearing at the laces of Veronica's outdoor shoes.

Veronica put the newspaper down. 'I don't think we're going to find suitable names for puppies in the births column,' she admitted. 'What we really need is one of those baby names books—'

She stopped suddenly, looking down at Ottilie who was still busily playing with the puppies on the other side of her desk.

'Nicholas Phelps has been arrested. Your lawyer's been arrested for attempted assault.'

Ottilie straightened up. 'Not my laywer any more, V. Not for some time.'

Veronica handed her the newspaper. 'Just as well. It seems he's quite definitely not safe in taxis.'

Ottilie stared at the item in the newspaper, and for a second found herself wondering if she should not have been as brave as the woman who was now taking Phelps to court, but then she remembered how little she herself had to go on, nothing at all really, less than nothing. She gave the newspaper back to Veronica without saying anything. Veronica seemed to understand because a few minutes went by before she said, 'I'm glad you dropped him. I never really liked that Phelps, you know.' She pushed her spectacles back up her nose. 'Too smooth.'

Ottilie sat back on the floor again and after some minutes, during which she played with the puppies and they discussed more names for them, they eventually chose Amos and Andy.

The following May the weather was perfect. The kind of perfect, soft, early sunshiny Cornish days before tourists and the more mettlesome days of summer arrive, when the daffodils are still delaying their exit, and everyone has set to and finally finished scraping off last year from the bottom of their boats and put to into the water with slow easy strokes and smilingly decided that life is quite as good as they remembered it from the previous year.

On just such a day Ottilie and Pierre were married. The little church that they chose to be married in was filled with people, but not just their guests. It was filled with the people from past days, the Cornish saints, many of whom were buried within its sanctuary, the people who had known them both, and were there, who had loved them, but were now gone, but most of all it was filled with the happy promise that fills the hearts of those who have decided to hand destiny each to the other.

Afterwards, back at the Grand in St Elcombe, as the wedding breakfast spread into luncheon, and luncheon into tea, and tea into dinner and the dancing and the drinking continued unabated, Ottilie and Pierre, by previous arrangement and without more ado, crept off to the top suite. Here the sign DO NOT DISTURB stayed in place for so long that Nantwick was heard to remark that he thought it must be some sort of record. Everyone else however remained silent on the subject, only Amos and Andy being allowed up.

THE END

A SELECTION OF FINE NOVELS
AVAILABLE FROM BANTAM BOOKS

THE PRICES SHOWN BELOW WERE CORRECT AT THE TIME OF GOING TO PRESS.
HOWEVER TRANSWORLD PUBLISHERS RESERVE THE RIGHT TO SHOW NEW RETAIL
PRICES ON COVERS WHICH MAY DIFFER FROM THOSE PREVIOUSLY ADVERTISED IN
THE TEXT OR ELSEWHERE.

50329 4	**DANGER ZONES**	*Sally Beauman*	£5.99
40727 9	**LOVERS AND LIARS**	*Sally Beauman*	£5.99
40803 8	**SACRED AND PROFANE**	*Marcelle Bernstein*	£5.99
40429 6	**AT HOME**	*Charlotte Bingham*	£3.99
40427 X	**BELGRAVIA**	*Charlotte Bingham*	£3.99
40432 6	**BY INVITATION**	*Charlotte Bingham*	£3.99
40497 0	**CHANGE OF HEART**	*Charlotte Bingham*	£5.99
40890 9	**DEBUTANTES**	*Charlotte Bingham*	£5.99
40296 X	**IN SUNSHINE OR IN SHADOW**	*Charlotte Bingham*	£5.99
40469 2	**NANNY**	*Charlotte Bingham*	£5.99
40171 8	**STARDUST**	*Charlotte Bingham*	£4.99
40163 7	**THE BUSINESS**	*Charlotte Bingham*	£5.99
40895 X	**THE NIGHTINGALE SINGS**	*Charlotte Bingham*	£5.99
17635 8	**TO HEAR A NIGHTINGALE**	*Charlotte Bingham*	£5.99
40072 X	**MAGGIE JORDAN**	*Emma Blair*	£4.99
40298 6	**SCARLET RIBBONS**	*Emma Blair*	£4.99
40615 9	**PASSIONATE TIMES**	*Emma Blair*	£5.99
40614 0	**THE DAFFODIL SEA**	*Emma Blair*	£5.99
40373 7	**THE SWEETEST THING**	*Emma Blair*	£4.99
40973 5	**A CRACK IN FOREVER**	*Jeannie Brewer*	£5.99
40996 4	**GOING HOME TO LIVERPOOL**	*June Francis*	£4.99
50429 0	**KITTY AND HER BOYS**	*June Francis*	£5.99
40820 8	**LILY'S WAR**	*June Francis*	£4.99
40819 4	**A BITTER LEGACY**	*Margaret Graham*	£5.99
40818 6	**A DISTANT DREAM**	*Margaret Graham*	£5.99
40730 9	**LOVERS**	*Judith Krantz*	£5.99
40731 7	**SPRING COLLECTION**	*Judith Krantz*	£5.99
40945 X	**FINISHING TOUCHES**	*Patricia Scanlan*	£5.99
40947 6	**FOREIGN AFFAIRS**	*Patricia Scanlan*	£4.99
40942 5	**PROMISES, PROMISES**	*Patricia Scanlan*	£5.99
40483 0	**SINS OF THE MOTHER**	*Arabella Seymour*	£4.99

All Transworld titles are available by post from:

Book Service By Post, P.O. Box 29, Douglas, Isle of Man IM99 1BQ

Credit cards accepted. Please telephone 01624 675137,
fax 01624 670923 or Internet http://www.bookpost.co.uk
or e-mail: bookshop@enterprise.net for details

Free postage and packing in the UK. Overseas customers: allow
£1 per book (paperbacks) and £3 per book (hardbacks).